# JOVIAN

# JOVIAN

## DONALD MOFFITT

**ibooks**
new york
www.ibooks.net

DISTRIBUTED BY SIMON & SCHUSTER, INC.

An Original Publication of ibooks, inc.

Copyright © 2003 by Donald Moffitt

An ibooks, inc. Book

Distributed by Simon & Schuster, Inc.
1230 Avenue of the Americas, New York, NY 10020

ibooks, inc.
24 West 25th Street
New York, NY 10010

The ibooks World Wide Web Site Address is:
http://www.ibooks.net

ISBN 0-7434-5277-1
First ibooks, inc. printing January 2003
10 9 8 7 6 5 4 3 2 1

Jacket art by Bob Larkin
Jacket design by Mike Rivilis

Printed in the U.S.A.

# INTRODUCTION

J UPITER HAS been an intimidating subject for science fiction for at least forty years, ever since the medium's best writers sorrowfully came to grips with the fact that the solar system's largest piece of real estate was a howling hell with no solid surface to serve as a backdrop for human adventures. Add to this the giant planet's crushing gravity, extreme pressures, and lethal radiation belt, and you had an arena that no self-respecting writer of hard sf would dare to populate with mere humans. Oh, there were a number of ingenious stories about brief *visits* to Jupiter—notably Poul Anderson's "Brake," which had a disabled spaceship bobbing like a cork in Jupiter's upper atmosphere until it could be rescued, and Arthur C. Clarke's 1971 masterpiece, "A Meeting with Medusa," about a harrowing reconnaisance in a hot-helium balloon (and by a gravity-defying cyborg at that). But if you wanted to plant a colony, it was easier to move to the Moon or Mars. Or still better, to a planet revolving around another star, a world which could be tailored to plot specifications.

This wasn't always so. In the 1930s and 1940s, and right up through most of the '50s, sf clung to the notion that Jupiter was merely a larger Earth, and—gravity be damned—a fit landscape for human beings to roam. Often it was seen as a primitive version of Earth on which evolving humans—by the same curious convention that colored Martians red and Venusians green—were just like us, only blue. (I still remember with nostalgia the "Jovian Dawn

Man" in a swashbuckling *Planet Stories* novelette by Emmet Mac-Dowell.)

Pioneer and Voyager closed that particular book with a bang. And while human colonists were allowed to settle on Jupiter's moons in several excellent novels, the giant planet itself became a prop, used for other plot purposes. (Arthur Clarke turned it into a star. In my own 1977 novel, *The Jupiter Theft,* it was hijacked by galaxy-hopping aliens from Cygnus to serve as a hydrogen fuel tank.)

But where there's a will, there's a way. Galileo and continuing Earth-based observations taught us more about Jupiter. The temperatures in a narrow stratum of the upper atmosphere seemed quite salubrious. There was water ice, and the other ingredients for growing terrestrial plant life were readily available in the Jovian atmosphere. The same magnetic field that made Jupiter's radiation a killer also provided a radiation-free zone. Buckytubes came along, and with them the hope that doping them with other elements might make them still stronger. As for gravity, there are plenty of active people right here on Earth—some of them athletes—who carry around body weight in excess of four hundred pounds, without benefit of muscles hardened by a lifetime of two and a half g's.

I did the arithmetic on an aerostat that could support a city of 20,000 in Jupiter's hydrogen-helium atmosphere, and the figures came out right if I substituted hard vacuum for hot hydrogen. That was enough encouragement. I sat down and wrote the opening chapters of *Jovian.*

That was almost ten years ago. And then I put the chapters aside and went on to other things. *Jovian* might have remained in the drawer except for an unexpected and happy turn of events.

The Internet gave birth to a visionary company called ereads.com. Its premise was that there were thousands of out-of-print books—some of them fondly remembered classics, some merely good reads—that were ready to find a new audience. A new generation of readers was becoming accustomed to PC screens and palm readers, and for those who still preferred paper, there was a brave new technology called print-on-demand, which made it practical to custom-produce one book at a time, making costly warehousing unneccesary.

To my great delight and surprise, I became one of the beneficiaries of this upstart revolution in reading. *The Jupiter Theft,* which had seen its third and final printing in 1986, became one of 2001's best-selling e-books at Palm Digital Media. *The Genesis Quest* and other novels that I thought were dead and forgotten picked up steam as well. Convinced that there were still readers out there for hard-science space adventures, I dusted off the opening chapters of *Jovian* and finished the book.

Planetscapes, gadgets and abstract ideas do not in themselves a satisfying story make. Robert Heinlein taught us that a long time ago. No matter how riveting the original premise, the story needs to be about recognizable people living recognizable human lives. As Heinlein expressed it, "As a result of this (premise), new *human* problems are created, and our story is about how human beings cope with these new problems." For *Jovian,* I imagined a future in which the headlong pace of progress has slowed down a bit after the twenty-first century, as it has many times in the past, giving us a more recognizable world in which extreme technologies do not distract from the essential story. The aristocracy, after lying low for a few centuries following the Age of Enlightenment, have come to the fore again, resuming their traditional role in the human scheme of things and once again openly pulling the economic strings. Rough labor, however, will always be needed, even in a high-tech information-based society. This time around, the rustics willing to take the unwanted jobs are Jovians. Jupiter is necessarily a backwater. Its immense gravity well makes commerce with the rest of the solar system difficult and expensive. The people in the bubble cities live hardscrabble lives, and are thought to be unpolished by the sophisticates of Earth and Venus, who derisively call them "cloudhoppers." But their great physical strength and the frontier virtues of honesty and reliability make Jovians prized "workies" nevertheless.

It was a good place to start a story. The further adventures of

Jarls Anders take him to the hell of Venus (another planet whose image in science fiction has changed drastically), and to a palace revolution on Earth that provides the key to a revivified Jupiter. Luck was with me all the way. As I wrote, the German news magazine *Der Spiegel* published a report that lent weight to my speculations about the role of little Liechtenstein in Europe's financial future, and, just in time for the finale, the Lawrence Livermore National laboratory released information about the nature of metallic hydrogen that validated the assumptions with which I had begun.

I hope this brew of elements will make a satisfying read. My thanks to Richard Curtis, who performed the Lazarus maneuver on me, and to the folks at ibooks, whose motto, "The best of the past, the best of the future," has indeed turned a dimming past into a bright future and breathed new life into science fiction and other genres. My special thanks go to my wife, Ann, who egged me on and, more important, knocked herself out to make writing time for me.

And most of all, thanks to the readers, both old and new, without whose interest and encouragement *Jovian* would not have been written. I hope I've repaid them with a few hours of reading pleasure.

–Donald Moffitt
October 2002

# PART 1

# JUPITER

# 1

**A**STIFF HYDROGEN wind screamed past Jarls, making a din in his helmet and threatening to tear him loose from the floater's outer scaffolding. He tightened his grip on a strut and leaned cautiously outward for a respectful look at the immense salmon-colored cloudscape below him. Lightning flashed in its crevices; violent eddies of raw color churned its seething surface. Above, a tiny sun cast a broad shimmering path on the cloud deck. In the distance, Jarls could see Port Elysium, an iridescent bubble that contained farmlands, well-stocked lakes, and the villages of the twenty thousand people he called his neighbors. It was riding the storm well, twisting slowly in the maelstrom of the Great Red Spot's approach, but remaining stable.

A hand as hard as iron clamped itself around his upper arm, making itself felt even through layers of padded thermal suit. "Time to go inside," his uncle said through a howl of radio noise.

Jarls turned his head. The bulky shape clinging next to him was massively overdeveloped even for a Jovian, with a chest like a packing crate and treetrunk legs. Uncle Hector was a comforting presence to have on a work detail.

Jarls himself had grown to a pretty good size. On Earth he might have passed for a rather solid young man whose hobby happened to be weight lifting. But no earthborn weight lifter could have attained the density of muscle that bulged at Jarls's thighs and upper arms, or quite matched the thickness of his torso. The unyielding hardness of his body, molded by Jupiter's crushing gravity, was needed to support a Jovian weight of close to five hundred pounds.

"I'm going to ride it down out here," Jarls replied.

Hector lifted a shaggy eyebrow. "Sensible people don't take chances. I've got to stay outside to ride herd on the siphon. But even the latching crew's sitting out the descent inside the cabin."

"I want to know what it feels like, not see it through a porthole."

"All right." Hector cracked a grudging smile of approval. "I guess you're old enough to make up your own mind."

"Commencing to trim," a laconic voice buzzed in Jarls's ear. There was no second warning. On Jupiter, people learned early in life to pay attention.

The superfluous personnel on the work platform below started to file up the ladder to the floater's belly cabin. A half-dozen spread-eagled shapes remained clinging to the outside strutwork of the great silver egg, like Jarls and Hector. One of them began edging toward them. Jarls recognized the well-worn suit belonging to Gord Murdo, the foreman.

"Hang on," Uncle Hector said.

Jarls didn't need to be told. A thousand kilometers below the seething orange cloud deck lay the surface of a hydrogen sea that no man had ever seen, or ever could see. If you lost your grip and fell, you didn't have to worry about splashing into it. Long before you reached its indeterminate boundary the increasing pressure would crush you into a shapeless blob, and the steadily rising temperatures would cook what was left of you. Below that strange ocean lay a stranger realm yet—a core of hydrogen so compressed that it turned to a liquid metallic form. There, at pressures of more than three million atmospheres and temperatures above 11,000 degrees K, the dissociated molecules that once had been your precious self would float in eternal suspension.

Jarls wiped the unsettling image from his mind and waited. It took a long time to reach negative buoyancy. The vacuum shell was big—it had to be in Jupiter's lightweight upper atmosphere of hydrogen laced with helium. The early floaters had been little more than hot-hydrogen balloons. But the combination of hydro-gen and the inevitable oxygen leaks from suits and cabins had proved too dangerous. So the huge egg enclosed nothing but vac-uum—the one thing in the universe that is lighter even than heated hydrogen—and the trimming was done with helium filtered out of the outside atmosphere.

There was the tiniest of shudders, and the blimplike vehicle began to sink, almost imperceptibly at first. Jarls checked its progress with a glance at the floating anchor rig, hovering about a mile farther east. It was just visible past the curve of the floater's shell, a tall tetrahedron with a froth of flotation bubbles at its top. The thick monomolecular hose that ran from it to the floater was a looping arc that dwindled to invisibility after the first quarter mile.

"Pull in those lines!" the radio said sharply in Uncle Hector's voice. "Snub that hose end before you lose it!"

Jarls looked down at the work platform, where four burly roustabouts were struggling to restrain the gigantic coupling that had lifted dangerously on its fastenings when the descent began. He began automatically to inch downward to help; on Jupiter, you didn't wait to be asked.

"They can handle it," Hector said. The iron fingers gripped Jarls's arm again.

The work gang beneath hauled in on the guy lines, and with pure brute force wrestled enough hose inboard to wrap a bight around a stanchion. The hose was thick as a log and obstinately rigid, but Jovian muscles were equal to a task that would have taken a donkey engine on Earth. They lashed it efficiently into place. There was a jerk that made the floater sway, and then, as some distant capstan came unstuck, the hose commenced to unreel smoothly.

"Nice going," Gord Murdo said, coming up next to Hector and helping himself to a handful of strut. He acknowledged Jarls's presence with a nod. Jarls noticed that the foreman had made the crawl across the vac egg without bothering to use a safety line; a bad example, but it wasn't up to him to comment.

The roustabouts beneath received the compliment with raised

faces and a thumbs up. They were three men and a woman, hulking bruisers all of them.

Hector grunted. "We don't need a loose coupling whipping around. Not this close to the Spot."

"Lot of turbulence," Murdo agreed. "That's what probably pulled the siphon loose in the first place."

Jupiter's sloshy outer layers rotated at different speeds, depending on latitude, and the immense whirlwind that was the Great Red Spot periodically passed Port Elysium to the south. It never came closer than about 15,000 kilometers—a margin wider than the planet Earth—but that was close enough. Port Elysium always battened down during the passage. But the floating city couldn't do without its water and oxygen, and these could only be obtained from the ice crystal layers below the ammonia clouds.

Port Elysium had to tend its wells, no matter what.

A vast chasm opened in the layer of ammonia clouds, and the huge silver ovoid dropped straight through. Abruptly, the marble-size sun was cut off. The floater lay in deep shadow. Jarls caught his breath at the scary majesty of his surroundings. The cloud walls on either side were inky black, and darting forks of lightning crackled within them. There was an almost continuous roll of thunder in Jarls's ears now. Jupiter's hydrogen-helium atmosphere transposed sounds a couple of octaves higher, but there were always deeper sounds waiting on the threshhold of human perception to be heard in turn.

Ammonia snowflakes were beginning to melt against Jarls's helmet, making rivulets down his faceplate. He wiped them off with a sleeve. It was cold in the upper clouds—about 130 degrees below zero—but the pressure here was still a comfortable one atmosphere. About fifteen kilometers down, the floater reached the bottom of the rift and was swallowed by pink mist. The blankness was disorienting for someone used to Jupiter's vast horizons.

Then the floater broke through into another clear stratum. Jarls drank in the sight of a new cloudscape, stretching to infinity.

"Well, how do you like it, youngster?" Murdo said. "First time down this deep?"

The unbroken carpet of clouds was more brownish in color than the orange-pink ceiling above. It was composed of ammonium hydrosulphide crystals, precipitated out of the hydrogen atmosphere at the differing pressure and temperature levels here. Already, Jarls could notice that it was getting warmer. He switched off his suit heater.

"No, I've seen it before," Jarls replied. "But only through a porthole."

The foreman nodded soberly. "Nothing like the real thing, eh? I'll tell you one thing. It's a sight no Earthman will ever see with his own eyes."

Uncle Hector said sourly, "Earthies don't have to come down here. They can sit in their corporate dens on Callisto and Olympus Habitat and skim our wealth from orbit. And there's not a damn thing we can do about it."

"Come now, Hec," Murdo protested. "Jupiter gets a royalty on every load of hydrogen the mining satellites scoop out of our atmosphere. And the surface jobs we do for them help our credit balance. You've worked for them yourself."

"Royalties!" Hector exploded. "One tenth of one percent on a gigatonne? It's robbery! And we've only been getting *that* since '32, when one of Earthcorp's orbital siphons crashed through the North Equatorial aerostat and killed thirty thousand people. As for Earth wages, they can keep them! We're a source of cheap local labor for them, that's all. They treat us like peasants. We're being exploited. That's why Jupiter's the backwater of the solar system."

"You always were a radical, Hec," the foreman said. But his own face had clouded at the recitation.

The political talk made Jarls uncomfortable. It came from getting old, he decided, all this endless palaver about abstractions that had nothing to do with real life. Real life was about being young, and feeling your juices, and doing things and going places. He looked down at the giant planet spread around him. Now *that* was real—the hydrogen winds that tried to pluck you from your grip, the immensity of the roiling cloudscape below, the sound of thunder in your ears, the nagging lifelong pull of Jupiter's two and one-half gravities against your muscles and your body's joy in defeating it.

"We're being skinned and you know it," Hector said. "Jovian hydrogen keeps the solar system running, and everybody makes money on it except us."

"It's the gravity," Murdo said defensively. "That's what keeps us isolated. You know what it costs to raise a ship out of this gravity well. The whole planet doesn't own more than twenty ships, and it takes ten or fifteen cities going shares just to lift one. It's just too expensive for the rest of the solar system to trade with us. That's why off-planet goods are so high."

"They've got their foot on our neck," Hector growled. "We're here to be plucked. The South Temperate Zone consortium tried to break the hydrogen monopoly by orbiting a siphon of their own, and look what happened. They couldn't sell one miserable cargo anywhere in the solar system. It's all under the thumb of the Earth-Venus cartel. Twenty cities went broke, and their children are still paying for it."

"We're still a young planet, Hec. Some day the Deep Tap project will pay off, and Jupiter will take its rightful place in the solar system."

"You and I will never live to see it, Gord."

"The Deep Tap's technically feasible," Murdo insisted. "The hypercarbons able to withstand the heat and pressure have been around for a couple of centuries. We've reached depths of over a thousand kilometers. A lot of good men and women have died trying to sink more sections of it. If we could just get the financing to carry it through . . ."

Hector's voice sounded tired. "We'll never get the financing from off-planet. Not from the steely-eyed gnomes who run Earth. They'd be cutting their own throats. It's up to us Jovians, us against them."

"That kind of talk . . ."

Jarls was glad to be able to interrupt. "Look!"

They followed his pointing gauntlet. Some kilometers away, a flock of flapping dots flew in loose echelon, making a broad arc against the rust-colored clouds. There were twenty or thirty of them.

"A hunting party," Hector said. "Heading toward the Great Red Spot."

"A little out of their depth, aren't they?" Murdo said.

"Must've got caught in an updraft. But the air's soupy enough for them here. Feels like about six atmospheres."

Jarls had noticed the increasing thickness of the atmosphere himself as they sank. It slowed down your movements, but it also took away some of the terrible drag of gravity, like lying in a bathtub.

Hector's craggy face had come alive. "Good hunting for the flapjacks when the Great Red Spot comes around," he explained to Jarls. "Means an upwelling of organic molecules for fifty thousand kilometers around, and an explosion of the small life forms. And that attracts those big floating colanders that the flapjacks prey on."

Jarls strained to see the distant specks. Jovian life was plentiful, and the small thistledown forms that inhabited the upper atmosphere liked to congregate around Port Elysium. But he had seen these big hunters of the middle depths only on holo.

As he watched, the formation veered. Jarls's heart thumped in his chest.

"They're changing course!"

Hector nodded. "Looks like they're coming over for a visit."

# 2

T HE GREAT flapping shapes grew in size, matching the drop rate of the floater. Jarls could make out their contours plainly now—they were immense flat pancakes, easily acres in extent, undulating gently to stay aloft. Their scalloped outer edges served as limbs of a sort, curled around thousand-foot cartilaginous spears and coils of what looked to be rope. They wore harnesses, too, crisscrossed bands from which dangled carrying pouches the size of barns.

Jarls didn't fully appreciate the tremendous scale of the creatures until they came to rest about a quarter mile from the floater. Not one of them would have fit in the biggest enclosed space he could think of—Port Elysium's stadium. It dawned on him that the spears they carried must have come from the skeletons of creatures that were larger still. They arranged themselves in a shallow curve, obviously looking over the human vehicle with whatever Jovian natives used for senses.

Jarls could feel their attention, though their flat gray expanses were featureless. They maintained position against the gale-force wind with apparent effortlessness, billowing in slow rhythm. Jarls could see them making small adjustments by curling and uncurling the projections on their outer mantles. They tilted slightly toward the floater, blotting out sky and dwarfing the human artifact into insignificance.

"What do they want?" he asked his uncle. "Do they want to trade?"

Hector shook his head. "They're just curious. Came over for a closer look at us midges."

"Too bad," Murdo said. "We could make more money out of the exotic organics in just one of those skin bags than we're getting paid for this little repair excursion."

"That's not the way they like to do things," Hector said.

"I guess you ought to know, Hec," the foreman replied.

Hector had been a trader himself in his youth, among all the other jobs that Jovians had to do to scratch out a living; Jarls's father had been a partner in that and a host of other enterprises before the deep-fishing accident that had crippled him.

"You know how what old-timers call the Shadow Trade works, don't you?" Hector said to Jarls.

"Sort of." Jarls had heard the stories often enough while growing up.

But Hector was not to be deterred. "We send down a balloon loaded with trade goods, and leave it. They load it with things they think we might want—usually skins, or some of their cartilage artifacts. Then *they* leave. If we accept the deal, we take the stuff, and then they come back to collect. If we don't, they add more. If *they* don't like the deal, *we* add more. When both parties are satisfied, we make the exchange. Usually we never see the parties we trade with. They're cautious but honest."

"You're attributing too much intelligence to them, Hec." Murdo said. "A dog can be taught to fetch. We taught them a complicated reflex over the years, that's all."

Hector declined to rise to the bait, though Jarls knew he was a passionate believer in the reasoning capacity of the Jovian natives. Arguments could get pretty heated between opposing camps on the issue, but Hector limited himself to observing mildly: "There are different kinds of intelligence, Gord. It took us a couple of hundred years to learn that about dolphins."

A sudden gust tipped one of the flying pancakes, almost making it drop its spear. It righted itself with a casual ripple of its vast body and resumed its scrutiny of the floater.

"What if one of them bumps us?" Jarls asked nervously.

"No danger," his uncle said. "They're careful with their bodies. They're fragile despite their size. Lightweight, like all Jupiter's aerial life."

"I mean by accident."

"So do I. It's us humans who're clumsy. They're made for this environment. They've got keen senses, like any hunters. Right now they're bouncing sonar, radar, and God knows what else off us. And taking infrared snapshots with their whole bodies. They're probably tasting us by our stray molecules, too!"

Murdo gave a short bark. "You can't blame the youngster for being a little nervous. Those spears give me the jitters myself. What if they decided the floater was good to eat? Imagine one of those shafts through our vacuum bag."

"Now Gord, you know as well as I do that they don't do that. There's never been a recorded case of a flapjack intentionally harming a human being."

He turned back to Jarls. "Those spears they carry come from the keels of those floating sieves that strain out the atmospheric plankton. I once saw a flapjack throw one. Whirled around and around like a pinwheel, picking up spin, then let loose. Usually they position themselves in a circle above their prey and drop their harpoons straight down. In this gravity, they fall like thunderbolts. But this fellow's shaft must've been flying fast enough to straighten itself out. Ripped right through the big gasbag it was hunting. The other hunters got harpoon lines into it before it started to sink too fast, and they flew away with that mile-wide carcass hanging between them. Can't be many men alive who've seen such a sight."

It made a vivid picture. Jarls couldn't help glancing over at the line of disklike creatures hanging in loose formation around the floater. Most of them carried their spears sensibly at the vertical, well above the balancing point, but a few carelessly held shafts drooped like basket handles under Jovian gravity. Jarls tried to imagine the kind of kinetic energy it would take to straighten one out enough to be flung at the horizontal, and was impressed anew.

Hector was staring thoughtfully at the visitors too. "If only we could get them to work for us in some sort of reliable fashion," he mused. "We might be able to get somewhere with the Deep Tap project—and there'd be a future for this planet."

"Huh?" It came as a snort from Murdo.

"These fellows are fishers as well as hunters. They bring up catches that must come from all the way down to the hydrogen sea. The life chemistry's different from the aerial forms whose skins and lipids they usually trade."

"So what? All Jovian organics are weird. That's why they fetch a good price outside."

"My point is that we don't know how far down the flapjacks can operate, but it has to be a lot deeper than we can go. If we could get their help in setting up rigs just another thousand kilometers down—below the transition point between gaseous and liquid hydrogen, out of reach of atmospheric storms—we'd have stable platforms that might be able to take the Deep Tap down all the way."

"You're dreaming, Hec."

"They cooperate with one another. Why not with us?"

The hovering giants seemed to have lost interest in the floater and the tiny specks that moved around on it. With one accord, they tilted themselves on edge and dived down through the cloud bank below. The floater rocked with their passage, and Jarls found himself scrabbling for a better handhold until the swaying ceased.

The floater was falling faster now, and within two or three minutes it, too, was submerged in clouds. A brownish mist swallowed the vacuum egg and the people clinging to it.

There were several minutes of obscurity. Jarls used a mitten to wipe off the rust-colored scum of ammonium hydrosulphide forming on his faceplate. Then the floater emerged into blue sky, with cottony white clouds billowing below.

"There's our water-ice layer," Hector said to him. "Now all we've got to do is find the pumping station."

The flock of natives was nowhere to be seen. Jarls scanned the broad sandwich of a horizon and found no trace of them.

The floater stopped its headlong descent with a jerk, and Jarls had to try for a new grip. The vacuum egg was drifting west along with the scudding clouds. The long tether of hose vanished obliquely into the sky, punctuated every few kilometers by brightly colored, hot-hydrogen balloons.

"How are you taking the pressure, youngster?" Murdo asked.

"He's taking it just fine," Hector answered for him. "He's a Jovian, isn't he?"

The air was thick as syrup by now. It dragged at Jarls's every movement. He maintained a stoic silence. People worked down here all the time, and the pay was better than it was upstairs. Hector had had to pull a few strings to get him the job.

"We're about a hundred kilometers down at this point," the foreman informed him. "Pressure's about twenty atmospheres here. An Earthie would have to wear a hard suit to get down this far. We don't go much lower ourselves without hard suits. Gets a lot hotter from here on down, too."

Sweat was already trickling down Jarls's face and neck. It was like a steambath inside his suit. Jarls resisted turning on his suit's thermoacoustic cooler until he saw that Hector and Murdo had already turned on theirs.

"There's a buoy," Hector said suddenly.

Jarls saw a brightly painted balloon, red with yellow bands. It was perfectly spherical, not onion-shaped, which showed that it was a small vacuum shell rather than a hot-hydrogen balloon. The less maintenance the better at these depths.

"It's too low," Murdo said. "The pumping station's sinking."

Jarls kept his eye on the bright marker, and after several minutes it became apparent that it was being pulled down through the stratum of white clouds. He could sense the foreman's frustration at the floater's inability to move faster, though it was squirting hydrazine at full throttle. The striped ball disappeared through the cloud blanket just before the floater reached it.

"We're going to have to dive for it," Murdo called over the general frequency. "Everybody hang on."

The floater pilot didn't bother to wait for a formal order. The silver egg lurched downward as its empty buoyancy cells sucked in atmospheric helium at high velocity. Droplets began to form again on Jarls's helmet as they plunged through the clouds, only this time it was water ice crystals that were melting.

Hector saw him wiping his faceplate off. "You're looking at Port Elysium's life," he said. "Never forget it. The flapjacks' life, too. The cold weather flora and fauna we see upstairs is ammonia-based."

A dim squarish bulk rushed at them through the fog, and the floater halted its fall with a whoosh of exhaled helium. They hovered just above a rack of long vacuum pontoons, while the pilot fought the winds that were trying to tear the vehicle away. Already, roustabouts were climbing down extension ladders and beginning to latch the floater in place.

Jarls saw twisted wreckage, gaping holes in two of the pontoons. The shredded remnants of what had been the rig's other marker buoys were whipping in the wind, somewhere underneath the hanging fields of condenser plates.

Murdo studied the damage, sucking his lip. "You can see why the rig lost its siphon hose—there's a whole corner torn off. But there are pontoons breached along one side, too. What could have caused that kind of havoc?"

Jarls couldn't understand it either. Jupiter's atmosphere was violent, but there was nothing being flung around by it that was substantial enough to have caused the jagged destruction he was looking at now. Even one of the mile-wide dirigible creatures, caught in a sudden gust, would have ripped its gauzy tissues to tatters against the rig's hard edges.

"I'll tell you what caused it," Hector said harshly. "It was one of the hydrogen consortium's orbital siphons, dropping its hose end where it wasn't supposed to be."

"No, Hec, it couldn't be," Murdo said. Jarls could hear the shock in his voice.

"What's orbital velocity at the heights the mining satellites skim? Must be something like fifty thousand kilometers an hour. Probably the nozzle just grazed the rig. At that speed, it'd be enough."

"They're supposed to stay away from the inhabited latitudes. It's in the treaties."

"Since when have treaties meant anything to Earth?"

Jarls was stunned by the enormity of the danger to Port Elysium. Old holo images of the North Equatorial aerostat disaster of '32 raced through his mind . . . a whole city crumpling and falling like a stone into the Jovian depths.

He blurted, "Isn't there anything we can do?"

"We'll tell the City Council when we get back. They'll lodge a protest through the Jovian League."

"In the meantime we've got to stabilize this rig before we lose it," Murdo cut in. "There aren't enough hard suits to go around, so we'll have to work fast . . . before it sinks much further. We'll need every man and woman."

"We can use the spare buoyancy pods we brought along for the hose and dippers," Hector said. He did a calculation in his head, comparing the lifting power of hot hydrogen and vacuum. "About forty of 'em plus our own vac egg ought to buy us enough time while a couple of crews seal those pontoons and pump them out."

Murdo was already barking out orders. People bustled in slow motion under the pressure. More of them poured out of the floater's belly pod and swarmed down the extension ladders to the crippled pumping station.

Murdo's eye fell on Jarls. "More than you bargained for, eh, youngster? You can help the roustabouts wrestle girders. The pressure's going to go up another ten atmospheres before we stop sinking, and the wind's getting worse. Think you're up to it?"

"Of course he's up to it," Hector said gruffly. "He's strong as an ox."

The phrase had persisted, though there were no oxes on Jupiter—or any other large terrestrial land animals either. Actually, it was a misstatement. Any Jovian male Jarls's age was a good deal stronger than an ox.

As Jarls turned to go, there was the sudden, bright snap of a spark in the vicinity of Hector's faceplate; Hector jumped and said, "Damn!"

"You've got an oxygen leak, Hec," Murdo said. "You'd better see to it."

"It's this old suit. Been patched too many times. It's not serious. Just a loose hose connection. It'll hold up till we finish this job. I've just been trapping too much gas between me and the eggshell by staying in one spot too long and jabbering with you, that's all."

"Go on inside. You can take one of the hard suits."

"It's tough enough to move around in this molasses. Save the suit for someone who's used to them."

"All right. But keep moving. And stay away from electrical equipment. You can hang balloons."

Jarls left them and clambered down to the work platform, refastening his six feet of safety line every few rungs, as Hector had impressed on him. The roustabouts put him to work without ceremony. "Grab the end of that beam and hold it in place until Maryann can weld it."

Jarls did as he was told. Maryann was a brawny giantess, freckled and red-haired. Her welding torch used no oxygen. It would have been insanely dangerous in a hydrogen atmosphere, even with controlled release. Instead, the torch simply forced a stream of available atmospheric hydrogen between two electrodes, tearing the molecules into single atoms. When the atoms recombined into the molecular form, you got the intense heat you needed.

"That oughta hold the sucker," Maryann said cheerfully as she finished. "Wanna get me another girder, kid."

Jarls soon found that his safety line was a luxury. It slowed him down too much and made his coworkers impatient with him. None of the roustabouts used them for traverses, except to cross really tricky gaps. Where they were useful was when you were working in one place and wanted both hands free. Otherwise you trusted to an iron grip and good reflexes.

But the tilt of the pumping rig was improving as more balloons tugged at it, encouraging overconfidence. And maybe fatigue was starting to set in, though Jarls's workmates wouldn't admit it. At one point Jarls found himself carrying one end of a girder with a taciturn slab of meat named Brok. Brok missed his footing between handholds. Unfortunately, he'd been shifting his grip on the girder at the same time, and he went windmilling backward, made another false step, and took a pratfall over eternity.

Jarls dropped his end of the girder. His right arm shot out without his thinking about it, while his left hand retained its grip on the handhold he'd been using. He snagged Brok by the toolbelt. The jolt almost pulled his arm out of its socket. But he had five hundred pounds of roustabout dangling from his fist.

The two men at the other end of the girder couldn't hold on after Jarls let go—they were now at the end of a very long lever. The girder went tumbling down through the wispy fog, picking up speed like a bullet. Jarls watched it for a full two seconds before it was swallowed up. The swiftness of its departure was a useful reminder of Jupiter's special perils.

By then the other two men were at his side. One hooked an arm around Brok's thick waist, the other grabbed an ankle, and in short order, they had Brok beached on a level surface.

Brok picked himself up and dusted himself off. He didn't bother to thank Jarls. The only comment was from one of the other roustabouts, who gave Jarls a fishy look and observed that Murdo was going to give them hell for losing a girder.

Maryann was already calling for more steel—the term was still used, though the girders were actually an aluminum-matrix composite. Jarls went back to work on the double.

When he had a breathing space, he looked around to see what was happening. The pumping rig was almost level now; one of the pontoons was fully repaired, and enough of the temporary buoancy pods had been hung to make up most of the difference. There had been another mishap—a swinging hook had smashed someone's ribs, and she was now out of action in the cabin—but otherwise Jupiter had claimed no victims.

Jarls looked for Hector and found him about fifty meters away, sitting astride a projecting girder. He was making fast a tether for one of the last of the hot-hydrogen balloons. The balloon itself was swinging below him like a pendulum, waiting to be inflated. He hadn't taken a break yet. The end of Jupiter's ten-hour day was approaching, and Murdo wanted to get the trickiest portion of the job finished before dark.

Hector saw him and waved, a wide squarish figure silhouetted against a background of cottony mist, veined with the constant flicker of lightning. Jarls waved back, and Hector pointed out over the abyss.

Puzzled, Jarls followed the gesture, and then he saw what Hector had called his attention to—a scattering of shadowy flat shapes hovering just at the limits of visibility.

"The flapjacks," he said to Maryann. "They've come back."

"Huh?" She gave a disinterested glance, then went back to an inspection of her last weld.

"I wonder why they're hanging around."

"Maybe they're hoping we'll drop another girder."

It was Jarls's turn to say, "Huh?"

"Yeah, they like metal. They'll scavenge it whenever they get the chance. It's funny, they won't steal it from our rigs, even though we couldn't stop them, but just drop a hammer overboard and they'll dive for it. I don't know how something that big sees something that small."

"I wonder why they're so interested in metal—I mean metal especially."

"They never saw any before humans arrived on Jupiter. I guess it must seem some kind of miracle to them—something that dense and hard. They make ornaments out of it, polished mirror-bright. And knives. The lucky ones that get it, they use it to edge those big triangular bone knives of theirs."

"How can they work it without a forge?"

"You can work metal without a forge—just beat it long enough, cold, the old-fashioned way."

Jarls pondered a moment. "If they can see something as small as a hammer, then I guess they can see us, too. I mean, notice us as separate individuals."

"Yeah," she said dryly, "they're fascinated by us. Look, you wanna grab that can of flux over there and hand it to me?"

Over where Hector was working, the anaerobic burner had ignited, and the balloon was inflating. Unfortunately, a gust of wind had caught it as it started to rise, and the still-sagging gasbag had ensnared itself in its own guylines. It lay trapped under the far end of the girder, pushing futilely upward as it continued to fill. A bluish discharge of Saint Elmo's fire crackled along its upper surface.

Hector waved off a roustabout who was coming to help. He wrapped an arm and leg around the girder and started to inch upward along the inclined surface to free the guylines. The inflating fabric billowed around him as he worked.

A nearby fork of lightning made the Saint Elmo's fire flare up, as electrical potential around the floater increased. Hector's face was invisible behind the reflections in his helmet, but Jarls had the eerie feeling that Hector was looking straight at him.

What happened next could not have been said with any certainty. Perhaps Hector's exertions had loosened the leaky air hose further. Or perhaps there was an increased oxygen buildup because of the richer mixture everybody was breathing at these depths.

There was an abrupt, blinding flash where Hector had been. Jarls blinked his vision back in time to see a swirl of black ashes whipping away into the wind. The balloon was gone, too. A few shredded pennants flapped at the blackened end of the girder.

The natives had taken off like a flock of startled birds at the moment of the flash. They came fluttering back one by one and settled down to their watching.

The general frequency had gone silent. The only sound came from somebody who was breathing hard, and then he switched off too.

After a while Murdo came on. He sounded shaken. "All right, people, that's it," he said. "Go back to work." He had no special word for Jarls. Port Elysium was a small place, and a quarter of the people aboard the floater were probably related to Hector in some degree or another.

There was no time to mourn. That could come later. Jarls clamped his jaw and wrestled steel for Maryann. She bent over her torch, her wide freckled face hardened into an inexpressive mask.

Darkness came swiftly with Jupiter's rapid rotation, and the outside spotlights were switched on. There were two night shifts in every Jovian working day, but on a job like this, not even the crassest of legal quibblers was keeping track of his time sheet. Jarls worked straight through like the rest, moving through a daze of fatigue and aching muscles.

Pure bad luck and the vagaries of orbital mechanics stepped in at that point. The consortium's atmospheric mining satellite came around about every five hours in its skewed orbit, which meant that it returned to approximately the same vicinity twice a day, with a variation of only a few thousand miles. It was an arrogant gamble by the consortium—it was easier for them to keep track of their property that way, and minimized the chances of a collision with any inhabited aerostats when they strayed beyond their allotted five percent deviation from equatorial orbit. Jupiter was a big place. They thought the odds were with them, despite the North Equatorial tragedy of '32.

The siphon nozzle would have whizzed by once already while the floater crew worked, but it must have passed too far away to have been noticed. Now it was due again, and again the odds should have kept it from striking twice in the same place.

Jarls was out on a spar, waiting to receive a crossbeam that was being poked at him from below. The wind had died down somewhat, and he stood with feet braced far apart in order to leave both hands free.

He glanced around to see an unnaturally straight incandescent line drawn against the sky. It was brighter than lightning, and getting rapidly brighter.

Jarls had a fraction of a second to realize what it was. He grabbed for support, but it was too late. The thing flashed by at a distance of less than fifty meters and was gone, leaving nothing but a thunderclap and a glowing afterimage on his retinas. The wind of its passage blew him off his perch.

He tumbled into emptiness, picking up speed at the rate of fifty miles per hour every second. Above him, the rig's outline shrank with alarming suddenness and disappeared.

He could still feel the scorching heat of the siphon's transit on his face as he fell. Atmospheric friction at this depth would be terrific.

And then he was aware only that he was falling like a stone into Jupiter's crushing depths.

The rushing air plucked at the fabric of his suit. He was still accelerating. Soon he would burn up, a living meteor. Stoically, he counted out the few remaining seconds of his life.

And abruptly, there was a blanket under him, a gray blanket that stretched for acres.

It matched velocities with his and broke his fall gently. He sank into rubbery flesh. Not more than twenty seconds had passed since he'd fallen off the rig. But in that time he would have fallen some five kilometers, and would have been traveling at close to supersonic speed.

The flapjack lofted him upward, its outer edges working with powerful strokes. He raised his head cautiously. He was sprawled in the center of a vast, rippling, glossy landscape. It felt tough and resilient underneath him. Its temperature was noticeably feverish—it must be heating hydrogen in its internal spaces. Across the gray vista, near one edge, he could see a girder, small with distance. The crossbeam he'd been working with must have tumbled overboard with him. The flapjack was keeping one of its scalloped projections curled protectively around it; it was toothpick-size in the creature's colossal grasp.

As the living carpet rose through the mist, Jarls had time to examine the harness the being wore. The straps were as wide as roadways, and were made of something that could have passed for leather. There was a crossroads near him; he crawled gingerly over for a closer look. The juncture was decorated with some kind of badge or buckle of beaten metal. It was hammered wafer-thin, with a diameter of about thirty feet. Jarls remembered what Maryann had said, and decided that the individual he was riding must be an important one to have so much metal at his disposal.

The flapjack didn't like his touching the badge. The ground under Jarls twitched and deposited him a short distance away.

Jarls wanted to be sure. He got to his hands and knees and started to crawl toward the ornament. Again there was a Brobdingnagian shrug, and Jarls found himself at a distance.

This time he crawled ten meters in the opposite direction and sat down again. There were no more twitches.

It was a primitive form of communication. Jarls had shown that he understood. The flapjack had exerted itself twice to make a point. Three exchanges constituted a kind of dialogue. It occurred to Jarls that except for the Shadow Trade, this might be the first time in Jovian history that human and flapjack had ever engaged in that direct a give-and-take.

It gave him another idea. He unclipped his tool kit from his belt. There was a hammer in it, pliers, a couple of screwdrivers, a small pry bar. He pushed it away to arm's length, then again retreated a few meters.

It seemed a pathetically small amount of metal to offer to a flying island, but Maryann had said that the Jovian behemoths coveted even a dropped hammer.

The edge of the flapjack folded itself over—it still seemed perfectly able to fly in this lopsided fashion—and one of the scalloped serrations came questing inland toward the toolbox. Jarls backed off another couple of meters.

The fleshy protrusion hesitated, then curled around the toolbox. It swallowed it up, like a human hand engulfing a grain of rice, and tucked it away somewhere in its harness. The flapjack flattened itself out again and went back to flying in its normal mode.

Jarls let out his breath. He'd gone to a second stage in the conversation. It was a simple abstraction this time. The flapjack had saved his life; he'd given his permission for it to take his toolbox. It was payment for a service—not quite the same thing as exchanging goods.

For a brief, wild moment he felt a rush of elation at the thought of telling Hector. Hector's vision of getting flapjacks to work for humans on the Deep Tap project might not be a pipedream after all. Then he remembered that he would not be telling Hector about this, or about anything else, ever.

He rode upward in a black mood. The adrenaline that had sustained him had begun to wear off, and he was bone tired. Thinking had become an effort.

A square shape loomed overhead through the clouds. The platform of the pumping rig. It was big, though it couldn't compare with a flapjack. The creature came up level with it in a delicate maneuver. Jarls could see running figures, pale dots of faces turned in his direction. It must have made an awesome sight, this tremendous circular leviathan breaching the hydrogen depths and coming to a hovering halt just a few meters away.

The flapjack tilted carefully and spilled Jarls out on the platform. Hands reached out for Jarls, grabbed him. The flapjack, with a rippling movement around its entire circumference, pushed itself off and disappeared.

Murdo was one of the blurred faces around him. A pair of mittened paws squeezed his shoulders. "Jarls, boy, we thought you were a goner!"

Jarls's tongue was thick. "The flapjack saved me," he said stupidly.

"Yeah, they've been known to do that." Murdo's tone was offhand.

"No, I mean it came after me."

"I notice it caught the girder. Probably it was after that. You're a lucky fellow."

"I gave it my toolbox." Jarls knew he wasn't making sense.

Murdo scrutinized him, concern showing in his bluff face. "Yeah...don't worry about losing it. We'll get you another. Look...are you all right? No broken bones, sprains? You had the wind knocked out of you. Maybe you better go back to the cabin, lie down."

He was looking past Jarls at one of the repair gangs. His expression was distracted.

"I can work," Jarls said.

Murdo let off a little steam before turning away. "That damn siphon. They're not going to get away with this. Hec was right. Earth killed him. We never would've been working this deep on an ordinary repair. And they damn near killed you."

The job was finished in another five hours. Darkness had come and gone, and a new dawn was sending pink shafts of light through the cloud layers. The floater cut loose and rose slowly and majestically. It would be a long ascent. Everyone was purged of nitrogen anyway by the deep-breathing mix, and getting the bends wasn't a worry, but Murdo wasn't a man to take chances.

He sought Jarls out in the cabin. Most of the crew had crawled inside to collapse, and it was crowded. He picked his way through a tangle of stretched legs and recumbent bodies. Jarls was sprawled out, exhausted, a warm beer in his hand.

Murdo cleared his throat. "Tough about Hec."

"Yes." Jarls was too numb to think of any further response.

"He was a good man."

"Yes, he was." Jarls stopped short of saying thank you. That wasn't done.

Murdo cleared his throat again. "What are you going to say to your family?"

"I don't know," Jarls said. "I'll think of something."

# 3

PORT ELYSIUM grew larger, a translucent sphere of shifting rainbow colors set among puffy white clouds. It was a beautiful sight, but there was no pleasure in it for Jarls.

The others standing at the rail had moved aside to give him a little space, whether out of respect for his feelings or simply out of normal Jovian awkwardness. But now one of the suited figures edged closer in what seemed to be an attempt at manners.

A raspy voice broke into Jarls's proximity circuit. "Almost there. Be glad to get this suit off and hit the showers."

Jarls was surprised to see that it was Brok, the hulking roustabout he'd saved from falling overboard. Brok was not a garrulous type, and had been even less so after the rescue.

"Me too," Jarls said with matching clumsiness. "These suits weren't meant to be lived in for three Jupiter days straight."

Brok seemed relieved to be answered at all. He cast about for something else to say.

"Can't complain, though. Lucky to get any kind of work, the way things are."

Jarls nodded agreement. Port Elysium was a nice place to grow up in, but times had been hard for as long as he could remember.

"I've been thinking of migrating to South Polar City," Brok confided. "I hear there're jobs opening up there. They've just landed a big new maintenance contract from one of the Earth mining companies on Callisto."

There was nothing in Brok's conversational efforts that remotely suggested gratitude for Jarls having saved his life, or even an indirect allusion to what had happened. Chewing on a neutral subject was concession enough for a Jovian.

"The polar settlements always get first crack at Earth contracts," Jarls assented. "Seeing that all the off-planet traffic has to come in at the poles to avoid the radiation belts."

"They're always looking for people to man the Amalthea repair station. Three-month tour. Pay's high. I might get lucky."

Jarls said nothing. Amalthia was an irregular chunk of rock that whirled around Jupiter about once every twelve hours, not far above the cloud-scraping orbits where the Earth-Venus cartel's mining satellites plied their assigned courses. The satellites were recalled there for service, and it also served as a transshipping point for cargoes of hydrogen being sent sunward.

Earthmen never set foot on the place; it was manned entirely by contract labor from Jupiter. It was bathed in Jupiter's radiation belt. You used up a lot of your lifetime rad allowance just getting there in a shielded cocoon, and ran entirely out of rads in three months, even if you never left the deep underground burrows where the work bays were. But of course there were always chores nearer the surface, and the foremen weren't fussy about keeping track of radiation dosages. And the tours tended to stretch out past the stipulated three months because the pay was good and labor was always short—and what did a few more rads matter.

You could always see a few Amalthea veterans around Port Elysium—pathetic wrecks who had lost too many brain and retinal cells to the bombardment of charged particles, and who showed the further biological effects of spending time in a strong magnetic field. When Jarls was growing up, Hector had taken care to point them out. "Never be suckered into taking a job outside the atmosphere," he'd warned. "We're made for Jupiter. We're not made for the magnetosphere. Jovians get the dirty jobs, sure, but that one's a little too dirty."

"Maryann and I are trying to get a stake so we can start out,"

Brok went on. "We're not getting any younger. She says she'll come with me to South Polar City."

It was none of Jarls's business. "Well, I wish you luck," he equivocated. "Maybe something will open up closer to home."

"You got a girl?"

Jarls thought it over and decided that Kath qualified. They'd never actually made a commitment in so many words, but they'd known each other since childhood, and everyone assumed they'd marry some day.

"Yes."

"That's the ticket. You can't spend your whole life waiting for things to work out before you settle down. Sometimes you have to take chances."

Port Elysium filled the entire sky now. It looked as insubstantial as a soap bubble, but that was an illusion. The crystalline hyper-carbon skin was only a few inches thick and you could see moving shadows through it, but it was the strongest material in the universe. Mars's orbital elevators were made of it, and some day Earth's would be made of it as well.

Light though it was, it was rigid enough to form a perfect sphere, thirty miles in diameter. Almost all of it enclosed vacuum. The habitat section was a lidded bowl—the bottom 1/1,200th of the sphere by volume. That was big enough. Air, water, soil, and structures averaged at a little more than a thousand times the weight of hydrogen. But vacuum weighs exactly nothing, and there was 1,200 times as much of it. With ceilings averaging 500 feet, Port Elysium boasted 124.39 square miles of living and farming area—twice the size of Liechtenstein, and everyone knew that Liechtenstein was one of the great powers of Earth. Elysiumites learned that statistic in school, and they tended to sound smug when they recited it to outsiders.

Bubbles like Port Elysium were still called aerostats, through old habit. The first primitive habitats of the early Jovian settlers, three centuries earlier, had indeed been balloons of warmed hydrogen, with sealed-off inner living sections. But air and hydrogen were always in hazardous proximity at the interfaces, and despite triple locks and other stringent precautions, accidents happened. There was a series of flaming disasters—whole populations incinerated in the blink of an eye. The anniversaries were still observed as days of mourning by the entire planet. For a time the entire Jovian colonization program seemed in question. But then the hypercarbons came along, and it became practical to enclose large volumes of vacuum.

"I better find Maryann," Brok said, and pushed his way through the crowd that was waiting to disembark.

A docking crew was waiting to make the lines fast and lug a gangplank into position. The waiting disembarkees moved aside as a pair of litter bearers came through, carrying the woman whose ribs had been smashed. They'd suited her up again for the transfer. Jarls winced involuntarily; she must have been a tough one to refuse an ambulance airbox.

Murdo was trotting along beside them. He slowed down for a moment when he saw Jarls and said, "I had to radio in about Hector, but I told the dispatcher to sit on it until you had a chance to notify your family."

Jarls nodded a minimum Jovian thank you. Murdo hurried after the stretcher bearers.

Jarls waited for the others to clatter down the gangplank. He didn't feel like fighting the tide. When he emerged into the holding area, showered, freshly coveralled, and carrying his duffel, Torbey was waiting.

"Hello, Jarls," he said uncomfortably. "I . . . that is, I heard."

Torbey worked in the dispatcher's office. Jarls took his reply to mean that he had intercepted Murdo's radio message about Hector.

"Where's Kath?" he said, looking around.

Torbey looked unhappy. He was a pale, serious youth, slopeshouldered and relatively slight for a Jovian, though on Earth he could have picked up a wrestler in either hand. He and Jarls were two different types, but they'd been best friends since childhood.

"I thought maybe you might not want to see her until you'd had a chance to . . . uh . . . straighten things out at home. So I told her the floater wasn't due back yet."

That had been imaginative for Torbey. Jarls's heart warmed. Good old dependable Torb!

"Okay," he said. "That's fine."

Torbey looked relieved. "Want me to go with you?"

"No, I'll do it alone. You can drop by later."

Torbey nodded. "I'll walk you as far as the Green."

A mile's walk through the dock sector took them to the first air-wall. They went through and followed the pedestrian lane to a droplift that took them down through several levels of farmland and fish lakes, past a couple of villages, and finally to the enclosure that contained Middleville.

The two of them halted by the bordering row of gnarled trees. Torbey said, "Well, I'll leave you here," and they exchanged an awkward handshake.

Jarls cut across the Green toward home. The plot of common land was faced on three sides by small wooden houses that had grown up over the generations. Wood was the construction material of choice in the Jovian aerostats. It was light, strong, and plentiful—and cheaper than industrial materials. The ingredients for growing terrestrial plant life—carbon, nitrogen, and water—were readily available in the Jovian atmosphere, and Port Elysium's tame forests were an essential part of its air plant. The houses were of lightweight panel construction—there was no weather in Middleville. But they represented privacy and a necessary sense of owning one's own space. The gingerbread facades dripped with scrollwork and lacelike filigrees. Woodcarving had been a tradition among the early settlers, many of them Siberians and North American ethnics—something to while away the long winter nights—and generations of whittlers had tried to outdo their neighbors.

Jarls found his mother in her workroom, repairing gaskets on a spare airsuit. She had a job with the shell maintenance department that sometimes took her outside.

She looked up with a smile. "Hello, Jarls. You must be tired. I expected you back at last Jovelight. Have you had anything to eat?"

Marth Anders was an angular, handsome woman with graying

blonde hair. There was not an ounce of flesh on her that was not sinew or muscle, and she was blessed with a strong-boned, high-gravity frame that Jarls had inherited.

He kept his voice flat. "Where's father?"

"He's in his room. This isn't one of his good days." She scanned his face. "Isn't Hector with you? What happened?"

He told her in as few words as possible. She took the news in silence. He saw her eyes, above the wide cheekbones, squeeze shut, then open again, glistening with moisture.

Then she said, "I'll go in with you. We'll break it to him together." She compressed her lips. "He and Hector were always very close."

Jarls could remember when Hector had come to live with them. It was after Hector's wife, Neta, had died. They'd had no children. Jupiter's gravity was unkind to fetuses, culling out all but the strongest and fittest, and Neta had never been able to carry one to full term. At the time of her death, Hector had been partners with Jarls's father in a carbon seining venture, and it seemed natural for him to move in with them. Jarls had been five at the time. Hector had never remarried, and had stayed on as part of the household.

"We'll have to inform your uncle Jase," his mother said absently. "It's too bad he had that silly quarrel with Hector, but it doesn't matter now."

"I'll take care of it," Jarls said.

Jarls's father was dozing in his chair when they came in. His head snapped up at the sound of their footsteps, and he swiveled the chair around on its six broad rollers to face them.

Clete Anders was as massive above the waist as his brother had been, with arms and shoulders that were still powerful, but his legs had been crushed in a deep-atmosphere accident years ago when a trolling platform had collapsed and pinned him to the deck. Clete tried hard, and did what he could, but despite his upper-body strength, his condition had been steadily deteriorating in the last few years. In Jupiter's implacable gravitational field you had to stay active, and invalids tended to die young.

"What is it?" he said when he saw their careful faces.

Jarls gave him the same brief account he had given his mother. His father's voice, when he responded, was calm and reasonable.

"It happens. We take a risk every time we draw a breath on this planet."

"Murdo's going to file a claim through the League. He says we wouldn't have been working out there in the first place if Earthcorp's satellite hadn't strayed out of its assigned band."

His father's face was stony. "You can't blame Earth for everything. They didn't invent Jupiter. It's dangerous outside, period. I warned Hector about that old suit of his."

There was a whir of electric motors and the rollerchair abruptly turned to face the wall. Clete stayed that way a long minute, his breathing labored, then swung round toward them again.

"Does Jase know?" he asked.

"I'll go there now," Jarls said.

Wakes were bad form in Port Elysium, but people drifted by all next day on one pretext or another. By Third Dark, there was quite an accumulation. Although no food or drink had been set out, those who had brought their own bottles disappeared from time to time into the utility room to fortify themselves, and those who hadn't could readily get a nip from the ones who'd congregated there. As time went on, the gathering acquired a glow that Hector would have approved of.

"Who's the man talking to your father?" Torbey asked Jarls.

"Old workmate of Hector's. Name of Alik Paavo. He and Hector and my father were in business together once."

"There's Councilman Mak," Kath said. "He's working his way round the room toward you."

Kath and Torbey were sticking like glue to Jarls, for which he was grateful. They were standing off to one side, out of the traffic pattern between front door and utility room.

"Take him a while to get over here," Torbey said. "He's got to shake a lot of hands on the way."

"Oh, Torbey, don't be awful," Kath said.

"Mak's all right," Jarls said. "He helped my father get comp after the accident."

Kath squeezed his arm sympathetically. She was trim and neat, with glowing skin and straight, shining blonde hair. She went by the name Kath av-Kristen. The proud cognomen signified that her mother had been self-fertilized to create a genetic replica of herself—because, it was said, she could find no man whose child she wished to bear. Kristen av-Greta was a formidable woman with a talent for making people uncomfortable, including Jarls. Kath was just the opposite—accommodating, sunny, a good sport. But genes expressed themselves in different ways.

Mak arrived with a broad, snubnosed man in tow. "This is Dr. Chukchee," he said. "He studies flapjacks. He heard about your adventure."

They shook hands all around. Dr. Chukchee smiled warmly. He had choppy black hair and eyelids with pronounced epicanthic folds, a hallmark of some of the old Siberian families.

"We try to document all such encounters," he explained.

"I've spoken to Gord Murdo," Mak said. "I'll be introducing a motion at tomorrow's Council meeting that we file a formal protest to Earth about Earthcorp's satellite orbit. I don't think we'll get a unanimous vote in the League, though. The polar settlements are always afraid of offending Earth."

"It doesn't matter," Jarls said.

Mak sighed. "We may end up moving Port Elysium a few degrees farther south. But we're brushing up against the Great Red Spot as it is."

"Thanks for trying, anyway."

"You never know. Earthcorp'll be a little more careful for a while, anyhow. We'll send 'em a bill for the damages."

A constituent across the room had caught his eye. He switched on a politician's all-purpose smile. "I'll leave you to Dr. Chukchee now." With an inclusive nod to Kath and Torbey, he was gone.

Dr. Chukchee had been fidgeting. "They tell me you had quite a close call, young man."

"Uh . . . yes, I suppose I did."

"Your experience wasn't unique, you know. We've been able to document one hundred and seventy-four rescue incidents involving *Laganum volatilis*, going back three centuries. Stranded floaters being bumped back to their cities, and so forth. Your case makes the hundred and seventy-fifth. Of course that doesn't include all the tall tales and unverified anecdotal material." He beamed at Jarls. "What do you think of that?"

"Uh . . . I've heard stories about flapjacks saving people. I never knew whether to believe them till now."

Dr. Chukchee winced at the vernacular term. "Yes, even after all these years, we still don't know much about *Laganum volatilis*. 'A science without data,' as the saying goes. We have the observations of traders who rarely get within twenty kilometers of them, we have the occasional encounter like yours. We don't even know exactly how their metabolism works. The only specimen ever to be available for dissection was a partial carcass that was recovered by a fluke—and that was more than a hundred years ago. The investigators botched the job—imagine poking around in a quarter mile of rotting flesh swinging from balloons in a high wind. Generations of researchers have been poring over the stored data ever since, building ever more exquisite castles in the air from it. What we could do with a fresh tissue sample, or even a scraping!" He added hastily, "Though of course they're a protected species."

His bubbling enthusiasm had put Jarls, unaccountably, on the defensive. "I'm sorry I can't help you. I didn't have much opportunity to collect tissue samples."

"Heavens, I'm not an exozoologist! I wouldn't know what to do with a *Laganum* specimen if you brought me one gift-wrapped! I'm interested in their *behavior*!"

Jarls was thoroughly confused. "Oh."

"I've spoken to the dolphins about it," Dr. Chukchee confided.

"The dolphins?"

Port Elysium, like most bubble cities, had a small population of dolphins. They worked the salt water lagoons as fishherds, did underwater maintenance, and, with their built-in sonar, worked as structural integrity inspectors, patrolling every square foot of the bubble's outside skin in the mobile tanks that had been designed for them. Dolphins, in a sense, were better adapted to living and working on Jupiter than humans, since they were immersed in water, nullifying the terrible drag of gravity. They never slept, they didn't get tired, and they were always alert, which made them natural safety engineers.

"That's amazing, sir."

"Yes, in a way, they're better equipped to understand *Laganum* than we are. It's true that they're just as biologically distant from Jovian life forms, but their wild ancestors in Earth's oceans had much in common with *Laganum* nevertheless—a three-dimensional environment, a tradition of cooperative hunting, even the use of sonar."

"I never thought of it that way, sir." Dr. Chukchee seemed to be going a bit overboard on his subject, but he certainly had a knack for capturing one's attention.

Dr. Chukchee sighed. "I wish I could afford a dolphin research assistant. With the tremendous information storage capacity that nature gave them, they're uniquely suited to handling great masses of anecdotal data, and they're certainly more intuitive than computers. Some day they may provide the key to communicating with the native cohabiters of this planet, and a whole new world will open up for both species. Can you imagine what a human-*Laganum* partnership could accomplish?"

"That's what my Uncle Hector used to say. He thought the flap . . . uh, the natives could help us on the Deep Tap project."

Dr. Chukchee did not become solemn at the mention of Hector. He smiled warmly. "A wonderful man. He was quite interested in our project. He used to stop by the laboratory from time to time to add some reminiscence about his days as a trader. It's all in the data bank."

A sudden wave of loss washed over Jarls at the reminder that Hector was gone. But it was good to know that all his old stories would live on, if only in computer memory.

"Now, young man," Dr. Chukchee said, suddenly serious, "tell me exactly what happened."

Jarls dug into his memory and gave as complete an account as he could of his encounter with the Jovian giant. Dr. Chukchee became very excited.

"Yes, yes!" he exclaimed. "You were entirely correct in your assumption that you'd had a conversation with your rescuer. Your interchange proceeded in a structured series of responses on both sides, and that can be defined as a form of conversation."

"Is it that important?"

"That important?" Dr. Chukchee sputtered a while. Spots of red appeared on his flat cheeks. "It shows that communication is *possible*! Believe me, we have too many scenarios showing that communication between human and *Laganum* is inherently *impossible* because of the different wiring of our perceptual systems!" He became calmer. "We'll have to go into this at greater depth."

"I don't know what more I can add, sir."

"You'd be surprised." Dr. Chukchee smiled broadly, showing an expanse of square teeth. "We'll hook you up to a computer, have it prompt you, with our entire data base at its disposal. I'll see if I can borrow a dolphin for the day. Its presence may be useful. It may think of questions that wouldn't occur to me or the computer. And we'll let you interact with some holographs generated by dolphin sonar perception. How does all that sound?"

"Well . . ." Jarls hesitated.

"Good. It's settled, then. You can drop by the lab in a day or two. I'll let you know when I get it set up."

He squeezed Jarls's hand abstractedly and shambled off, nodding to himself in some interior conversation. Jarls turned around to find Torbey raising his eyebrows at him.

"Are you going to go?" Torbey asked.

"I guess so."

"Sounds crazy." Torbey snorted. "Talking to flapjacks."

"Oh well, it can't hurt. I don't have anything better to do with my time, anyhow."

"Don't you have anything lined up?" Torbey frowned.

"No. The job with Murdo's finished. He said he'd let me know if anything else turned up."

"What are you going to do?"

"I don't know. Things are tight right now in Port Elysium. I only got the job with Murdo because Hector put in a word for me." He shrugged. "One of the fellows I worked with was talking about trying South Polar City. He thought he might have better luck finding something there."

Kath spoke up quickly. "You belong right here, Jarls. Don't get discouraged. You've been out of work before."

"That's right," Torbey agreed. "Things are bound to get better sooner or later."

He trailed off awkwardly. Jarls knew what he was thinking. Torbey was one of the lucky ones with steady work. His job at the dispatcher's office would always be safe.

"Maybe I ought to try my luck off-planet," Jarls said, only half joking. "Like Ian Karg."

He nodded toward the door. Ian Karg, one of Port Elysium's acknowledged luminaries, had just arrived in his power chair, and already there was the usual eddy of hangers-on orbiting him at a respectful distance, hoping some of his luck would rub off on them.

"Don't talk foolishness," Kath said in alarm.

"I mean it," Jarls said perversely. "That's the way to do it. Enlist in the Executive Guards, put in your time, and come back to Jupiter to retire without a care in the world."

He eyed Karg with admiration that was entirely unfeigned.

Ian Karg was an impressive figure, though he was obviously unwell and rarely got up from his power chair. He had been away from Jupiter too long. Thirty years of Earth gravity had taken their toll, robbing him of Jovian muscle and giving him heart problems when he returned to Jupiter's greater pull. His complexion was gray, the lines around his mouth deeply incised.

Karg scanned the room with a professional sweep of his eyes and located Clete Anders. He spun the chair around and sent it marching on its rows of steel rods in a straight line toward Clete, managing to maintain an erect military bearing despite his seated position. The crowd parted before him, and a moment later he was parked chair to chair with Jarls's father, paying his respects.

"At least there's one thing Earth needs Jovians for," Jarls said, his voice harsher than he intended.

Torbey put on his reasonable expression. "The Guard recruiters only come around every twenty years or so. The chances of getting chosen are about one in ten thousand. And they like to take them young, so they can mold them from scratch and indoctrinate them with loyalty to the Pandirectorate. You'd be too old the next time they come around. Besides, Earthies think we're freaks. Best to stay on Jupiter, where you fit in."

"Yes," said Kath. "Here in Port Elysium you know who you are and what you'll be doing for the rest of your life. Everyone says you have a promising future."

Jarls had only been talking idly. He hadn't expected to be taken this seriously. But now he looked across to where his father sat broken in his chair, and he thought of all of Hector's brave schemes that had come to nothing, and his lips tightened stubbornly.

"There's no future on Jupiter," he glowered.

Kath let her impatience show. "I don't see why everyone kowtows to Ian Karg! Earth used him and threw him away. Do you want to end up like that, not able to walk ten steps without having to sit down . . . no family, no close friends?"

Jarls was taken aback by her vehemence. "He's one of the most important men in Port Elysium. He could be Head Councilman if he wanted. And he's better fixed than most people around here, that's for sure."

Torbey shook his head soberly. "That's only because his pension goes a lot further on Jupiter than it would on Earth. Earth's expensive. If he'd stayed there, he'd be living in a cheap room somewhere, pinching centimes and twiddling his thumbs. He *had* to come back."

"Why are we arguing anyway?" Jarls was tired of the subject. "I don't exactly see anyone falling over himself to offer any of us a berth sunward. It'd cost ten years' wages just to buy a ticket out of this gravity well."

On the other side of the room, Ian Karg had finished talking to Clete Anders. He spun his chair around, did his reconnoitering trick again, and started toward Jarls. A bold soul stepped imprudently into his path and attempted to start a conversation. From the stony look on Karg's face, the conversation wouldn't last long.

In the meantime, someone was causing a mild hubbub at the front door. The new arrival, unlike most of the crowd, had not stopped to change from his work coveralls before dropping by. Jarls did not recognize him. The newcomer shook off a couple of people who were trying to question him and made a beeline for Torbey.

"It's Tal Rikard from the dispatcher's office," Torbey said with a frown. "What's he doing here?"

Rikard was flushed and a little breathless when he finished pushing his way through the room. Some of the people he'd stopped to talk to at the door had followed him. He let himself be introduced to Jarls and Kath, hurrying impatiently through the amenities, then blurted to Torbey, "Have you heard the news?"

"What news?"

"There's an Earthman in Port Elysium. He just arrived about an hour ago. He's already met with the burgomanager and a couple of the councilmen."

"An Earthman?" Torbey's jaw dropped.

Jarls was electrified too. He'd never seen an actual, living Earthian. The rare visitor from Terra had sometimes appeared in one of the polar cities, and he had caught glimpses of them on the holovid, floating in their gel tanks or riding around in little powered tubs. But he'd never known one to visit Port Elysium before.

"What's he doing here?"

"He calls himself a labor contractor. Name's Stebbins. Been onplanet for a month and a half. This is his last stop. He's lifting off in a few days. Looking for a few people to sign on with him, so he says. They've given him the use of the Community Hall for a meeting."

The announcement caused a stir in the immediate vicinity. People started pressing in closer, mostly the younger men and women. Some of those who had followed Rikard from the entryway began firing more questions at him.

"Only has a few places left to fill, is what I understand," he said, addressing a general audience now. "Competition's going to be fierce."

Jarls looked at Torbey. "You going?"

"Guess so. Hear what he has to say, anyway."

Jarls turned to Kath, expecting to find her caught up in the excitement that was growing around them. He was surprised to see a frown on her face.

"Everybody'll be there," he said. "Will you come with me?"

"Yes," she said. "I think I'd better."

# 4

**S**TEBBINS TURNED out to be a large, florid, jowly man—taller and certainly stouter than any Jovian in the hall—who surprised everyone by standing on his own two legs to address the meeting.

He remained upright with the help of a powered exoskeleton that moved his limbs for him with minimum muscular effort, and that cushioned him in a fitted gelsac that was the next best thing to floating weightlessly in a tank of water.

Even so, the six weeks on Jupiter had clearly been a great strain on him. His round cheeks sagged with their unaccustomed weight, his eyes were bloodshot, his nose bloomed with broken capillaries, and only a turtleneck of gelpads kept him holding his head up straight. Jarls had to admire his guts.

"I thought he'd be in one of those walking bathtubs," whispered Kath.

"You don't dominate a meeting lying on your back," Councilman Mak observed. "First rule of politics."

He had paused at their seats while making his rounds. He glanced back at the stage, professional admiration showing in his expression.

"That rig must have cost a fortune," Torbey put in. "Never saw anything like it. Must be custom-made."

Mak smiled knowlegeably. "Not quite. It's adapted from one of those powered suits they use for high-pressure work on Venus.

Off-the-shelf job. Somebody ripped out the mechanical frame-work, substituted bladders of gel for the armor and life support. Good enough to let an Earthman navigate in our kind of gravity. But I'll bet he'll get himself back in a tank as soon as the meeting's over."

"Shhh," someone said.

Mak gave an obliging nod and continued on down the aisle, stopping here and there to lean across a row and greet someone else.

Stebbins had reached the podium, his movements a little jerky, like those of a puppet. The exoskeleton amplified his own muscle power, but there must have been a fraction of a second of resis-tance before the motors kicked in.

He looked around the hall, measuring his audience and exud-ing a genial self-confidence despite the terrible drag on his Earth-born flesh, a drag that was given away by the drooping of jowls and eyelids. The hall was packed. Extra chairs had been brought in, and there were standees ranged along the back wall.

"The name's Stebbins," he said without preamble. "Rolley Steb-bins. I represent an outfit called Solar Placement. We're based on Earth, but we do business all over the system. You might call us brokers. Our business is matching people to opportunities. And believe me, there are plenty of opportunities on Earth and Luna for ambitious young people who don't mind working hard."

He paused, letting the words sink in. He had the audience with him. Stebbins was a natural orator, with instinctive timing and delivery. The tremendous physical strain he must have been under did not show in his voice.

Jarls whispered to Torbey, "What do you think?"

"Smooth," Torbey whispered back.

Jarls thought so too. The chubby man was impressive. Jarls set-tled back in his seat to hear more.

"Why, you may ask, would we come all the way to Jupiter to recruit?" Stebbins continued. "Good question. We don't come that often. Actually it's easier for us to recruit in the Saturnian ring set-tlements or the Uranian sea cities in terms of energy expenditure, even though they're farther away. Jupiter's escape velocity makes getting people in and out expensive. From that point of view, you're the farthest planet in the solar system."

He scanned the audience benevolently. They were thoroughly warmed up now.

"But the Jovian reputation for honesty and hard work is much admired in the inner system, believe me. The old-fashioned virtues—that's what the word Jovian stands for where I come from! We've got plenty of jobs on Earth and not enough people to fill them . . . just the opposite of conditions here. Right now we're building a transPacific tunnel. Biggest project since the Pyramids. Want to know what a sandhog makes? Sixty leichtenfrancs an hour! At the current exchange rate, that works out to about two hundred Jovmarks."

A buzz went through the audience. Stebbins leaned back in his tubular support frame and waited with a satisfied expression for it to subside.

"That's right." He nodded sagely. "And that's not counting the double and triple overtime. Now sandhogging's a job that Jovians are uniquely suited for—you can handle pressure better than any Earthborn tunneler who ever lived. And work the longer hours that get you the overtime pay as well. Why, two or three years of working flat out and saving your money, and a person could come back to Jupiter and retire for life! And that's only one example . . ."

Stebbins went on for the next twenty minutes, painting a glowing picture of conditions on Earth, and the opportunities available to able young Jovians in a labor-short market. He worked skillfully to a crescendo. By the time he finished, the audience was hardly able to sit still.

"And we guarantee the jobs," Stebbins wound up. "We're so sure of it that we pay you from the first moment of liftoff. You're under contract to us, Solar Placement, you see. We're willing to gamble on you. We'll collect a commission on your salaries and deduct any money that we've advanced, of course, and if we transfer the labor contract to your employer, we'll collect a one-time commission on the sale. But that's to your advantage. What it means is that we work in your interest, because the more you make, the more we make."

His manner changed. He stared a challenge at the crowd.

"We lift off tomorrow. Do I have any takers?"

There was a surge forward. A couple of chairs were knocked over in the rush.

"Take it easy," Stebbins said with an amused smile. "We'll talk to everybody. We'll stay here as long as it takes. That's my assistant over there, Mister Enescu. He'll take your applications."

For the first time Jarls noticed the man sitting at a folding table at one side of the hall. He had a sallow, narrow face, but the thick neck and bulging muscles of a Jovian. A score of applicants were already milling around him.

Jarls started to get up.

"Where are you going, Jarls?" Kath said.

"I'm signing up," he said.

"Jarls, we've got to talk this over."

There was an edge in her voice that he hadn't heard before. For a moment the old, complaisant Kath disappeared, to be replaced by an image of the formidable mother who had cloned her. He shook off the impression with an effort.

The line in front of the table was getting longer. "I'll lose my chance if I don't get over there," he said.

"You'll be half a billion miles away. Have you thought about that?"

He shifted his feet uncomfortably. "It'll only be for two or three years. Till I get us a nest egg."

"Three years," she said, her lips tight. "I suppose that's nothing to you."

"You could come with me," he said. "We could sign up together."

She looked away. Jarls looked at Torbey for support, but Torbey wouldn't meet his eyes either. Jarls shrugged and clumped off heavily to join the mob churning in front of Enescu's folding table.

He got an application form, a stiff sheet of photoplastic that kept scrolling page after numbing page of the small print of a contract. A motionless island of space contained a few boxes to be checked and lines to be filled in. They seemed to want remarkably little information about him.

He took the application over to one side and started using the little quill that had come with it. A husky voice beside him said, "You signing up?"

It was Brok, the roustabout who had been going to try his luck in South Polar City. Maryann was with him, looking just as sizable out of her bulky airsuit. She gave him a comradely grin.

"Yes," Jarls said.

"Us, too."

Maryann pointed a chin in Enescu's direction. "I asked him what welders make. You wouldn't believe it."

"Maryann's coming with me," Brok said. "We figure we can build up our stake twice as fast that way."

"I've always wanted to see Earth," Maryann said cheerfully. "The Earthwomen on holo look like twigs."

"Your girl signing up with you?" Brok asked.

"No."

Brok looked at Maryann and got a warning frown from her. "Well that's all right too," he said. "Give you something to come back to."

Maryann signed the photoplastic form with a luminescent squiggle and said brightly, "We'd better get over there and turn these in before they fill their quota." Jarls completed his own form in short order and followed them.

Enescu had the approximate warmth of a block of ammonia ice. He glanced at Jarls's application without particular interest and said, "Press your thumb in the box after your name."

Jarls complied and felt the sting of microscopic pinpricks from the abrasive patch within the box. He looked at the bloody thumbprint and said, "What's that for?"

"DNA sampling and some other stuff," the sallow man said.

The photoplastic sandwich had finished processing whatever smidgens of information it had been programmed to extract. A red dot at the top turned green. Enescu peeled a flimsy layer off the back of the sheet and handed it to Jarls.

"This is your copy," he said. His eyes slid past Jarls to the next candidate.

"Is that all?" Jarls said.

"That's all."

"When will I hear?"

The Jovian factotum gave him a bored look. "You're hired," he said indifferently. "Report at docking bay C three hours before launch."

"You're of legal age now," his father said gruffly. "Over one-and-a-half. Old enough to make your own decisions."

It was not one of Clete Anders's good days. He held himself rigidly in his chair, moving as little as possible. Jarls could tell that he was in pain.

Jarls's mother busied herself silently in the background, getting her suit and equipment ready. She was due for her outside shift and didn't have much time. She'd maintained a resigned silence since Jarls had made his announcement.

"Three years," she said, raising her head. "That's a long time."

"Earth years," Jarls corrected her. "Only about a quarter year, Jovian."

"Or longer, you said."

"Yes, if I'm doing well."

His father tried to speak and had one of his wheezing spells. When he got his breath back, he said, "It's no use hashing it over. It's done." He mustered a bleak smile. "Good luck, Jarls. Do what you have to."

"Thank you, father," Jarls said.

His mother said in a carefully controlled voice, "I'll help you pack in the morning."

"They'll only let us take thirty pounds, Earthweight," Jarls said. "They said they'll supply everything when we get there."

"You'll be seeing Kath tonight, I suppose."

"No."

His mother gave him a surprised look, then suppressed it. She made no comment.

There was a whir of rotors as Clete Anders swung his chair around to face Jarls directly. He coughed. "There's something I want you to do before you go," he said.

"Yes sir," Jarls replied. "Certainly."

"I want you to talk to Ian Karg."

"Ian Karg?" Jarls said, caught off guard. "I didn't think we knew him all that well."

There would be a lot of good-byes to say, a lot of things to do before departure, and he was just starting to feel how limited his time was.

"We know him well enough."

"But why? What for?"

"For advice. He's the only person in Port Elysium who's lived on Earth."

"He was an officer in the Executive Guard. He must have served most of his thirty-year hitch stationed at the Pandirectorate head-quarters in Bern-Liechtenstein. Miles above any circles I'm likely to find myself in."

"You ought to see him anyway."

Jarls had the feeling that his father was holding something back. At any rate, he seemed to set great store by Ian Karg. He looked at his mother for guidance.

"Yes," she nodded in agreement. "It might be a good idea to see him."

"All right."

"I'll call him now," his father said. "He'll probably see you this afternoon."

His mother had gathered up her helmet and air tank. Jarls hoisted her toolbox to his shoulder and said, "I'll see you over to the lock."

At the door he paused for a backward look at his father. Clete Anders had let himself slump in his chair. His powerful forearms rested like deadweights in his lap. His granite face had gone slack. Jarls had not noticed before how suddenly old and unwell he looked. Perhaps Hector's death had taken its toll on his reserves.

His mother waited until they were outside before speaking to Jarls. "He's worse," she said, biting her lip. "Jarls, he won't be here when you get back from Earth."

"Mother . . ."

"It's all right, Jarls. He knows it himself. He wants you to go."

Ian Karg received Jarls in full dress uniform, as if for a formal occasion. The uniform must have been old, but it was well preserved, and the tailoring was impeccable. The black and silver tunic was austere, unrelieved except for the sleeves, which were slashed to reveal a multicolored striped underlayer—a vivid reminder of the Executive Guard's mercenary origins. The original uniform, it was said, had been designed by Michelangelo. The crossed silver pikes of the collar insignia were another nod to the Guard's long and honorable history.

Karg did not attempt to rise from his power chair. "Sit down," he invited, motioning at a faded settee.

"Thank you, sir," Jarls said.

He stole a look around the room. Karg's surroundings were plain, even drab. The ex-Guardsman lived a monastic existence. There was little furniture and the walls were bare of decoration except for some kind of a framed document with a seal and a few small photographs.

"Try some of this," Karg said, indicating a bottle and two glasses on a side table. "It's an earthwine called Burgundy. The one luxury I haven't been able to give up . . . though it wasn't a luxury on Earth."

Jarls accepted, uncomfortably aware that wine shipped from Earth must have been hideously expensive. There were no vineyards on Port Elysium, and most Elysians either made do with the local biosynthesized product or, if they were fussy and didn't mind spending money, with wine imported from one of the vineyard aerostats.

They sipped the wine in silence. Jarls did not know how to begin, and Karg did not seem inclined to start the ball rolling. Finally Karg said, "How do you like the wine?"

"What? Oh. Er, it's very good."

Actually, Jarls thought it tasted vinegary. But he put it down to his lack of familiarity with the finer things of life.

"Makes an appropriate farewell drink to see you off, don't you think?"

"Uh, yes sir, I guess so."

"It was the *vin ordinaire* of the Guard mess in Greater Liechtenstein. Part of our daily ration. Not a very good brand."

He drained his glass with a grimace and set it down on the side table. "So you're going to Earth?" he said.

"Yes sir."

"I can't tell you anything about this Stebbins person, I'm afraid. I've never heard of him."

Jarls said apologetically, "My father thought you might be able to give me some advice. About Earth."

"Your father and I were going to enlist together. We were both very young. Boys, really—hardly grown. Not of legal age on Jupiter, but that's when the Guard prefers to recruit its raw material."

"I never knew that, sir. My father never said anything about trying to enlist in the Guard when he was young."

Karg shifted in his chair. Under the tight uniform his muscles looked as rock-hard as any Jovian's, but the movement seemed to take more effort than it ought to have.

"There were half a dozen nominees from Port Elysium. Culled out by the Guard's advance men. The Guard doesn't like to take more than one recruit from any one city. It discourages hometown friendships. Injurious to discipline, you see. I was the only one chosen from here."

"I see." Karg seemed to have nothing useful to tell him. He was only being polite to a boyhood friend's son. Jarls began to think about how to take his leave gracefully.

"I served my thirty years and that was that," Karg said. "Another boy from Port Elysium made it to Earth on his own, I was told later, but our paths never crossed. There are a surprising number of Jovian transplants on Earth, considering our small population, but I had little contact with any of them. The Guard keeps rather apart from daily life."

Jarls started to get up. "Well thanks anyway. I appreciate your taking the time to see me."

Karg waved him back to his seat. "Earth may not be what you expect," he said.

"Uh, well, I haven't really thought much about it yet . . ."

"It's a very old civilization. Crowded and more jaded than ours. Hard for outlanders to find their way around in sometimes."

What was Karg trying to tell him? "Well of course I'll be careful, sir, keep my eyes open . . ."

Karg regarded him with a wintry expression. "Earthians can be devious. They're far beyond us in sophistication. Maybe that's why they set so much store by their Jovian help. We've got qualities they've lost."

"Sir?"

"Directness, honesty, lack of guile. In a perverse way, they value us for that."

"That's . . . sort of what Stebbins said. He said there were plenty of opportunities for Jovians on Earth . . ."

"Ah, opportunities." Karg's tone was harsh. "Yes, there's chiefly one thing Earthians value us for."

"What's that, sir?"

"Our strength."

Jarls waited for more, but that seemed to be the sum total of what Ian Karg had to offer in the way of advice. A vague and faintly bitter assessment of Earthian character, and nothing else. Jarls hid his disappointment.

"Thank you, sir. I'll certainly keep what you say about Earthians in mind."

He started to get up again, but Karg was not quite through with him. "Wait a minute." His chair turned on its myriad little steel legs and walked him over to a console. Karg tapped on the keys a while, signed the document that emerged, and sealed it in an envelope with a tamper-proof, high-security hologram. He handed it to

Jarls. "Here, take this."

Jarls glanced at the name Karg had scrawled on the envelope. It said *Leith Carnavan.*

"It's not likely that you'll find yourself in the Bern-Liechtenstein megalopolis," Karg said. "But if you ever have need, you can drop by Guard headquarters and ask for him. Mention my name. He's an old companion."

Jarls was completely at sea. He took the envelope and stuffed it into a pocket of his coveralls. "Thanks for giving me your time, sir. I know my father appreciates your seeing me."

"Your father's a good man. Try to live up to him, Jarls."

This flash of warmth disposed of, Karg went back to being a monument. Jarls's last impression as he left was of Karg sitting alone in the bare room, enthroned in his power chair, reaching for another glass of the wine from Earth.

A note from Dr. Chukchee was blinking on his screen when Jarls got home that night. He had been able to requisition a dolphin for the following afternoon, the scientist said, and he had set up the file of flapjack encounters on the computer. If Jarls was free, would he call him in the morning?

Jarls had forgotten all about Dr. Chukchee. He felt bad about having to disappoint him, but he was going to have to report to the docking gate at first Jovelight.

He punched his regrets into the commnet, with instructions not to deliver the reply until breakfast time. He'd be gone by then, he thought guiltily, and he wouldn't have to make any explanations or apologies in person. He had a feeling that Dr. Chukchee was waiting to pounce the moment his mailboard alerted him that he had a reply from Jarls.

His mother, wearing her padded sleepcap, poked her head into the room. "You'd better get to bed, Jarls," she said. "You're going to have to get up early."

"I know," he said. "Good night."

\* \* \*

Departure was brutal. A hydrogen-burning scramjet took a path halfway around the planet to build up the necessary escape velocity of 37.3 miles per second—5½ times the escape velocity needed to break free of Earth—and then had to fling itself into orbit from the pole—not the equator where the giant planet's 25,000 miles-per-hour rotation would have made things easier—because only by that route could a ship get through Jupiter's radiation belt before its passengers fried to death. Final acceleration piled on the G forces to a point that even a born Jovian could barely tolerate.

The scramjet was huge. It could afford to be. It had an unlimited supply of fuel at its disposal that it didn't have to carry—the hydrogen atmosphere of Jupiter itself. In a reversal of the way such transatmospheric craft worked on Earth, it carried its oxidizer rather than its fuel—in this case a dangerous load of liquid fluorine. The Jovian version of a scramjet had an advantage over its earthly counterpart: the volume required to store fluorine was many times less than would have been required for hydrogen, and the extreme cold of Jupiter's upper atmosphere helped to chill the cryogenic tanks. But fluorine was so reactive that ignition was spontaneous. This made for a simpler design for the scramjet combustion chambers, but a scarier machine to fly in. Port Elysium's docking authority didn't allow orbital scramjets within a hundred miles of the city. A floater had ferried Jarls and the others out to a jury-rigged spaceport where the craft from Callisto dangled on hooks from a floating rack. It had launched simply by dropping free and falling for a half-minute or so, by which time Jupiter's impatient gravity had accelerated it to the supersonic speed needed for ignition. For the last hour it had been picking up speed steadily on a shallow upward curve that would carry it to the outer fringes of the atmosphere for its final leap into space.

The giant palm that had been pushing against Jarls's chest pushed still harder. Around him, the scramjet's stripped interior was packed with some hundreds of people strapped into ordinary padded seats like himself. At the front of the cabin, a row of proper acceleration tanks, looking like oversize bronze coffins, had been left bolted to the deck, but such amenities were reserved for Earth-ians; it wasn't worth pampering a load of Jovians.

His seatmate had been staring silently ahead. "Is Mister Steb-bins in one of those?" Jarls asked, nodding at the coffins. Nodding was a mistake; it took a serious effort to straighten out his neck again and get his head settled in the cushions.

"Stebbins? Not likely. He won't be aboard this hernia factory. He'll be leaving on one of the charter flights that cater to Earthies and takes its time getting to orbit. That Enescu stooge and the other hired help grabbed the G-tanks for themselves."

"Where did you get on?"

"New Kalingrad."

Jarls raised an eyebrow. New Kalingrad was currently floating around somewhere on the opposite side of the planet, in the North Tropical Zone.

"How long have you been aboard this thing?" he inquired.

"About seventy-two hours."

Jarls politely refrained from wrinkling his nose. There was no denying that his new neighbor was a little overripe.

The man guessed what he was thinking. "No showers aboard," he said with a grimace. "Not for us, anyway. Toilets back there." He started to point a thumb aft, but gave up the attempt to lift his forearm from the armrest. "You don't want to visit them any more often than you have to, believe me. They've fed us, though. Twice so far. Earth-size portions. I guess they don't need as many calo-ries as we do."

"Rough," Jarls commiserated. "But we ought to make orbit pretty soon. Then maybe another couple of hours to the transfer station at Callisto."

"The crew's getting pretty irritable. At least seventy-two hours in Jupiter gravity. Usually they fly in and out, I guess. They've been floating in their eggs all that time, with their plumbing hooked up to a spaceman's johnny. They're beginning to feel the strain."

"You haven't seen any of them in all that time?"

"No, just one of Enescu's assistant stooges."

"What makes you think they're getting antsy?"

"Oh, the little announcements over the loudspeaker keep getting nastier. The pilot doesn't much like Jovians." He paused. "Calls us cloudhoppers."

"He's probably just trying to be funny."

"He's not trying to be funny."

There was an uncomfortable lapse into silence. After a moment Jarls said, "I'm Jarls Anders, by the way."

"Anton Stroz."

Neither of them offered to shake hands. Jarls turned his attention to the cabin interior. He spotted Brok and Maryann eight or nine rows ahead, in adjoining aisle seats. Maryann had tried to take her welding equipment with her, but had been told at the departure gate that she'd have to leave it behind. When she'd protested, saying, "I'm a welder, dammit—that's what I *do*," she'd been told that it didn't pay to haul unnecessary weight sunward, when tools could be provided at the work site. She hadn't been too happy about it.

Kath had shown up at the last minute to see him off. She couldn't let him leave without saying good-bye, she said. Her manner was oddly constrained. They'd exchanged an unsatisfactory kiss, both of them made awkward by Torbey's presence. Torbey had hovered closely by, maddeningly insensitive to Jarls's signals, and had pumped his hand at great length at departure. Jarls had promised them both to send a vidgram as soon as he was able.

"You're one of the ones from Port Elysium, aren't you?"

The voice belonged to the young woman in the other seat sandwiching him. He hadn't paid much attention to her as he'd stepped over Stroz, but rolling his eyes as far to the side as he could without turning his head, he had the blurred impression of a round, fresh face and a mop of brown hair.

"Yes."

"Don't mind poor Anton. You'd be grumpy, too, if you'd been cooped up in here as long as he has."

"Are you a Kalinetska?"

"No I got on later, at Southhaven. We're about forty thousand miles behind Port Elysium, right now, at thirty degrees, and catching up. But I'm pretty wilted myself."

"I guess we Elysians are having it easy, compared to you folks."

"Oh, I don't mind. At least I'll get to see Callisto." There was unabashed elation in her voice. "That's something I never thought I'd do in this lifetime."

Jarls was looking forward to seeing Callisto himself. It had a reputation of being one of the glamour spots of the solar system. Outside the worst of Jupiter's deadly magnetosphere, the icy satellite was field headquarters for the great Terran corporations in the Jovian system, and their executives lived well.

"We might not have a chance for much sightseeing," he cautioned. "It's just a transfer station. I don't know how long we'll be there."

"All I want is to be able to say I've been!" Her laugh had an underlayer of wistfulness. "My, won't they all be jealous back in Southhaven!"

Her name was Cam, and she'd done some kind of factory work back in Southhaven. That was about all he gleaned from her in the next few minutes, except for the fact that she had two brothers, and that they'd been raised by a grandmother who had died within the last Jovian trimester.

A loudspeaker crackled overhead and a voice with the residual gurgle that came from being submerged in an oxygenated bath and speaking through a contact mike drawled, "Listen up, cloudhoppers. Brace yourselves for orbital insertion. Thirty seconds at twenty gees, then weightlessness. You'll find your Jovian feedbags in front of you. Make sure to use them if you have to. We get enough complaints from the maintenance crew at Callisto about having to clean up after cloudhoppers as it is."

"The bastard," Stroz muttered beside him.

The deck tilted sharply upward, and Jarls was slammed back in his seat with crushing force. For the first time in his life he was unable to move against gravity. His vision blurred. There was a pain in his chest as he labored to draw breath.

Then, suddenly, there was silence. The scream of atmosphere could no longer be heard. They were in the vacuum of space. Jarls could hear groans around him.

His weight was gone. They were coasting in orbit. Jarls started to float against the restraining straps. To his left, someone's duffel bag had broken free and was rising into the air.

The falling elevator sensation went on and on without stopping. Free fall was a special hell for Jovians. To a Jupiter-bred inner ear, it meant only one thing: a fall from a height so great that final impact would leave nothing but a mash of red pulp.

He fought nausea. Others around him were not so successful. Beside him, Cam sat hunched with her face buried in the bag the pilot had taunted them about, her shoulders heaving. Someone else farther back hadn't been quick enough; the explosive result sailed overhead and splatted into a bulkhead.

Jarls released the latches on his safety corset and levitated involuntarily to a quasi-sitting position in midair. He swallowed hard and anchored himself again. Weightlessness was going to take some time to adjust to, when you'd spent your entire life with all the crushing load of Jupiter sitting on your shoulders.

Stebbins's three Jovian hirelings had emerged from their coffins, looking as miserable as everyone else. Enescu came floating back, shoving himself from handrail to handrail, his pasty face turned a sickly yellow.

"Get used to it," he said vindicatively before disappearing through an overhead hatch. "We're coasting all the way to Callisto."

"It's not fair," Cam complained. "To come all this way and not even get to put down on the surface!"

They were moving through a flexible transfer tunnel in the midst of a mass of fellow Jovians who were wriggling their way toward the ship's airlock like a school of clumsy minnows. Cam was still miserable with weightlessness, her face pale and drawn, but she was a determined young woman with a lot of spirit.

"There may be a viewport somewhere ahead," Jarls consoled her. "If it's facing the right way, you might get a pretty good view of the Valhalla basin. Some of the above-ground structures ought to be visible from orbit."

"Viewport!" she said in disgust. "I thought we'd land, get to spend at least a few days in Valhalla and see how Earth people live."

"I guess the ship was already waiting for us in orbit. They aren't about to ferry a crowd like this down for sightseeing."

Stroz came drifting up from behind and bumped them before he could stop himself. "Couple of thousand people already aboard," he said. "I wormed that out of one of Enescu's goons. We're the last scramjet load. Some of them've been waiting here for six weeks. Stebbins shipped them into orbit as fast as he could recruit them, before anybody could change their minds."

He grimaced at Cam. "They didn't get a chance to see Valhalla either."

One of Enescu's burly deputies was suddenly floating beside them. "Move along, move along! No time for chitchat!"

Stroz spun ponderously on his vertical axis to face him. "You're not thinking of using that prod on me, are you, friend? If you try, I'll wrap your fibula around it."

The man's face colored. "Oh, it's you again, is it? The talker."

Stroz stared him down. The man's knuckles whitened around his pushstick, but in the end he only used it to shove off again and went wriggling down the corridor, yelling at people to hurry along.

Jarls pulled himself along with the last trickle of passengers from the scramjet. There was a pileup at the airlock door. He waited his turn, then ducked through. Before he had time to take in his surroundings, the door clanged shut behind him.

An almighty stench assailed his nostrils—a pervasive reek of stale bodies, overworked toilets, and an acrid underlying aroma of spacesickness. He was inside a yawning steel cavern—nothing but a bare cargo hold, but one big enough to take an entire habitat module or cometary ice tanker. Clouds of people drifted like midges against the far walls, staying away from the vast central spaces. Tiers of bunks were stacked all the way around the cylindrical circumference, suggesting that there would be weight once the journey started. A glance at the nearer bunks showed that no attempt had been made to segregate the sexes. Some attempts at privacy had begun, in the form of improvised curtains and partitions. There were easily two thousand people sharing the spartan accommodations.

"A cattle boat!" Stroz's voice rasped from somewhere in the clot of people just ahead of him. "It's nothing but a stinking cattle boat!" The reference was unfamiliar to Jarls.

The last stragglers were being funneled through an openwork tubular chute to a checkpoint where Enescu and an assistant were ticking off names on a palmscreen. Stroz was holding things up again.

"You can complain when you get to Venus," a bored-looking Enescu said.

"Venus?" Stroz exploded. "I didn't sign up for that hellhole! I'll be damned if I'll go there!"

Enescu's expression was bland. "You don't have much choice, do you? Unless you want to get out and walk." He preoccupied himself with the palmscreen. "Next."

"Why you . . ."

Stroz surged forward, but Enescu's sidekick immobilized him by the simple expedient of lifting him away from contact with the deck and leaving him hanging in midair.

A rising babble of voices was growing around Enescu as the import of what he had said dawned on those in line. Jarls squeezed through and said, "What's this about Venus?"

Enescu stared through him as though he didn't exist. "Your work contracts have been assigned to Solar Oxygen. You'll be working in their Venus operation."

Jarls was bewildered. "Mister Stebbins never said anything about Venus. He promised us jobs on Earth or Luna."

"Did he? I never heard him say anything like that."

"But . . ."

"Read the fine print in your labor contract. It says you can be assigned at the will of the contract holder."

Jarls, at long last, was coming to a slow boil. "We want to see Mister Stebbins. We'll see about this."

A chorus of voices around him echoed his demand.

Enescu was amused. "Stebbins? You won't find him aboard *this* tub, that's for sure. He's on his way back to Earth by now."

Jarls never saw Stebbins again.

# PART 2

# VENUS

# 5

**S**O THAT'S where our Jovian hydrogen goes," Maryann said in a hushed voice, her face lit by the enormous crescent of Venus looming outside the observation wall.

"Most of it, anyway," agreed Jarls.

He gaped unabashedly along with her. Venus was a dazzling sight from close orbit, a blinding expanse of swirling yellow-white cloudtops that filled the void. Then you had to shiver as you remembered that beneath those brilliant clouds was a dull red hell that would melt lead and crush an unpressurized steel tank like an eggshell.

They were walking through a long curved gallery that led from Venusport's busy docking hub to one of the elevator spokes. The gravity here was only a minute fraction of Earth-normal, but the long trip from Callisto had taught the Jovians the shuffling gait that helped them keep their feet on the ground. Most of the Port Elysium people were sticking together in a loose group, as were people from the other cloud cities, but a certain amount of mingling had begun during the long voyage from Callisto.

Anton Stroz came shambling alongside. "Here's one for you," he said biliously. "What's the rarest thing in the known universe?"

Maryann smiled at him distantly. Jarls said, "What?"

"A Venusian on Venus."

He shuffled off again. Jarls saw him catch up to another batch of Elysians ahead and slow down for a similar brief exchange.

"Your friend has attitude," Maryann said. "He won't last long with that chip on his shoulder."

Brok said uneasily, "What'd he mean by that business about Venusians?"

"He means they can't take the pressure and the weight of the equipment. That's why they mostly use Jovians for surface work."

Jarls defended Stroz reluctantly. "He's all right. He just likes to talk."

"I've seen that kind of resentfulness before. It's dangerous in a work gang. It makes it too easy to slip up. You've got to get along with the people around you. We're stuck here in Venusport for a while. We'd better learn to live with them."

"You've got a beef coming yourself," Jarls said. "They wouldn't let you take your welding equipment. Seems a waste to use a skilled worker like you as muscle."

"I've done it before, and worse. There was only some kind of misunderstanding, that's all. I'll get it cleared up eventually."

Brok made a grunting sound. "Wait'll you fill out an evaluation form. They don't know what they've got yet." He moved protectively closer to her.

"I'm sure it'll work out," Jarls said. "Like Maryann said, we've got to get used to the Venusian way of doing things."

The corridor gave way to an open area with a row of elevator doors at the far end. A Venusian functionary was waiting for them, a stringy man who looked impossibly frail to Jarls's Jovian eyes, until he reminded himself that Venusport's gravity—matched to the planet it orbited in brave anticipation of the generations that would one day descend to the surface—was even weaker than Earth's by a factor of almost ten percent.

"This way," the Venusian said, in an accent that stressed the sibilant. He was dressed in clothes that on Jupiter would have been considered impractical and overfancy, with too much extra fabric that you could trip over—certainly not clothes that you could work in. But in gravity as weak as Venusport's, of course, a fall did not necessarily mean broken bones, even for such lightly built folk as these.

He herded them to the elevators. "Last five cars," he said.

Jarls crowded himself with twenty or thirty others into a large bare car that looked as if it was intended for freight. The door slid shut and the car began its descent. The sensation of weight increased steadily until, at the end of the ride, it was approximately what Jarls had gotten used to on the Callisto-Venus run during the long stretches when the ship had been under spin.

Another Venusian functionary was waiting for them when the doors opened. This one carried more flesh, but it was fat, not muscle—extra weight that the man's slight frame could never have carried under Jovian conditions. Jarls was beginning to feel thick and lumpish next to these overdressed fops.

"This way, Jovies," their new escort said in the same sibilant accents. "Follow me and stay close together."

They walked for at least a mile down a wide thoroughfare lined with luxury shops, restaurants, and parklike open squares with greenery and flowers. The vista ahead was unobstructed for several miles, where it ended in a series of rising garden terraces. The curve of Venusport's enormous outer rim was not readily apparent, so large was the habitat's diameter. At most there was the illusion of a slight uphill slope at the end of the avenue.

Gorgeously dressed strollers, in costumes as bright and gaudy as the flowers in the plazas, turned to watch the throng of Jovians as they clomped by, drawing back fastidiously to avoid contact when they had to. Jarls was in a group of about two hundred. The other groups being assembled at the elevators would be starting to pour out after them by now.

There was still no sign of Enescu. Jarls had not seen him since the freighter had emptied its human cargo at the hub terminal.

They took a turn down a side avenue, following their attendant. This thoroughfare was less inviting than the broad promenade they had left. It seemed to be some kind of warehouse or commercial district, faced with blank walls and scarred doors. The alleys that led off of it were narrow and ill-lit, with a neglected, rundown look.

"Through here," their guide said.

He led them through a barred gate that slammed down behind

them when the whole group was through. Inside, the appointments were more luxurious than Jarls had expected, with a high-ceilinged, thickly carpeted reception area and plush seating arrangements for the fewscore people waiting there.

They weren't allowed to dawdle. Their attendant shooed them down a side corridor, through some kind of holding area, and into a fan-shaped hall with tiered seats at the perimeter. The raised area at the focus was divided by waist-high railings that resembled pens. Several hundred people in bright Venusian clothing were seated or wandering through the hall.

"What is this place?" Jarls asked, snagging the Venusian escort on his way by.

"Labor exchange," the man said.

He looked at Jarls's hand on his arm with distaste, shook himself free, and hurried off. Jarls followed his progress to a small cluster of tables where a number of people sat with keyboards or lightpads and styluses. Jarls blinked. Enescu was there, head to head in close discussion with a couple of Venusian dandies.

Jarls started over, but was stopped by a clerk with a datapad.

"Over there. Stay with your group."

In short order he was given a lot number and an identification disc to hang around his neck, and assigned to one of the pens. Brok was there, arguing with one of the Venusians.

"I told him I didn't want to be separated from Maryann," he explained to Jarls. He turned back to the Venusian. "Listen, I'm going over there now," he said. "You can do whatever you like about it."

He tried to open the little gate, and a railing came off in his hand. Brok stared at it in chagrin. A man in some kind of iridescent uniform and wearing a weapons harness came hurrying over, a two-pronged rod in his hand.

"Trouble, messer Jeem?"

"No, no, it's all right, Hari, we'll let it go." He sighed. "What makes them want to be so difficult. All right, go on, fellow. I'll change your lot number."

Brok didn't know what to do with the broken piece of railing.

He set it down gently on the floor, and with an embarrassed shrug for Jarls, shuffled off to the pen where Maryann was standing with a couple of dozen others.

Another batch of Jovians had arrived in the meantime, and were being sorted out. A brisk, authoritative man, in a jeweled tabard and shirred blouse with enormously puffed sleeves, rapped for attention and said in an amplified voice, "We won't wait any longer, messers and mistrees. Bidding on the first lots will begin in five minutes. In the meantime, interested buyers may examine the contractees."

There was a silken rustle of movement from the front tiers of seats as some of the spectators rose to their feet and began threading their way forward.

The clerk who had been annoyed at Brok was still within earshot.

"What did he mean, buyers?" Jarls asked, catching the man's eye.

"They're here to bid on your labor contracts," the clerk hissed back at him. "What are you using for a brain, fellow? Stand up straight and try to look lively. See if you can fetch a decent price for yourself."

Ears burning, Jarls peered at the front rank of spectators. The Venusians were splendid in rich brocades and twinkling kaleidofabrics that were gathered into all sorts of fantastic puffs and pleats. Their weak, overbred faces, almost lost in the profusion of finery, were burnt dark by ultraviolet. They twittered like birds at each other, their quick gestures glittering with jeweled rings and bracelets. Jarls was acutely aware of the grimy singlet he wore, of the grubby appearance he and the other Jovians must present after their months in the hold of the freighter.

A beribboned fop, his chin buried in a neck ruff, was coming toward him with an elaborately gowned and coiffed woman in tow.

"Magnificent in their way, aren't they, Lilth my dear?" he drawled. "All that meat in the form of a human being."

He leaned across the railing and began to feel Jarl's upper arm muscles, as impersonally as if he were examining an animal. He had not yet addressed Jarls, or even looked him in the face.

"A fine specimen," he said. "If they're all like this one, I'll bid on the entire lot for Vanius."

Jarls stiffened. On Jupiter, one did not touch another person without permission. Venusian customs were different, he told himself. He made himself remain motionless while the man poked and prodded at him. The man finished his examination. "Hard as steel," he said with satisfaction. "You'd expect them to soften up a little during the trip. Just feel him, my dear."

To Jarls's horror, she proceeded to do just that, running her hands over his biceps and thigh muscles and squeezing them.

Her face was like a porcelain mask. There was no expression on it that Jarls could read. "Oh Ralf," she said, "could we get him for the household?"

Ralf laughed unpleasantly. "Up to your old tricks, are you, Lilth my sweet? No, I shan't split up the lot. This is on Vanius's tick, not mine."

They moved on down the railing, pausing here and there. They had left a heavy scent of perfume behind. It made Jarls all the more conscious of the smell of stale sweat that still clung to him. The competition for the freighter's makeshift shower arrangements had been intense before docking. He longed fervently for a long, hot shower in whatever quarters would be assigned to him.

Several pens away, Brok was getting the same treatment Jarls had just undergone, and taking it badly. Jarls saw him flinch as a jeweled and caparisoned gentleman handled him. Brok's blunt face darkened alarmingly and his nostrils flared like an animal's, but to Jarls's relief, he held himself in check.

The Venusian finished with Brok and went on to Maryann, and this time it was too much for Brok to take.

A low growl came from his throat and he laid a sausage-fingered hand on the Venusian's wrist to pry him away. Jarls could see that he was trying to be gentle—Jovians were careful with their strength, like all powerful creatures—but the Venusian yelped in alarm.

A monitor in an iridescent uniform appeared with one of the two-pronged instruments and touched Brok briefly with it. Brok's entire body gave a violent jerk, and he went reeling. He would have fallen, but the man next to him caught him and kept him on his feet. He had a slack, vacant expression, and didn't seem to know where he was. Maryann sprang to his side and helped support him until he seemed able to get his legs under him again.

The monitor stepped back and studied Brok for a moment through narrowed eyes. Satisfied, he turned and walked away.

The hall was buzzing. The dandified auctioneer rapped sharply and said, "An unfortunate incident, messers and mistrees. But not typical, I assure you. The Jovie intended no harm, I'm sure. They're a tractable and even-tempered people. But they don't know their own strength." He smiled genially. "We may take it as a useful reminder to exercise ordinary caution in managing them."

The Venusian who had felt Brok's grip was rubbing his wrist and looking somewhat pale. The auctioneer said to him, "My apologies, messer. Do you want the contractee punished? No? You're very generous, sir."

The auction proceeded. It was a confusing business, full of terms Jarls did not understand. He watched the crowd and tried to imagine how he and the other Jovians must appear to them—a throng of slab-muscled, thickset people looking somewhat seedy in the brief garments they had been wearing too long and laundering too infrequently. No wonder they were being treated like meat!

"...come now, messer, Solar Oxygen guarantees equity for rescission, so you need not hesitate..."

"...executed by parole, with proper manifestation of assent under applicable statutes..."

"...yes, messer, you may be assured that the subcontract guarantees the buyer unconditional *purum et merum dominium* under the labor code, with power to have, hold, sell, alienate, exchange, rent or unrent, and do with for the term of the original contract or in perpetuity under applicable provisions for renewal..."

The frayed copy of the contract that Enescu had given to him contained much of the same legal language, all of it just as incomprehensible. He had it in his beltpack now, read and reread, folded and refolded, until some of the words had become illegible along the creases. Jarls sighed and shifted his attention from the audience to his fellow hirelings. Across the way, Brok still acted stunned, but Maryann was staying close to him and holding his hand. Jarls located Anton Stroz in a pen nearby. If Jarls had thought of anyone as a troublemaker, he would have nominated Stroz, but the man from New Kalingrad was subdued, his face busy with his own thoughts. Jarls looked around for the young woman from Southhaven, Cam Finn-Myra, but couldn't find her. His own pen contained several people from Port Elysium, including some men and women he'd worked with on the floater, on the job with Murdo that had killed Hector.

"Come, good messers and mistrees, be forthcoming in your bids," the auctioneer was wheedling. "The lot I'm offering now is a truly exceptional buy. According to the manifest, it includes work gangs used to working at pressures of twenty atmospheres or more and at temperatures exceeding a hundred degrees Celsius—and all this in the most primitive thermal suits, mind you! Not quite as extreme as conditions on our own Venusian surface, I grant you, but as long a way toward them as you'll find in the solar system. And these are Jovians, able to move around in gravity three times ours! That gives them a big advantage in working in the soup we've got down there! You've often heard it said that Saturnians are just as good for surface work, but the fact is they're just not as strong as Jovians. No one is. So let's hear a serious bid. Do I have twelve hundred megaducs? Who'll give me twelve hundred?

Jarls paid little attention. His eyes strayed to the table where Enescu sat with the Venusian clerks, a hulking presence that made them look stringy and elongated by comparison. He was in conversation with one of the bidders, a gaunt man in spiral-striped tights. Jarls saw him nod and tap data into his palmscreen.

"Increments of a hundred minimum if you please, good gentlees," the auctioneer was saying. "I have fourteen hundred. Who'll raise me to fifteen?"

His eyes flicked to the gaunt man, whose face remained impassive as a servant touched palmscreens with Enescu to transfer data.

"Fourteen once, fourteen twice, going . . ." the auctioneer said with a sigh. "And gone. I congratulate you for a fine bargain, sir."

Jarls didn't realize he'd been sold until an auctioneer's assistant came to open a gate in the enclosure holding his group and lead them away.

"They wouldn't let me stay with Maryann," Brok said dully. He seemed listless, slow. Whatever the pronged instrument had done to him hadn't worn off yet.

"These are just temporary barracks," Jarls told him, putting more confidence into his voice than he felt. "They didn't make any provision for couples. They're moving us out tomorrow, I heard."

"We've never spent a night apart since we hooked up," Brok said, shaking his head. "Even in the freighter, we pushed our bunks together. I wonder how she's taking it."

"Maryann's very adaptable," Jarls said, hiding his misgivings. "It's just a night in the women's barracks. We'll have quarters of our own. It's in our contract."

He wondered if the women's barracks were any less crowded than the men's. He stared unhappily down the length of the long, narrow space they'd been crowded into. The rows of bunks were stacked three high, without much aisle space between. It was the vertical arrangement that bothered Jovians. Though they'd had ample experience of Venus-standard gravity in the transport ship that had brought them here, it was hard to adjust to the notion that a fall from a height was not as serious a matter as it was on Jupiter. The mattresses were something else. Thin as they were, they ought to have been adequate in nine tenths of an Earth gee, but they seemed unaccountably hard nevertheless.

Anton Stroz, who had wangled himself a lower bunk across the aisle, laughed harshly. "It's slavery," he said.

Jarls frowned at him. Brok didn't need that kind of talk after what he'd been through. None of them did.

"Come on, now," he said. "That's nonsense."

"It's slavery," Stroz repeated stubbornly. "No matter what you want to call it. We've been bought and sold, and we don't have any say in our work assignments."

"We get paid a salary," Jarls said. "We're free to quit when the contract's finished."

"Are we?" Stroz thrust out his jaw. "Not if you owe the company money."

Jarls was getting tired of Stroz. "Then the trick is to not owe them money, isn't it?" he said. "To be frugal and save your pay."

"They charge us for every little thing. Have you tried to spend anything against your pay yet in this orbital paradise?"

Jarls was silent. He had, in fact, slipped out of the barracks after supper to look for a public terminal where he could send a vidgram home, reporting his safe arrival. He had been shocked at the cost. It had almost wiped out his balance.

Then, on the way back to the men's barracks, he had been stopped by one of the shiny-suited cops, who had asked him where he thought he was going. Jarls had explained his errand and the cop had grudgingly let him go, after first advising him to stick close to the barracks and not wander around in other neighborhoods. "It's too easy to get into trouble, if you know what I mean," he'd said, eyeing Jarls's shabby singlet and Jovian bulk until Jarls's ears burned.

Stroz gave a twisted smile. "I thought so," he said.

"All right, my balance was smaller than I thought it was," Jarls said. "There was a deduction for something called maintenance on the trip from Callisto. And we were only on half pay during transport. We go on full pay after we start working."

"You see. They've got it all worked out. So that there won't be any way to get ahead."

"That's crazy."

"They deduct for what we eat. They deduct for where we sleep. Before long we'll be charged for the air we breathe. Have you ever studied Earth history? Debt bondage, they used to call it. A condition of permanent indenture."

"You're exaggerating."

"Slavery," Stroz pronounced, his jaw set. "Just as I said."

He turned his face to the wall and made a show of trying to get to sleep. Jarls was glad not to disturb him.

\* \* \*

A chime sounded somewhere. "Rise and shine, rise and shine," a disembodied voice said.

A rustle of movement interspersed with creaks and groans filled the barracks. Jarls opened his eyes, and for a moment couldn't remember where he was. His neck was stiff. One could do without a cushioned headcradle in Venusport's light gravity, but Jarls hadn't been able to shake the habit of sleeping with his neck held rigidly straight and unmoving.

He swung his feet over the edge of his bunk and dropped the short distance to the floor. He'd at least gotten used to the fact that you could do that in Venusian gravity without it jarring your spine and rattling your back teeth.

Brok, who had also drawn one of the narrow bunks, was already on his feet in the narrow aisle, scratching and yawning. He turned a pair of red-rimmed eyes toward Jarls and said, "When do you suppose they feed us around here?"

He seemed his old self again, and Jarls heaved a sigh of relief.

"First we'd better get to the showers. The crush is starting already."

When they emerged from the shower room, a man was passing out clean coveralls from a stack on a table behind him. From his cyanotic complexion and bristly haircut, he looked like a Uranian.

"Here you go, cloudtoppers," he said sourly. "You may as well throw away those—" He wrinkled his nose. "—*things* you've been wearing. You won't need them any more."

Jarls frowned at the term "cloudtoppers." He was sensitized enough by now to know that it was only a slightly sanitized version of the "cloudhoppers" sobriquet he'd heard from the scramjet pilot—still meant to be offensive, but without the courage of its prejudice. It seemed to him that a fellow citizen of the outer planets should not indulge in that kind of talk.

"I'll keep these, thanks," he said, hanging on to the singlet and shorts he'd laundered at the sinks. They were worn, but still serviceable. Venusport might be rich, but on Jupiter one didn't throw things away lightly.

The Uranian sniffed. "Suit yourself, fellow. Mess hall down the corridor to your left."

The mess hall was a high-ceilinged chamber painted in faded institutional pastels. The cloudy face of Venus swung by every three minutes or so, filling the tall windows. Brok brightened visibly when he saw Maryann sitting at one of the long trestle tables across the room. She spotted him at the same time and waved vigorously. Brok started single-mindedly toward her, and Jarls grabbed his arm.

"Better get a tray first," he said. "The line's getting longer fast."

Brok reluctantly allowed himself to be led over to a service window where a sweating individual in a grimy apron was loading trays with large helpings of starchy foods. Jarls looked at his own tray critically. He identified a succotash made with wingbeans and chimeric corn, a bowl of steamed rice drowned in some sort of gravy, a couple of greasy soyburgers, a mound of mucilaginous glop that he guessed was bacterial protein. None of it looked terribly appetizing, but there was plenty of it.

"Whaddaya want, seconds?" the counterman growled. "Move on, move on." The harsh accent was neither Venusian or Uranian, and Jarls didn't think it was Saturnian; it might have been one of the countless dialects of Earth, one of the few other places in the solar system able to supply imported labor capable of working in Venusport's simulated gravity.

He caught up with Brok and slid into an empty space on the bench opposite Maryann.

". . . I asked the section head about my filling out a new evaluation form," Maryann was saying. "You know, about getting reassigned as a welder. But he said I'll have to wait till we get to Cloudhab One."

Brock sat peacefully beside her, stolidly shoveling chimeric gruel into his mouth, content to let her do all the talking.

"What's Cloudhab One?" Jarls asked.

Stroz, sitting a few places away, raised his head and said with malicious satisfaction, "I'll tell you what it is. It's the anteroom to hell."

# 6

**A**FTER TWO centuries, Cloudhab One was showing its age. The paint of its ancient corridors was flaked and peeling, spiderweb cracks spread across its sagging ceilings, and doorways were out of plumb from the constant buffeting the station took from Venus's violent upper atmosphere.

And, Jarls thought, perhaps Stroz hadn't been too fanciful in describing it as the anteroom to hell. A sulfurous stink hung in the air, somehow managing to get past the station's seals from the incessant sulfuric acid drizzle outside.

The Jovian quarter was on the lowest levels, well below the turtle-shaped structure's center of gravity. Cloudhab One was big enough to be stable, but there was a noticeable sway at these depths—enough to make a sensitive person seasick when Venus's atmosphere acted up. The pitching and rolling was less apparent in the upper levels, where the Venusian supervisors lived.

"You Jovies should be used to aerostats," said the shift boss, a bristle-headed Uranian named Sykes. "At least you got a headstart in learning to live in them."

Jarls said nothing, remembering the tidy dwellings and manicured village greens of Port Elysium. No one could truly call Cloudhab One a home—not even the Uranians, who served out their twenty years between its grimy decks, no doubt dreaming all the while of the boiling oceans and ship cities of their gloomy native planet.

"Bachelors' barracks here," Sykes said, stopping at a long, narrow compound that had been built out from the wall of what once might have been an agricultural space. He consulted a list. "Okay, you're signed up for it, Anders, Arne, Haig, Rudi, Stroz, Yashi . . ." He read off another dozen names. "You'll get along fine here. Good bunch of boys in Barracks Five, show you the ropes."

He forced the semblance of a smile, trying to put them at ease. Sykes wasn't a bad sort for a Uranian—at least he wasn't always rubbing it in about the supposed backwardness of Jovians. The Uranians had their own neighborhood several levels above the Jovian quarter and the slums that housed the Earthian riffraff, though they still came nowhere close to commanding the luxury and open space of the topmost residential level where the Venusian supervisors and their families lived during their tours of duty.

That was another difference between Venusian aerostats and the Jovian variety. In Venus's dense atmosphere, ordinary breathable air was enough to keep a habitat like Cloudhab One aloft. Consequently, most of its volume did not have to be a sealed-off bubble of vacuum, like a Jovian floating city, and the upper-level elite had the benefit of vast open spaces, complete with an imitation sky.

"I guess we say good-bye here," Jarls said, shaking hands with Brok.

"We'll see you in a day or two," Maryann said, sticking close to Brok's side. "As soon as we get settled in."

The two of them had opted to live together in private quarters, despite the big bite it would take out of their pay. They'd also put in a request for joint work assignments.

"How's your application for a welding job coming?" Jarls asked Maryann.

She frowned. "I haven't heard anything yet."

"It'll probably take a while," Jarls said uncomfortably.

"Yes, that must be it."

"She's not going outside in a refrigerator suit," Brok said with a beetle-browed scowl. "I told her that."

"Oh Brok, don't be foolish," she said. "There's not going to be much opportunity for inside work at the base camp. What do you think they want us down there for?"

"Plenty of inside maintenance work in a place like that," Brok said stubbornly. "Things breaking down all the time from the heat."

Jarls fervently hoped that would be the case, for both their sakes. It was obvious that there would be no call for welding skills on the Venusian surface itself, not when the flux would melt as soon as you stepped outside.

"Okay, inside, you singlers," Sykes groused. "I can't hang around here all day."

Jarls cut short his good-byes and filed inside with the rest of his group. He found himself in a large, L-shaped dayroom that led into a long, narrow corridor partitioned off into sleeping cubicles. He could glimpse a dining area, kitchen, and small gym down another corridor. The dayroom was spartan and bleak, made all the more cheerless by someone's attempt to brighten it up with illustrations printed out from an entertainment bank.

"What are you doing here, Herk Tyler?" he heard Sykes rasp. "I thought you liked to do tour-on-tour down below and build up your overtime."

"Someone must have slipped up, Sykes," said a lazy voice. "Heads will roll over this."

Jarls saw a white-haired man who must have been in his fifties. He was a rough-looking character with a broken nose and a left cheekbone that must have been crushed in an accident or fight.

The Uranian's bluish complexion turned violet. "Same smart attitude as always, eh, Herk? I thought the last session in the hot-box would have taught you a lesson. Just don't start any trouble up here in Barracks Five."

"Don't worry about it Sykes," the other said. "I'm sure I won't be here long enough to corrupt your little lambs."

The Uranian opened his mouth to say something, then turned on his heel and left. The older man went back to reading a bound printout that, from its thickness, must have eaten up a good chunk of his credit balance.

He caught Jarls squinting at the title page and held it up for him to see.

"*Spartacus*," he said. "An old book. I'm surprised it was still in the data bank."

"I'm afraid I'm not familiar with the name," Jarls said politely.

"He was a Thracian gladiator who revolted against the system."

Jarls knew what a Thracian was. There were inhabitants of Port Elysium who claimed Thracian ancestry. "It must have happened a long time ago."

He got a wry smile in return. "A very long time ago. Before the colonization of the solar system. Obsolete information."

Jarls thrust out his hand. "Jarls Anders," he said.

His hand was engulfed in a powerful grip that would have crushed the fingers of an Earthian or Venusian. "Herk Tyler. Welcome to Venus, Jarls."

"What's it like down there on the surface?"

"Hot. Pressure about five times what we're used to working under on Jupiter. Acid drizzle that eats away at equipment. Visual distortion. The ground glows."

"How long have you been here?"

"Thirty years."

"Thirty years?" Jarls exclaimed in astonishment. He might have imagined someone staying on for a term of five years, or even ten if they were money-mad enough to want to pile up savings and benefits. Stebbins, in his recruitment speech on Jupiter, had talked about a three- or four-year maximum. But to choose to spend thirty years of your life in a dreary place like this was beyond reason.

"What made you stay on so long?" Jarls asked delicately.

"I owe too much to the company store."

"Company store?"

"Another ancient term. Only not so obsolete, it seems."

"I don't understand."

"Negative credit balance."

Jarls was shocked. Negative credit balances were the stuff of sermons and cautionary tales. Yet Herk Tyler did not seem to be a particularly self-indulgent person.

He had thought he had kept expression from his face, but the broken-nosed man said, "Hard to understand how it happens, isn't it?"

"None of my business," Jarls fumbled.

Tyler smiled. "I'm afraid you're about to find out how the system works," he said.

"It won't happen to *me*!" Jarls burst out with a vehemence that surprised himself.

"Good luck."

Jarls was reluctant to pursue the subject, though Tyler had invited it. "But ... but you *could* work your way out of it, even now, couldn't you?" he said.

"Too deep in the hole by now," Tyler said equably. "It adds up after thirty years. Anyway, at this point I'm not sure I'd want to leave, even if I could."

"You can't mean that!"

"The system needs someone like me to balance it out. I don't particularly like the idea, but I guess I'm stuck with it. That's the thing about ideas. They're stronger than anything else in the universe."

Jarls couldn't tell if he was serious. "Why do you think it's up to you?" he asked warily.

"Somebody's got to give the bastards a hard time. It took me a long time to accept that burden." He saw the puzzlement in Jarls's eyes and laughed. "Never mind, Jarls. Maybe I just enjoy being contrary."

He seemed to be through with the subject, to Jarls's relief. Jarls let his gaze wander around the dayroom. Stroz was already picking a fight with someone, to judge from the angry gestures he was using, while some of the others had discovered the dayroom's scanty selection of game screens and VR helmets, or were heading for the gym.

Herk Tyler sighed. "Let's find you a bunk and locker, and then get some early chow. You better get a good night's rest. We go downstairs tomorrow."

"So soon?" Jarls said, startled.

"They're supposed to give you two weeks of survival training, but you're going to have to learn on the job. You'll have to learn fast, all of you. Venus is good at killing people who don't."

"So is Jupiter."

"Don't get too smart. You might think that experience at working under high pressures and high temperatures gives you an edge, especially since you don't have to fight Jovian gravity at the same time. The Venusians think so—that's why they use Jovians for the scutwork. But low gravity can kill too—overconfidence is a deadly sin in an environment like the surface of Venus. So can visual distortion. Refraction in a heavy atmosphere like that can trick you. And those are just two of the tricks that Venus has up her sleeve."

"We'll be careful—all of us."

"I hope so. Stick close to me tomorrow. I'll try to keep you alive."

"Aren't you here for rest and rehab?"

"I just cut it short."

"But you don't have to . . ."

"Oh yes," Tyler said with wry resignation. "Oh yes I do."

Stroz had wandered over, his face still angry. Jarls could see two red splotches on his cheeks.

"Do you know what I just found out?" Stroz demanded. "They're sending us all down to the surface tomorrow! Without even a chance to catch our breath here on Cloudhab. That Uranian bastard knew it all the time!"

"Stroz, this is Herk Tyler," Jarls interrupted. "He's offered to show us the ropes."

Stroz nodded ungraciously at the older man and said, "Thanks, but I don't need anyone holding my hand." He returned to his tirade. "Well I can promise you that toadying blueboy's going to get an earful from me the next time I see him. Him and any of those other Uranian flunkies who think they can push us around."

"It won't do any good," Tyler said amiably.

Stroz gave him a pitying look. "Some of us still have a little fight left," he said.

* * *

Base Camp Two was a hundred square miles of refractory plumbing in the highlands of Ishtar Terra. Maxwell Montes, the highest spot on Venus, brooded invisibly over it, hidden by the opaque atmosphere. A river of glowing lava skirted its southern border and emptied itself into the plains below. Lightning crackled endlessly in the orange sky, where a hazy overhead patch of illumination indicated the dim presence of a sun that would never break through the clouds.

Jarls marched with dreamlike slowness along the banks of a streamlet of molten lead, pushing his way with effort through the thick syrup of the atmosphere and keeping the man ahead of him in sight at all times. The suit, with its powered limbs, was supposed to do most of the work. But pressure inside the suit was high—about 20 atmospheres—enough to give a Jovian an edge in the 90-atmosphere outside pressure.

It was actually cold in the suit—too cold for comfort. But you didn't want to try to fine-tune a Maxwell's Demon. Not when it was fighting temperatures of 900 degrees plus. It worked logarithmically, and the line between too hot and too cold was a delicate one.

Jarls stumbled and caught himself before he went sprawling. The molasses-like air buoyed his fall and gave him time to get his legs under him. He reprimanded himself for his carelessness and reminded himself that Venus, like Jupiter, didn't give a person many second chances.

The man ahead of him had stopped, and behind him the other armored figures were starting to bunch up. Herk, at the front of the little procession, must have stopped to get his bearings.

"Take a five-minute break," Herk's voice came through a crackle of static. "Don't anyone move from the path. There's a pool of metal blocking our way—it must have eaten its way through the bank since the last time I came down this way. I'm going to try to find a way around it. In the meantime, stick together and don't stray."

Jarls took advantage of the respite to look around at the scenery. He'd looked at very little except his feet since they'd left the refrigerated vehicle on the other side of a ravine, about a mile back.

The baked landscape around him was strewn with rubble—chunks of solidified lava that had crumbled under heat and pressure. The light was bad. Objects around him rippled in the heat waves, like things seen through a jiggling lens. On top of that was the distortion caused by the refraction of the immensely thick atmosphere. Though he knew he was standing on fairly level ground, with only the gentlest of downward slopes, there was the unsettling illusion of being at the bottom of a vast bowl, with everything tilted toward him, including the men who were walking down the trail in his direction. Venus was a place where you didn't dare trust your senses.

Then the sky caught fire.

"Incoming," said Herk's lazy voice in his ear.

From zenith to horizon, a blinding sheet of flame wiped out even the constant flicker of lightning. The gloomy landscape was bathed in brilliant light. Jarls couldn't help flinching. It was hard to get used to, even though it happened once or twice an hour on the current schedule. Down the trail, the advancing figures had frozen in place. After a few moments, they started walking again.

The flames raced across the sky for several minutes before breaking up into isolated cells of fire. The smaller cells began to die out. The thunder arrived then, rolling on and on without stopping, shaking the ground and visibly raising dust and ashes.

A hundred miles above, it had started to rain. But the rain would never reach the ground. It would sizzle and evaporate as soon as it dropped below the cloud layers and remain in the Venusian atmosphere as superheated steam. The *real* rain would come a couple of centuries hence.

In the meantime, the crushing weight of the carbon dioxide atmosphere was being removed little by little as $CO_2$ was split into carbon and oxygen by installations like Base Camp Two. The liberated oxygen combined with incoming hydrogen from Jupiter to form water, while the carbon ash, frustrated in its attempt to recombine with the oxygen, drifted in the soupy atmosphere for years before settling to the surface as a fine soot.

And one day, if the terraforming project continued, the Venusians would at last come down from the sky to live on the surface of their reborn planet.

Jarls craned his neck at the sky. Somewhere up there, a small worldlet made of frozen hydrogen had miraculously dissolved in a flash, ending its decades-long journey through space in a violent union with a fountain of Venusian oxygen. And behind it was an endless chain of other worldlets, like a string of cosmic pearls, waiting for their turn to disappear.

"They're getting rich on our hydrogen, the bastards," said a sour voice in his ear.

The armored figures behind him had closed the gap. Jarls tore his gaze from the flaming sky to face Stroz and Brok. It was Stroz, naturally, who had spoken.

"They're getting rich on their oxygen," he said reasonably. "They've got the solar system monopoly."

"*Somebody's* getting rich on our hydrogen," Stroz retorted. "It sure as hell isn't us."

Beside him, Brok stood silent and motionless as a blackened statue, letting his suit do the work of supporting him. He'd been quieter than usual since they'd arrived on the surface. Maryann had not been sent down to Base Camp Two with him this tour. He'd managed to spend exactly one night with her since they'd disembarked at Venus.

"What's taking him so long?" Stroz complained. "We stand here much longer, we're going to start charring around the edges."

"Take it easy, Stroz. We got a couple of hours left in these suits."

A fourth man had joined them. It was Yamaguchi, who'd been at the end of the column. He was a relatively seasoned veteran of three years on Venus and its habitats.

"I'm baking inside this damn thing," Stroz snapped back. "I've got two puddles of sweat in my boots."

"You shouldn't have changed the setting on your demon,"

Yamaguchi said with a shrug in his voice. "Those little loudspeakers that chase the gas molecules are tuned to within a hair."

Stroz wasn't listening. "I'm going to have a look-see over past the other side of that outcropping," he said. "I'll bet there's another way around whatever it is that's holding us up."

"Herk told us to stay on the path," Jarls reminded him.

"I'm tired of hearing about what Herk said!" Stroz flared. "Who appointed him our keeper anyway? He's just an indentured stiff like us. Only dumber. He hasn't figured out how to get out of this Venusian trap after thirty years!"

Jarls, to his discomfort, realized that Stroz was not bothering to use his laser proximity circuit, but instead was talking over the general radio comm. But if Herk had heard him, he gave no indication of it.

Stroz was already striking out toward the raised surface feature that had caught his eye, moving with characteristic impulsiveness in the thick air. He kept trying to bull himself through the resistance by sheer strength, then overcompensate and have to recover his center of balance.

"Don't be a fool, Stroz!" Yamaguchi yelled after him. "Any outcropping on Venus is liable to be dangerous! The surface is still plastic. There's a lot of viscous creep around hot spots. Whatever pushed that formation up from below might still be active!"

But Stroz wasn't good at taking advice. Jarls watched him move in jerky slow motion out onto the field of glowing rubble, clambering over boulders and threading his way between active fissures.

"Fellow like that can get others killed beside himself," Yamaguchi said on the proximity circuit. He hadn't waited until Stroz got out of range, and Jarls wondered if that was deliberate. "If he gets himself into trouble, we'll have to go after him."

"Maybe he won't wander too far," Jarls said.

Stroz had managed to cover a few hundred yards by now, and already he was looking blurred and indistinct around the edges. He slipped on a rock, and Jarls heard a grunt of pain on the radio band. But Stroz picked himself up and struggled onward through the viscid air. Minutes later he was around the outcropping and out of sight. Jarls strained to listen, but the radio signal had been cut off, and there was nothing in his ear but a roar of static.

They waited for some minutes. Then, on the path ahead, the man who had been second in line after Herk waved at them to advance. A moment later, Herk's voice came over the radio band.

"Yeah, we can get past the lead pool," he said. "It's going to be a little tricky. There's a narrow spot we can bridge one at a time. Better close ranks now."

"Herk, we've got a little holdup here." Jarls explained the situation to him.

"I heard it. Can anyone see him?"

"No. But he can't have gotten too far."

Brok stirred out of his statue-like immobility. "I'll go look," he volunteered. "You two stay here."

"Wait a minute," Jarls said.

There was an indistinct motion around the edge of the outcropping. A few moments later, like a stretching of taffy, the refracting atmosphere separated a moving blob from the larger mass. The blob developed arms and legs, and showed that it was walking toward them.

"There's a lake of lava on the other side," said Stroz's strained voice. He was panting with effort—not a good sign. He still hadn't learned to pace himself in these conditions. "It's impassable in that direction."

"Herk found a way across," Jarls said. "We're forming up now."

"I'll be there in a couple of minutes," said Stroz. "Go on and get started. I'll catch up."

Herk had been listening. "Take it easy, Stroz. We'll wait for you. There's plenty of time."

"Sure. And then you'll be saying that I held things up."

The blurred figure across the plain started bounding toward them, if its sluggish progress could be called bounding. For all his effort, Stroz was managing no more than a fitful alternation of sudden spurts and retarded motion.

"Slow down, Stroz," Yamaguchi warned. "Remember that you

still have all the mass you had on Jupiter, no matter how light you feel. It'll catch up with you if you have to stop suddenly or change direction."

"You sound like Herk," Stroz's scratchy voice replied. "I know all about operating in dangerous environments. I've worked on the Deep Tap. I've probably been down farther than any of the rest of you."

"This is Venus, not Jupiter," Yamaguchi said evenly. "We're talking about inertia, not pressure."

"Go soak your head, Yamaguchi."

The man-shaped blob continued to forge ahead, skipping from rock to rock, windmilling its arms for balance. Jarls watched as it came gradually into sharper focus, turning into an ash-smudged refrigerator suit with the hump of the demon on its back.

Then, when Stroz was about halfway across, his foot slipped on a rounded rock. He tried to stop, but was unable to brake in time, and continued flailing in the direction of his motion. Inexorably, he slid down the rock. His foot sank into the doughy ground at the base of the rock, and he sat down hard. Jarls saw with horror that Stroz's leg was buried up to the thigh.

"What happened?" Herk said over the comm.

"He's stuck," Yamaguchi answered. "Like a fly in honey."

Stroz was trying to pull his leg out, but he couldn't get a footing with his good leg, and he couldn't get a handhold on the slippery surface of the rock.

"I'm all right," Stroz said, sounding irritated. "The suit's keeping my leg cool. I'll get loose in a minute."

"The chilling action of the suit's going to harden the magma," Herk said urgently. "You've got to pull him out while it's still plastic."

"I'm all right, I tell you!" Stroz said. "I'm working it loose now!"

Jarls was the first to move. Brok and Yamaguchi followed close behind, the powered legs moving like pistons.

"That's right, you've got a nice pace going," Yamaguchi said. "Just keep it up."

Jarls hadn't tried to move this fast in a suit before. He'd had only a few days' practice in it. The speed of response of the powered limbs was a function of the force he could apply in the shortest possible time, and it was rough going when you had to fight the 90-atmosphere outside pressure, the 20-atmosphere inside pressure, and the resistance of the feedback servos all at the same time. Jarls knew he was on the edge of being in control, and he silently cursed Stroz. The only difference was that he had a healthy respect for the risk he was taking, while Stroz was careless.

He was puffing by the time he reached Stroz, and he could hear the wheezing of the other two in his ears. Stroz hadn't made any progress in freeing himself. In fact, he seemed to have embedded himself even more deeply.

Time was of the essence. In addition to the problem of the magma firming up with Stroz's leg in it, there was the problem of the demon itself. It was working too hard to dissipate the extra heat that the trapped leg and Stroz's prone position on one of the solar system's hottest griddles had imposed on it. Jarls could see the rippling effect caused by the hot $CO_2$ exhaust rising like a column from between Stroz's shoulders. On Venus, there was no convenient outside vacuum or thin, chill atmosphere that would carry off excess heat the normal way. Radiator fins would merely absorb outside heat and cook the man inside the suit. Instead, the Maxwell's demon sucked in the outside air, batted the fast molecules outside again through a tube filled with sound waves, and circulated the slower molecules through the suit's cooling network. But there was too great a strain on the demon now, particularly if the fall had resulted in pinched ductwork. If it broke down, Stroz wouldn't last five seconds.

Despite the alarm bells going off in his head, Jarls forced himself to take a moment to survey the situation. The only firm purchase within ten feet of Stroz was a little shelf of rock on the other side of the boulder that Stroz had slipped on. It didn't look as if it was soft around the edges.

He didn't have to explain. Brok took his hand in a steely grasp as Jarls scrambled over the boulder, then braced himself between two rocks and stretched his other arm toward Yamaguchi, who had already wedged his toes under the shelf.

Jarls grabbed Stroz's wrist in an acrobat's grip, ignoring his protests, and growled at him until he closed his fingers around Jarl's wrist in a reciprocal grip. Jarls heaved. Behind him, the two-man human chain tugged. Stroz was no help. There was nothing he could push against.

There was a moment of resistance. Jarls felt as though his arm was being pulled from its socket. Then something gave, and Stroz was drawn free. Jarls and Brok went sprawling. Stroz flopped like a fish on the rock's smooth surface.

"There wasn't any need," Stroz bellowed. "One more minute and I'd have . . ."

"Shut up, Stroz," Yamaguchi said. "Just shut up."

Jarls stared in fascination at the dimple Stroz's leg had made in the magma. It was curling slowly inward, but not closing up all the way.

"Let's check out your suit," Yamaguchi said.

"It's okay," Stroz said. "No harm done."

Yamaguchi made a visual inspection anyway, over Stroz's objections. "How's the leg?" he said. "Not getting hot, is it?"

"It's all right, I tell you."

Yamaguchi turned to Jarls and Brok. "Better look you over, too. You both took a fall."

He checked their suits for contusions, examined the screening over the demons' intakes and outlets. "How's it look?" came Herk's voice over the radio band.

"Okay, as far as I can see," Yamaguchi answered. "We can check the suits over when we get back."

"We need new equipment anyway," Herk said. "These units have been around too long. They've taken a beating."

"Good luck," Yamaguchi said. "You didn't get anywhere last time."

"I'll threaten a strike," Herk laughed. "That always scares them."

"And gets you put in the hotbox."

Herk laughed again. "I do some of my best thinking there. Come on. We'd better get going."

They picked their way back across the stretch of rubble, keeping an eye on Stroz. He didn't seem particularly chastened, but he didn't try to skip ahead.

"Now you know what I meant about hot spots and viscous creep," Yamaguchi said. "You've got to learn to read the terrain."

Stroz made a rude sound. "I'll tell you what, Yamaguchi. *You* shut up."

They regained the path and caught up with the man ahead. Herk had returned; Jarls could see him about a hundred feet ahead, motioning them on. They closed ranks further. Presently they came to the pond of molten lead that Herk had mentioned. There was a narrow place forming a channel between two pools, and a slender neck of solid-looking ground projected almost all the way across, but there was still a gap of six or seven feet.

"There's the spot," Herk said. "Follow in my footsteps, and don't stray more than six inches to either side. The ground's deceptive. There's a thin crust that formed over the molten lead bordering that little peninsula, and it's covered with dust and ash. It looks solid, but it isn't."

The lead pond looked as if it were boiling in places, but Jarls knew it couldn't be *that* hot. It had to be trapped gases bubbling up from underneath. In fact, the lead had to be cooler than the rocks it had been leached out of by the furnace that was Venus. Still, you wouldn't want to fall into it. Jarls edged up behind Herk and the others. He still didn't see how they were going to get across.

Yamaguchi and Herk were arguing. "I'm taller, Herk," Yamaguchi was insisting, sounding irked.

"Yeah, but I'm meaner," Herk said. "I get the honor."

Abruptly he raised himself on tiptoe and stretched both arms to the sky. "Here goes," he said, and toppled over like a tree.

His fingers scrabbled at the rim of the opposite bank, digging holes in the ground. Instantly, Yamaguchi was kneeling, grasping Herk's ankles to steady him. "Go!" Yamaguchi bellowed.

Brok, standing immediately behind him, jerked into motion and loped across Herk's broad back to the other side. Immediately he flung himself prone and pinned Herk's wrists.

"Go, go!" Yamaguchi screamed.

Jarls woke up. He sprinted across the human bridge and reached the opposite side in two or three quick steps. He could feel Herk's body sag beneath his feet, and wondered why Herk hadn't locked the suit's joints. The servos helped, of course, but Herk still had to push against them by brute force to support a quarter-ton extra of Jovian and refrigerator suit.

Two more men were right behind Jarls, and ten seconds later, everyone was across except Stroz and Yamaguchi.

"Get going, dammit!" Yamaguchi bawled, but Stroz still vacillated, either unsure of himself or being stubborn. Yamaguchi planted two mittened paws in the small of his back and shoved.

"Hey!" Stroz roared. He took two tottering steps across, dancing to keep his balance. Jarls grabbed him by the harness and hauled him bodily across the gap. One of the other men caught Stroz in his arms to keep him from sprawling face down in the glowing alluvium. "I could have fallen in!" Stroz said indignantly, but no one was paying attention to him.

Yamaguchi was last. He wasted no time. He was across in a couple of bounds, and kneeling beside Brok at Herk's clawed hands.

Herk had lost his toehold even as Yamaguchi was stepping on him, and now, to Jarls's horror, his feet slipped down the bank and he was up to his hips in molten lead. Brok and Yamaguchi yanked with all their might, and dragged him up the shallow bank. Molten droplets spattered Jarls and the other men. But Herk was sitting up and struggling to his feet. A crust of cooling lead had formed on his legs, like a thin layer of ice. Herk flexed each leg in turn, and the hardened lead fractured and fell off.

"Nice going," he said. "We'll make live veterans of you yet."

Jarls wondered why he hadn't chewed Stroz out, but they were on the move again, and there was no time to think about that. Another flash of fire in the sky lit up the landscape, and he was walking through a flickering hell, putting one foot ahead of another and trying to keep up with the man ahead.

The ground shook some minutes later, and someone said, "That was too close. What if somebody in the orbital switchyard miscalculates and we get hit by a load of magnesium? Hydrogen's one thing, but getting rained on by solid ingots is something else."

"Don't worry about it," Yamaguchi said. "Tell them, Herk."

"There's no danger," Herk affirmed. "They do it on a rotating schedule. The last load for Ishtar Terra arrived weeks ago. They won't start dumping again at this location for another thirty days. Right now, all the incoming from Mercury is raining on the Aphrodite Terra depot."

"That's what they say," said the other man, a north equatorial Jovian named Haig, whom Jarls didn't know very well. "But that's a lot of metal to field. Trillions of deliveries. Easy for a few million to get by you."

"They keep track of every chunk," Herk said dryly. "It costs money."

Stroz cut in. "In contrast to us," he said savagely. "Jovians come cheap."

Herk said mildly, "If you think we have it tough here, pity the poor bastards who get shipped to the mines on Mercury. It makes this place look like a resort."

"Yeah, they don't last long on Mercury," Yamaguchi agreed.

"Our Jovian brethren there need to be organized," Herk said. "Nice little strike in the Caloris Basin smelting operation. It would cut off their credits from Venus. *That* would make the Mercurian powers-that-be sit up and take notice."

"Keep it up, Herk," Yamaguchi said. "Just keep on agitating and *you'll* get yourself shipped there."

"Not a chance," Herk shot back. "I'm too old. They wouldn't get their money's worth out of me."

Another twenty minutes' walking took them to the borders of the ingot dump. Dump was rather an understated characterization for an area of some two million square miles that stretched halfway to Aphrodite Terra and provided a margin of error for the bombardment from Mercury. Fortunately the problem they had been sent to fix was a minor one that was as close to the Ishtar $CO_2$-splitting installation as the celestial pitching team on Mercury and in Venus orbit dared to aim. A problem any deeper inside the broiling wasteland of Leda Planitia would have required a convoy of long-range refrigerated vehicles, and that would have been expensive.

Jarls looked around. Visibility was about a hundred yards in any direction, but within that circle of hellfire was a chain of seething fumeroles that marched out of sight into the enveloping fog. Ingots were strewn all over the landscape—coffin-size lozenges of plastic-wrapped magnesium, some of which still had the remnants of solar sails and descent parachutes attached to them.

"There's the cart over there," Herk said. "It just went off track."

Jarls could just about make it out through the mist. It was a boxy shape about forty feet long and twelve wide fitted out with flexible metal mesh wheels. Somehow it had failed to sense the edge of a steep slope and had overturned, spilling its load of ingots across the ground.

"Is that what they sent us for?" Stroz complained. "One of the robot loaders could have picked it up in a second."

"Robot loaders?" Herk's tone was sardonic. "They're valuable pieces of equipment. You don't send them into unknown situations where another piece of equipment's gotten itself into trouble."

They waded through the heavy air for another hundred yards and gathered around the tipped dump truck. It was a massive thing, built for heavy-duty service. Herk found its tiny brain behind a heat-resistant panel, put it on manual, and observed that the oversized mesh wheels turned properly. "Still operational," he said. "Okay, let's set it upright."

First they emptied it of its remaining ingots. Magnesium was light—lighter than aluminum—but each of the wrapped bars weighed tons.

Jarls teamed up with Herk. Together they horsed one of the coffins around, levered it upright, and toppled it over the side of the truckbed.

"Why the plastic?" Jarls grunted as the ingot hit the ground with a thud. "It can't keep out the heat."

"To keep the atmosphere away from the metal during reentry. Magnesium burns in $CO_2$. Don't want to waste it until there's a shipment of incoming hydrogen to react with the oxygen it releases. Otherwise, no water, and the loose oxygen just goes looking for carbon again."

The flimsy wrapping was pretty badly shredded in spots, with long streamers of plastic peeling off. The rough handling hadn't helped any.

"Didn't hold up too well, did it?" Jarls said.

"Doesn't matter any more. It's well below the ignition point of magnesium when it isn't being a meteorite."

They heaved another ingot over the side. The trailing ends of the shrouds for the solar sail were still attached. A small lump of plastic slag at the fork must have been the pea-brained guidance system.

"Talk about waste," Jarls said. His Jovian sense of frugality was offended.

"Oh, they stamp out those control packages cheap. Mercury's got all the energy in the world."

The truckbed was empty. The eight men ranged themselves along the sides and took a grip.

"One, two three . . . *heave!*" Herk said.

The Jovians lifted the vehicle bodily and put it down on level ground. It bounced ponderously on its enormous latticework wheels and settled down. The men stepped back out of the way, and the truck, after taking a few seconds to figure things out, rolled off in search of a loading machine to fill it up again.

"That's that," Herk said. "Let's get going. We've been out here too long."

"That's all?" Stroz said sarcastically. "I thought you were going to ask us to load it up again."

"No, I wouldn't do that to you, Stroz," Herk replied equitably. "I'm no Uranian straw boss."

He turned on his heel and began walking back along the

scuffed trail their boots had made. Jarls and the others followed, and after a momentary hesitation, Stroz did the same.

Jarls had to fight a tendency to hurry. He was, he realized, too eager to be away from this nightmarish plain. So were the others. The line was bunching up in places, people bumping into one another.

"Slow down," Herk's voice came back. "There's plenty of reserve left in our suits. We'll get there."

The ragged line gradually straightened itself out and spaced itself out more evenly. Jarls slogged on, keeping his eye on the back of the man ahead as he climbed the endless slope of the illusory bowl that refraction had scooped out of the landscape.

"Here's the spot where we crossed," Herk said. "Looks like part of the bank broke away. We've got some fast water, but we'll be all right. The bottleneck's still there."

He was waiting just at the edge of visibility, letting them catch up. When Jarls got there, he could see what Herk meant. The shore of the further pool of molten metal had crumbled just beyond the narrow channel, opening the floodgates. The liquid lead was rushing through the gap, then churning around in a wide, slow circle until it spilled over a low waterfall.

"Stay close," Herk said. "I want to test the shore."

He and Yamaguchi were kneeling together, poking at the ground with a short rod. Jarls watched them for a minute or two, then looked around to see Stroz wandering along the bank.

Herk looked up and saw him too. "Stroz, stay away from there," he said sharply.

"Just having a look," Stroz said.

"It's mud, made of liquid lead and crumbled lava."

"Looks solid to me."

Stroz took another step. As always, his movements were too abrupt. His feet slid out from under him and he tumbled into the torrent of lead.

Herk moved fast, scrambling after him in a half crouch, with Yamaguchi right behind. Jarls pounded after them, one step ahead of the others.

But it was too late. Stroz was swept away even as Herk flung himself on his belly and reached for him. Stroz was still active. His armored paw stretched toward Herk's hand and closed on air.

"We've got to get him out!" came Brok's agonized voice. "His exhaust's under the surface. It could get clogged, just like that!"

Herk stood up. "I hope so," he said. "It'll be fast."

Jarls stood back and watched helplessly as Stroz's struggling form was carried further out of reach. Stroz was kicking and splashing. A hand rose, clutching furiously at the sky, then fell back.

"Lord, but he must be mad," Yamaguchi whispered.

Stroz sank out of sight. There was a wait of thirty seconds or so. Then the surface of the molten pool burped up a bubble of superheated steam—the vaporized contents of the refrigerator suit. The bubble burst with an audible pop, and the vapor that had been Stroz disappeared in a flash.

"He didn't feel anything," Herk said. "Let's go."

Jarls was in the exercise room, constricted in a heavy-duty penguin suit that resisted every move he made, while running on a treadmill with one of the 200-pound yokes on his shoulders. It was only a rough simulation of Jovian gravity, but two hours a day of it for the last 30 years had kept Herk from going soft, like some of the other Jovians you saw on Venus, and Jarls was determined to follow his example.

The older man grinned a challenge and forced the pace again. Two or three of the others on the treadmill groaned, but Herk wasn't even winded yet. Jarls grinned back at Herk and raised the pace another notch. Another man dropped off, but the rest of them stayed with it.

A Uranian in neat coveralls with a supervisor's badge pinned to his chest came through the door and looked around. When he saw Herk, his sharp features tightened, and he pushed his way through the exercise machines to stand in front of the treadmill.

"I hear you've been shooting your mouth off again, Tyler," he said.

Herk stepped carefully off the treadmill and looked the Uranian in the eye. "He should never have been sent out there, Smithers. A man like that. You know that."

The Uranian's bluish complexion deepened a shade. "I never heard of a delicate Jovie. Everybody pulls his weight down here, mister. You musclebound freaks are here to work, not admire the scenery through a porthole."

"He needed to be broken in. Light duty around the base for a week or two till he knew how to handle himself outside."

"Shut up. You had to go file a complaint, didn't you?"

"It's my right," Herk said evenly.

"You know what happens to your complaints. But in the meantime they accumulate in the computer, like sediment, till I have to go to the trouble of getting them expunged."

"You didn't like him," Herk said, as still as stone.

"He was a troublemaker. Like you."

"He was a loudmouth. Nobody took him seriously."

The Uranian was breathing hard. "I don't like complainers. They breed other malcontents."

"So you admit it, you son of a bitch. You didn't like him, so you sent him out there."

The Uranian swung at Herk. It was like hitting a rock. The Uranian yelped and rubbed his knuckles.

Herk smiled contentedly and threw a return punch. It connected, despite the hampering counterforce of the penguin suit. Even so, he must have pulled it. The Uranian went staggering backward and fell over an exercise machine. He landed heavily on his narrow backside, still conscious, but unable to get up.

Herk stood quietly in the half crouch that a penguin suit imposed when the wearer was at rest, making no further attempt to move. Jarls and the others on the broad treadmill looked at one another, then he and Brok got off it and started toward the Uranian to help him up.

"No," Herk said. "They'll say you touched him."

Jarls wavered, not knowing what to do. A moment later, four

armed guards, big men for Uranians, pounded into the exercise room, their helmet lights flashing and their whooper alarms making a racket. Two of them went over to the fallen straw boss, Smithers. Jarls saw that he had some sort of beeper clutched in his hand.

Smithers, still too winded to speak, nodded in Herk's direction. "Them too?" one of the guards said, looking over at Jarls and Brok, and Smithers shook his head in a weak "no."

All four of the guards piled on Herk, clubs swinging. He could have shrugged them all off, even with the penguin suit, but he endured the beating, only raising one thick forearm to protect his head and face. When one of the guards got too enthusiastic and tried to ram the end of his club into Herk's eye socket, Herk caught it in the palm of his hand and said indulgently, "You don't want to get carried away, Grimes. Think of the paperwork. Besides, you might make me mad."

The beating lost its steam then. The guards dragged Herk's unresisting form toward the doorway then, two of them raining a few halfhearted blows on his back and shoulders.

"What happens to him now?" Jarls said to Yamaguchi.

"He gets put in the hot box."

"What's that?"

Yamaguchi's face twisted. "They call it 'detention.' There's no such thing as cells or dungeons on Venus. To get sent to jail, there has to be a hearing up in Cloudhab, or even all the way back to Venusport if it's serious enough." He gave a bitter laugh. "But it has to be labeled a crime to do that. It's amazing how there's never any crime on Venus. Just 'work discipline.'"

"But what *is* it?"

"Just a little storage room at the perimeter of the station. Too small to stand up in and just wide enough to stretch out in. But it just happens to have one hell of a thick steel door and a spy eye in the ceiling, so it's perfect for, uh, detention. Oh, did I tell you that the demon for the little blind alley the storage room is in doesn't work? Somehow they never got around to fixing it. So there's just about enough cool air filtering in from the rest of the station to keep an egg from frying."

"But they can't *do* that!"

"Can't do what? Didn't I tell you that it's only temporary detention. Just in the interests of keeping the detainee from 'harming himself or others' is the way they put it. There's token medical monitoring, if only to save themselves the trouble of hauling out a corpse. Though it happens. And of course, the person inside gets the full mandated ration. It's the law, isn't it?"

Jarls stared. "Well . . . yes."

"The full *mandated* ration, that is. No extra fluids. So if a person is smart, he doesn't eat his rations."

"This is monstrous!" Jarls blurted.

"They're very kind, actually," Yamaguchi went on. "They try to tempt your appetite with delicacies. Like anchovies."

"How long will they keep him there?" Jarls said, his jaw tight.

"Don't worry about Herk," Yamaguchi said. "He's smart. He's gotten out alive every time."

Jarls slept badly that night. He kept visualizing Herk, squatting in the center of the hot box so as not to touch the scorching walls, the sweat streaming down his naked body, his expression blank so as not to give any satisfaction to the watching eyes, as he contemplated ancient books about ancient injustices, or whatever it was that kept him sane.

And then, all of a sudden, he realized who it was that Herk reminded him of with his white hair and massive frame and uncomfortably radical ideas.

It was his uncle Hector.

# 7

**J**ACK STRAW," Herk's voice said in the darkness. "John Ball. Watt Tyler. They were the leaders. They called it the Peasants' Revolt, and for a time it brought justice to the country that was known as England. But in the end, the charters of freedom were revoked, and seven thousand peasants were hanged to punish them for their effrontery. Jurors who failed to find them guilty were hanged too."

There were groans from the surrounding bunks and someone said, "Have a heart, Herk. We appreciate the bedtime stories, we really do, but it's a half hour past lights out. Save the rest of the seminar till tomorrow."

"Have it your own way," Herk said genially. "If you want to remain unenlightened, it's up to you. But remember that oppression feeds on ignorance."

There were more good-natured groans from the darkness.

"Okay, pleasant dreams, peasants," Herk said. "I'll pass out printouts in the morning."

He was answered by yawns and the rustle of shifting bodies, replaced within minutes by the sound of snores.

After an interval, Herk whispered, "Jarls, are you awake?"

Jarls stirred restlessly in his bunk. He had been having trouble falling asleep the last week or two, despite the fact that he was always bone-tired at the end of his shift.

"Yes," he said.

"I saw our friend Smithers order you out on a repair detail today after you'd done your legal fourteen hours. He's riding you, you know."

"I can take it."

"He's got it in for you. He's seen you palling around with me and Yamaguchi. Maybe you better keep clear of us for a while till he cools off."

"I don't avoid my friends."

"Nice sentiment. But it could get you killed. You don't want to get yourself posted on old Weasel Face's permanent list of dangerous assignments."

"Why not? You are. And so is Yamaguchi. And you've both managed to stay alive."

"We've got more experience. You've got the stuff, but you're not ready yet. Give it a little more time, and you can start tweaking the system too." Jarls could imagine him grinning in the darkness. "Yamaguchi thinks you're the one who could take over from me when they finally get me."

"I don't plan to stay that long," Jarls snapped, and immediately regretted it. It sounded as if he were rubbing it in about Herk's failure to break away from the trap of Venus.

There was a pause. Then Herk said, "I think I can get Smithers to ease up on you for a while. I happen to know he's been fiddling with vouchers—diverting small balances to an account he set up and then erasing the trail. And I know how he does it."

Jarls was startled. He listened uneasily to the snores around him and wondered if anyone nearby was awake.

"Does he know that you know?" he whispered finally.

Herk gave a muffled chuckle. "He will tomorrow."

"Don't do it, Herk," Jarls pleaded. "He has enough reason to hate you, right now. Don't give him any reason to be afraid of you too."

"I was going to use it some time. I might as well use it for this."

"It's not worth it. I'll take my lumps. Don't make more trouble for yourself. That last session in the hot box almost did you in."

"It's not yourself you're worried about, is it?"

"Me? No." Jarls was affronted.

"Then it's settled." There was another soft chuckle. "I'm going to enjoy turning up the heat on that Uranian toady another notch." He changed the subject. "I'll need some help distributing those printouts tomorrow. Will you stuff some into the lockers at your work site?"

"Sure." Jarls had the sense of having been manipulated. "Aren't you using up an awful lot of your credit on accessing old books and printing out these pamphlets, though?"

"What's money for, if it isn't to get yourself in debt with? Get some sleep, youngster. They're going to sweat us tomorrow. There's a new cycle of incoming hydrogen on the way."

Jarls lay awake a while longer. The images of the Peasants' Revolt wouldn't leave his head. Perhaps Herk's quixotic campaigns were having an effect after all.

"I see you're at it again, smartass," Smithers said. The bruise Herk had given him in the exercise room had not yet completely faded, making a darker blotch against his cyanotic face.

"At what?" Herk said innocently.

"Don't give me that, you Jovian lump! This is your work, and we both know it!"

He waved the printout under Herk's nose. The paper was wrinkled, as though it had been violently crumpled, then smoothed out again.

"So what?" Herk said. "The right of free expression is guaranteed in the Venusian articles, if a copy of them still exists any more."

"This is subversive garbage!" the Uranian straw boss erupted. "We found it in every locker on this level. We're going to search the entire compound and confiscate every copy."

"It's a history lesson. And even an indentured Jovian is allowed by law and company regulations to have any reading material he wants in his locker."

Jarls thought he should step in at this point. He started forward, but Herk waved him back with a peremptory gesture. The gesture was not lost on the straw boss, who fixed Jarls with a long, baleful look before turning back to Herk.

"The law's whatever Solar Oxygen says it is, Jovie. And there's a company regulation against, quote, 'possession or distribution of any materials tending to compromise safety or efficiency, thus causing a monetary loss to the corporation.' Unquote."

"You're in no position to talk about compromising safety, Smithers. Especially not after sending an inexperienced man out to get parboiled."

A vein twitched in the Uranian's narrow forehead. "Don't try to spar with me, you damn barracks lawyer. I'm tired of dealing with you. If the hotbox doesn't impress you, try a citation for maliciously causing undue expense to the company. You think I'm tough? They'll turn your life into pure hell."

Herk laughed. "I'm terrified, Smithers. What are they going to do to me? Add another million megaducs to my existing debt? Make me work it off for another fifty years after my death?"

Smithers exploded. "You've got all the strikes against you that're allowed, you joker! I'm going to see to it that you're shipped to Mercury as an incorrigible. With your record, one little word from me is all it'll take for them to reassign your labor contract." He glared at Herk. "They know how to handle your sort on Mercury."

"All right," Herk said quietly. "But first we'd better have a little talk."

"No talk. You can get back to work—for now!"

Herk's answering look was almost regretful. "Seems to me you're under a labor contract too, Smithers. Let's have a little discussion about vouchers."

The Uranian almost choked with fury. "Why you . . ."

"Not here. Let's have a little privacy."

He took the Uranian by the elbow and led him off to the side of the big lock chamber. Smithers went without visible resistance. Watching them, Jarls thought that they looked almost like two friends having a private word together.

The discussion didn't take long. Jarls saw the Uranian nod in response to what Herk was saying. There was another brief exchange, and this time Herk nodded. The two men looked each other in the face for a heartbeat, and then Herk started back toward Jarls. Jarls didn't like the way Smithers stared at Herk's back the whole way.

"What happened?" Jarls said.

"It's all fixed. "He'll ease up on you—for a little while, anyway—but you won't get away with anything. That's understood."

Jarls nodded.

"You'll have to watch your step, though. He has it in for you now."

"What about you?"

"Oh, he'll go right on riding me. That's understood, too."

"But . . . aren't you going to be sent to Mercury?"

"Me? No." Herk gave a short, harsh laugh. "We're used to each other, Smithers and I. He'd be lost without me."

Smithers and the other straw bosses were striding up and down the line now, bawling orders. "All right, suit up, everybody! And be quick about it! Incoming's in six hours. We don't have much time."

The inner door to the airlock was a twenty-foot circle, noticeably hot to the touch. When it swung open, a heat wave rolled through, and the temperature of the hanger-size antechamber immediately went up to about 150 degrees—hot enough to make any unsuited men gasp for breath—and the big industrial-size demons began laboring to sort out the air molecules.

The vehicles went through first—immense eight-wheeled capsules pulling powered trailers. The suited men followed them up the ramp and into the yawning inner lock. The door clanged shut behind them, and they waited while the chamber built up to Venusian pressure.

Jarls had been paired with a new man, a young South Polar Jovian named Doolan. Jarls found it a little disconcerting to be looked upon as an old Venusian hand, after only a few weeks on the surface, but Doolan had even less experience than he did, and Jarls took seriously the responsibility of looking after him.

"I don't mind saying I'm a little nervous," Doolan confessed. "It'll be my first time that far from the station."

"We won't be that far out," Jarls reassured him. "We'll be inside the vent perimeter, and no matter what part of the grid they drop you off at, you're never more than a couple of miles from a bunker."

The pressure inside the lock had about equalized by this time, and the crushing Venusian atmosphere had them firmly in its grip. Jarls listened to the complaining creaks and pops of his suit and reflected that no deep sea diver on Earth had ever felt this kind of pressure, and none ever would, unless they gave that job to Jovians too.

"I can hardly move," Doolan said. "How are we supposed to work like this?"

"Just move slowly," Jarls said. "Exert a steady pressure against the suit's feedback. And don't make *any* move without thinking about it first. There are no prizes for hurrying. Except maybe one you wouldn't want to collect."

It came to Jarls with a rueful flash of recognition that he must sound exactly as Herk or Yamaguchi had first sounded to him. Seasoned. Avuncular. A little bit didactic.

The outer door slid open. There was a swirl of volcanic dust that took its time about settling to the floor. Venus glowed dimly beyond. It was like looking into an oven.

"That's our carrier there," Jarls said, pointing at one of the capsules.

They hauled themselves up its bulging flank to the broad encircling fender and grabbed a handrail.

"It's a good idea to change hands every once in a while," Jarls advised, feeling self-consciously pedantic. "The grip's supposed to be nonconducting, but theoretically, prolonged contact with *anything* at ambient temperatures could burn through a glove."

Doolan snatched his hand away as if it had caught fire, then sheepishly grabbed for the bar again to keep from falling.

"That's all right," Jarls said. "I only meant every five minutes or so."

He ran his eyes down the length of the capsule. Herk was hanging nearby, and he could see Brok beyond him. Yamaguchi was nowhere in sight. He might have been on the opposite side of the capsule, but Jarls thought it more likely that Smithers had decided to split him and Herk up, and that Yamaguchi was riding one of the other vehicles.

The train of capsules and trailers began to move out into the landscape. Jarls felt a lurch, and his vehicle followed. For the next few miles, the lumbering procession threaded its way through a forest of blackened industrial shapes: angular towers, gigantic overhead pipes, smoking vents, squat storage tanks made of refractory concrete, huge snail-like pumping stations fed by thick conduits. The tremendous structures leaned toward them as they approached, loomed overhead, then leaned backward to disappear into murk.

Then the industrial scenery thinned out and turned into the familiar Venusian wasteland, only sparsely punctuated by an occasional man-made structure. The colossal tunnels that shortly would be delivering hurricanes of pure oxygen, Jarls knew, were buried under the surface, a gargantuan engineering feat of two hundred years ago that was more astonishing, even, than Earth's transatlantic tunnel of the same period.

There was a jolt as the eight-wheeled vehicle bounced over a rut. Jarls tightened his grip on the handrail. The bare expanse of seared rock that lay ahead seemed somehow more intimidating now that the $CO_2$-splitting installation, as ugly as it was, was out of sight behind them.

"It must be nice to ride inside," Doolan said beside him, making a brave and almost successful effort to conceal a slight quaver in his voice.

"That's only for supervisors," Jarls said. "A Uranian couldn't get around in one of these suits. Hell, they couldn't even get *into* one of these suits."

"Smithers came along with us for this trip," Herk cut in over the proximity circuit. "I saw him climb aboard before."

"How come?" Jarls said. "He usually does it by radio."

"I don't know. He has some reason for riding herd on us more closely. Maybe he's getting flack from upstairs. I heard that one of the high muckamuks from one of the families that controls Solar took up residence in a luxury suite in Cloudhab. A young blood named Paes. These Venusian grandees don't visit Cloudhab any more often than they have to. It's a hardship tour for them."

"Think he'll make an inspection trip down here?"

Herk cackled. "On the surface of *Venus*? Not likely!"

The carrier vehicle was slowing down. Jarls's radio crackled into life, and Smithers's voice broke in.

"Anders, Doolan, you get off here. That's your location over to the left. When you finish, you'll find a bunker about 800 yards further east. You can't see it from here, but there's a marker visible from the site. You wait there, and there'll be a vehicle to pick you up before Incoming."

"What do we do?" Jarls asked.

"You've got to replace a gasket. You'll find a kit on site. Do a diagnostic on the valve and fix anything else that needs to be done."

Jarls could see the housing at the edge of visibility, near a line of ridges that were muzzy with atmospheric distortion. Evidently the refrigerated vehicle was not going to make a detour for him and Doolan. And, he soon realized, evidently it was not going to come to a full stop for them either.

"Hang," Jarls told Doolan. "Get the legs of your suit going in rhythm. Match pace with the wheeler. Touch ground. Then drop."

"Get off, I said," Smithers's abrasive voice cut through. "Never mind the talk."

Jarls took his time, and hoped Doolan was doing the same. Hanging by his arms, he gingerly made contact with the ground and slowly transferred weight to the soles of his boots. When it felt about right, he let go. He stumbled involuntarily forward a few steps, fell to his hands and knees, and bounced upright.

He took a step sideways to give the big wheels plenty of clearance, then turned to look at Doolan. Doolan was dangling straight down, still hesitating, but doing everything right. He was still a little short on practice, and he took a worse tumble than Jarls. But,

Jarls was pleased to see, he had the presence of mind to roll out of the way of the wheels, and he got back to his feet without delay.

"You all right?" Jarls said.

"I've got bruises between my bruises, but nothing's broken." He gave a shaky laugh. "On me or the suit."

"Good man."

Jarls watched the refrigerated vehicle rumble by, its trailer jouncing along behind it with a limited cybernetic judgment of its own that let it sidestep potholes and small obstacles. It picked up speed again until it was out of sight in Venusian haze.

He took his bearings. The small delay had carried them a few hundred yards past the drop point, but it wasn't much of an extra walk.

With Doolan close behind him, he trudged toward the installation. It took the form of an enormous incurvate cone uncannily resembling a volcano. Which it was, of course, in a manner of speaking.

There was an access panel along the near slope. Jarls and Doolan had to shovel away a lot of accumulated Venusian ash and grit, using the telescoping spades from their belt toolkits, then pry the door open with crowbars.

"Fused into place," Jarls grunted. "But not too badly. I've seen worse."

It was dark inside, and they had to switch on their helmet spotlights, using up more of their power packs than Jarls would have liked, until he located the main lighting switch.

The gasket was a flexible disk the size of a house foundation. Jarls and Doolan got on opposite sides and wrestled it into position. It wasn't a hard job for Jovians in Venus's weak gravity. They could have done it without their powered suits if the climate had been less inimical.

"First we've got to loosen the main fitting and slide the old gasket out," Jarls said. "Then we can just slide this one into place."

The bolt heads were the size of kegs. There were twenty-four of them, about five feet apart, around the circumference of the fitting. Jarls found a two-man lug wrench with a six-foot handle in the repair locker, and he and Doolan fell to work.

They leaned into the handle with all the strength of their suits, but nothing gave. "Frozen," Jarls grunted, not stopping to reflect on the incongruity of the word in an environment like this.

There was no such thing as a lubricant on the surface of Venus. "What'll we do?" Doolan said.

Jarls paused to think a moment. Then he undid the safety on his Maxwell's demon. There was a nipple valve with a short length of tubing at the business end of the thermoacoustic cylinder. It was for emergency use. If a man's demon failed, you could bypass the cold air gate and hook him up to an auxiliary demon that would keep him alive until you could get him to safety. You had all of ninety seconds to make the exchange before you had an oven-baked corpse on your hands.

Doolan saw immediately what he was up to. "Aren't you taking a chance?" he said.

"A thirty-second blast of cold air. That's all I'm going to give it. It might shrink the metal just enough to make a difference."

"It's not worth the risk."

"I've got plenty of time if I don't panic. I once saw two men sharing the same demon, attached together like Siamese twins. They walked a half-mile, arm in arm. When the medics got the suits off them, their body temperature was over a hundred and four. But they both were fine after a night's rest. There's plenty of reserve capacity in a demon."

He did not mention the fact that the two men had been Brok and himself. Afterward, Yamaguchi had said, "Never try a damn fool stunt like that again."

Jarls fished out the length of tubing and unscrewed the nipple. It was clumsy work in his thick gauntlets, even though the logarithmic response of the motorized fingers was eggshell sensitive at the low end of the scale, and he prayed that he would not fumble when it came time to reconnect. The stream of cold air that shot out coated the bolt head with carbon dioxide frost. Jarls counted out the seconds, making himself hold the tubing in place as it became more and more uncomfortable inside the suit.

"Thirty," he said aloud, and managed shakily to screw the nipple back in place without dropping it. His skin felt as if it were on fire, and he could hardly breathe. A medical monitor beeped disapprovingly at him, telling him that he had a high fever and should report to sick bay at once.

Relief was immediate. Jarls gulped a mouthful of cool air to quench his searing lungs. "Quick!" he said. The CO-2 snow had volatized instantly, and the chilled bolt was absorbing Venusian heat again.

They flung themselves like maniacs against the handle of the two-man wrench. Nothing happened, and they strained to the limit. The bolt creaked, resisted, and then turned easily.

Jarls and Doolan grinned at each other through their faceplates. Jarls had been afraid that the bolt head would snap off, and he was sure that the same thought had passed through Doolan's mind.

It went fairly quickly after that. The next half-dozen bolts turned without any fuss at all, and then they came to another frozen one after that. Doolan wanted to contribute cold air from his suit, but Jarls wouldn't let him. All in all, Jarls only had to unhook his demon four times. When they finished, he was dizzy and drenched with sweat, and he allowed himself the luxury of sitting down for a few minutes until his medical monitor quieted down. He took a long drink of water from the spigot at his chin, and started to feel better.

"You'd think they would have left a powered wrench here," Doolan said.

"Too chancy," Jarls said. "Power tools don't last long in the heat. Muscle power's more reliable. That's why they need Jovians on Venus."

He was sounding more and more like Herk every day. He stopped himself before he started to go on to Herk's standard introductory lecture on exploitation.

"We're not through yet," he told Doolan. "We've still got the diagnostics to go through."

It took them another hour to check out the operating systems of the auxiliary delivery valves that would add a portion of powdered magnesium and calcium to the geyser of pure oxygen that would shortly fountain into the Venusian troposphere. All told, the job had taken some three hours.

"We'd better get out of here," Jarls said, as he finished tightening a last loose connection. "It's not going to be very healthy around here in a little while."

They tidied up, and sealed the access door behind them. A marker was dimly visible about 800 yards to the east, as Smithers had promised—a slowly flapping aluminum pennant that was intermittently lit by lightning flashes. Without it, they might easily have missed the low hump of the bunker nestled between declivities. All bunkers were supposed to be equipped with directional transponders having a range of several miles, but in Venus's freakish conditions, you couldn't always depend on them working.

They had to lean into an east to west wind to get there. The surface breeze of about three miles an hour was negligible, but the air was so thick that it was like pushing their way through gelatin. They crowded into the airlock and logged in by displaying the bar code on their helmets to the scanner. When they emerged through the inner lock, they found a dozen men already inside, waiting for the eight-wheeler to come by and collect them. Nobody had bothered to crack their suits because it would have taken too long to crank down from the 20-atmosphere suit pressure and then repressurize again, but the bunker gave them an opportunity to cool off their suits, take a load off their demons, and recharge.

Jarls spotted Brok. "Where's Herk?" he asked.

Brok frowned through a faceplate streaming with condensed moisture. "We were almost here when Smithers ordered him back out to fix a stuck valve on a pumping station about a quarter-mile past where we'd been working. Herk told him that his suit needed recharging first—that he couldn't get all the way there and back with the charge he had left—and that he'd go out again after he checked in at the bunker. But Smithers told him he'd be picked up in plenty of time. He said the eight-wheeler would detour for him on its way back from picking up the men at the outlying bunkers, and he could plug into the outside umbilical during the ride if he was really that low." He shook his big head. "I wanted to go myself, but my suit was even more used up than his was."

"How long ago was that?"

"About an hour."

Jarls pursed his lips. "Smithers should have let him recharge first. You don't cut it that close on Venus."

"He said there wasn't enough time. Incoming's on final approach trajectory."

Jarls glanced at his helmet clock dial. "The eight-wheeler'd be due about now. It probably won't be long."

He joined Doolan at the spouts and flushed out his suit with fresh air. When he had a good flow going, he plugged in the umbilicals to recharge his demon and top off his air reserve. He was standing there watching the dials go round when Brok came up beside him.

"You better hear this," Brok said on the proximity circuit. "Switch on your radio."

Jarls tuned in to the general comm. There was a lot of outside noise—faint voices from a dozen sites fading in and out—and then Herk's voice came in clear and strong.

"Where the hell are you? I'm running out of reserve."

Static made a sound like a spitting cat, and then Smithers' voice said, "Sit tight, Tyler. We've had a breakdown. We'll get to you as soon as we get it fixed."

"Sit tight, hell! I'm going to walk for it!"

"We'll get to you in twenty minutes, tops. I promise."

"I haven't got twenty minutes. I'm leaving now."

There was a pause for more static, and Smithers said, "You'll use up your reserve faster walking than staying put. You wait there. That's an order."

"Sorry, Smithers, I can't hear you. I thought you said you

wanted me to wait here until I ran out of time, but even you wouldn't expect me to be such a jackass."

Smithers cursed. "At least leave your directional on. We'll pick you up on the way."

"Sure. And pigs have wings."

Jarls could hear the sound of labored breathing as Herk got himself moving, and he realized that Herk's safeties must have switched to minimum support.

"Wait a minute! Did you fix the valve?" Smithers sounded querulous.

"Funny thing, Smithers. It didn't need fixing. Your monitors must have been out of whack."

Herk switched off, leaving only the empty hissing sound of the carrier wave.

Jarls stared at Brok and said, "He'll never make it."

"Shut up," Brok said.

Both of them were pawing at their suit latches, fastening seals and getting the internal pressure started up again. They scrambled for the airlock door. Others were right behind them. Four or five of the most agile squeezed into the lock with them, and then they closed the door against those who were still trying to get inside.

Nobody was up to the full twenty atmospheres of internal suit pressure by the time the outer door opened, but there was a lot of redundancy in the armor, and nobody's suit buckled. Jarls swallowed hard to relieve the stabbing pain in his ears, then swallowed again.

There was a rack of spare demons in the lock. Jarls shouldered one and stepped outside.

Beside him, Brok grabbed his arm, an obsolete reflex for someone in a powered suit.

"That way," Brok said, pointing. "He'll be coming from that direction."

"Fan out," Jarls said. "Stay in sight of one another, and don't get ahead of the line. Maybe we can meet him halfway. Somebody should stay behind in case we miss him."

"You chums go on ahead," came a radio voice from a second batch of rescuers still inside. "One of us will stay near the lock."

"Thanks," Jarls said. "We're moving on a front about five hundred yards wide."

"All right. We'll move out on either side in case he gets past you."

The line of armored figures began advancing. Jarls could see two more men besides himself who were toting the big, heavy cylinders that contained spare demons. That was the important thing. If Herk's power gave out, they could carry him in, if necessary. In fact, he wouldn't put it past Herk to keep walking inside a dead suit, carrying it along by sheer muscle power.

His expression grew somber as he realized that Herk was probably pushing some dead weight already. When a suit's power began to fail, the computer gave priority to the demon.

"Herk, can you hear me?" he said. "Come in if you read this."

There was only radio silence to answer him. "He's turned everything nonessential off," Doolan said from somewhere in the line. It took a new man to bother stating the obvious. Still, Jarls thought with a small appreciative part of his brain, Doolan was proving to be a fast learner.

"He had about two miles to walk," Brok said gruffly. "Keep your eyes peeled from here on out."

The wavering shape of the bunker was still dimly visible behind them when someone shouted, "Look! Over there!"

Jarls searched the swirling mist and saw a speck of motion ahead. He fine-tuned his filters and made out the distant outline of a man staggering toward them.

The line of rescuers broke into a run. The run was a frustrating slow-motion lope, with the gluelike atmosphere pulling at their feet, but they covered ground with snail-like persistence. Jarls saw Doolan stumble and fall, pick himself up, and keep plodding forward without missing a beat.

Herk tottered toward them with nightmare slowness, moving like a run-down mechanical toy. His radio was still switched off, but he raised one arm to show that he had seen them.

Then Jarls saw him suddenly stop and stand stock still. He stood frozen in place, the arm still upraised.

Before Jarls had time to think, the motionless figure exploded. The hard suit burst outward against the pressure of boiling body fluids and rained metal and plastic parts on the scorched landscape.

"Oh, God!" Jarls heard someone moan.

Jarls got himself moving again. When he reached the spot, there was nothing except a pair of boots standing in a circle of soot that was still drifting slowly downward.

# 8

**Y**AMAGUCHI WORE a sorrowful expression on his face, like an old hound dog. "What's that you've got on?" he asked. There was the faintest hint of disapproval in his tone.

Jarls was sliding down a catenary slope with the wind whistling in his ears, picking up speed as he headed toward the axis of the $y$ coordinate. The slope was in brilliant hues of blue, shading to violet at the bottom, against a pale yellow void. He had tuned the setting low enough to let in the real world as a ghostly background image, and enough of Yamaguchi's voice got through for him to hear the words.

He took off the veeyar helmet and set it down on the low table beside him. The feedback glove gave a final twitch as the helmet faded to a clear bubble, and there was a beep to tell him that the program was on hold.

"It's a study holo," he said. "Engineering. Elements of stress theory."

Yamaguchi made a disparaging gesture. "You're wasting your time. You'll never use it. You'll never be anything but unskilled labor to a Venusian."

"There's nothing wrong with wanting to improve yourself."

"How much did you spend on that study holo?" Yamaguchi demanded. "And the others before it?"

"Not that much," Jarls said defensively. "It'll just take me a little longer to work it off, that's all."

"That's what Herk used to say before he decided he was never going to get out of the hole. And what about the vid you sent to Jupiter? That must've cost you a week's worth of credit."

"I just wanted to let them know that everything's fine and I'm doing all right."

"You're lying to them and you know it. That outfit you bought that you'll never wear again except to send another vid. How many months did *that* set you back. Tell me something. Did that girl ever answer you?"

Jarls regretted ever having told Yamaguchi about Kath. "Well, no. Not exactly. My mother said she said to say hello in the vid she and my father sent."

"I thought so," Yamaguchi said.

"Kath has better things to do with her money than waste it on high-density vids!" Jarls retorted angrily. "I'll probably get a laser-gram from her any day now." He frowned. "We've still got an understanding."

"I'm sorry. None of my business. It's just that I hate to see you give up on what Herk taught you."

"I haven't given up on what he taught me. But Herk's been dead for half a rotation now. That's what his ideas got him. I can't fill his shoes, and neither can you. I only want to get along and make the best of a bad bargain. And maybe get out of here some day."

"I see," Yamaguchi said evenly.

"Look, Taki, we've still got another week of recoop here on Cloudhab. I just want to relax a little, hoist a few beers, and enjoy the amenities, such as they are. Let others worry about the social order for a change."

"A few of us are having a meeting tonight. We've got an anti-surveillance loop set up in a storeroom behind Barracks Four. At least come to that."

"Sorry. I've got other plans."

"That girl you met on the transport from Callisto?"

Jarls flushed. He still felt a little guilty because of Kath, though the friendship he had struck up with Cam Finn-Myra had so far done nothing to compromise his self-imposed loyalty.

"I'm meeting a few friends at the tavern in the rec corridor for drinks, that's all," he said.

Yamaguchi shook his head. "Another way to use up your credit," he said. It was his parting shot. He rose heavily to his feet and headed for the dayroom door.

The Red Spot was a dark, low-ceilinged dive at the far end of the Jovian quarter, crammed between a used goods exchange and a dream shop. It was run by a flabby, manumitted South Equatorial Belter named Fitz, who had somehow managed to squirrel away enough credit over a thirty-year period to pay the rent on the space and keep it running at a marginal profit. It was said that untaxed gambling went on in the back room, and also that Fitz loaned money on the sly, but for some reason the Venusian authorities left him alone.

Brok and Maryann were sitting across the room with Doolan, nursing beers in thick cryomugs. Maryann spotted Jarls at the door, and waved him over. Jarls squeezed his way between scarred plastic tables and joined them. He signaled Fitz for another mug and pulled out a chair for himself.

"Where's Cam?" Maryann asked.

"She had to work the dogwatch at the maintenance depot," Jarls said. "She'll be along later."

Fitz's waiter, a little Earthman nicknamed Skink for reasons unknown, brought Jarls's beer. "There's a good deal on eight-hour pops," he said, leaning over.

"No thanks," Jarls said, and Skink shrugged and went away. Jarls caught a glimpse of an illegal stunner sticking out from under the little man's smock. Skink was scrawny, even for an Earthman, but Fitz depended on him to keep order among Jovian clientele. Jarls had seen him quiet an unruly Jovian even without resorting to the neurospray—simply by a well-aimed rap across the side of the head with the lead-filled sap he also carried under his smock.

Doolan said, with a nod of approval, "That's bad stuff. It saps the will. They say the Consortium encourages it unofficially because it tends to make people pile up debt faster."

Doolan, Jarls had found, was fanatically frugal. He was determined to pay off his five-year labor contract and go home to Jupiter on schedule. So far, he was holding his own. Jarls did not have the heart to tell him that Herk had begun his long servitude with the same idea.

"They don't just encourage it," Jarls said. "They rake off a profit on it." He'd learned that much from Herk, anyway.

"God, I miss Jupiter!" Doolan said. "The sun coming up over the cloud tops! The colors! The lightning flashing below! The moons in the sky like jewels on black velvet! Proper weight on your feet, and air that doesn't taste like sulphur!"

Brok made a low rumbling sound of agreement, and Jarls could see the attempt to suppress the emotion that was trying to break out on his blunt face.

"Have you made a decision about, you know . . ." Jarls began.

"About the baby?" Maryann said, finishing it for him. "It was a bad idea. It would mean we'd given up. If I had a baby here in this feeble excuse for gravity, we could never take it home with us to Jupiter. We'd have to stay here for the rest of our lives. We'd be condemning our child to slavery." She tossed her head defiantly. "We'll wait. We'll get home somehow, and have the baby on Jupiter."

Brok's square jaw worked. "No child of mine is going to be a slave," he said gruffly.

Jarls said delicately, "How are you doing?"

"Oh, we've had a few small setbacks," Maryann said. She took a swig of her beer and wiped her mouth on the back of her hand. "Like when I broke my arm trying to lift that earthmover without a jack and it slipped and fell on me. They docked me a month's pay for the bone-growth matrix and another month for general med."

"Yeah," Brok said. "And the time I was dumb enough to sign for the new sleeping couch they told me went with the cubbyhole they call married quarters."

"But nothing major," Maryann said. "We'll make up the debits in no time at all."

"I don't suppose you've heard anything about your welding application?" Jarls said.

"No. I've given up on that," she said cheerfully. "Common laborer, that's me." She took another swig of beer and wiped off the suds again.

Jarls finished his own beer and called for another. Doolan looked at him disapprovingly. He was still trying to stretch out his first drink. Skink arrived with four beers on his tray, and Jarls signed for the round with his credit transfer locket, wincing when it chirped to indicate that it was overriding the negative credit balance buffer. Brok and Maryann drained their cryomugs and traded in the empties. Doolan's expression remained carefully frozen. No doubt he was thinking that it would be his turn to buy a round all the sooner.

The background hum of conversation and clink of glasses that was the Red Spot's usual ambience was interrupted by the sound of loud voices and unpleasant laughter at the entrance. Patrons turned to look for the source of the disturbance, then looked prudently away.

Jarls turned to see a party of four or five Venusian aristocrats pushing their way through the doorway, prattling all together in penetrating, artificial tones meant to impress one another and the world at large. They were young men, ribboned and jeweled in the Venusian manner, dazzling in bright, puffed clothing.

"Here's trouble," Skink murmured, and disappeared with his tray.

The newcomers had come to a restless standstill just inside the entrance, bumping into one another and darting impatient glances around the crowded room. A couple of them were noticeably unsteady on their feet. One of them said something witty, and the others twittered with laughter.

Fitz came hurrying toward them, wiping his hands on his apron and projecting an obsequious eagerness to please that Jarls had never seen before.

"It's an honor to have you here, messers," Fitz said nervously. "How can I serve you?"

One of the young dandies looked down his nose at the tavern-keeper. "Do you have anything decent to drink in this pigsty?" he said in a contemptuous drawl.

The others sniggered. "None of that swill they brew for the Jovians, Vanius," one of them shrilled. "You promised."

"For you, Messer Paes, nothing but the best," Fitz burbled. "I have a bottle of the finest vintage spirits, imported at great expense from Earth and still with the original seal, that I've been saving."

"Save it no longer," Paes said lazily. He lifted a tufted eyebrow toward the big corner table in the back. "We'll take that table over there."

"I'm so sorry, messer," Fitz temporized. "That particular table is occupied, but . . ."

"Unoccupy it," Paes said.

Fitz shrugged, and signaled Skink. The little Earthian scurried over to the table and spoke to its occupants, three Jovian couples who seemed to be having a quiet little celebration of some sort, with a bottle of cheap Venusport champagne in front of them and another unopened bottle in a cryobucket beside one of the chairs.

Jarls expected trouble. The fellow next to the cryobucket started vehemently to object, and rose halfway from his seat. But Skink said something to him that made him sit down again. Skink gathered up their glasses and the opened bottle, and gave the table a swipe with a wet rag. Finished, he added the heavy cryobucket to his tray, and the three couples followed him docilely to a couple of tables that he pushed together for them.

Fitz led the Venusians to the table, bowing and scraping all the way. He produced a tablecloth—the only one Jarls had ever seen at the Red Spot—and smoothed it over the scratched plastic tabletop. Skink materialized on cue to take their orders and received a dressing-down from Fitz for being slow.

The Venusian dandies watched the proceedings with amusement, making rude comments. The one called Paes kept a handker-

chief to his face as a critique of the presumed odor of his surroundings. The promised bottle of Earthian spirits arrived in a protective nest of basketry, and Paes made a show of inspecting the
label and seals before permitting it to be poured. Fitz, looking
relieved, mopped his forehead and took his leave.

The Venusians sipped their drinks, looking restless and bored.
Jarls felt the gaze of one young popinjay light on him, and quickly
looked away.

"What are they doing in the Jovian quarter?" Doolan said.

"Slumming," Jarls said.

"What for? Aren't there enough amusements in the upper levels
for them?"

"They get sent to Cloudhab to look after the family interests
and they find there's not enough excitement for them in their own
neighborhood. So they come downstairs here, looking for trouble."

He was only parroting what Herk had told him once, but
watching the Venusian bluebloods show off for one another
brought the words home.

"I wonder what that bottle of scotch costs," Doolan said.

"Plenty," Maryann said. "Drink your beer."

It wasn't easy to ignore the Venusians. They were several tables
away, but their loud, intrusive voices cut through the Red Spot's
cheerful din.

"I've never had a Jovian woman," one of them was saying.
"There, I admit it. What do you see in them, Vanius?"

"They're so . . . solid," Paes said, and the others snickered. "It's
like making love to a boulder."

"That doesn't sound very appetizing. Rather austere, in fact."

"Of course that's only the outside," Paes said, and there was
another burst of laughter.

"I prefer my soft little Rheans," the other said with a smirk.
"Yielding, pliable, easily positioned. They have to spend as much
time as possible lying down in our gravity, poor darlings. I've got
three of them now. Mother gave me another one for my birthday."

"Oh, these Jovian wenches have a certain low-slung charm,
Giro," Paes said with a grin. "Sturdy, immovable—that's what

makes it such a pleasure to tame them. They're innocent creatures, you know. Easily intimidated by wealth and authority. And for those who can't be cowed by one's name and position, there's always a touch of stun spray to neutralize their advantage in brawn."

Giro shuddered. "You're a braver man than I am, Vanius."

Paes took a fastidious sip of the scotch from Earth. "All in all," he said reflectively, "I rather think I prefer to use the neurospray. It adds a certain spice to the proceedings. All that superior muscular strength lying there helpless. Those bewildered eyes darting about. It's quite delicious."

"Vanius, you almost persuade," said another member of the pack, a pimply fellow with gold ringlets. "But isn't the use of a stunner in such circumstances illegal?"

"You're always joking, Darrold. The authorities won't take the complaint of a Jovian trull seriously."

Jarls had watched Doolan's face grow redder and redder. "The bastards!" Doolan burst out.

"Take it easy," Jarls said.

"I know the type," Maryann said. "Those little pipestem men. They're fascinated by Jovian women. They find us exotic in some perverse fashion. I've had to fend one off more than once."

Thunderclouds gathered on Brok's brow. "If someone's tried to lay a hand on you . . ."

She touched his hand. "It's all right," she said. "It's nothing."

The Venusians finished the bottle and called loudly for the check. Fitz brought a readout slate over himself and laid it before them with a flourish. Paes did not deign to look at it. In some fashion there was the cricket chirp of credit being transferred, and the five Venusians rose to leave. Jarls watched them cross the room. A couple of them had developed a pronounced wobble, but Paes did not seem at all drunk.

Fitz came over to Jarls's table. "It's a bad business," he said. "They came here looking for women. I told them I don't keep women here—to try Rosie's Place under the bypass. They got ugly about it."

"Who are they?" Jarls asked.

"The one at the head of the pack, his father controls the board of one of the big atmospheric mining corporations. Triplanet. That's the Paes family. The curly haired one, he's the heir to Venusbank. He's titular prez, but his mother's regent till he comes of age—sometime when his hair turns gray. Even his family doesn't trust him. He's a bad one—hurt a little entertainer at Hari's pretty bad on his last trip to Cloudhab. It was hushed up, but he almost put Hari's out of business just out of spite."

Fitz realized he was talking too much, and closed his rubbery lips. He shook his head and left. Jarls saw him at the table of the party of six who had been displaced by the Venusians. It looked as if he were offering an apology. He summoned Skink, who arrived with a bottle of champagne. From the label, it looked like the good stuff.

Jarls sat through another round of drinks with Maryann, Brok, and Doolan. Maryann caught him looking at his chron for the fourth time. "Cam?" she said.

"I wonder what's holding her up."

"They might have kept her at the depot. She'll probably be along later."

"Maybe I'll call it a night. If they're keeping her this late, she probably won't want to go out again anyway. I can stop off at her dorm on my way back to the barracks and leave a message with her roomie."

He stood up. Doolan looked relieved. The next round was going to be on him.

"Are you sure you won't stay for one more?" Doolan asked bravely.

"Another time." Jarls felt suddenly tired. The Venusians had put a damper on the evening.

Cam's shareroom was in one of several residences for unattached women scattered around the Jovian quarter. She had been attracted to it because it was cheap, clean, and offered limited privacy, if you could find a congenial sharemate. Jarls let himself in through the narrow vestibule and followed the dimly lit corridor that led to Cam's pigeonhole. All the doors down the corridor were tightly closed, and he found that unusual, because ordinarily there were a few that had been left ajar to invite sociability. A door ahead of him opened a crack, then quickly closed again. He heard the latch click as he passed, and that struck him as odd, too, because a lock meant nothing to a Jovian, particularly the flimsy variety provided by Cloudhab's landlords; in the Jovian quarter, good manners substituted for locks.

He stopped at Cam's door and raised his hand to knock. There were muted voices and scuffling sounds on the other side of the door, and something fell over with a crash.

He hesitated, his hand still poised to knock, and inadvertently pushed the door open a crack. He saw that the doorframe was splintered where the lock had been forced, and he pushed the door all the way open and stepped through.

The little room was filled with people. His eyes absorbed it all in a flash. The crash he'd heard had been Cam's roomie toppling to the floor. She lay sprawling and helpless, her mouth agape, her limbs making feeble jerking motions, her blouse hanging in ribbons. Her name, Jarls remembered vaguely, was Margriet. The five Venusians from the Red Spot were distributed through the room in various arrested postures, their bright clothes vivid against the drab surroundings. One of them sat on the floor weeping and hugging his ribs, his face bloody. Paes and two of the others were hovering over one of the beds. Cam was lying there, inert and motionless except for the rise and fall of her chest. Paes was in the process of ripping her jersey open from neck to hem. Jarls saw the stunner resting on the night table where Paes had set it down for the moment.

"What's going on?" Jarls demanded.

Paes raised his head. "Get out of here," he said. "And close the door behind you."

"Vanius," sobbed the man on the floor. "I think she broke my ribs, the bitch."

"Oh, do stop blubbering, Morin," Paes snapped. "The other one gave Darrold a bloody nose before I could use the spray on her, and you don't see *him* sniveling." He gave Jarls an annoyed glance. "Are you still here? Get *out* of here, you Jovian clod! Giro, give him some money."

His eyes widened in alarm as Jarls started toward him. He made a grab for the stunner. Jarls reached him in one swift step and took it away from him before he could use it.

"Take your hands off me, fellow!" Paes sputtered. He struggled ineffectively in Jarls's grasp. It was the first time in Jarls's life that he had used his strength against a non-Jovian, and he had to force himself to overcome his inhibitions.

He frog-marched Paes across the room to the door, half lifting him off the floor. He gave him a good shaking before releasing him, and propelled him down the corridor with a final shove.

The pimply one with the blond ringlets had been beating on Jarls's back with his fists all the while. He made a whimpering sound when Jarls reached out and seized him by the wrist. Jarls saw that he had wet his ballooning pantaloons. "Don't hurt me!" he squeaked. Jarls gave him a shaking, too, and booted him outside.

There was a jolt as someone broke a chair over Jarls's head from behind. Jarls turned with a frown. It was the one called Giro, the one who liked Rheans. He started backing away. "Get away from me," he said in a voice that was used to telling people what to do.

Jarls spun him around and picked him up by the belt and the scruff of his neck. He carried him to the door, holding him at arm's length.

Giro kicked and flailed his arms. "Do you know who I am?" he demanded, his voice rising.

"Yes," Jarls said.

He swung him back and forth once, and heaved him out into the corridor. He turned back to the room without waiting to see how Giro had landed.

There were two of them left. Jarls pivoted to face the one who was standing.

"I'm going!" the Venusian yelped, holding out his hands to ward Jarls off.

Jarls made a quick grab for the pleated neck ruff and twisted. The Venusian started choking and gagging. Jarls hauled him over to the door, slammed him against the doorframe to give him something to remember, and sent him on his way.

He swiveled around, but he wasn't fast enough this time. The one whose ribs were thought to have been broken scrambled with alacrity to his feet before he could get to him. Jarls made a snatch at him, but the man got past him with surprising agility and scurried out the door.

Jarls went out into the corridor to make sure they were gone. He saw them standing around uncertainly in a little group about halfway down the passage, trying to decide what to do.

With a bellow, he took a step toward them. They bolted and ran, losing any remaining shreds of dignity.

Jarls turned back to the room. He picked Margriet up off the floor and carried her to a chair. She flopped loosely in his arms, limp as wet spaghetti. He propped her up in the chair and found a blanket to cover her up with. Her eyes rolled, and she tried to say something, but nothing came out except a rasping sound.

Cam's eyes were alert, but she couldn't move either. She had a nasty bruise on her cheek and scratches on her arms, but otherwise seemed unharmed. He covered her with another blanket, averting his eyes, and put a pillow under her head. He squeezed her hand and thought he felt the tiniest answering pressure.

"It'll wear off soon," he said to them, and forced an encouraging smile. The only thing he could find in the room that looked anything like a stimulant was tea. He brewed a pot on the little countertop demon and tried to get a few spoonfuls past their lips, but gave up when the tea ran out of their mouths and dribbled down their chins. "Sorry—that wasn't such a good idea," he said, and settled for rubbing their hands and feet.

After a while they found their voices, though they still couldn't make their limbs work.

"Are they gone?" Cam asked hoarsely. The effort took all her breath.

"Yes," he said. "Don't worry, they won't be back."

"I've got pins and needles all over."

"That's the feeling coming back. Just hang on."

"That one with the blond curls—he hit me in the face after I was paralyzed. He said it was to pay me back for giving him a bloody nose. He said that when they were finished with us, he was going to do something to hurt me." She shuddered. "He didn't say what it was."

The shudder was a good sign. It showed that the neurospray was wearing off. Jarls helped her to a sitting position and adjusted the blanket to keep her covered.

"Looks like you both got in a couple of good licks before they zapped you. What happened?"

Margriet spoke from the chair. She was able to clench and unclench her fingers by now. "They were drunk. They were prowling up and down the hallways, banging on doors and demanding to be let in. They offered money and they were laughing at first, and then they started to get angry and yell about how important they were, and they'd come here to have some fun, and no flock of musclebound Jovian trollops, by God, was going to defy them. I opened the door to see what all the fuss was, and when I saw what was going on, I closed it and locked it, like the other women were doing. But one of them saw me, and then the whole bunch of them was concentrating on our door, hammering and kicking, and saying that they owned us and we had to let them in. I told them to go away, and they broke the lock and all rushed in and swarmed around us like puppies. They were making jokes about how firm Jovian women were, and about how we had huge bulging muscles and barrel chests and breasts like dinner plates, and so forth, and what a novelty we were. And then they started touching us all over."

"That's when I hit the blond one," Cam said. "I tried not to hurt him too much, but he started bleeding all over the place, and the other one, the one who was egging them on, aimed that thing at me, and I just fell down like a sack of flour, and I couldn't move a finger."

"And then I hit the little nasty one to get him off me, and I tried to get to Cam to help her," Margriet said, "but that bantam rooster with the stunner thing turned it on me, and I dropped."

"Three of them huffed and puffed and got me lifted onto the bed," Cam said, "and they were starting to rip my clothes off when you came in."

The color was coming back to her face and she was able to move enough to clutch the blanket to her, but Jarls thought it would be a while yet before she would be able to stand on her feet by herself.

"I'll stay with you until you're out of the woods," he said. "Then I'll go and report this to the block warden."

"Don't do that, Jarls!" There was fright in Cam's face. "I heard them talking. They're very influential. You'll get yourself into trouble."

He thought of the drubbing he'd given the Venusians, and the way Paes and his cohorts had scurried without dignity down the corridor.

"I'm already in trouble," he said.

Yamaguchi stuck his head around the corner of the partition. "They found out who you are," he announced. "You won't be charged with assault. Paes doesn't want to be made to look foolish, given the circumstances. But he's a vindictive bastard. From here on out, you get the treatment."

"I've had it before," Jarls shrugged. He turned the broken strap around in his hands and went on with his mending chore.

"Not like this, you haven't." Yamaguchi sat down on the bunk opposite. "This isn't like dealing with some blueboy strawboss like Smithers. The big boys upstairs have now deigned to notice that you exist. You've been tagged as a troublemaker. They're out to break you."

"I can handle it."

"The hell you can." Yamaguchi sighed. "I'm sorry, Jarls. I sniffed around to find out whatever I could. For starters, you're on permanent surface duty, starting right now. God knows when you'll ever see Cloudhab again. They're sending a couple of armed proctors to the barracks in an hour or so to escort you downstairs."

"I won't give them any trouble."

"Doesn't matter," Yamaguchi said. "They'll be looking for it."

# 9

**J**ARLS SPAT out a bloody tooth and tried to sit up. It was an awkward proposition, with his hands taped behind him and his ankles hobbled by a plastic cord with only about eight inches of leeway.

The proctors who had dumped him on the floor warily backed away from him, keeping their flat little riot guns trained on him. They were serious guns, the orange tabs showing that they were loaded with thousand-round clips of explosive microflechettes, not splatter pellets laced with neuroinhibitors.

"Just stay calm, boys," one of the proctors said to the Jovians bunched together against the far wall of the barracks. "One of you can cut him free after we leave."

A surge of angry muttering from the clustered men made one of the proctors hesitate. "He resisted detention," he said defensively, and they both hastily left.

Jarls achieved a sitting position. His left ear was still ringing from the parting smack he'd been given with a gun butt.

He grinned crookedly at his fellow Jovians. There was nobody there he recognized.

"Hold still," said a straw-haired young giant, leaning over him with a little sawtoothed box knife. "I'll have you loose in a jiffy."

Someone else had produced a torch and was busy melting the plastic cord that tethered his ankles. A molten drop splashed on his skin but he kept himself from flinching.

The reciprocating blade was slicing through the tape that bound his wrists. "Hyperfilament strapping tape," the straw-haired youth grunted. "Heavy duty. The kind they use for attaching booster rockets. They weren't taking any chances with you, were they?"

"They had handcuffs," Jarls said. "I guess they didn't trust them on a Jovian."

The last crystalline carbon strands fell away, and Jarls's hands were free. He flexed his swollen fingers, and was rewarded with a tingling stab of purest agony as circulation tried to return. His hands were an ugly purple, the knuckles buried in puffed flesh.

"Tight," the other said, sucking in his breath. "They had it in for you. What'd you do?"

"Nothing," Jarls said.

He had offered no resistance, remembering Yamaguchi's warning. But as soon as they had him trussed up, they had given him a working over anyway. "Messer Paes said to remind you never to put your hands on your betters," one of them had informed him as he clubbed him on the side of the head. "Nothing personal, fellow."

"Yeah?" said the man who used the torch on the leg cord. "You're Anders, aren't you? The word's been passed. Nobody's supposed to talk to you, you know."

"Hell with that!" came an angry voice from one of the other men in the group surrounding Jarls. "We're Jovians! Nobody tells us who we can talk to or what we can say!"

Jarls thought he sounded like a recent arrival, but there was a general murmur of agreement from the others. Perhaps they were all relative newcomers in this barracks. Probably the idea was to isolate Jarls from his old friends.

"Still, they can make it pretty rough on you," said the straw-haired youth. He thrust out a hand. "I'm Rufe Arris. I've heard stories about you from some of the old-timers in the other barracks. And about what happened to a long-timer named Herk, was that his name?"

Jarls felt a stinging in his eyes. "Yes, Herk." He lifted his head. "Is there still a straw boss named Smithers here?"

There was an exchange of uneasy looks among the others. "He's gone," Rufe said. "They came and took him away one day. Something about him being caught stealing. There's a new straw boss. Another Uranian. Name of Terrill."

"What's he like?"

"He's a bastard. Aren't they all? If anything, worse than Smithers."

Jarls rubbed his chin. "So I'm supposed to be in Coventry, am I?"

"Yeah. Don't let it worry you. You heard what Sven said. We're all Jovians here. We stick together."

"Thanks," Jarls said. "I won't worry. Not about Jovians."

The first attempt on his life was childish. Somebody had cut the sensor wire to the $CO_2$ scrubber in his suit and concealed the break with a smear of non-conducting gunk. Jarls would not have detected the $CO_2$ buildup because the safety light was served by the same sensor. The idea, he supposed, was that he would have gotten woozy without realizing it, and made some fatal misstep on his next outside job. The error would have been put down to worker carelessness, and not sullied the records. But Jarls knew every splice and patch in his equipment by heart. He fixed the break without saying anything to anybody, and waited to see which straw boss would find a reason to put him in harm's way, out of reach of a workmate. He was not surprised to find that it was Terrill. Paes would have found it easier, of course, to bribe a new man coming down from topside. Not that Jarls could afford to trust any of the Uranian supervisors, but Venuscorp officially frowned on private revenge, and if Jarls had to watch his back, it was useful to narrow it down somewhat.

Jarls retaliated deliberately, just to show he wasn't intimidated. That night he preached a little sermon to his new barracksmates on the subject of the oppressed and downtrodden throughout Earth's long and dusty history.

He took as his text the serfs of the Middle Ages and their various attempts to break out of their bondage—the peasants' revolt in England led by Wat Tyler, the peasants' war in Germany a century and a half later. Jarls knew he was no great thinker, like Herk, and that his knowledge was sketchy. But he strained mightily to remember what Herk had said in his infamous after-hours "seminars," as he had called them, and he was able to repeat some of Herk's more stirring phrases verbatim. "No man has the right to own another." "Chains are chains, whether made of iron or debt." "It is a self-evident truth that all men are created equal, and are endowed with certain inalienable rights . . ."

He was astonished to find that his audience listened respectfully, as if he were an historical figure himself; they had already heard stories about Herk from some of the older hands, and Jarls had figured in some of those stories.

Jarls's little disquisition was calculated to drive Terrill and his Venusian overlords into a fury. Surely word of it would have gotten back to the Uranian—if not through an eavesdropping device, then through some unwary barracksmate spreading the story around to other barracks. But there was not a peep the next day from any of the straw bosses, as there invariably had been whenever Herk had shot off his mouth.

Jarls grinned to himself all through the morning shift. He was getting to them.

The next attempt on his life was crude and brutally direct. He'd been sent out into the wilds of Ishtar Terra with a small crew to scavenge magnesium ingots that had gone wide of the target area. The crew scattered, each of them paired with a nonhuman partner—a six-legged loader with an ant's brain and tungsten-steel jaws the approximate width of a barn door. With its long jointed neck and a row of demon exhausts making a ridge along its humped back, the loader looked like some armored creature out of a nightmare paleontology. Jarls told the monster what to do through a small palm control programmed for about two dozen basic tasks; the tiny brain took care of the details.

The loader followed Jarls at a walking pace, lumbering along with a low-bellied, straddle-legged gait, its clawed feet flexing for purchase in the friable soil. He paused to point out a coffin-shaped ingot half-buried in the loess, but the loader had already seen it and stretched out its neck to pick the metal wedge up. Jarls let it trot behind him with the ingot in its jaws, like a dog with a bone, until they reached a flat stretch where he could see four or five stray ingots fanned out within an acre or so of moderate visibility. He decided it would be a good place to establish a temporary dump until the truck could get to him.

He signaled the loader to drop the ingot it was carrying, but the idiot machine wouldn't let go. It stood there, holding the slab of metal in its teeth, its neck swaying from side to side as if it were trying to make up its mind.

Cursing, Jarls used the laser pointer to show the loader where he wanted the ingot placed and stabbed the button again. Again nothing happened, and he tried a third time. The questing neck stopped, reared back, and the recalcitrant jaws finally let go.

Jarls jumped back just in time. A ton of metal hit the ground with a thud that he could feel through the soles of his thick boots. The metal slab tottered on end and fell over not inches from where he'd been standing.

Jarls stared at the loader thoughtfully. Loaders had rudimentary shape recognizing ability, and a suited man was certainly high up in their limited catalog. He sent the machine scurrying after another ingot, and this time he stepped well back while it deposited its load at the designated spot.

Inside of a half hour he had a nice little pile of Mercurian magnesium started, and the truck still had not arrived. He could make out a few more slabs at the edge of his bowl-shaped bubble of visibility, but he could not get the loader to go after them.

Jarls sighed. He supposed that the laser pointer did not cut sufficiently through the dust and ash suspended in the heavy air, and resignedly he trudged across the glowing waste with the loader following on its radio leash.

He got the balky machine to pick up five or six more ingots and stow them in its saddlebags, then sent it back to unload while he scouted the perimeter of his optical bubble for more salvage.

Then he couldn't get the idiotic loader to come back to him.

Laser pointing was no good at these distances. He stationed himself by his next find and began wagging his arms and doing scissors jumps to summon the loader. The machine's miniscule brain contained a basic vocabulary of hand signals—the same ones used by human beings operating heavy machinery—and it had pretty good eyesight.

The loader hesitated, then started galloping toward him, its neck extended and its jaws open. Jarls stood waiting—until it dawned on him that the machine was making a beeline for him, not the ingot he had pointed out.

It was hard to be certain, with the optical distortion of Venus's refracting atmosphere, but he had stationed himself a cautious twenty feet to one side of the ingot. He renewed his hand signals and stepped another thirty feet away.

Now there was no mistake. The loader veered on its six pumping legs and raced directly toward him.

He waited until it was almost on him, then threw himself prone and rolled to one side. There was a lot of inertia in all those tons of machinery. The huge jaws snapped at empty air, and the machine skidded to a stop.

The long neck began questing, the clustered photoreceptors located him, and the thing lunged at him again.

Jarls rolled out of the way and scrambled to his feet. He edged out of reach while it was still busy extracting its jaws from the dent it had made in the soil.

It began seeking him again, its steel mandibles twisting at the end of their flexible stem. Jarls stood poised, trying to guess where and how it was going to strike next.

There was no mistaking its malevolence. This was no machine error caused by program breakdown or faulty sensors. The loader's actions were purposeful. A human being had overriden the machine's limited volition and was controlling it with murderous intent.

Whoever was operating the machine was bouncing radio signals off a satellite. The fractional delay was the only reason Jarls was still alive.

The long neck stretched itself out at ground level and made a quick swipe at Jarls, like a bat trying to hit a ball. It was a clever move, but Jarls had anticipated it when he saw the neck trying to outflank him, and instead of trying to dodge out of range, he had run toward the loader, getting himself inside the swing.

The jaws and neck scuffed up about a ton of Venusian soil, making a fan-shaped furrow about a foot deep. But Jarls was safely pressed against the flank of the loader, hunched down where the angle of the neck gave him five feet of leeway.

The jaws tried to get at him, but the articulated neck was not able to double all the way back on itself. There was a pause, during which Jarls could almost feel the frustration of the remote operator. Then the machine took a shuffling step on its stumpy legs, trying to crush him.

Jarls moved with the machine, staying close to the curved hull. The operator tried changing direction several times at random, but thanks to the few seconds' grace given by transmission delay, Jarls was able to outguess him each time.

What next? He could try to climb aboard, but the jaws would be able to reach him almost anywhere along the loader's back or flanks. There *was* an inaccessible spot on the spine, just behind the base of the neck, where the machine could not scratch its own itch, but getting to it fast enough would be a problem.

The operator got lucky. The machine backed away at high speed, leaving Jarls exposed, and the massive jaw housing tried to swat him. Jarls barely avoided being mashed into the ground. The machine took another swipe, but he was able to get back into its blind spot.

This could not go on. The operator would soon realize that he had to move off to a distance and try to run him down. It might take a while, but Jarls couldn't dodge the machine forever. Eventually the loader would run him into a state of exhaustion, powered suit or no, and pulverize him.

But his adversary hadn't figured that out yet. He was still trying to move the loader back and forth at random, hoping to get lucky again, while the metal jaws opened and shut futilely, like a dog trying to nip at a flea.

Then the operator got smart, and the moment Jarls had been dreading arrived.

The loader backed off a good one hundred yards, revved up, and took a high-speed run at him.

Jarls had a choice. He could stand his ground, and at the last moment dodge either to the right or left. With the satellite delay of a few seconds, he had a fifty percent chance of guessing right.

So did the remote operator.

The odds were awful. It was the same as flipping a coin. You might win once, twice, three times. But how many times can you flip a coin before coming up wrong?

Jarls broke and ran. To Terrill, or whoever the distant assassin was, it must have looked as if he had panicked. The odds were the same. Except that now Jarls had to keep looking over his shoulder.

Jarls pounded along at full waldo amplification, his thick boots throwing up little spurts of Venusian ash. Out of the corner of his eye, he saw that he had a witness. The truck had arrived to pick up his collected ingots. It had just topped a rise a couple of hundred yards away, at the limit of visibility.

The loader's operator either didn't see it or didn't care. A Jovian witness didn't count for much. The machine kept coming at Jarls, its belly low to the ground, its six stumpy legs drumming.

When the approaching truck driver saw what was going on, he floored it, trying to put his lumbering vehicle between Jarls and the attacking loader. He was a Jovian, after all. But heavy-duty machines like that weren't built for speed. He didn't have a whisper of hope of making it in time.

The loader was gaining on Jarls. He could see its reflection in his helmet visor without turning his head. He pounded onward, hitting at least thirty miles an hour with his suit's amplified strides and jarring leaps, despite the danger of a tumbling fall that would kill him as surely as the loader would if it caught up with him.

There! Ahead and to the left he could see the patch of ground he had noticed while he was scouting for ingots. He hadn't paid much attention to it at the time, and he hoped his impression was correct. There was a telltale flatness to the patch, as if it had been recently liquid. That could mean that a pool of lead had collected there—lead that had leeched out of rock and trickled in streamlets until it had found a hollow. Over a period of time, dust and ash settled on such pools, leaving a deceptively solid-looking surface. Under the coating of ash, lead would cool off enough to form an eggshell-thin veneer. But underneath, the lead would still be liquid.

Men on foot learned to avoid such patches. Sometimes the crust was thick enough to support a man, sometimes not. Jarls prayed that this one had been cooling long enough. He had no choice.

His six-legged pursuer was only a few yards behind him now, and quickly gaining. Its forward end was low to the ground, the jaws yawning wide to give it more impact area.

At least, Jarls thought dizzily, a collision at this speed would breach his suit and kill him instantly. He wouldn't feel a thing when the steel legs trampled his fried remnants into the ground.

His foot broke through a frozen crust of lead. Jarls pitched forward and almost fell. But he recovered, pulled his foot free in the same instant, and danced precariously over the thin veneer without breaking through again.

Behind him, the onrushing machine was moving too fast to stop, even if its distant operator could have seen what happened with no time lag. It thundered onward, closed the gap, and made a final lunge that would have flattened Jarls.

He felt the ground shiver. Hot lead splashed his back and instantly solidified. He stumbled forward a few more yards, seeing a scary web of cracks spread out all around him.

But the crust held. Jarls brought himself safely to a stop without falling over, and slowly turned around.

The loader was sinking. It was a deep pool. The frantically pedaling legs disappeared, then the metal hips, and it came to rest with only its broad many-finned back showing above the fiery surface.

What passed for its head emerged from the pool, dripping molten lead, and swiveled to face Jarls. He imagined that he could feel its hatred. But that was ridiculous. Any such emotion belonged to the operator, miles away at Base Camp Two. Besides, a thin film of lead was already solidifying over the clustered sensors behind the jaws. The feeling that the thing was glaring at him could only be an illusion.

Still, he kept well out of range of the dripping jaws as he skirted the hole the loader had made in the crust. He got back to solid ground without mishap.

The truck driver had parked a safe distance away from the bad patch. Jarls trudged over to the gigantic vehicle and let a hydraulic lift take him up to the cab. He squeezed into the miniscule airlock behind the cab and stayed inside it while his suit cooled off and the 90 atmospheres of Venusian pressure cranked down to the 20 pounds of compensating pressure retained by his suit. At the moment he was a hot stove, and could not be admitted to the cabin proper.

The driver twisted around in his seat and looked at Jarls through the transparent panel. It was Yamaguchi.

"Well, you've got yourself into a pickle, haven't you?" Yamaguchi said.

"When did you get here?" Jarls asked.

"Yesterday. They put me right to work." He nodded at the embedded loader, slowly entombing itself as its chilled metal hardened the lead around it. "Terrill's playing rough, isn't he?"

"What do you know about it?"

"Oh the word's out that young Paes doubled the ante on you. He's getting impatient. Terrill's in a hurry to finish the job before one of the other straw bosses decides to try to claim the bounty."

"I see."

"We talked it over. We'll try to get you moved in with us so we can watch your back for you."

"Who's 'we'?"

"Brok's here this tour. And Doolin. And some of your other old bunkies."

"I'm with a good bunch now. They'll look out for me."

Yamaguchi took a breath. "I know they're a good bunch. That's not the point. They're new. They don't have the experience. You're better off with your old friends."

"Is Maryann here this tour?"

"Yes."

"I thought Brok made arrangements to bunk with her when they were down here together."

"They don't mind being separated temporarily. They both said so. Maryann said it would save them money."

"I doubt you could get me transferred. You'd only draw Terrill's attention."

"Jarls, don't be stubborn. We can get into the computer, juggle work assignments . . ."

"I can look after myself."

"Is that your last word?"

"Yes."

"Have it your way," Yamaguchi said stiffly. "We'll do what we can for you."

"We'd better get back to work. I've got a pile of ingots over there you can pick up. You'll have to borrow one of the other loaders."

"I'll take care of it. In the meantime, you're riding in the cab with me till we get back to base."

"Terrill won't try anything now, if that's what you're thinking. Not the same thing twice, anyway. Loaders are expensive machines."

"You're riding with me anyway."

Jarls started to argue, then gave in. "All right, Taki. Thanks."

He threw it back in their faces again that night. This time his text was the Serfs' Rebellion in seventeenth-century Russia.

"Serfdom," he said. "Chattel slavery under another name. The serfs were theoretically free, but they were so bound by ever-increasing indebtedness that for all practical purposes they were the property of their masters, and could be sold with the land. Sound familiar?"

Jarls realized, as he repeated Herk's old harangue, that he didn't really know what he was talking about. But it seemed to go down well with his barracksmates, and he resolved to study the old texts, as Herk had done. His next topic, he decided with a sour grin, would be Spartacus, the gladiator who had led the slave rebellion against Rome. He'd have to bone up on it, though. He remembered the ruinously expensive printout of the ancient book that Herk had been reading when he first met him. The printout had disappeared after Herk died, along with the rest of his painfully acquired library. The Uranian supervisors had cleaned out all of Herk's possessions, leaving no trace to show that the maverick Jovian had ever existed.

But Herk did still exist, Jarls thought fiercely. He existed in Jarls's brain, and in the brains of all the others he had made an impression on.

There was no help for it, Jarls thought. He'd just have to pay for another search and printout himself. He was already so far in debt that another charge against his negative balance wouldn't matter that much.

"Tell us more about Boris and the false Dmitri," came a voice from the surrounding darkness. "And why did the serfs let themselves get bamboozled again?" It was Rufe Arris. The big yellow-haired youth had proved to have a keen and probing mind as well as an oversupply of muscle.

A murmur of assent came from several of the other bunks. "Yes, Jarls, did the serfs ever get emancipated?"

That was the way, Jarls thought. Turn it into a story. That's what Herk had done.

"Tomorrow night," Jarls promised. "That's enough gab for now. We've all got to get some sleep."

The next morning, Jarls found that he had been charged with the cost of the disabled loader. "Lost through worker carelessness," was the way the report put it. He was past even the slimmest hope of redemption now. It was a lifetime debt.

No matter how long he lived.

"We'll just check out the seal ring and connections for you before you suit up," Rufe said.

"I've already done it," Jarls said.

"Can't be too careful," Rufe said firmly.

He and Sven Bjorn were already going over the big torso gasket inch by inch for cracks and examining all the electrical and fiberoptic leads that connected the two halves of the coolsuit.

Jarls let them. They were very earnest. He didn't want to hurt their feelings.

"All okay," Rufe announced. He wrestled the lower half of the suit to a standing position and levered it over to where Sven was hoisting the torso on the suiting rack.

Jarls thanked them gravely.

"You can never tell about seals," Rufe informed him. "Just one drop of some caustic, and they can develop a brittle spot."

Word had gone round quickly about the loader's attempt on Jarls's life. Jarls had told Yamaguchi about the monkey business with the $CO_2$ sensor in his suit, too, and Yamaguchi must have spread that around as well. Now the entire roster of Jarls's barracks had appointed themselves his babysitters, thinking they were being discreet about it. It could get to be a bit stifling at times, but Jarls, touched by their concern, endured it.

Otherwise, his life was actually a bit easier than it had been on previous tours of the Venusian surface. There was none of the petty harrassment that he and Herk had suffered under Smithers. Terrill ignored him most of the time. He seemed to have trouble meeting Jarls's eye. Even Jarls's subversive little sermons after lights out had gone officially unnoticed.

Jarls was not deceived, however. The official inattention was more chilling than any overt persecution would have been. It showed that Terrill had already written him off as a dead man. He wasn't worth venting any more spite on. Terrill was saving his efforts for some major, well-planned attempt, one that would not fail.

"I'm sure the suit's all right," Jarls said.

Rufe nodded. "Terrill probably won't try anything else," he said. "He must be in all kinds of hot water over losing a loader like that. I understand he got an encrypted face-to-face call from Vanius Paes the day after it happened. The commlink clerk's a Jovian, you know. She doesn't know what was said, but Paes must have given Terrill a royal chewing out. Paes isn't Lord Chairman of

Solar Oxygen yet, but he's heir apparent, and he looks out for his father's interests. Loaders don't come cheap, even by a Venusian grandee's reckoning."

Jarls said nothing. Rufe evidently was under the impression that Terrill's attempts on his life were part of some kind of personal vendetta. That they might have been ordered by some spoiled puppy higher up the ladder hadn't occurred to him.

"At any rate, we'll keep an eye on you this morning all the same. Though I can't see how he could get to you. We'll just be tunnel walking today. There'll be Jovians all around you, and there won't be any loaders or other machines whose controls he could override."

Jarls nodded. He climbed into the bottom half of his suit and, arms held high, let Rufe and Sven lower the torso shell into position. They stood back diplomatically while he fastened the latches himself.

The big refrigerated transport vehicle began dropping them off in groups of five or six after they passed the main pumping station and the above-ground structures started to thin out. Jarls was amused to find, when he checked the assignment sheet, that he had been appointed taskmaster in charge of a work gang. Pariah or not, surface experience counted for something out here in the Venusian hell.

"That'll be our substation just ahead," he told his crew, pointing out the tremendous dome sticking up out of the tortured plain. "We've got the first impeller stage where it branches out to D Sector." He glanced at the work sheet. "There's supposed to be a stuck vacuum door—that whole section of tunnel's still under full Venusian pressure—and then all we have to do is walk the tunnel to the next impeller stage. Nice little Sunday stroll. About seven miles. There'll be transport waiting for us there. Then we leapfrog the next four substations—there'll be other crews working those sections of tunnel—and do the section after that."

"What happens if you get caught in a tunnel when the oxygen buildup starts?" Rufe Arris asked.

"Nothing much. It takes hours and hours to build up the terrific head of pressure that's needed to create the oxygen geyser that meets the incoming hydrogen at the top of the atmosphere. You'd always have time to walk to the next substation and get out. Anyway, they're not due to start cycling oxygen for another four days. Incoming isn't due for a week."

"It would be quite a hurricane inside the tunnels though, wouldn't it?" Rufe said.

"Yeah. But they've got to pump out the CO2 first. Get rid of as much Venusian atmosphere as possible. And don't worry about that, either. They never get down to full vacuum. One or two percent of Venusian pressure's about as much as is practical. About Earth pressure, in fact. Your suit can handle that easily. Even if you don't bother to bleed off the 20 atmospheres you're carrying yourself."

"So no blowouts, then?"

"No blowouts, no matter what."

A bulky figure in a dented suit shoved in, completing Jarls's contingent of five men. "It's not blowouts you have to worry about," the man said. "It's other things. Like maybe an impeller blade starting up while you're standing next to it. Impeller blades can be switched on by remote."

"Brok, what are you doing here?" Jarls said, blinking. "You're supposed to be with Yamaguchi's gang."

He rechecked the work roster to be sure.

"I reassigned myself," Brok said. "I had a little talk with Sven, and we switched places."

"You can't do that."

"I can't, huh? Tell that to Yamaguchi. He gave me a checklist of everything he could think of that Terrill could fiddle with. Like the impeller blades. You could boobytrap them with a motion sensor."

"I'm not going near any impeller blades. Unless I cut off the circuit first."

"Fine. But Yamaguchi said to stick close to you. There'll be someone tomorrow, too."

"Listen, Brok . . ."

"It's all right, Jarls," Rufe Arris said. "I think it's a good idea."

Jarls gave in gracefully. "Okay, then. But we're only going to be walking a tunnel and eyeballing it for cracks. I never heard of anybody being attacked by a patch kit."

They reached the base of the gigantic dome and skirted its perimeter until they found the service door. It was fastened shut with a simple outside latch.

"The rest of you stand back a minute till I check it out," Jarls said as he undogged the door.

"I'll go first," Brok said, brushing past Jarls. He gave him a push hard enough to send him sprawling.

"Hey!" Jarls yelled.

Brok was inside before he could stop him. "What the hell is this?" Jarls heard him say. "It's full of pure oxygen at Venus pressure. My sensors are going crazy."

Jarls's own sensors were getting a whiff of oxygen escaping from the doorway. "Brok, listen to me . . ." he started to say, struggling to his feet. Before he could get up, Rufe Arris and two of the others were on him, pinning him down.

"They must have flooded the tunnel from C Sector prematurely," Brok was saying in a puzzled tone. "The vacuum door's not stuck. It's jammed open. You guys wait out there a second till I get it shut and open the outlet door."

"Brok, get out of there!" Jarls shouted.

He threw the three men off him and hurled himself at the entrance. He reached it in time to see Brok stretch a gauntleted hand toward the vacuum door. There was the bright crack of a spark, and then Brock's suit was enveloped in a brilliant sheet of flame.

"Oh God, I'm burning!" came Brock's agonized cry.

Jarls tried to reach him, but he was hurled back by a violent rush of wind caused by the sudden expansion of superheated air. Jarls landed flat on his back, with a clang of his helmet against the concrete floor. The next fifteen or twenty seconds of lying supine were what saved his life.

Half-stunned, he watched in horror as the fire blazed and crackled, shot through with a dazzling glare that he recognized as a carbon arc. It was feeding on the diamondlike hypercarbon shell of Brok's suit.

The fire was greedy. It was reaching out for anything that would burn in an atmosphere of almost pure oxygen at ninety Earth pressures. But there was precious little within its grasp in the refractory interior of the dome. The great hypercarbon impeller blades were insulated by a few crucial yards of distance that put them just below the ignition point of pure carbon. Jarls was similarly protected by his prone position. Even so, the added heat, on top of Venus's 900 degrees, was almost more than his Maxwell's Demon could cope with; in his helmet display, the warning bar edged close to the red line of failure.

So the fire fed on Brok's suit and any nearby electrical insulation or other non-refractory materials it could find.

As Jarls, dazed, raised himself on his elbows, he saw a thin line of fire streak upward and race along the ceiling of the dome, following some wiring channel. Melted plastic dripped fiery globules across the floor. But the thread of flame snuffed itself out before it got halfway across.

The fire winked out as abruptly as it had started. It had lasted less than 30 seconds. Venus's carbon dioxide blanket had rushed in to replace the expanded oxygen that had whooshed out of the door, and it had smothered the flames. Thick black smoke billowed through the chamber. Plastic still bubbled in the puddles where it had splashed.

Jarls staggered over to the blackened thing that had been Brok. It was a large cinder, roughly man-shaped. It continued to smolder, glowing embers fading on its pitted surface. Jarls saw the place where the carbon arc had started, a smear of melted wire still spitting sparks at the edge of the metal door. There was no reason that he could see for insulation to have abraded or gotten scraped away at that point to cause a short circuit. When Brok had reached for the door to push it shut, the arc had leaped toward his outstretched hand.

The others had fought their way into the smoke-filled chamber and crowded in behind him, despite the intense residual heat that was making their demons labor. Jarls heard some unlucky individual being sick in his armored coolsuit—a small catastrophe for whoever it was.

Rufe stared at him, white-faced behind his visor. "It was meant for you, Jarls," he said in a shaky voice.

"It was meant for all of us," Jarls said grimly. "The bastard didn't care. He didn't care at all."

There were tears in his eyes.

Yamaguchi was waiting for him when he got back. "It was pretty blatant," he said. "I don't know how they're going to cover it up. The whole section had to be flooded four days early, two separate safety systems had to be overridden, and somebody had to be paid to manually scrape away the insulation and set the booby trap with the open door. The impeller blades weren't damaged, but they'll have to shut down the whole sector for repairs. That means that at least thirty or forty percent of the next consignment of hydrogen from Jupiter's going to be wasted—hundreds of trillions of tons. Even Triplanet can't take that kind of loss without wincing. Paes's father's going to have to answer some awkward questions from the board, Lord Chairman or not. Young Paes will be taken to the woodshed, and if he doesn't come up with some good answers, Terrill's head's on the chopping block. Paes must've leaned on Terrill pretty hard to get him to stick his neck out like that."

Jarls wasn't paying attention. "I'll break it to Maryann," he said.

"She's already gotten word. She's in their quarters. One of the women is with her."

Jarls made no reply. Yamaguchi saw the look on his face, and stepped aside as Jarls shouldered past him.

The private billet that Brok and Maryann had pooled their resources for was little more than a cubbyhole, with room for a bed, a small scarred table and two mismatched chairs, some shelves for personal possessions, and a compact sanitary module behind a privacy curtain. Maryann did their cooking on a two-burner hotplate, which was now stowed on a lower shelf.

Jarls's throat tightened as he saw the few brave touches Maryann had provided to make the place homelike: a blurred and scratched window holo looking out on an imaginary forest glade, some bright cheap pillow covers for the bed, a plastic bowl with an arrangement of paper flowers set in a layer of polished Venusian pebbles. She had pestered Yamaguchi, Jarls remembered, to teach her how to make the flowers.

Maryann was sitting on the bed, looking drawn and pale. Her freckles stood out against her pallor, and her red hair seemed dull and lifeless. Jarls didn't know the woman who was sitting with her; she was big—as big as Maryann—with impressive musculature and a jagged scar down the side of her neck.

"She's doing all right," the woman said. "She just needs some time."

"You don't have to screen for me, Rhia," Maryann said with a tired smile. "I can speak for myself."

Jarls planted himself in front of her. "I was there," he said harshly. "I couldn't stop it from happening." He bit his lip. "It should have been me."

Maryann took both of his hands in hers and held on to them tightly. "Brok always talked about how you saved his life that time on Jupiter when he fell overboard," she said. "He said he owed you one."

She gave his hands a squeeze and let go.

"What are you going to do?" he said.

She took her time about answering. "I'm pregnant," she finally whispered.

Jarls gave a start of surprise. "But you said . . ."

"I know. We were fools to let it happen."

Jarls's mind raced. "Maryann, we've got to get you back into Jovian gravity right away. I'll talk to Yamaguchi and the others. We can all chip in, buy back your labor contract . . ."

He stopped as he remembered his own negative credit balance. Yamaguchi was a lot better off, but he was below the line too. Of all of those he could think of, only Doolan was still in the black, but he was relatively new, and frugal as he had been, his margin would still be miniscule.

"It's good of you to think of that, Jarls, but it's too late," she said.

"But if you're still in your first month, fetal development can't be that advanced! There'll still be time to give the baby a Jovian start in life . . ."

She looked at him with weary patience. "Have you forgotten how many months it takes to get back to Jupiter?"

"You could . . ."

"No. The baby's Brock's. I'll get him out of here somehow, if only to Earth one day. I won't let him grow up a slave!"

"Maryann . . ." Jarls began helplessly.

He fell silent. What was the use of going on? Maryann could never return to Jupiter now. Not with a baby who would have to be submerged in a bathtub filled with gel, and whose heart probably wouldn't take it for more than a week or two, even then.

"It's all right, Jarls. There are just some things you can't do anything about."

The woman with the scar, Rhia, put a hand on Maryann's shoulder. "She needs to sleep now," she said to Jarls. She turned her attention back to Maryann. "Best not to think, for now," she said in a sensible voice. "There'll be time for that later."

Maryann nodded. Her powerful body slumped. Exhaustion showed in her mottled face.

Jarls stayed a moment longer, staring at her. Then he turned abruptly and left.

"Where's Terrill?"

Jarls stormed past a startled dispatcher, not waiting for an answer. The dispatcher stared after Jarls's broad back, open-mouthed, then punched an alarm button.

Jarls paused at a corridor junction, trying to decide which way to go. To the left there seemed to be nothing but a darkened utility area. The short corridor to the right had a closed office door at the end of it. He lowered his head and plunged forward.

A security guard stepped out of an alcove and barred his way. He was not a Uranian, but a hard-looking Earthian, so overmuscled that he might almost have passed for a Jovian. "You can't go in there, Jovie!" he challenged.

Jarls pushed him out of the way and kept going. The security guard staggered backward, fumbling for his gun. Jarls took the gun away from him in mid-stride and crushed it into a ball of metal and plastic scrap in his fist. He tossed it aside, planted his hand in the Earthian's chest, and sent him sprawling.

He charged on without looking back, and reached the door in time to hear an electronic security bolt click shut. He growled. He enveloped the knob in one sizable hand, placed the other hand flat against the door, and shoved. The door gave way with a groan of twisted metal.

Terrill was sitting behind a desk at the far end of the room. He was a fortyish, slope-shouldered man with the characteristic bluish tinge and bristling haircut of a Uranian.

He tried to stare Jarls down. "You're off limits, cloudhopper," he said. "Get back to your kennel."

"You son of a bitch," Jarls said.

There was a sickly pallor of fear underneath Terrill's cyanotic hue, but to his credit, he stayed put in his chair without flinching.

"It was an unfortunate accident," he said unblinkingly. "Some insulation rubbed bare. There was an oxygen buildup because of a faulty seal. A worker failed to observe proper safety procedures. Now go back to your barracks while we investigate the incident."

With an incoherent roar, Jarls leaped forward and grabbed Terrill by the front of the shirt. He lifted him out of the chair and batted away a nasty little splinter gun that had appeared in Terrill's hand. Terrill screamed as the blow shattered his metacarpals. Jarls threw him at the wall, and Terrill screamed again as an arm snapped, and then the room was full of security.

Jarls whirled to face them, just in time to see the weighted net that they cast over him. He raised a thick arm to ward it off, but it was already contracting as the high-speed micromotors around the rim drew the mesh tight.

His strength was no good against the diamond fiber and the microscopic ratchets that prevented the minigears from being reversed. He ended up in a tight ball, squeezed into the smallest volume that flesh could endure.

The security men kicked at him a long time, until their fury spent itself. One of them called for a med to tend to Terrill. Four of the others picked Jarls up like a sack of soywheat and carried him out.

Corridors rushed by, as the four men grunted and puffed under their burden. Jarls hung face down, the floor inches away, bumping his forehead every time the net sagged.

"Where are you taking me?" Jarls yelled.

"Shut him up, Grig," one of them said.

They dumped him on the floor. He got a skinned nose out of it. One of them squatted, located his face, and sprayed him with something. There was the stinging of a thousand bees, and then Jarls's consciousness fled down a long tunnel, drained away into a dark hole at the end of it, and vanished.

When he woke up, he was in the hotbox. They had taken his clothes from him, and he could watch the perspiration drip from his naked body and pool on the floor. The pools visibly shrank as he watched, and evaporated away.

After an interval that might have been an hour or more, he felt able to move. His head was beginning to clear. He groaned and sat up. He made the mistake of trying to lean his back against a wall, and got a painful reminder that prolonged contact with a vertical surface was an invitation to slow-cook yourself. Getting enough sleep was always a problem in the hotbox.

He judged that about twelve hours had gone by when they brought him his daily portion of the mandated ration. The door opened, and a warder in a ballooning plastic coverall cooled by a small demon cautiously slid a tray across the floor. A guard stood behind him with a gun, motioning Jarls to remain at the far end of the box. The warder backed out and the door closed. The demon's exhaust had made the room even hotter.

Jarls examined the tray. The required beverage was a cup of water that he drank at once. It hadn't occurred to them to salt it this time; that might come later. The rest of the ration he pushed aside. There was a mush of soycorn and beans, sprinkled with artificial bacon crumbs, no doubt well salted in the bargain, and for a treat, a slice of anchovy pizza that would look good on any report of detainee treatment, in the unlikely event that there ever were a review. They had even thoughtfully provided a little packet of salt with the tray.

Jarls counted the trays. There were five of them before the door opened to let in a quartet of armed and hard-shielded security guards. They had no trouble handling him. He was half delirious from dehydration. He stumbled along in their midst, dimly aware of the delicious sensation of cool air on his naked skin.

"In here," one of them said.

They pushed him through a doorway into a shabby room that gave the impression of being used as a temporary office. There was a comm terminal, a couple of desks, a plastic couch from storage.

Jarls blinked when he saw the man who was standing next to one of the desks, fastidiously avoiding contact with the dusty furniture. It was a Venusian in extravagant dress, with huge puffed sleeves and pantaloons in shimmering kaleidofabrics, all tricked out with ribbons, chains, and glittering jewels.

For a moment, Jarls thought he was hallucinating. He had never seen a Venusian on the actual surface of Venus. Nor had anyone else he knew ever seen one here. The Venusian gentry considered that they were roughing it when they paid their brief visits to the perfumed upper levels of Cloudhab One.

The Venusian regarded him with distaste. "Is this the man?" he asked one of the guards.

"Yes, messer," the guard said.

"Can I have a glass of water?" Jarls croaked.

He didn't expect any small mercies. He was surprised when the Venusian said to the guard, "Get him water."

"But messer," the guard protested, "he could go another two, three days before showing any signs of vascular shock."

"Do I have to repeat myself?" the Venusian said coldly.

The guard nodded at one of his fellow gorillas, who disappeared into a small lavatory and came back with a cloudy glass of water. Jarls forced himself to drink it slowly. A shudder went through his body.

The Venusian cocked a ringleted head at Jarls. "You've caused more trouble than you're worth," he sighed. "Poor Vanius's father is furious with him, and has *forbidden* him even to *talk* to any supervisory personnel or employees of Solar Oxygen or Triplanet. His allowance has been frozen for the time being, which is a dreadful inconvenience, given the size of his debts, and there's even talk of sending him on a holiday to Terra till things cool off."

Jarls recognized him then. He was the Venusian fop whose woman had tried to get him to buy Jarls for her as a household pet the day Jarls had been sold in the labor exchange. His name was Ralf. He was a friend of Vanius Paes, and had been there in Paes's behalf, to buy up one or more lots of Jovians for him.

"What happened to Terrill?" Jarls asked.

Ralf was entertained by the question. "He'll recover," he said. "You broke his arm and his hand will have to be put into nano to reassemble the bone fragments, but Solar will foot the bill. We don't want a bitter man spreading stories, eh? He'll be kept in isolation till he's healed, of course. And then he'll be shipped back to Uranus early, with a bonus and his labor contract paid up, so you can congratulate yourself for actually doing him a favor."

"The bastard!" Jarls said.

"Tut, tut," Ralf said. "You committed a serious offense, you know. You laid hands on a supervisor. We can't have that sort of thing. And we can't have word of such a thing going around. Not with a Jovian labor force. Jovians are supposed to be gentle and docile, rather like large dogs."

"What are you going to do?" Jarls said.

The Venusian shook his head. "No, no, my dear primitive. The question is, what are *you* going to do?"

"When I get out of the hotbox, I'm going to file a complaint against Terrill and Vanius Paes," Jarls said. "I'm going to ask for a charge of murder."

"He'll never get out of the hotbox alive," the Earthie guard said. "We can promise you that."

The Venusian waved a hand to silence him. "Of course you wouldn't get anywhere with such an accusation," he said to Jarls. "I'm sure you already understand that. Oh, the likes of Terrill might *conceivably* be sacrificed—under other circumstances—but Vanius's name would never appear in any database."

"I don't care," Jarls said. "I'll keep trying. Over and over. Whatever your joke of a legal code allows."

"Oh dear, you Jovians are so humorless," Ralf sighed. "You've turned yourself into a tiresome inconvenience."

He signaled to the guards, who closed in on Jarls on either side. Jarls tensed as they seized him by the arms. He wondered if he should bother to resist. As weak and shaky as he was, he was still stronger than the four of them put together. But they were bristling with weapons, high-tech restraints and chemical pacifiers. If he was going back to the hotbox, he didn't want to be trussed up in diamond fiber or turned into a helpless jellyfish by neurosprays.

The guards hustled him through a maze of corridors. People going about their business paused to look at the spectacle. Jarls began to regret his decision to be rational. If he was going to be cooked to death, he might as well make it as hard for them as possible.

He gathered his remaining strength, waiting for the right moment to make a break for it.

Then his keepers took a couple of unfamiliar turns, and he realized, incredulously, that they were not returning him to the hotbox after all.

"Where are we going?" he said through a dry mouth.

The Earthian guard spat. "Don't worry about that, cloudhopper. In a little while you may be sorry we didn't put you back in the broiler."

They jerked him forward with unnecessary force, and Jarls fell silent while he tried to work it out. Of course! They couldn't simply let him die in the hotbox now. Not after Paes's father had exerted himself behind the scenes in behalf of a hothead of a son who didn't know how to manage things discreetly. It was too late to pass Jarls off as just another Jovie with a weak heart who had failed to emerge from "detention" alive, or as the victim of an industrial accident in a brutal environment. Now Paes and his strutting friends had the elder Paes to consider. It would be an embarrassment to the Lord Chairman, and open up all sorts of doors that he had been busy closing.

Jarls tried again. "What do you mean?"

The Earthian gave Jarls an evil grin. "I've seen you hard cases before. Let's say the hotbox is too quick for you."

Jarls felt his hackles rise. He was right. They had something else in store for him.

"What's this?" Jarls said. "That's not a flyer."

They had given him clean coveralls and allowed him to drink his fill at a water tap. Then they had chivvied him into a waiting ground vehicle, one of the transport busses used for meeting the landing vehicles that ferried labor contingents back and forth from Cloudhab—except that this time Jarls and his guards were the only passengers. He was properly shackled this time, hand and foot, in clinking vanadium chains, as befitted a dangerous prisoner who had physically assaulted supervisory personnel.

Now, as the bus slowed and Jarls looked through a viewport at the bulldozed stretch of Venusian plain where the landers parked, he had expected to see one of the fleet of turtleshelled transfer vehicles that floated through the thick atmosphere on tiny wings and ridiculously small helium cells. Instead, he saw an orbiter, a stubby delta-winged ramjet with auxiliary rockets for the final leap into space.

"Didn't we mention it, Jovie?" the Earthian said. "You're going upstairs."

"I thought you meant Cloudhab."

He got an ugly laugh in return. "What, and lie around in the Jovie barracks? Not this time. You're going all the way to Venusport. You'll wait it out in the lockup there."

"Wait? Wait for what?"

"Why, for the next ship to Mercury," the guard replied with obvious malice.

"Mercury?" Jarls said, stunned.

"You've been labeled an incorrigible," the Earthie said. "You're not worth anything any more. They're getting rid of you."

# 10

**A**T NIGHT, the guards would come and lock them in dingy little cells in pairs or threes, but during the day, they were allowed to circulate in a big, bare bullpen, pretty well unsupervised. The system had its drawbacks—once, one of the crazies came out of his apathy, went berserk, and started attacking his fellow inmates. He managed to stab someone with a plastic knife he had honed out of a toothbrush before the guards could rush in and subdue him. But by and large the chief danger was boredom.

Jarls sat on one of the hard benches that comprised the dayroom's essential furnishings, ignoring the background drone of the afternoon holodrama that someone had switched on across the way, and stared listlessly around the room at his fellow detainees.

There were eighteen of them at present. Most were Jovians—the scrapings at the bottom of the barrel. These were men who had been labeled intractable by reason of stupidity or stubbornness, or who had been caught in some petty crime. But there was a sprinkling of others—a square-bearded Saturnian who refused to believe what was happening to him, and who kept insisting that there must be some mistake; a spidery Martian who had been caught in some sexual infraction; a couple of beetle-browed Earthian laborers; a Tritonian woman whom someone had gotten tired of; a twitching wreck from the asteroid confederation who was reputed to be violent, but who was kept medicated.

Rumor had it that there was even a Uranian in detention, who had somehow earned himself a one-way trip to Mercury, and who was separated from the others for his own protection.

Jarls resigned himself as he saw the Saturnian heading in his direction. The Saturnian was an overtalkative bore, who made it plain that he considered his present company to be beneath him. Somehow he had singled Jarls out as someone worthy of his confidences.

The Saturnian sat down heavily beside him. "It's outrageous to put us in with types like those," he said indignantly, rolling his eyes toward a couple of Jovians who were shooting dice with the Earthian laborers. "Now don't misunderstand me," he added hastily. "I'm not saying anything derogatory about Jovians as such, just obviously low types like those. You seem to be a decent, well brought up sort of chap with some education."

The Saturnian was a fairly new arrival. He had been brought in only three days earlier, sputtering with indignation. His muscular, high-gravity build showed him to be from one of the cloud settlements on Saturn itself, not an emigrant from Titan or one of the other moons.

Jarls made a noncommittal sound in his throat. He shifted position, moving an inch or two away, and the Saturnian immediately took advantage of the space to settle in more comfortably.

"I'm not used to the kind of swill they've been feeding us," the Saturnian complained. "At Lord Director Roiz's table, the household staff dined as well as the family itself."

Jarls didn't think that the food served to the detainees deserved to be called swill. It was pretty much the same ration that was served to the Jovian working force. It ran heavily toward starchy items like soycorn and snow rice with gravy, but though monotonous, there was plenty of it.

"Oh, the food's not too bad," he said.

The Saturnian paid no attention to his reply. "I've heard that there'll be a ship for Mercury ready in a few more days," he said. "They've been refitting it in a parking orbit farther out for the last month. It's just been moved to Venusport's docking hub. You understand that this is in strictest confidence."

"Yes, I've heard the rumor too," Jarls said.

"I'm sure my master will correct this unfortunate error before then," the Saturnian said. "I'm a trained servitor, not a common laborer. The Mercurians have no refinement. None at all. There'll be no proper work for me on Mercury."

"Yes, I'm sure it will all be straightened out," Jarls said.

He felt sorry for the Saturnian. There was only one job for bondsmen on Mercury—the mines. The Saturnian would be sent to Caloris Basin with the rest, to sweat away his life electrolyzing molten rock to separate magnesium from the feldspar. Gravity was only 38 percent of Earth-normal on Mercury. A Saturnian, born and bred in a gravity field three times higher than that, could not compare in strength to a Jovian, of course, but he would be a workhorse, and nothing but a workhorse, to the puny Mercurians.

As for Jovians, Jarls thought with a bitter smile, they were better than heavy machinery on a planet like Mercury. And cheaper.

"Somebody must have been telling lies about me, that's all there is to it," the Saturnian said plaintively. "Lord Director Roiz is bound to realize that, when he has time to consider the matter. I've always been a loyal servitor, faithful to my master's interests. Why, I would never . . ."

He fell suddenly silent. He swallowed hard, and Jarls wondered if a realization of his plight was starting to catch up with him.

The Saturnian recovered his aplomb. His gaze wandered about the room, looking for some new topic. "Here comes that scurvy Martian," he hissed sharply to Jarls. "An unsavory type if I've ever seen one. Don't give him any encouragement, and maybe he'll go away."

Jarls looked up. He saw the Martian limping toward them, his long spindly legs and underpowered muscles trying painfully to cope with the Venusian gravity. He'd no longer be handicapped on Mercury, Jarls thought. The gravity there would be about the same as it had been on Mars.

But otherwise, unfortunately, a Martian would find Mercury to be as hellish as everybody else did. It was almost as hot as Venus on the sunward side, without the amenities of orbital habitats like

Venusport. And because Mercury was still very much a frontier society, despite the great wealth it derived from its metal-rich crust and its unlimited supply of free solar energy, conditions there were harsh and primitive. For a Martian, used to a chilly planet and a remote, tame sun, there would be the special gut terror of an immense blinding ball of fire beating down from less than thirty million miles away at perihelion.

But the Martian, as he approached Jarls's bench, did not seem at all worried by his prospects. He acted like a man who was confident of landing on his feet wherever he might find himself.

He gave the Saturnian a brief, perfectly sociable smile, and turned to Jarls and said, "May I?"

Jarls made room for him, and the Martian sat down. The Saturnian scowled his annoyance.

"I wonder if our Mercurian hosts will be as gracious as the Venusians have been," the Martian said, with an ironic lift of his eyebrow to indicate their surroundings.

"I doubt it," Jarls said.

The Martian sighed. "I fear you're right. Work us to death, throw us away, and buy up another batch of misfits, cheap. That's their way."

"See here . . ." the Saturnian objected, bristling at the "misfits."

"No, our Venusian hosts can't wait to get rid of us," the Martian finished with a sigh.

"There are still laws," Jarls suggested. "The Mercurians will still have to abide by the terms of our labor contracts."

"Oh, and they will," the Martian agreed. "To the letter. Humane treatment and all that. We'll be paid in leichtenfrancs at the exchange rate specified, and we'll be able to charge extras like air and water against our accounts. Know what a bottle of water costs in converted leichtenfrancs on Mercury? About a week's pay. One hears of the occasional manumission on Venus or Earth, but no one's ever come back from Mercury."

"Nonsense!" the Saturnian blustered.

The Martian smiled sadly. "Life on Mercury is nasty, brutish, and short, as the saying goes. Unless you're a privileged Mercurian, living in one of the protected burrows at Mozart, Michelangelo, Chekhov, or some such location . . . Odd that the Mercurians should have inherited all the nomenclature of human culture when they have none of it themselves." He cocked an oversize head on a long skinny neck. "No, my friends," he said with a sigh, "they don't last long in the magnesium mines."

Life for the Martian on Mercury would be shorter and nastier than most, Jarls thought, looking at his stringbean physique. Unless he could somehow get himself sent to one of the artistically named Mercurian underground cities. The Mercurians, Jarls suddenly realized, looked a lot like Martians, with their frail, elongated bodies.

The Saturnian got stuffy again. "I don't want to hear any more," he asserted. "That kind of whining doesn't accomplish anything. And I'll tell you this—you won't get anywhere by criticizing your employers. No wonder you've been reassigned to Mercury. Your sort deserves it." His lip trembled. "Not like some of us."

He turned to Jarls. "I'm sure it wasn't your fault either that you've been reassigned. Probably they'll find it was a mistake, just as in my own case. What was the reason for their selling *your* contract?"

The question took Jarls by surprise. He didn't mind it. But in detention, one didn't ask personal questions unless invited. The Saturnian was going to get his face smashed by one of the violent types if he wasn't careful.

He was saved from having to frame an evasive answer by the Martian, who turned a bland smile on the Saturnian and said, "He beat up his supervisor. Injured him quite severely, I believe. Before that he had a reputation for subversive utterances in the barracks."

The Saturnian got up hastily. "Excuse me," he said, and walked away.

The Martian laughed. "I hope you didn't mind my sending him packing," he said to Jarls.

"No," Jarls said. "How did you know that about me?"

"One hears things," the Martian said vaguely.

"Bad break for him," Jarls said, motioning after the Saturnian's retreating back. "Bad break for all of us. What did he do?"

"He didn't do anything," the Martian said. "That's what got him in trouble."

Jarls looked puzzled.

"Priggishness," the Martian explained. "He virtuously refused his owner's wife. Well, she couldn't have him around after that. He might spill the beans to His Lord Directorship. So to protect herself, she invented some story about him. About him having eyes above his station, or some such. So he got the blame without having played the game."

"I take it you don't think much of . . . priggishness."

"Me?" The Martian laughed. "Heavens no."

"Mercury's no picnic," Jarls said. "I hope you don't mind my saying so, but it's going to be harder on you than the rest of us."

"I'll survive."

Jarls's raised eyebrows showed his skepticism.

The Martian spoke carefully, his eyes on Jarls's face. "Mercurians are an unrefined lot. Still unpolished, rather like you Jovians, but without your endearing qualities. But they are still susceptible to human folly."

Jarls decided to leave it at that. "The Saturnian says that they're planning to ship us out in only a few more days," he said, to change the subject.

"He got it wrong. We're leaving tomorrow."

"So soon? I thought we'd have some warning."

"They don't want to give us time to become restless."

Jarls thought he had been prepared, but it was a shock. "Well then, that's it," he said.

"Maybe not. There might be another chance for you. A slim one."

"What are you talking about?"

"There's an Earthian labor contractor here now—just passing through. Looking for bargains. Name's Makay. He's one of the vultures who specializes in hard cases—a 'man tamer,' he calls himself—and unloads them at a profit to some unsuspecting buyer. He'll be allowed to look us over before we're shipped, take his pick of the cream of the crop, and make the Venusians an offer."

"How can that be? My labor contract's already been sold to Mercury."

The Martian gave him an indulgent smile. "Do you think the Venusians are that scrupulous about honoring contracts? If they can make a few more leichtenfrancs off of you, they'll do it."

"I'm not that marketable. Or hadn't you heard?"

"Your little history of insubordination? That won't bother Makay. His boast is that he can break any man. You'll be certified tame when he foists you off on one of his Earthside customers. Jovians are in vogue there. All he cares about is that you behave yourself during the sale. So if you'll take my advice, make yourself look good for Makay's inspection. Show off your muscles. Act agreeable, and a little stupid."

"I won't kowtow to anybody!" Jarls said angrily.

"Up to you. But anything's better than the magnesium mines."

"Are you going to . . . make yourself look better?"

"No. Mars is the second oldest civilization in the solar system, but we're raw tyros compared to Earthians. My master . . . or mistress . . . would see right through me. Besides, Earth is even heavier a planet than Venus. I prefer Mercurian gravity."

"You might not have anything to say about it."

"Makay won't want me." The Martian, despite his bravado, let his mask slip for the first time, and Jarls could see that he was frightened at the chance he was taking. "Martians don't fetch a particularly good price on Earth. We're weak there, and our other attributes don't compensate. But Jovians are another story. And you're an even better specimen than most."

"I'm not a piece of merchandise!" Jarls exploded. "You might think of yourself that way, but I don't, and I never will!"

"I'm sorry," the Martian said, shrinking back from Jarls's fury. "But what you think doesn't matter. It doesn't matter at all."

"On your feet," the guard said. "The messer wants to get a better look at you."

He prodded Jarls with his baton to emphasize his words. Jarls gave him a cold stare, and the guard changed his mind about prodding him. He let the baton drop and took a step backward.

Jarls took his time about getting up. He pushed the bench back and stood impassively, his thickly muscled arms hanging loosely at his sides, staring above and beyond the men who had paused in front of him.

"He's the one I warned you about," the Venusian sales agent said, waving a ring-encrusted hand in Jarls's direction.

The Earthian labor contractor, Makay, nodded. "Dumb insolence. I've seen it before. We'll knock that right out of him."

Makay was a bony man with tight lips and a permanently furrowed brow. He wasn't particularly tall for an Earthian—not much more than a few inches above Jarls in height.

"It's not just that," the Venusian said. "He's dangerous."

"Yes, yes, I've read his file," Makay said impatiently. "It doesn't worry me. I've dealt with far worse."

He turned to Jarls with a scowl. "You, Jarls!" he barked. "Now's your chance. You're thinking you could snap me in two this very minute, aren't you? Go ahead and do it if you're going to. I couldn't stop you, could I?"

Jarls, against his will, felt himself starting to flush. The fact was that the thought *had* occurred to him. Though the Earthman and the Venusian were both taller than he was, he far outbulked them. Like all inner planet people, they were frail and brittle-boned compared with a Jovian.

He thrust the rogue thought from his mind. All of his Jovian instincts constrained him to be careful about touching or handling such fragile folk. He took a deep breath and felt the flush start to fade.

Makay laughed. "See what I mean?" he said to the Venusian. He looked Jarls over more closely. "Impressive brute, even for a Jovian," he said with satisfaction. "The only Jovian I've seen who can outmatch him is my own mandriver, Tunk." He jerked his head toward the enormous Jovian at the other side of the bullpen, busy lining up the other prisoners whom Makay had singled out.

"Just so it's clear that we warned you," the Venusian said.

"I guarantee that he'll be meek as a lamb by the time we land on Earth," Makay said. He thumbed a data slate. "Hmm. He seems to have some education and skills according to this. And he's shown some interest in self-improvement, to judge by the record of learning veeyars he's rented. Not that intelligence is always a plus—sometimes it can make them more difficult to handle. But with a little luck, I might be able to dispose of him at a premium, once he's been housebroken."

He looked into Jarls's face. "How would you like that, boy?" he said. "Maybe a little step up in the world instead of wrestling rock in a hardsuit until your heart bursts."

Jarls clamped his jaw shut and stared straight ahead.

"Stubborn, eh?" Makay turned to the Venusian sales agent with a thin smile. "This one might take a little work, but Tunk will straighten him out."

"Your problem now," the Venusian said.

"Get over there and get in line with the others," Makay said curtly to Jarls.

Jarls stayed put. He had taken an intense dislike to Makay. He would rather, he decided, be shipped to Mercury.

"Tunk, come over here," Makay said without raising his voice. He clasped his hands behind his back and assumed a waiting posture. To Jarls, he said, "We can carry you aboard if you wish. Wrapped up in stickytape if you insist on it."

Across the room, Makay's huge assistant paused in his tasks and turned around. He was the biggest Jovian Jarls had ever seen—as tall as any Earthian, but with the bulk and solidity of all born natives of the giant planet. An extra bulge of soft flesh around his waistline gave away the fact that he had been away from home too long, but there was a compensating girth of upper arm and thigh muscle to show that he had exercised fanatically in penguin suit and with other spring-resistance devices to keep up his Jovian strength.

Jarls had kept up his strength too, but Venus's gravity was not quite as demanding as Earth's, and he had not yet fully recovered from his session in the hotbox. And Tunk was a lot bigger than he was. The conclusion was foregone.

Jarls stepped forward and joined the line for Earth. Tunk looked disappointed.

He looked back across the room. Makay was consulting his data slate, but he seemed to be finished with his selection. The Martian was still sitting there on one of the hard benches. He had guessed correctly. He was going to Mercury. If he were sent to the magnesium mines in the Caloris Basin, it would mean certain death for him. But he didn't look like a man who expected to die.

The Saturnian was still there, too, looking desolate. It had finally dawned on him that his master was not going to rescue him from Mercury at the last minute, and he had made a nuisance of himself when Makay had shown up. Earth, with its wealth and its great families, had suddenly looked good to him. He had puffed himself up and harangued Makay about his superior qualifications as a trained servitor. But Makay, it appeared, was interested only in Jovians. The Saturnian had grown shrill and insistent, and in the end, Tunk had had to pry him away from Makay and sit him down forcibly on a bench.

Jarls turned his eyes away, embarrassed for the man. He shuffled forward with the rest of the shipment for Earth. Makay had chosen about a third of the most presentable Jovians, ignoring any history of violence or insubordination in their records. There were worse cases than Jarls. The hulking fellow ahead of him in line, Remmer, had killed a man. The only reason he hadn't been executed and sent to organ retrieval was that the man he'd killed had been another Jovian.

Remmer turned around and sized Jarls up with a belligerent stare. "I saw what you did," he said. "Practically daring that Earthie bloodsucker to send you to Mercury. Stupid!"

"Maybe," Jarls said.

"Stupid," the man reiterated. "Me, I'm meek as a lamb till we're aboard ship in Earth trajectory and nobody can do anything about it. Just let them try to lean on me then. I can take that overgrown ape, Tunk, any time. Size don't mean anything. Did you see that gut of his? Soft."

"I wouldn't underestimate him," Jarls said. "Either of them."

Remmer curled his lip contemptuously. "Yeah, I saw you back down as soon as he gave you a look. And they said you were tough."

"No," Jarls said. "I'm not so tough."

"Just keep your nose clean till you get to Earth," the other taunted him. "And maybe they'll give you a nice soft job as somebody's tame Jovie."

He turned away from Jarls as the line started to move toward the exit. Jarls fell in step with the others.

Earth, he thought, fabulous Earth. The place he'd been hearing about all his life. Maybe when he got there, things would be better.


"Why do you want to do this?" Tunk pleaded. "It always ends the same way."

Jarls didn't waste breath answering. He broke free from Tunk's grip on his upper arms long enough to drive a fist into the big Jovian's middle with a force that would have shattered stone. His fist sank into rubbery flesh up to the wrist, then hit something firmer.

Tunk grunted, looked annoyed, and caught Jarls by the wrist. He gave Jarls an open-handed smack on the side of the head that left his ears ringing. The blow would have snapped the neck of anybody but another Jovian. It left Jarls disoriented long enough for Tunk to shift to a more comfortable grip, back him up against a bulkhead, and begin methodically to punch him in the belly, diaphragm and ribs in some sort of predetermined rhythmic pattern. Through a haze of pain and the roaring in his head, Jarls retained enough consciousness to realize, with a sense of revulsion, that the man was counting out the blows. ". . . twenty-four . . . twenty-five . . . twenty-six . . . twenty-seven . . ."

Tunk stopped to rest. He was breathing hard, and there was a small trickle of blood at the corner of his mouth from the blow Jarls had landed earlier. He made the mistake of shifting his grip again.

Jarls kicked him in the shin and tore loose from his grasp with a sudden violent twist that put enough space between them for Jarls to hit him squarely in the face a second time.

Before Jarls could follow up, Tunk wrapped his tremendous arms around him, and together they toppled to the floor. With his arms pinned to his sides and the big Jovian's weight on him, Jarls was unable to move. Tunk was out of breath—a small victory.

"Don't make me do this," Tunk said in an exasperated tone.

"There's no easy way," Jarls said. "You know that."

"You're crazy," the mandriver complained. "That's all there is to it. I don't enjoy grinding down other Jovians like this. But it's my job."

"You chose it," Jarls said.

He tried to wriggle free, but the big man slammed him down with a force that knocked the wind out of him.

"All I want to do is save up enough to go back to Jupiter," Tunk said, looking as if he were about to cry. "Buy a little plot on a farm deck. Grow vegetables. Raise quadrachicks."

"How long have you been away?" Jarls wheezed.

"Fifteen years now—Earth years."

"You better get on with your job, then," Jarls gritted.

Tunk shook his head resignedly and drew back a big fist. He had to change his grip to pinion Jarls one-handed, and Jarls used the opening to lash out at his face. Jarls had the satisfaction of seeing Tunk flinch—another small victory that would have been unthinkable at the beginning of the voyage—and then the fist descended on him.

"What did you want to go and make me do this for?" Tunk said unhappily, and proceeded to beat him to a pulp for the fifth time that voyage. Through the rain of blows, Jarls smiled with bruised and bleeding lips. He was wearing them down.

* * *

"I told you not to mark him," Makay reprimanded his mandriver. "Scars are a dead giveaway."

"I couldn't help it," Tunk said defensively. "He wouldn't stay down. Anyway, look at *me*."

He had a split lip, a splint over a broken nose, a torn ear. The intimation that he was less than invulnerable had made his job harder with the other recalcitrant cases, and he had had to deal out more bruises than usual this trip.

Makay looked up from his paperwork, and leaned forward across his desk. "You're stupid, and you're costing me money," he said to Jarls. "I could have gotten you a house job. Hall boy, porter, gatekeeper. Lots of the big Earth households like to keep uniformed Jovians around in the visible positions—beefs up their regular security. The Jovian looks tough, so much the better—so long as he's certified tame." He shook his head in disgust. "But I can't risk it. I've got a reputation to consider. You're good for nothing but cheap muscle."

"That's fine with me," Jarls said.

Makay folded his hands. "I don't understand it," he said. "I thought Remmer was going to be the tough nut to crack on this trip. But he gentled down nicely after a bad start. I was able to place him as a second footman in a Lord Director's town house in Bern. His Directorship doesn't mind employing a murderer— lends him a certain cachet with his friends. But an incorrigible like you is worthless to me. I should have let them send you to the mines."

"Maybe you should have," Jarls said.

He felt vaguely ashamed for Remmer, though it was none of his business. Remmer had caved in after the first beating, and spent the rest of the trip trying to justify himself to Jarls.

"I got you a better deal than you deserve," Makay said tiredly. "You're going to do stable work on one of the country estates of a great lord. The stablemaster will work you till you drop, and you'll be kept out of sight of the family."

Jarls met Makay's eyes with an even stare.

"By God I could have broken you down with a little more time!" Makay burst out. "I wish I had you for one more month!"

"But you don't," Jarls said.

# PART 3

# EARTH

# 11

**Y**OU'LL START by mucking out the elephants' stalls," Jock Drummond said. "After that, it'll be your job to exercise them every day." He looked Jarls up and down with a critical eye. "It takes a lot of strength to handle the beasts. That's why I told Makay I'd take you on. But I'll make no allowances for you. Do we understand each other?"

Jarls gave him a cursory nod. "Yes." He shifted his attention to the enormous gray creature on the other side of the barred gate, busily shoveling straw into its mouth with a long, snakelike appendage. "I thought elephants were extinct."

"Ay, they were," said the wiry little stablemaster. "For more than two hundred years. But his lordship decided he wanted a herd of them for foxhunting. His neighbors have only horses, you see. So he had twenty of them cloned from old elephant DNA in museum artifacts. You can't imagine the expense. They aren't much good for foxhunting. He only uses them once a year for his gala weekend at Strathspey. But they make a grand impression on the other gentry."

Jarls was a bit dazed. So far that morning, in the few hours since he'd arrived at Lord Chedforth's country estate, he'd seen horses, cows, camels, sheep, even a caged bear—all the semi-mythical animals of Earth that he'd seen in his childhood nature holos on Jupiter.

And now elephants! His Lordship, Tomo Hirakawa, the forty-eighth Earl of Strathspey, was a bit of a collector, it seemed.

At the end of the line of stalls was a tall cage with heavier bars set in concrete. A muscular Earthman, stripped to the waist to show peeling, sunburned skin, was pitching straw through the bars to a gigantic hairy beast moving about restlessly within.

"Well, what do you think?" Jock Drummond said with a hint of pride in his voice.

Jarls moved closer. He saw a shaggy creature that looked something like an elephant, only bigger, with immense curved tusks that were half again the length of a man. When it saw Jarls, it blared at him with an ear-splitting trumpet sound that made him involuntarily take a step backward.

"What is it?" he said.

"A mammoth," the stablemaster replied. "They were extinct twenty-five thousand years before the elephants disappeared. His Lordship had to move heaven and earth to get the DNA sample. But there's no stopping him when he has his mind set on something. He cut through the red tape as if it didn't exist—national sovereignty, biological regulations, corporate proprietorships. They couldna' said no to the Laird! His family's not only had the peerage in an unbroken line since it was sold to the Hirakawas four hundred years ago, but he has connections to the Japanese imperial line and to the house of Liechtenstein as well. In fact—" Drummond lowered his voice confidentially. "—His Lordship is an eighth cousin to the Megachairman himself!"

Jarls was impressed. "Franz Joseph XXIV?" he exclaimed.

"Ay. And we Drummonds have been around a long time too. We have been gillies and gamekeepers and stablemasters to the Earls of Strathspey since the first Hirakawa took over the title."

"When will I see Lord Hirakawa?" Jarls asked.

"Ye'll remember your place!" the stablemaster said with sudden harshness. "His Lordship is not concerned with the likes of you! He doesna' even know that you exist. And on those occasions when he comes to visit Strathspey, you will keep out of his sight. Do you understand?"

"Yes."

Drummond turned grumpy, aware that he had been boasting

too freely to a mere stableboy. He jerked his head toward the caged mammoth and said gruffly, "You've never seen an animal that size, I'll wager."

Jarls thought of the flapjacks of Jupiter, remembered riding those acres and acres of living flesh through the ammonia clouds on that day, long ago, when the Jovian native had saved him from a plunge to oblivion.

"No," he said. "No terrestrial life form, anyway. The biggest Earth creatures we have that could stand the gravity are the dolphin workers. And they spend their lives in fluid."

But Drummond had already turned away to talk to the the barechested stablehand, who was taking advantage of the break in routine to lean on his pitchfork and chew ostentatiously on a straw.

"Why is the beast so nervous, Grier?" he demanded. "You havena' been teasing him, have you?"

"Me, Jock? Never." Grier was the picture of innocence.

"It's Mister Drummond, if you please," the stablemaster said with a frown.

"It's that sorry I am, *Mister* Drummond," Grier apologized. "I just forgot myself, is all."

Drummond looked at him suspiciously, but there was nothing in Grier's demeanor that could be tagged as outright insolence.

"That'll do, Grier," he said. He looked back and forth from Grier to Jarls, turning it into a scolding for both of them. "Remember that these are valuable beasts, and verra sensitive, for all their great size. We've lost more than one through stress, and I willna have them abused." He scowled at the mammoth. "There are worn patches in his fur," he said. "His Lordship won't like that. Has he been rubbing against the bars?"

"Throwing himself against them, is more like it," Grier snickered. "He wants to get out, he does."

As if to punctuate Grier's words, the mammoth trumpeted again, making Jarls jump a second time. But this time its beady little eyes—surprisingly small for so large a creature—were fixed on Grier. There was intelligence in them, and hate.

If Drummond noticed the look, he didn't show it. "This is the new number-three stableboy," he said to Grier. "He's called Jarley. With him and Bert to pitch in, I'll expect no more excuses. These stalls are a bloody disgrace. Show him where things are, will you? I've already given him a job to start him off."

Drummond stomped off. Grier turned to Jarls, the humble posture gone. "You're a Jovian, are you?" he said, taking in the immense muscles, the huge shoulders, the thick neck.

"Yes," Jarls said.

"Thought so." Grier spat in the straw. "Don't get any ideas. We've got house Jovies up at the manor, but you're not one of them. You're general dogsbody around here. Do you understand?"

Jarls didn't know the term, but Grier's meaning was plain enough. "Yes," he said.

A sly look passed across Grier's face. "Pretty strong, are you? That's what they say about Jovies."

"I suppose so," Jarls said.

Grier grinned with satisfaction. "Come with me. I'll show you where the tap is. You can help me out by watering the beasts."

"Mister Drummond told me to start by mucking out the stalls."

"Forget about that for now. You'll water them, I say."

Jarls shrugged. He followed Grier to a dank, concrete-floored room crowded with battered tools and equipment. There was a lone dripping tap at the far wall, surrounded by a jumble of buckets and jerry cans.

"His Lordship hasn't seen fit to extend the water lines to the elephant barn," Grier said in a mocking tone. "The expense, you see. There used to be a system of pipes to the stalls, but the elephants were marvelously clever about turning on the taps. And, not having to pay the bills and fill out the forms about water use, they tended to leave the taps running. When we tried locking the taps, the beasts only tore out the pipes."

"What about a cutoff valve at this end?" Jarls suggested.

"Isn't he the brainy one for a stableboy," Grier said. "Tell me, are they all that brainy on Jupiter?"

Jarls saw no point in replying, and let it pass, but Grier was not finished with him.

"Ye'll do what you're told, and leave the thinking to others," Grier said. "Plumbing's expensive, and stable boys are cheap." He handed Jarls a five-gallon bucket and said, "You'd best get started. You've a lot of trips to make."

"Haven't you anything larger?" Jarls asked.

"Listen to the man!" He grinned as he got Jarls a ten-gallon pail. "Here you are. Half as many trips. This one holds eighty pounds of water. But then, you're one of those Jovians, aren't you."

Jarls ignored the proffered bucket. He rooted around in the clutter and came up with a thirty-gallon metal drum. Two hundred and fifty pounds of water, he thought sardonically. But then, he was one of those Jovians.

He hoisted the drum to his shoulder. "This will do," he said.

Grier was not pleased at having his joke spoiled. "I have no doubt you'll be able to lift it and carry for a time," he said with a scowl. "But do you know how many trips you'll still have to make?"

"Fewer," Jarls said. "How much water do I give them?"

"You'll keep fetching till they stop drinking," Grier said with a scowl. He swaggered off through the elephant barn. A few moments later, Jarls heard one of the big animals bellow.

It took a long time to fill the drum. Jarls heaved mightily and lifted it to his shoulder. He heard his joints crack. It felt good to be doing heavy work again. He'd soon be getting back the strength that had been stolen from him by the space voyage. He walked a straight line through the utility room, balancing the drum with easy grace, and emptied the water into the drinking trough of the first stall.

The elephant's long appendage came through the bars and rested briefly on his shoulder in a curiously human gesture. Then the beast began siphoning water and squirting it into its mouth. It seemed very thirsty. Before long the trough was empty, and the beast fixed Jarls with its small intelligent eyes and snorted at him for more. Resignedly he trudged back for another load, and was dismayed when the elephant used ten or twenty gallons of the water to give itself a shower.

The other elephants, alerted by the smell of water, had begun trumpeting by now. They seemed frantic, and Jarls wondered how long they'd been neglected.

It took five hours of nonstop hauling before the creatures were satisfied. It would have taken longer, except that halfway through his labors he found a wheeled dolly, able to accommodate three drums per trip, that Grier had neglected to tell him about.

He took care of the hairy mammoth last. He was a little apprehensive. He had seen the way Grier had been careful to stay out of reach of the long, muscular trunk when he was pitching hay. The beast looked frankly murderous, and glared at him with tiny red-rimmed eyes as he walked up to the reinforced cage. He approached the bars cautiously, prepared to leap back quickly, but the mammoth stood quietly, only shifting its weight from side to side while Jarls filled its drinking trough. He spoke to it—a few meaningless soothing words—and was gratified to get a long, low rumble in return.

Drummond reappeared as he was finishing with the mammoth, and yelled at him angrily. "What are you doing? The beast's dangerous! Why are you not staying at a distance and using the hose?"

"Hose?" Jarls repeated stupidly.

"Did Grier not tell you about the hose? It's in that closet at the end of the row of stalls. Why are you mucking about with barrels?"

"I . . ."

"And why are the stalls not swamped out yet? The brutes should have been in the exercise corral all this time while you were working!" Drummond's meager face was red with fury. "Now you'll have to run them about after supper—if you ha' time for supper, that is!"

"I'm sorry."

"I'm sorry, Mister Drummond, if you please."

"I'm sorry, Mister Drummond. I thought they needed water first."

"That was Grier's job. In future, ye'll do what I say before you start letting Grier take advantage of you. Do you understand?"

"Yes."

Drummond was somewhat mollified. "I'll see that they bring you something if you're not finished by supper," he said.

He shook his head in generalized disgust and stamped out. Jarls, sweat still streaming down his face and torso in great rivulets, took a half-gallon swig of leftover water, lifting the thirty-gallon drum with both hands and letting it pour down his parched throat. He returned the drum to the tack room, where he had found it. There was a closet with a hose where Drummond had said it would be. Jarls unreeled the hose; it would make the job of cleaning the stalls a lot easier. He went around to the back of the building and shot the outside bolts that led to the stalls. The elephants knew the drill, even if he didn't. They shuffled out one by one and gathered in the exercise corral, a fenced-in area of trodden earth that was easily several acres in extent. The elephants filed past Jarls without bothering him, and it did not occur to him to be afraid of the massive creatures. One of the gray giants, on its way to join the others, paused to push gently at Jarls with its trunk, testing the new human's strength. Jarls pushed back, and though he might not have been able to resist the elephant's sheer weight had the animal decided to make it more than a contest of simple muscle power, was able to hold his own in the brief shoving match. The elephant stored the data away for further consideration and went to catch up with the rest of the herd.

Jarls set to work to clean up the stalls with shovel, pitchfork, and hose, and added the results to the impressive mountain of manure in back of the barn. The mammoth's cage gave him pause. Drummond had told him to stay away from it, but Grier had obviously been more than usually neglectful of his difficult charge, and Jarls could not leave the poor creature standing amidst piles of filth. The outside door was padlocked, but a holding pen of sorts had been constructed in place of an adjoining stall.

The empty pen was filthy too, and Jarls scrubbed it clean before proceeding further. Then he was faced with the problem of transferring the prehistoric beast.

There was a steel lift bar between the two cages, with its end baffled to keep the mammoth from reaching around and fiddling with it. The baffle itself was secured with four thick eye bolts. It was a primitive safety measure, probably improvised by Drummond; the eye bolts would have to be unscrewed one by one and the baffle removed, and then Grier, before the mammoth realized it could get at him, would have time to cross to the other gate, climb it, and while perched on top, lift the crossbar with a chain-and-pulley contrivance. It would be a lot of trouble; maybe that was why Grier was so lazy about cleaning out the mammoth's cage.

While Jarls pondered the arrangement, the mammoth's trunk curled around the bars and unscrewed the four eye bolts.

Jarls retreated without undue haste to the other gate, and waited to see what the mammoth would do next. The primitive beast was cleverer than it looked. It could get at Grier any time it chose. It also had the capacity to bide its time. Why it had decided to demonstrate its abilities to Jarls was more than he could fathom.

Was it waiting for Jarls to take the next step and raise the steel crossbar?

Jarls wondered if what was now happening constituted a form of dialogue with the mammoth—as his implicit consent for the Jovian flapjack to take his toolbox as a reward for saving his life on the day he had fallen overboard had constituted a form of dialogue with the flapjack.

At least Dr. Chukchee, the flapjack expert back at Port Elysium, had considered the incident to be an authentic example of interspecies communication.

When another thirty seconds went by without Jarls lifting the bar, the mammoth snaked its trunk around again and raised the bar itself. Jarls saw no reason to scramble to the top of the gate, as Grier would have done. He waited as the mammoth pushed the connecting door open and ambled into the holding pen.

Jarls stood motionless while the hairy monster sniffed him all over with its trunk. When it finished, he stood on tiptoe and scratched one shaggy ear, then walked unhurriedly past it to the other cage. He decided regretfully that he would have to warn Grier about the animal's ability to unscrew bolts.

He swung the gate shut behind him and set about the onerous job of swamping out the dung-filled pen.

Earth's oversize sun had long since set by the time he finished his chores. It had been a long day—more than twice as long as a Jovian day. Jarls was bone weary and his muscles ached from the hours of continuous work, though Earth's puny gravity had put no strain on them.

He wandered outside and sat on a bale of hay to enjoy his first Terran evening. The sky was a velvety black, flecked by dim ghostly clouds, and there was an enormous moon overhead that made the night as bright as a Jovian day. The air was warm and humid on his bare torso, and heavy with the smell of growing things. He inhaled Earth's rich perfume with a sense of reverence; even a farm deck on Port Elysium didn't smell like this! There were mysterious musical piping sounds in the night, and he knew intellectually that they must be birds.

He looked at the twinkling lights sprinkled across the Scottish landscape, using them to trace the shape of the rolling hills that surrounded Lord Hirakawa's country estate. Earth's horizon was small and near compared to Jupiter's, but nevertheless, the planet had a spacious feel to it. This was the world that the human race had come from, and Jarls reminded himself that more people lived on Earth than on all the other planets, moons, and habitats of the solar system put together.

He twisted his head to stare at the lights of the big house, almost a quarter-mile away across expanses of neatly trimmed lawn and stunning formal gardens surrounded by geometric borders of ancient pavement. He had been amazed that morning, when he had arrived, to see the army of gardeners it took to mow the grass, clip the shrubbery, and otherwise maintain the grounds for Lord Hirakawa's pleasure. Though the Laird visited Strathspey only intermittently, Jarls had learned, the staff could never tell when he might arrive, and consequently the grounds had to be kept always in a state of perfection. Jarls marveled at the wealth that must be concentrated in one man to pay for such lavish upkeep, but then, Earth was immeasurably rich—richer even than Venus.

He heard footsteps crunch on the path and a moment later there was a young woman at his side, carrying a large covered wicker basket.

"You'd be the new stableboy?" she said.

"Uh, yes," he said.

He examined her in the bright moonlight. She was tall and slender, like so many of the Earth women he'd seen since his arrival at the Singapore space elevator terminal the day before. She was attired in some kind of uniform—a black dress with a white apron and tiny ruffled cap.

"Mister Drummond said to bring you some supper. I got Missus Macintyre to put up a hamper." Her voice turned accusing. "You were supposed to have your supper in the annex with the rest of the grounds staff."

"I'm sorry," he said.

She cocked her head at him. "You're a Jovian, then?"

"Yes."

"What's your name?"

"Jarls."

"I'm Mary." She lifted an eyebrow. "What are you doing here?"

"What do you mean?"

"We have Jovians at the house. They're under Mister Karsen's direction. Lord Hirakawa likes to have Jovians around. Lots of the gentry keep them. He thinks they make a good appearance in their uniforms. But we've never had one on the grounds staff before. We once had one on the household staff as odd man, but he was too clumsy. He didn't know his own strength and he was always breaking things. Lady Hirakawa finally had to sell him to one of our London neighbors, Lord Shrewsbury. He's a bachelor. He said he didn't mind. He took him on as hall boy, so it was a step up for him."

"I see," said Jarls, thoroughly mystified.

"Oh, and we've got a Jovian scullery maid, too. She's not under Mister Karsen, though. She's under Missus Macintyre. Her name's Magda. She's as strong as a man. Stronger. Missus Mcintyre uses her for all the heavy lifting and things that otherwise she'd have to ask Mister Arthur, the butler, to loan her a hall boy for. She doesn't like to be indebted to Mister Arthur, because it gives him an opening to stick his nose into the kitchen. Do all Jovian women have muscles like that?"

"Well, growing up in Jupiter gravity . . ."

"I swear, she's built like one of those wrestlers that Lord Hirakawa owns in Japan. Even her breasts are hard." She sniffed disapprovingly. "You wouldn't think that sort of thing would be attractive to men, but there's one of the footmen, Harold, who's always sneaking around trying to have himself a little accidental feel, if you know what I mean."

She peered closely into Jarls's face, looking for a response.

"Well, I suppose . . ." he began, but got no further.

"I have to admit she always puts him in his place. But she'd better watch her step. There's one of Lord Hirakawa's nephews, the black sheep we call him, who has his eye on her. He was in a scandal with a Jovian woman who belonged to the Duke of Cornwall when he was a weekend guest there, and they say he hurt her some way, but it was hushed up. Has odd tastes, I suppose. Missus Macintyre's given Magda fair warning. She's been able to keep him at a distance so far, but it isn't easy to say no to a gentleman."

She paused for breath, and Jarls took the opportunity to ask a question. "This Mister Karsen who has a staff of Jovians under him—what's his title?"

She looked at him as if he were an idiot. "Why, he's chief of security."

"Chief of security?" he repeated stupidly.

"Of course. What else would he be?"

With that, she smoothed out her apron and went flouncing off. He followed her progress up the path until the dusk swallowed up her form.

He turned his attention to the wicker hamper she had left for him. Inside was an assortment of covered dishes separated by starched napkins. Lord Hirakawa's servants ate in style.

He took the lid off the first dish, and frowned at its contents. It seemed to be a plate of raw fish in a nest of rice. A tiny bowl of some pungent sauce went with it.

He sampled the rice dubiously. It tasted of vinegar. Some kind of English fare, he supposed. The raw fish didn't taste too bad after he dipped it in the sauce.

All of a sudden, Jarls discovered that he was ravenous. He hadn't eaten for over twenty-four hours—his last meal had been a soggy plastic-wrapped beanburger that they'd handed out to the labor contractor's tired little flock as they'd emerged from the Singapore space elevator.

He wolfed down the fish and rice, and found that it was delicious. The other dishes, though unfamiliar, were just as tasty. There were transparent noodles speckled with flecks of something green, a beautifully arranged platter of paper-thin slices of what looked like natural meat, tiny dumplings, a generous slice of some kind of mega-bean smothered in a rich sauce. It was a change from the starchy, monotonous rations the Venusians served their workers, but just as plentiful. Jovians needed a lot of fuel if you intended to work them hard.

Comfortably full, Jarls sat back and thought about all he had seen and heard on this, his first full day on Earth.

The servants' politics seemed complicated, with each faction struggling for advantage. But Lord Hirakawa, like other rich Earthians, evidently maintained a private security force of uniformed Jovians, with a fellow named Karsen in charge.

On Venus, an indentured Jovian was automatically consigned to the rank of common laborer. But here, in Earth's older civilization, the ruling aristocracy fell all over themselves to emulate the Megachairman, Franz Joseph XXIV. The palace guard in Bern-Liechtenstein had for more than two centuries been composed of hired Jovians. Earth had a tortured history of power struggles, and Jovians, though barbarians from a backward planet, had always been considered incorruptible.

Jarls thought of old Ian Karg, who had served thirty years in the Executive Guard, and in consequence had become Port Elysium's most celebrated success story.

What had Karg tried to tell him? It had been some oblique warning about Earth, he was sure of that now. Jarls suddenly remembered the sealed letter that Karg had given him, should he ever need help. It had been addressed to an Executive Guardsman in the Bern-Liechtenstein megalopolis.

Jarls fished around in his belt pouch for the letter. Yes, he still had it. There it was, buried under a lot of accumulated litter that included some crumpled Venusian credit chits, the tattered copy of his joke of a labor contract, and similar useless debris.

The envelope was twice folded over, creased, and much the worse for wear. But it was still sealed with the high security hologram that made it worthless if anybody except the addressee opened it.

Jarls squinted at the name written under the hologram in Karg's impatient scrawl: *Leith Carnavan.*

He smiled a thin smile. He had about the same chance of ever getting to the Executive Palace in Liechtenstein as one of Lord Hirakawa's recloned elephants had of flying to the moon under its own power. Less. The elephants, at least, were allowed off the estate during the fox hunting season.

He was tempted to open the envelope, just to see what Karg had written about him. Surely it didn't matter, since he would never get a chance to deliver it. But some impulse, some twinge of superstition, stopped him.

After a moment of hesitation, he refolded the envelope and put it back in the bottom of the pouch.

Just at that moment, Jock Drummond appeared. "There you are!" he said irritably. "What are you doing, idling about like this? There'll be more than enough to do tomorrow. You'll have to be up at sunrise, ready for an honest day's work. Come wi' me, boy, and I'll show you where you can sleep."

Jarls followed the little stablemaster to a hayloft over the elephant barn and gratefully took the blanket that was offered him. He was glad enough to turn in. Earth had a long day.

It was about a month later that the mammoth tried to kill Grier.

Jarls had become aware early on that his fellow stableboy tormented the huge beast whenever he thought he could get away with it. He had caught Grier prodding the mammoth with the sharp end of a ten-foot elephant goad when there was no reason for it, deliberately aiming for sensitive spots, and jerking the long pole out of reach when the mammoth became enraged enough to try to grab it. Jarls knew, too, that Grier sadistically withheld water from the giant animal. More than once he had found the poor creature half mad with thirst, sucking at a dry trough. Jarls had silently rectified the situation, filling the trough with the hose, while Grier looked on, grinning derisively. And once, though Jarls could not prove it, Grier had put hot pepper or something similar in the mammoth's hay. Jarls had spent a quarter-hour sluicing out the mammoth's gaping mouth with the hose and trying to calm the distraught beast down. After that, the mammoth had refused to touch food given by Grier, and Jarls had quietly taken over the job of filling the hay rack. Grier had smirked, but had not dared to object.

When Grier had made sure that Jarls would not report him, he became bolder. Grier, in fact, seemed to delight in provoking Jarls. Jarls had walked in on him one day, loitering around the mammoth's cage with a canvas sack dangling from one oversize fist.

"What have you got there?" Jarls said.

Grier gave him a sly wink. "A rat," he said. "Want to see it?"

Before Jarls could reply, Grier squeezed the bottom of the sack, gripping something tightly through the heavy canvas. A high-pitched squealing came from inside. Grier loosened the drawstring and peeled back the mouth of the sack. Jarls saw beady eyes and a sharp, whiskered face. The rat was scrabbling frantically with its forepaws, trying to escape, but Grier had a firm grasp of its hindquarters. Frustrated, the rat doubled back on itself and bit its own haunch.

Jarls was repelled. There were no rats or other vermin on Jupiter, but some buried racial memory made him react with disgust.

"Where did you get it?" he said.

"Oh, there's a nest of them in the grain room. Hard to catch. You've got to be patient. And quick."

"Mister Drummond won't like this. There's not supposed to be any vermin in Lord Hirakawa's stables. He's a stickler for cleanliness. The bins are supposed to be sealed tight, any spilled grain swept up immediately."

He'd had it drummed into him during his month on the estate. "*Kirei de nai.*" "This is not clean." "*Kitanai.*" "This is dirty." He could repeat the Japanese phrases in his sleep.

"The Drummond doesn't have to know, does he?"

"What are you talking about. Of course he has to know."

"And who's to take the blame, then? You're the new slavey around here. There were never any rats before you came. I'd watch my step if I were you, muscle boy."

"That's ridiculous! I don't even have the key to the grain room."

He stopped. Grier was the one with the key. But he was an expert at twisting things around, shifting blame.

"All right," he said angrily. "But we clean up the grain room right away. Today."

"What's the hurry, Jovie?" Grier said softly. "We can have a bit of fun with the creatures first."

"Fun? What kind of fun?"

"Now I've heard," Grier said, scratching the stubble on his chin, "that elephants, for all their size, are afraid of mice. The woolly beastie is a kind of elephant, isn't he, only bigger? I wonder, now, if he'd be afraid of rats."

Before Jarls could stop him, Grier flung the rat into the mammoth's cage. The results were electric. The mammoth squealed like a gigantic pig and reared up on its hind legs. It danced precariously to keep its enormous bulk balanced, its trunk curling upward some twenty feet above their heads. The rat, confused, continued to run straight at it. One of the dancing feet came down on the rat and crushed it. The mammoth, unable to stay upright any longer, dropped down on all fours with a crash that shook the barn. It went wild then, continuing to stomp the rat's body until there was nothing left of it. Gradually its frenzy abated until at last it stood trembling, its great flanks heaving to draw in air, the thick trunk twitching from side to side.

"It's true, then," Grier said. "Who would ha' thought it?"

"You sorry son of a bitch," Jarls said.

The mammoth was staring at Grier, its deep-set red eyes burning with hate. It raised its trunk and emitted a trumpet blast that sent a chill down Jarls's spine.

"Oh, you will, will you?" Grier said. With a thin smile, he picked up the twelve-foot elephant goad lying at his feet and started toward the cage.

Jarls grabbed the end of the pole and wrested it out of Grier's grasp. He snapped the pole in two like a matchstick and flung it away. He took a handful of Grier's shirt in his fist and lifted the man's two hundred pounds into the air. He held Grier there, one-handed, breathing hard. Grier stayed very still. Finally Grier said calmly, "Put me down, you stupid bugger. *Now!*"

Jarls held him a moment longer, then let him drop.

Grier dusted himself off. "Now look at what you've done," he said. "You've gone and broken the bloody elephant hook. How are you going to explain that to his nibs?"

He walked away, holding himself stiffly and not looking back.

Jarls stayed with the mammoth, speaking quietly to it. Drummond showed up a half hour later. He saw the broken elephant goad, lying where Jarls had left it, but did not comment on it.

"Is everything all right here?" he asked.

"Yes," Jarls said.

Drummond's weathered face swiveled toward the disheveled beast. His lips tightened. "Seems nervous," he said. "Better keep your distance for the time being."

He turned and left. Jarls let himself into the mammoth's cage and swept out the trampled, bloodstained hay. The mammoth retreated to the far wall and did not molest him.

Jarls was sure that Drummond suspected what was going on. But Grier was too clever to be caught red-handed. Bert, the number two stableboy, was no help. He wanted no trouble with Grier. He went about his duties, blandly pretended to see nothing, and kept his mouth shut.

The mammoth bided its time. Jarls could sense its rage. He kept an eye on it as best he could, and tried not to leave Grier alone with it, but he could not be everywhere at once.

He was swabbing out the holding pen next to the mammoth's cage one morning, prior to one of the periodic transfers of the animal, when he was called away by Bert.

"Jock wants you down in the north pasture," Bert told him.

Bert was a large, slow-moving, phlegmatic man in his fifties, chosen, like all of Drummond's crew, for his size and strength. He had accepted Jarls's Jovian primacy in the muscle department without apparent resentment, and worked amicably with Jarls on jobs requiring two men.

"All right," Jarls said. "As soon as I finish mucking out the pen."

"Right away," he said. "He's waiting for ye."

"What's the hurry?"

"You're needed to drive fenceposts for a new corral there."

Jarls set down his mop. "What's wrong with the pile driver? Is it in the repair shop again?"

Bert grinned, showing gaps where missing teeth had, for some reason, never been regrown. "He says you do a better job. And without all the bother of getting the steam hammer running and positioned."

Jarls grinned back at him. "He's just too cheap. He doesn't want the use of the pile driver charged against his accounts."

"Aye, there's that, too," Bert said. "Ye'd better come, lad."

Jarls followed Bert to the meadow. Drummond was waiting impatiently beside a large stack of sixteen-foot posts that had been deposited there by an estate truck. A fifty-pound sledgehammer, its head as big as a beer keg, leaned against the pile of steel fenceposts.

"Took you long enough," Drummond said.

"I was cleaning out the holding pen," Jarls said. "We're moving the woolybeast this afternoon."

"Best get to work, then. You've got fifty posts to drive."

"I'll need someone to hold them straight till I get them started."

"That'll be Bert," Drummond said. "You don't mind, do you, Bert?"

"Just don't miss your aim, lad," Bert said cheerfully to Jarls.

"Drive them deep, boy," Drummond said, moving away. "Six feet, at least. They've got to be firm enough to hold back an elephant stampede."

He got into his flywheel cart and set off toward the horse and zebra barn, about a half-mile away.

Jarls picked up the first post and wrestled it into position without Bert's help. It only weighed a couple of hundred pounds. When he had it on the marker, Bert came over without comment and braced it at the vertical. Jarls wheeled over the portable scaffold. It was an old aircraft boarding ramp for one of Lord Hirakawa's jets that Drummond had scrounged from the lord's travel secretary, but it was the right height for the job.

Jarls climbed to the top of the platform with the oversize sledgehammer, took judicious aim, and hit the posthead a mighty whack. It sank about two feet. Down below, Bert gave a grunt.

"Is it still plumb?" Jarls asked.

"Aye, it is," Bert said. "That were the hard part. Best not hit it so hard now, lad. Just tap it down. If you hit a rock, you're liable to bend the post."

Jarls swung again. This time the post sank a foot. Bert grunted again, but did not complain.

By midmorning, they were sweat-soaked and burned by the sun. The pile of steel posts had shrunk considerably, and they were halfway to the corner marker in a geometrically straight line. It was a job for machinery, but a pile driver still needed a man at the controls. On Earth, just as on Venus, there would always be work that could be done more cheaply by a Jovian.

"Where's Grier working this morning?" Jarls asked while they swigged water from the gallon jugs that Bert had brought along.

"He were curry combing the zebras wi' me earlier. We were about finished when Jock sent me to fetch you. Grier took off when he seen Jock coming. 'Fraid he'd give him another job to do. Said he had work to do in the elephant tack room." Bert lowered his voice. "Work, my foot. He keeps a bottle there. He can always grab a rag and look busy if Jock walks in on him."

Jarls stood up. "I'll be right back."

"Where are you going, lad? Jock wanted this section of fence finished by noon."

"I'll sink steel faster," Jarls said. "Wait here for me."

He set off at a trot for the elephant barn. A look inside the tack room told him that Grier was not there, but saddles, bridles, stirrups, and other foxhunting gear were spread out across the twenty-foot workbench, along with a can of polish and some buffing cloths to create an illusion of labor. Jarls looked for a bottle and found an empty one hidden under a pile of saddle blankets.

The elephant barn itself was unnaturally quiet, as if the great beasts were waiting for something to happen. Jarls hurried down the broad central aisle, past the rows of silent gray shapes, and came to a halt at the twin reinforced cages in the rear.

"Grier?" he said.

Grier was alone in the holding pen, standing a little unsteadily. Trailing from one hand was something he'd taken from the tack room—a twenty-foot lash that was ordinarily used by the whipper-in to control the pack of foxhounds from his lofty perch on the lead elephant's back.

"What did you think you were going to do with that?" Jarls demanded.

"I'm here to finish cleaning out the bloody pen," Grier snarled at him. "Walked away and left it for me to do, didn't you, mister high and mighty Jovian?"

Jarls took a step forward. "Grier, give me the whip," he said.

Grier jerked his hand. The whip writhed like a snake along its entire length and cracked at the tip.

"Keep your distance," Grier said, his speech slurred. "Even a Jovie's thick hide c'n be laid open to th' bone by a li'l touch of this. I've cut a watermelon in half with it."

The whip writhed along the floor again. Grier staggered but stayed upright.

"Grier, drop it." Jarls took another step forward.

"Stay back, I said."

Out of the corner of his eye, Jarls saw stealthy movement. The mammoth was quietly unscrewing the heavy ringbolts that held the baffle for the crossbar.

Jarls leapt forward. Grier, squinting blearily at him, tried to use the whip, but Jarls snatched it from his grip and flung him across his shoulder like a sack of grain. By that time the mammoth had lifted the crossbar and flung the gate open. Grier gave a terrified yelp as the mammoth's hairy trunk curled around his ankle. Jarls played tug of war with the mammoth for a while, and then pulled Grier suddenly free, either because the mammoth had tried to shift its grip or had deliberately let go.

"Easy, boy," Jarls said, backing away.

He found his back pressed against a set of thick steel bars. The mammoth shook its huge shaggy head from side to side and came at him, its trunk extended. Without hesitation, Jarls sprang for the top of the bars, twenty feet overhead, with Grier slung over his shoulder. The mammoth bellowed in frustration and reached for Grier again, but Jarls pulled himself over, dropped to the other side of the bars, and scrambled out of reach of the mighty trunk.

Grier was struggling feebly, but Jarls held on to him until he could get him out of the cage and some distance away from the mammoth. He deposited Grier on the corridor floor, between the elephant stalls, and made sure he was going to remain on his feet. Fifty feet away, the mammoth crashed repeatedly against the bars, making the whole barn shake. Grier was trembling, and babbling to himself under his breath.

"Bloody, sodding, filthy bugger!" Grier sobbed. "I'll kill the bastard!"

"Shut up, Grier," Jarls said.

Drummond was coming down the concrete aisle toward them, with Bert behind him. Bert gave Jarls an apologetic shake of the head.

"What happened here?" Drummond fumed.

The mammoth was bellowing in anger and continuing to fling itself against the bars.

"The bloody monster tried to kill me, that's what!" Grier said.

Drummond turned to Jarls in disgust. "Get him out of here," he said. "Take him back to his quarters. He's staying there till he sobers up."

"But Jock . . ." Grier began a protest.

"You're not to open your mouth," Drummond said. To Jarls, he said, "You'll make sure he gets there. And then you come back here. I want to talk to you."

Jarls took Grier by the arm. Grier flinched. "Come on," Jarls said. Drummond was already striding off for a closer look at the mammoth.

When Jarls returned to the barn, he found Drummond alone. Bert had been sent away. Drummond frowned sternly at Jarls. "All right, Jarley lad. There's no one here to carry tales. You can speak freely. What happened?"

"Nothing," Jarls said.

Drummond swore. "You workies stick together, don't you? There's no point in going out on a limb for Grier. He's in for it, no matter what. Lord Hirakawa's verra particular about his animals not being mistreated. He'd expect me to hand out punishments all around. But I'm prepared to go easy on you, boy."

"Nothing happened," Jarls said stubbornly.

Drummond's face turned beet red. "Do you expect me to believe that? The animal's having fits. He'll be off his feed for a week. There's a hunting whip lying on the stall floor. Now what was Grier up to?"

"The mammoth wasn't harmed," Jarls said.

"Do you know I could have you flogged?" Drummond screamed at him.

Jarls maintained a stony silence.

Drummond stared at him in disbelief for a moment, then stomped noisily away.

Grier was flogged the next morning.

The entire household staff and all the grounds workers were summoned by the steward to witness his punishment. They gathered by the hundreds on the south lawn, where a flogging post had been erected by the carpenters. The household physician, a stout man in powder blue livery, stood next to it, chatting with the head butler, Mister Arthur.

Jarls stood to one side, in the midst of a crowd of gardeners, nurserymen, lawnkeepers, and other outside workers. His fellow stablehands seemed to be avoiding him. He saw Bert, about twenty feet away, chewing on a straw. Bert caught his gaze and looked away.

Jarls looked across, toward the household staff. He rarely got to see them this close. There was an army of them—footmen, under-butlers, hall boys, scullery maids, laundresses, and daily maids, all in Lord Hirakawa's livery. He caught sight of the kitchen maid who had brought him his supper the night of his arrival. Mary, her name was. She did not appear to notice him. She was flirting with one of the odd men, a big, burly man in breeches, shirtsleeves, and vest, but without a coat.

What caught his attention was the Jovians. There were twenty or thirty of them, standing in a disciplined, cohesive group. This would be the security staff Mary had told him about, under the command of a Mister Karsen. They were not wearing livery. They were wearing what looked like military uniforms in severe black and gray, with high-necked tunics and shiny black boots.

He picked out Karsen without trouble. The security chief was an older man with gray at the temples, and he wore an unobtrusive insignia of rank on his collar. But he looked rock-hard, like all Jovians, and he held himself rigidly straight, keeping his powerful muscles under restraint in Earth's feeble gravity.

Some of the Jovians in the group, Jarls knew, must be second or even third generation. But they had been selected for body type by centuries of harsh Jovian conditions that reached into the womb and killed the weak. The bone mass, the muscular potential, were there from childhood. Even an earthborn Jovian could retain a good part of his heritage through unrelenting exercise. And Karsen, Jarls thought as he studied the security chief's stony face, would be just the man to enforce an unmerciful training program.

Jarls felt homesick. These were the first Jovians he had seen since leaving Venus. He longed to go over and talk to them. But reality intruded. He had been a workie on two planets long enough to know his place. The Jovian household guards might be indentured, as he was, but they were inside staff, not outside workers. That was what mattered. Everybody on Earth clung to his little scrap of status. The household servants did not mingle with the rough laborers.

A stir went through the crowd, and the background chatter died down. Jarls turned his head with the rest and saw two sizable footmen propelling Grier down the path. They each had a firm grip on an arm—unnecessarily, Jarls thought, since Grier was cooperating, though they were dragging him along faster than he wanted to walk.

The footmen were pretty big, but so was Grier. Jarls wondered why, if rough stuff were needed, the job hadn't gone to a Jovian. Wasn't that what security guards were for?

He stole another glance at Karsen. Karsen stood, still unmoving, watching the spectacle with a visible expression of distaste on his face.

The footmen dragged Grier to the base of the flogging post, and while one of them held him, the other stripped him of his shirt. Grier offered no resistance. He seemed in shock. His wide face was drained of color behind the permanent sunburn, giving it a mottled appearance. He stared around him without seeming to see anything.

Mister Arthur, the head butler, stepped forward. He nodded at the footmen, and they clapped manacles around Grier's wrists.

At that, Grier seemed to come to life. He struggled wildly, panic in his face. One of the footmen gave him a clout on the side of the head to quiet him down, and they hauled on the chains until Grier hung with his feet just off the ground, his wrists fastened to the crossbar and his naked back exposed.

Grier twisted his head around. "I didn't bloody do it!" he sobbed. "I didn't do a bloody thing!" Spittle ran down his chin.

Mr. Arthur said sharply, "Quiet, Grier! Mind your tongue, man," and Grier subsided immediately.

The footmen stepped away from the post. Mister Arthur looked around at the assembled servants and cleared his throat. He must have been wearing a wireless microphone in his lapel, because Jarls could hear his amplified voice echoing from loudspeakers somewhere on the marble steps that rose to the south facade of the house.

"We are gathered here on this melancholy occasion to receive an object lesson," Mister Arthur said loftily, looking out across the crowded lawn. "I hope each and every one of you will take that lesson to heart."

He paused for effect, then nodded curtly toward Grier's dangling figure.

"This unfortunate man has betrayed Lord Hirakawa's trust. We need not dwell on the circumstances of his betrayal, nor should any of you engage in undue speculation. Suffice it to say that he has committed an offense against Lord Hirakawa's property. And an offense against Lord Hirakawa's property is an offense against Lord Hirakawa himself."

He let the enormity of Grier's betrayal sink in for a moment then continued sorrowfully:

"We take no pleasure in punishing this foolish person, but there is no choice. His punishment must be a reminder to all of us of the loyalty we owe to Lord Hirakawa. Remember the three virtues. *On*—duty to one's master. *Giri*—our indebtedness as servants. *Gaman*—endurance of our lot in life. And remember also the motto on the Hirakawa family crest. 'In obedience is happiness. And in perfect obedience is perfect happiness.'"

He beckoned to someone in the nearby swarm of underbutlers and housemen, and a man in a silk hood, carrying a knotted whip, pushed his way forward.

"Fifteen lashes," Mister Arthur said.

The hooded man moved toward Grier, flexing the whip. He was squat and wide, with an apelike build. Jarls judged, from the plain shirt and breeches, that he was some sort of kitchen scullion or household menial, chosen for the extra reach his long arms would give him. The hood was a formality, meant to give him the illusion of anonymity. But Jarls was sure that the other servants had no trouble identifying him—from his conspicuous physique if nothing else.

The crowd of onlookers stirred with sudden attention. There was a brief surge of whispers and subdued babble that soon died down. Jarls looked over at the cluster of women where he had seen the kitchen maid, Mary, and saw her leaning raptly forward, her lips parted.

The hooded man took a step backward and swung the whip with all his might. Jarls heard a sharp crack and an involuntary grunt from Grier as the breath was driven from him.

"One," Mister Arthur said.

A red welt had appeared magically across Grier's back, with pockmarks where the knots had bit into flesh. The hooded man pivoted a quarter turn for extra force and swung again. Again there was the slap of leather on flesh, and a groan from Grier.

"Two," Mister Arthur said.

By the fifth blow, Grier was screaming. Lash laid over lash had opened up furrows in his back, and blood welled up in the cup-shaped depressions. Jarls turned away, sick.

One of the underbutlers saw him. "None of that," he said sharply. "Everybody's got to watch."

Jarls turned back reluctantly. Grier had gone limp, his head lolling on his chest.

"He's passed out," someone near the flogging post said.

The stout doctor snapped his fingers and a lackey brought a step stool. The doctor mounted it with an assist from a footman and raised Grier's head by the chin. He lifted an eyelid, peered for a moment, then let Grier's head drop.

"He's shamming," the doctor announced. "Somebody bring a bucket of water."

He climbed down, puffing. The footmen passed a bucket of water down the line and the doctor's lackey dashed it in Grier's face. Grier jerked his head back, coughing and sputtering.

"Commence," Mister Arthur said.

The hooded man finished the fifteen lashes as Grier struggled and writhed on the flogging post. Somewhere around the tenth or eleventh blow, Grier passed out for real. His body sagged and the screams stopped. But the whipping continued as the head butler remorselessly counted out the lashes.

When it was over, Grier's back was a mass of raw flesh, crisscrossed with furrows and ridges. He moaned feebly as the footmen unshackled him and lowered him to the ground. At a nod from Mister Arthur, they picked him up like a sack of flour and carried him toward the kitchen entrance, with the house physician trotting at their heels.

Jarls found that he was trembling with rage. On Venus he had seen men beaten up often enough, and he himself had taken a couple of beatings when the Uranian guards had him tied up and helpless. But he never had seen someone deliberately trussed up as Grier had been, to be whipped as a public spectacle.

He did not like Grier, but he found it sickening that a man could be flogged in such a cold-blooded fashion. No human being, workie or not, deserved that kind of treatment.

The crowd was breaking up now. The little gaggle of kitchen maids were twittering with excitement as they straggled back unwillingly toward the manor house, their outing over. Jarls caught sight of Bert heading back to the stables with the other hands, but Bert still would not meet his eye. Bert had not said anything, but Jarls knew that he blamed him for Grier's predicament.

Jarls's gaze drifted back to where the footmen were hefting Grier's slack form up the broad marble steps of the rear terrace. Even at this distance, you could see the raw stripes on Grier's back.

He clenched his fists till his nails drew blood. Grier had meekly surrendered to the flogging as if he were some kind of domestic animal. What kind of people were these Terrans, to be so tame?

Jarls spat on Lord Hirakawa's manicured lawn. By God, he thought, he would die before he allowed himself to be flogged! He was a freeborn Jovian, not some Earthie slave, ground down by centuries of subservience! Herk had taught him that much, at least.

As he followed the dispersing crowd, he caught another glimpse of Karsen, standing apart with his retinue of uniformed Jovians. The household security chief was staring at him with an odd expression on his face. But before Jarls could decide what to make of it, Karsen's face went professionally blank.

# 12

**J**ARLS WAS pitching hay for the elephants when Bert came into the barn looking for him. "Come along, lad," Bert said. "You don't want to miss it."

"Miss what?" Jarls said, pausing with a fifty-pound clump of hay balanced on the end of his fork.

"It's the laird's new beastie. They're unloading it now at the receiving dock. Hurry, lad."

Jarls had rarely seen Bert exhibit this much excitement. The laird's new beastie must be a sight worth seeing indeed.

"All right," Jarls said. "You go on ahead. I want to take care of the mammoth first."

Bert left with another admonition to hurry. He was back to being friendly with Jarls. He had relented after a few weeks, deciding that Jarls had not informed on Grier after all. Neither he nor the other stablehands had much sympathy for Grier anyway. Grier had always been a bully and a drunk.

Jarls got between the shafts of the antique haywagon and hauled it toward the rear of the barn. The wagon was another of Lord Hirakawa's toys. It was usually pulled by a tractor, but was occasionally hitched to an actual team of horses when the Earl wanted to play country squire for his guests.

He stopped at the mammoth's cage. The giant beast trumpeted its pleasure at seeing him, and fanned out its huge ears in greeting. Jarls flung his arms wide in a reciprocal gesture, and the mammoth thrust its hairy trunk through the bars to kiss him delicately on the mouth, elephant style.

"Hello, Jumbo," Jarls said. "I've got your dinner here, old fellow."

Jarls was in charge of the mammoth now. Drummond would not allow Grier anywhere near it. Grier had been demoted to third stableboy, and Jarls had assumed many of his duties, though without any change in his rank or his hypothetical pay. Grier was drinking more heavily now, and spending more of his time brooding.

Jarls filled the mammoth's feeding rack with fresh timothy hay, and finished by offering the beast a bunch of carrots that he had cajoled from the kitchen maid, Mary. She had protested that stealing food was a floggable offense, but Jarls gathered that the house servants did it all the time, and that the majordomo was lenient as long as it didn't get out of hand.

The mammoth signaled its appreciation with another trumpet blare, and the carrots disappeared into its maw. It would not let Jarls leave until he had engaged in a brief, playful tug of war with its trunk wrapped around his forearm.

He sauntered to the receiving dock, about three quarters of a mile away, where a mag-lev terminal emerged from the side of a low hill, nestled out of sight where it wouldn't spoil the view. Lord Hirakawa had his own mag-lev link to London and the Channel ports.

The mag-lev car came into view as he rounded the hillside. It was a big freight capsule, about a hundred feet long, resting in a concrete trough next to the loading dock with its landing wheels retracted. One curved section of the hull had swung down to become a heavy-duty ramp.

An expectant crowd of gardeners, groundsmen, and other outdoor workers was being held at a distance by a row of striped barriers. Jarls joined them and found Bert.

"They haven't unloaded it yet?" Jarls asked.

"Nay," Bert said. "There's some difficulty."

An enormous deep-throated bellow came from inside the car. It was like nothing Jarls had ever heard before. A moment later, Jock

Drummond came backing down the ramp, waving his arms and fussing at someone inside. The object of his displeasure appeared a moment later: a man in heavy protective gear, with a helmet and opaque plastic face shield. The bulky figure was not intimidated by Drummond. He motioned the little stablemaster back, and after a moment Drummond complied, stomping down the ramp in obvious ill temper.

"First time I've seen Jock flummoxed," Bert said.

"I suppose the laird's new beastie needs a special handler," Jarls replied.

"Aye. It must be that valuable."

Drummond came stomping over to them. But he stayed ostentatiously on the other side of the striped barrier.

"Stupid, stupid, stupid!" Drummond fumed. "I tried to tell him that an animal that size and weight, and with no brain to speak of, needed a nose ring to control it. I even had one made up by the blacksmith out of carbon steel. But he said that his orders were that he was to deliver the creature undamaged. He took that to mean that the septum couldn't be pierced."

"As if the laird would care," Bert said placatingly. "We put a nose ring in all His Lordship's prize bulls."

Drummond fumed on. "So he's got the creature fitted out with some kind of idiotic halter arrangement. Made of titanium-belted artificial leather, if you can believe it! The brute keeps trying to shake it off."

"Look!" Bert said. "They must have gotten it moving."

Jarls followed Bert's pointing finger. The bulkily clothed handler was backing away from the gaping cargo door, making semaphore signals with his hands. A moment later, a huge yellow machine with clanking caterpillar treads came inching backwards out of the freight capsule. It held a jointed boom aloft, trailing a heavy chain.

"That's a hell of a big crawler," Jarls said, impressed.

"It has to be," Drummond said. "The beast weighs eight tons."

A snout like an ancient battering ram emerged from the opening. There was a horny beak like a turtle's, and three wicked curved horns, one at the end of the nose and two longer ones thrusting forward from the armored skull. The massive head was the size of a passenger car, and rising behind it was a bony ruff ringed with spikes.

"What is it?" Jarls said in wonder.

"It's called a triceratops. A kind of dinosaur dating from the late Cretaceous. They've been extinct for a hundred million years."

The tractor pulled the rest of the animal out into the sunlight. It resisted all the way, dragging the machine backward every few yards to a sound of scraping treads. It was about thirty feet long, with a barrel-like body, legs like tree trunks, and a stubby tail. Jarls took note of the imitation leather bridle that had so incensed Drummond. It looked secure enough, with a thick strap anchoring it behind the spiked neck plate.

With the creature out in the open, the overhead boom cranked the chain short, forcing the triceratops to lift its ponderous head, and after that it trotted tamely down the ramp after the tractor, its head held high.

"Ill-tempered beast," Drummond said. "It's already killed a man. It's good for nothing, but marvelously expensive."

" 'Twill need half a ton of hay a day, I'll wager," Bert ventured.

"At least," Drummond said.

"What does Lord Hirakawa want with it?" Jarls asked.

Drummond gave a tight smile. "It's that pesky neighbor of his, Lord Cumbrough, west of here. He's only a viscount, but he's got above himself again. When Lord Hirakawa instituted foxhunting with elephants, Cumbrough tried to steal his thunder by showing up with a zebra at race week. And zebras aren't even extinct. Many collectors have them. So when the laird had the mammoth cloned, Cumbrough stretched his purse to the bursting point and ordered himself an animal called a rhinoceros. Rhinoceroses have only been extinct for three hundred years, and there's plenty of their DNA lying around, but they're an unusual-looking beast and it caused quite a stir in the district. So Lord Hirakawa hit on the idea of a triceratops. They look something like a rhinoceros, but they're four times the size, and they've been extinct for a hundred *million* years. At first it wasn't certain that enough triceratops DNA could be found, but then there was that lucky discovery in North America, with bones that hadn't been contaminated yet. And enough bones, from what had been a sizable herd, so that they could extract sufficient DNA fragments without a lot of fill-ins and guesswork."

Drummond's smile broadened. "It drove the paleontologists wild. Eight almost-complete skeletons had to be sacrificed. But you don't say no to Lord Hirakawa. He got the royal families in Japan and England behind him, and called on his connections in Greater Liechtenstein, and there wasn't a thing the paleontologists could do."

The triceratops had balked at the foot of the ramp. It dug in its stubby toes and shook its great head. The raised boom swayed dangerously back and forth, and the heavy crawler rocked on its treads. The armor-suited handler made frantic arm signals and the crawler operator cranked the chain up another notch. After a few stubborn moments, they got the behemoth moving again.

"It's a handful," Jarls said.

"There's no beast that canna' be managed, Drummond snapped. "We'll put it in the new corral behind the elephant pens. Lord Hirakawa will be flying in from London tomorrow to inspect his new plaything. It's possible there may be royals in his party—perhaps even Prince Alfred and the Duchess. The Prince is said to take an interest in prehistoric beasties. The big house is making preparations for the visit now." Drummond's expression grew sly. "Lord Cumbrough will be here. He's been specially invited as a neighborly gesture. The laird likes to rub it in. Cumbrough willna say no to a chance to meet the royals."

"What do you want us to do?" Jarls said.

"Do? Ye'll stay well back, that's what ye'll do. There's no need for the laird and his party to sully the grand spectacle with the sight of a grimy stableboy. That goes for you too, Bert."

"Aye, Jock," Bert said, looking hurt.

Drummond relented. "But it won't hurt for the two of you to take a bath and put on clean clothes. You can pass the word to the rest of the stablehands, as well. The laird and his guests may want a closer look at the mammoth and the rest of the stables while they're here, and I'll want you all looking your best."

The big house was up at dawn to get things ready for the visit. Jarls was shaken awake at first light by one of the groundsboys, who said: "You'd better get over to the kitchens right away if you want breakfast. There'll be no time to spare for any of us this morning. And then Mister Drummond wants you to report to the tack room."

Jarls dressed quickly. Through the tiny window of the hayloft he could see the estate gardeners at work washing outdoor statuary and clipping hedges that had just been clipped to a fare-thee-well the day before.

He hurried across ten acres of manicured rear lawn, and past the tennis courts and squash courts, where maintenance people were hosing down the pink marble tiles. As he came nearer to the broad rear terrace with its carved marble railings, he could see liveried footmen scurrying back and forth with armloads of cut flowers. A gardener's tractor was parked nearby, with a train of flatbed trailers heaped high with fresh blooms from the laird's greenhouses.

The kitchen wing was a madhouse. Sweating lackeys staggered about with hampers of delicacies while underbutlers barked orders, footmen in shirtsleeves were sitting at a bench polishing silver, and at the row of antique iron sinks, an octet of harried scullery maids in starched caps and aprons were scrubbing pots and pans. Jarls looked for Mary, but she was nowhere in sight.

An underbutler eyed him frostily, and Jarls slid past him to the low annex off the servants' hall, where the outdoor staff was fed. The long tables were occupied by only a sprinkling of estate workers, some of whom were already wiping their mouths and rising from the benches.

Jarls seated himself at the end of one of the nearer tables, and a distracted kitchen slavey unceremoniously set a bowl of boiled rice and pickled vegetables in front of him. "That's all there is this morning," she said. "No time to spare for anything more, though the butlers had their bangers and eggs."

Jarls fell to with a hearty appetite. It was only a simple country breakfast, but there was plenty of it. Before he finished, the slavey returned with a steaming pot and ladled out more rice for him. After looking around, she dug into a corner of the pot and added a couple of sausages to Jarls's bowl. "They was left over from the butlers' breakfast," she said, leaning over. "They'd only ha' gone to waste."

Jarls thanked her and wolfed the sausages down along with the rest of the rice and pickles. He wiped his mouth and got up to leave.

He had to pass the unfriendly underbutler on the way out. "Hold on a moment, fellow," the man said. "Stand over there and wait." Jarls stood against the wall while the underbutler scanned the surrounding hubbub. He spotted the head butler passing by and snagged him. "Oh Mister Arthur, do you have a minute?"

The head butler came to a reluctant stop. "What is it, Wilkins?" he said impatiently.

The underbutler reddened. "I'm sorry to interrupt you, Mister Arthur, but we're desperately shorthanded for lunch in the lower dining room. Mister Phipps has commandeered all the spare odd-men for the golf and boating excursions, and there's no one to carry the heavy trays except Edwin. This fellow looks strong, and he's clean. What do you say?"

Mister Arthur looked Jarls over impersonally and said, "Of course he's strong. He's a Jovian. But he'd never fit into livery. He'd burst it at the seams. Besides, his lordship prefers tall men on the serving staff."

"But . . ."

"No, Wilkins, he won't do. He's one of Mister Drummond's workies. If I were to commandeer him, Drummond would make a terrible fuss."

With that, Mister Arthur turned on his heel and disappeared into the turmoil. The underbutler turned to Jarls and said, "All right, fellow, you can go."

Jarls made his escape into the open air and headed for the stables. Drummond was in the tack room, fluttering about. "There you are," he said when he saw Jarls. "We have only a few hours.

You'll help Grier polish all the leather and brass, and then you'll groom the mammoth and put him in an outside pen."

It had not escaped Drummond's notice that Jarls had achieved the unthinkable with the prehistoric beast; though still thought to be dangerous and unapproachable, the mammoth not only allowed Jarls in its cage, but allowed him to use a currycomb on its long, tangled hair—and even seemed to enjoy being groomed.

"All right, Jock," Jarls said. "I'll have him looking his best."

Drummond left. Jarls could hear him shouting orders outside to the Scottish mahouts; the elephants, it seemed, were to be hosed down and made ready to be saddled in case any of the laird's guests wanted to go riding after lunch.

Jarls sat down next to Grier and began polishing harnesses. He could smell whiskey on Grier's breath, but Grier still seemed fairly sober.

"So you're to be in charge of the mammoth for Lord Hirakawa's visit," Grier said. "That used to be my job."

Jarls shrugged. He wanted no trouble with Grier.

"Well, have you nothing to say?"

"Be reasonable, Grier. The animal won't let you anywhere near it. Jock's told you to stay away from it."

"It needs to be taught who's master, that's all," Grier said savagely.

Jarls sighed. He turned his head to look directly into Grier's bloodshot eyes. "I'd have thought you'd have been the one to learn a lesson," he said, trying not to sound unkind.

Grier flushed and turned away. The two of them worked in silence for a few minutes, then Grier reached into the pile of straw behind him and drew out a bottle. He took a long pull on the bottle and rose unsteadily to his feet.

"Bugger you," he said, and left with the bottle, wobbling a bit as he walked.

Jarls worked on alone for a couple of hours and finished the job of polishing the harnesses. Then he got the currycomb and a long-handled brush and went to attend to the mammoth.

\* \* \*

There was the crack of a giant's whip in the sky, and Jarls looked up in time to see a tiny needle glinting in the distance.

"There's the laird now," Bert said. "He's gone subsonic."

The needle grew quickly into a sleek transatmospheric craft, painted black to help dissipate heat during reentry. The glint came from the shiny white of its unpainted ceramic underside. It looked big, even from the ground. It circled the valley swiftly, shedding speed with its nose up, and dropped out of sight behind a hill to land at Lord Hirakawa's private spacedrome on the other side of the valley.

"That's a lot of aircraft for such a short trip," Jarls said.

"Aye, that it is," Bert agreed. He squinted into the sun. "He'll be here in about five minutes. There's a pneumatic tube from the spacedrome. It comes out in the basement."

Jarls looked over at the manor house, a tiny cube of sugar cake from here. A sprinkle of colored dots was spread out over the immense green lawn, making a border on either side of the central portico—the hundreds of household servants and retainers who were presenting themselves for the lord's inspection.

Jarls would have imagined that an arriving master would walk past these assembled ranks going *into* the house. But, alerted by Bert, he was ready a few minutes later when movement appeared in the doorway, and another sprinkling of colored motes emerged, fanning out behind a minute fleck of gray in the lead.

Lord Hirakawa and his entourage moved past the array of servants without pausing, and seemingly without noticing them. It appeared that they were heading directly for the stables. As soon as they passed, the dusting of colored motes broke up and flowed back into the house.

Bert was grinning. "If the Prince is with him, it must be a new experience using the back door," he said. Drummond caught him grinning, and he quickly assumed a sober expression.

Drummond gave them both a warning glare, and hurried across the enclosure to wait for the lord, cap in hand.

Jarls strained to make out details. At a hundred yards, he could see that Lord Hirakawa was a tall man in a gray morning suit, wearing a strange cylindrical hat that must have had hundreds of years of tradition behind it. The smaller, pastel-clad figure beside him must be Lady Hirakawa. Her garment seemed to be an impractically long robe with a broad sash around it.

Jarls picked out what he guessed was the royal party. The Prince was tall and erect, like Lord Hirakawa, and he, too, was wearing one of the stiff gray suits out of Earth's past and a high-crowned cylindrical hat. The Duchess, in contrast to Lady Hirakawa, wore a short-skirted floral dress that showed off a big-boned figure and a floppy hat decorated with flowers.

And, exiled to one side, was a portly figure that had to be the unfortunate Lord Cumbrough, the upstart who had dared to resurrect a rhinoceros. He kept trying to edge up to the royal party and bumping into the Prince's buffer personnel.

Lord Hirakawa's guests, about thirty of them, ranged themselves along the fence, jockeying for good viewing positions, while the lord, with a courtly bow, ushered the royal couple through the gate into the enclosure. Lady Hirakawa, hobbled by her long robe, followed, trailed by a maid who held a flowered parasol over her head.

Drummond, by his posture and gestures, looked as if he were trying to dissuade the lord from his station within the enclosure, but Hirakawa waved him aside with a negligent sweep of his arm. Jarls couldn't see why Drummond had bothered; the fence wasn't made for anything more powerful than elephants, and if the triceratops ever were to get loose, the fence would be no barrier at all.

Drummond gave in, made a jerky little bow, and headed toward the barn at the rear of the complex where the triceratops was kept.

There was a lengthy wait, and then Jarls heard the engine of the big tracked vehicle cough into life. There was a spine-chilling bellow of protest from the triceratops, and shouting human voices. Jarls peered past the corner of the elephant barn, and saw the tractor backing across the elephant yard, dragging the horned beast behind it.

The spectators behind the fence strained forward for a better view. As the triceratops came into sight there was an excited twittering. The Prince raised a pair of binoculars for a closer look, then passed the binoculars to the Duchess. Lord Hirakawa himself stood with perfect nonchalance, as if this were an everyday occurrence.

The tractor had to pass the elephant barn to get to the enclosure, and as it did so, there was a frantic chorus of trumpeting from the elephants inside. They could sense the proximity of the prehistoric beast, and they didn't like it. The triceratops didn't like them, either, and it let out another enraged bellow.

The elephants were still trumpeting when Jarls saw the double doors at the end of the barn part, and a man come running out.

It was Grier, and he was running for his life. A moment later, the doors burst open all the way, and the mammoth came charging through after him.

What had Grier been up to? There was no time to think about that now. Jarls moved into action, running to intercept the mammoth.

He was dimly aware that the twittering from the little crowd of spectators had stopped. All of them—and Lord Hirakawa, too—must have been astonished at the indecorous spectacle of a running stableboy, and then they had looked past him to see what he was running toward.

Jarls pounded on, not knowing what he was going to do. He waved his arms and shouted, "No, Jumbo, stay, stay!" But he was too far away, and the mammoth was in a rage. It caught up with the fleeing Grier, knocked him over with a swing of its trunk, and trampled him into the dust.

Jarls felt a wave of despair. He kept on running hopelessly, but the mammoth, still in a rage, kept on stomping Grier's broken body. Jarls was still fifty yards away when the mammoth finished with the bloody rag doll that had been Grier and looked around for a new enemy.

"It's all right, boy, come to me!" Jarls sobbed as he ran. But the mammoth was too maddened to notice him. It caught sight of the yellow machine and the colossal beast trotting behind it. The great ears flapped and the mammoth raised its head and blared a challenge.

The operator in the machine's enclosed cab became aware of

the situation and tried to change direction. But the triceratops, its attention caught, stopped dead in its tracks and dug in its columnar legs. The crawler's caterpillar treads spun uselessly, stirring up dust. The beast's armored head swung around, dragging the machine a good six feet to the side, and the triceratops bellowed a challenge of its own.

Across the yard, the mammoth snorted once, lowered its head and charged, the formidable curving tusks ready to slash upward into an opponent's belly.

The ground shook. The triceratops tossed its head to get rid of its tether, tugging to the side. The titanium-belted bridle that Drummond had deplored held, but the chain connecting it to the crawler's raised boom levered the machine over on its side, trapping the operator inside the cab. Another energetic yank, and the chain snapped where it was attached at the top of the boom, and the creature was free, trailing about thirty feet of useless chain.

The triceratops lowered its own head to meet the mammoth's charge. It was twice the size of the mammoth. Tons of flesh met with a crash, and before the mammoth could use its long tusks, the armor-plated beast jerked its head upward and impaled its hairy opponent.

For a moment, the triceratops seemed not to know what to do with the great weight it was carrying. Then, with a snort, it tossed its burden over its head, freeing its horns. It worried the carcass for a while, poking at it with its nose and a forefoot. Then it dawned on it that it was free of the anchoring machine.

Two hundred yards away, the crowd of onlookers was scattering in a panic. Women were screaming. The triceratops sniffed at the disturbing noises and motion—a confusing blur to its nearsighted eyes. Something deep within the primitive head simmered, then boiled over. The triceratops gave a deep rumble, then charged.

Jarls, still running at an angle toward the scene, saw the Duchess scrambling athletically over the fence, while the Prince tried to give her her a boost. They'd never make it, and even if they did, the triceratops would crash right through the flimsy fence and run them down—assuming it took it into its pea-brained head to swerve in its course and go after them. But it was heading straight toward Lord and Lady Hirakawa.

Lady Hirakawa refused to flee. She stood her ground, looking utterly composed, with her hands folded decorously within the long trailing sleeves of her robe. Lord Hirakawa stood protectively in front of her, waving his ridiculous hat, as if it would turn aside eight tons of thundering death. Jarls had to admire them. Flight would have been useless, but not everyone could have resisted the temptation to turn and run.

The triceratops rushed by, only yards past Jarls's face. It did not appear to have noticed him. The long chain it was trailing rattled by in the dust. Jarls flung himself upon it before it was gone and wrapped it around his forearm. Immediately he was jerked violently off his feet and dragged. His Jovian strength was no good to him here. He didn't have the weight to slow the beast down.

The overturned tractor was right ahead of him. He was going to slam into it at thirty miles an hour.

Jarls twisted, and the tractor's hard edges scraped painfully along his ribs. His shirt caught on something and was torn away. Before he was dragged past the tractor, he grabbed a steel stanchion and anchored himself to it with an arm and a leg.

The sudden wrench almost tore him apart. But he held on with grim determination. He could feel the violent strain on his joints and tendons. But his tough Jovian muscle tissue was the equal of the best synthetic elastomers. He tensed with all his strength and the strain eased. The headlong rush of the triceratops slowed.

It was enough to break the charge. The great beast came to a halt, its anger spent, and stood panting and motionless. Quickly, Jarls wrapped several feet of slack chain around a stanchion. The battered machine operator climbed out of the cab through a side window and helped him to make a firm hitch.

Jarls moved aside, aching in every joint. He was bleeding at the scrapes along his torso, but not too badly. The machine operator was looking at him in awe. "I never seen anything like it," he said, and began babbling.

Jarls paid no attention. His eyes sought out Lord and Lady Hirakawa, only a dozen yards away now. The Lord had taken both her hands in his and was talking earnestly to her. Prince Alfred, his hat gone, was moving with self-conscious dignity to join them, but the Duchess was nowhere in sight. Jarls could see her floppy hat lying on the ground.

Drummond came running at him. "What ha' ye done?" he demanded, red-faced and scared-looking.

"Grier's back there," Jarls said, pointing with a hand whose steadiness surprised him. "What's left of him. He spooked the mammoth somehow. He couldn't leave it alone."

All of a sudden he wanted to sit down, right there in the dust. He made himself stay on his feet. He knew that to Drummond he must seem impassive, an unfeeling stone statue, but it was too much trouble to explain.

"The mammoth's dead," Drummond said hoarsely. "The triceratops may be damaged. To say nothing of an expensive machine. The laird humiliated in front of his guests. Someone's got to pay."

Jarls looked past Drummond. Lord Hirakawa was staring hard at him. He was close enough so that Jarls could see the grim expression on his overbred face. The stare lasted a long time. Then the Lord took Lady Hirakawa by the elbow and escorted her out of the enclosure. The Prince, heir to the throne and theoretically high above a mere Earl like Lord Hirakawa in the peerage, followed like a lackey.

"D'ye understand, lad?" Drummond implored.

"Yes," Jarls said.

The command to the big house came an hour later. The summons was delivered by a lowly underbutler. The Lord hadn't bothered to send a member of the uniformed security force to fetch him. He expected to be obeyed.

Jarls put on a clean shirt while the underbutler waited impatiently. One didn't face the Lord bare-chested. He thought the bleeding had stopped, but a couple of spots came through. It couldn't be helped. He dashed water in his face and smoothed his hair back. He remembered the vow he had made after Grier's flogging, and filed it away in his head.

"All right," he said to the underbutler. "Let's go."

Drummond looked at him with a miserable expression. "I'm sorry, lad," he said.

# 13

THE UNDERBUTLER took him through an unobtrusive side entrance in the currently unoccupied east wing, presumably to avoid prying eyes. Nevertheless, they encountered a few servants on the way: maids with dustmops preparing the guest-rooms, footmen carrying vases of flowers. None of them dared to look at Jarls. One of the maids was Mary. When Jarls passed, she looked the other way and pretended not to see him.

They climbed a flight of stairs to the second floor of the main house, and passed down a long corridor. It was lined on either side with marble busts of the previous Earls of Strathspey, mounted on pedestals. Jarls counted forty-seven of them as he strode along. The carved features changed at about the twentieth earl from western to eastern, and then began gradually to metamorphose back to the western again about a dozen earls later.

"The Lord will see you in the drawing room," the underbutler said nervously. It was the first time he had spoken to Jarls since they had entered the house.

They were in a large domed antechamber hung with armorial bric-a-brac. Straight ahead was a paneled door at least sixteen feet high. On either side of the door stood a thickset Jovian guardsman dressed in a tight-fitting black and silver uniform with a slash of rainbow color at the sleeve.

"Go ahead," the underbutler whispered. "Don't keep him waiting."

The underbutler pushed him forward and made his escape with undignified haste.

Jarls crossed the antechamber. Neither of the Jovians spoke to him. One of them pushed the heavy door open. Jarls stepped through. The Jovians fell in on either side of him. Of course. The Lord might expect a dangerous man who had been summoned for punishment to appear obediently before him, but his security guards would not leave that kind of wild card alone with their master.

Lord Hirakawa was sitting about fifty feet away, on a spindly settee in front of a bay window. Lady Hirakawa sat erectly beside him, her hands folded in her lap. The Lord gave an imperceptible nod. One of the security guards prodded Jarls, and he advanced toward the settee, with the two Jovians keeping step with him.

Hirakawa was a handsome man, though a bit pasty-faced. He had plastered-down black hair, parted in the middle, and a small mustache. Lady Hirakawa was a stunning beauty: small, delicate, with smooth, flawless skin and an elaborate arrangement of jet-black hair, lacquered in place.

Lord Hirakawa spoke. "You were the young man in charge of the mammoth, were you not?"

"Yes," Jarls said. There was no point in making excuses, or trying to explain about poor Grier. To a person like Lord Hirakawa, it would seem to be only an attempt at evasion, to be regarded with distaste.

"What! Not yes, Lord?" Hirakawa reprimanded him. "Did you have any idea how expensive the animal was, how difficult it was to manufacture it?"

Jarls looked past Hirakawa at the bay window. He could vault over the settee, hurl himself through the glass. It was a twenty-foot drop to the ground, but twenty feet was nothing to a Jovian. It would be like an eight-foot fall to an Earthling. Then what? He could make a dash for the river, where Lord Hirakawa entertained his guests with boating parties. He realized that he knew nothing of what lay beyond the laird's valley. But the river must lead to the great city of London. He could hide until dark, steal a boat . . .

But the Jovian guards were a complicating factor. He would have to be quick, before they could grab him. And then he would have to run across open lawn, with the likelihood of being shot in the back.

No matter. It was better than being flogged, like Grier. He stole a sidelong glance at the Jovians. They were both armed with long-barreled pistols of some sort. They looked like competent men.

But they were house Jovians. Fit as they looked, they had been on Earth longer than he had. They might even be second generation. They wouldn't be quite as strong or fast as he was.

He took a deep breath and waited for his chance. He would watch for some tiny moment of inattention.

Lord Hirakawa was waiting for an answer.

"Yes, your lordship," he said.

That brought a thin smile. "Better," the Lord said. He poured himself a drink from the cut-glass decanter in front of him. "The triceratops was even more expensive. A rarity. I'm told it wasn't harmed. But the handler will have to be punished. Drummond was right. The restraints weren't adequate, and the machine wasn't heavy enough."

Lady Hirakawa spoke up. "You can't punish the handler, Tommy darling. He doesn't belong to you. There would be all those tedious apologies to make." Her voice was surprisingly deep and husky for such a small woman.

Lord Hirakawa was annoyed at being contradicted. "The chairman at Retrogenesis Labs, Ltd. is Binky Hargrave. He's a good chap, and he owes me a favor. He'll see that I get my *kosei fukushu.*"

Painted eyelids lowered perfunctorily. "Quite right, darling." She took a sip from an eggshell-thin cup. "I'll never forget the sight of that hideous beast charging straight toward me," she said in her husky voice. "And then the incredible vision of one small man dragging it to a halt, like some dragon-slaying *eiyu* from the old legends!"

"Well, here's your gladiator now, my sweet," Lord Hirakawa said.

Jarls tensed. What was going on? Were they toying with him?

He knew all about gladiators from Herk's historical harangues on Venus. The revolt of Spartacus. They were slaves, dangerous slaves, and in the end they were all crucified as an object lesson.

Lady Hirakawa leaned forward. "Do you have any education, fellow?" she said.

"Yes, my lady," Jarls replied.

She turned to Lord Hirakawa. "It's a shame to waste him in the stables, Tommy," she said.

Lord Hirakawa sighed. "Very well, my dear." He turned to Jarls. "Have you any weapons training?" he said.

Jarls was startled. "No, my lord."

Lady Hirakawa intervened. "He can learn that, darling. Karsen will train him."

"Oh, very well," the Lord said. He turned a bored stare on Jarls. "You've done me a great service, my boy. You'll find that her ladyship and I are not ungrateful. You'll report to Mister Karsen. He'll tell you what you have to do. Do you have any things at the stable? Tell Mister Arthur. He'll send someone to fetch them."

One of the Jovians nudged Jarls, and he backed away from the settee. Outside the drawing room, the two looked him over. "Born on Jupiter?" one of them said, speaking to him for the first time.

"Yes."

"I thought so. How long on Earth?"

"A couple of months."

"Well, you'll learn. Come with me. We'll go see Hannes."

They found Hannes Karsen in the gymnasium, lifting weights. The estate's security chief was bare-chested and glistening with sweat. He lowered the barbell to the mat easily, without so much as a thump, and turned to face Jarls. Jarls stole a look at the weights and guessed that they added up to about a ton.

"You'd be Jarls Anders, then," Karsen said.

"You know my name?" Jarls said in surprise.

"Oh, yes." Karsen shot a look of inquiry at Jarls's escort.

"He's off the hook, Hannes," the guard said.

"I see," Karsen said. "Anders, come this way with me. Czoznek, you can go back to perimeter duty. Sector H."

"Right," Czoznek said, and left. Jarls followed Karsen to a small office. The security chief toweled himself dry, and put on a plain tunic without insignia. He was an impressive figure, tall for a Jovian, with a dignified touch of gray at the temples, and a chest as massive as Jarls had ever seen on the home planet.

"Now, then," Karsen said. "What exactly did Lord Hirakawa say to you?"

"He asked me if I'd ever had weapons training."

"And what did you tell him?"

"That I hadn't. And then Lady Hirakawa said it didn't matter, that you'd teach me."

A frown crossed Karsen's face at the mention of Lady Hirakawa, then disappeared as quickly as it had come.

"That I will. And not just weapons training. All sorts of armed and unarmed combat—three thousand years of it. Kendo, quarterstaff, judo, knuckle-fighting, *salle d'armes*. And security techniques: crowd control, electronic surveillance, anti-incursion strategy—the lot. Strength isn't enough in a job like this. You've got to be quick and smart, too. Up to it?"

"Yes."

"You'd better be. Otherwise we'll throw you back. We Jovians have a standard to uphold on Earth. We're the incorruptible barbarians from far away. Terrans don't trust one another any more, so they leave their security in our hands—the way overbred societies have always done on this planet. The Turkish sultans with their janissaries, the Egyptians with their Mamelukes. See this uniform you'll be wearing?" Karsen smote himself on the breast for emphasis. "You'll find a similar one on the private security force of every aristocratic household on Earth. It's an imitation—as close as the law will allow—of the uniforms worn in Greater Liechtenstein by the Executive Guards who protect Franz Joseph XXIV. Jovians have been protecting the Megachairman for two hundred years, and the uniform hasn't changed in all that time."

Karsen's bitter outspokenness, here in the Hirakawa household to someone he could not be sure he could trust, surprised Jarls. It echoed what old Ian Karg had said to him long ago on Jupiter, and he remembered the sealed letter of introduction that Karg had given him.

He wondered if he ought to show the letter to Karsen. But Karg had been an authentic Executive Guardsman, and the letter was addressed to one of his old comrades in Liechtenstein, not a household security chief in a backwater like England. Jarls decided to wait a while and see what the future brought.

Karsen had said more than he had intended to, and he bit off his next words. Instead, he said, "I'm stuck with you for the time being. You're raw and untested. We'll start you off on the lowest rung and see how you do."

"Thank you, sir."

"Don't thank me. You're here because Lady Hirakawa wants another uniformed Jovian in the household guard. Some of the lesser households resort to imitation Jovians—musclebound Terrans who couldn't take candy away from a Jovian three-year-old. The uniform is a status symbol, Anders. Live up to it."

"I will, sir."

Karsen cast a critical eye over him, and Jarls unconsciously squared his shoulders.

"All right, then," Karsen said. "Let's get you to his lordship's tailor."

# 14

**K**ARSEN WAS as good as his word. First he turned Jarls over to his weapons master, a squat, bullet-headed man named Harkins, who told him: "You don't get to even hold a gun until I'm satisfied you can handle yourself without one. Don't be too impressed with yourself because you're a Jovian. Muscle isn't everything, especially on Earth. Hmm. Where did you get those scars?"

"On Venus."

"Suit scars? That explains all the little broken capillaries. What about the big burn mark across the latissimus dorsi?"

"Hot box."

"What were you doing in the hot box?"

"Straw boss tried to kill me. The booby trap got a mate of mine instead. I threw the straw boss at a wall."

"And you're still alive and your mate isn't. Maybe you're a fast learner. Can you control your temper now?"

"Yes."

"Hit me."

"I beg your pardon?"

"Hit me. In the face. As hard as you can."

Jarls hesitated. A blow from a Jovian could break another Jovian's nose.

Harkins's fist lashed out, a blur too fast to follow, and hit Jarls in the mouth. Jarls threw a punch at Harkins in the same instant.

Something happened that he couldn't follow; somehow Harkins's thick wrist was under his, and all the force of the blow was deflected upward toward the ceiling instead of straight ahead. With Jarls's arm raised, Harkins tapped him lightly on the ribs with his fingertips, two—no, three—times.

"Not bad," Harkins said. "Pretty fast, considering. I'm sending you over to the kendo *sensei* to sharpen you up, and then we'll try some *kara te*—empty hand work."

In the next six weeks, Jarls worked harder than he had ever worked in his life. He was up before sunrise, after four hours sleep, to spend the morning in a blurred daydream practicing all the ancient techniques of bare-handed and barefooted fighting that the human race had devised in its long, violent history. After a spare lunch of rice or noodles, he immersed himself in the use of every possible variety of primitive weapon, from bamboo sticks to a short, basket-hilted sword called an *epee*. He learned where to rap a man with a club or his hand to quiet him down without damaging him. In the evening he was drilled unmercifully in the technical details of the estate's security devices: surveillance cameras hidden in the outdoor statuary, satellite links to law enforcement data bases all over the planet, retinal pattern readers that could check a person's identity without his being aware of it—and to avoid offending the rich and powerful, butyric acid sniffers that would have put a bloodhound to shame, perimeter defenses mediated by nearly autonomous artificial intelligences. Lord Hirakawa would not allow surveillance devices within the house itself—it was explained to Jarls that the Lord considered this an offence against hospitality, an idiosyncrasy that made it essential that Karsen's security force be honed to a fine edge.

After six weeks of hell, the weapons master grudgingly conceded that Jarls was ready for modern weapons training.

"The big pistol is just for show," Harkins told him. "You'll wear it on guard duty and ceremonial occasions. Impresses the hell out of our patron and his guests—fits their idea of how a Jovian ought to be armed. Don't get me wrong. Sixty caliber will blow one hell of a hole in a man. Very messy. But messes have to be cleaned up, and they leave a bad taste in the mouth. The preferred weapon is this little needle gun. Fits in the palm of the hand. Goes in this unobtrusive little square case that you wear west of your belt buckle. Lethal or nonlethal, depending on circumstances. You can dial it either for a tranquilizer or a neurotoxin. Both as near to instantaneous as you can get. But you've got to hit bare flesh, or at least summer-weight clothing. Face, neck, or hands are the best hits. The magazine holds one hundred and twelve darts, each about the size of a bee's stinger. So if you don't have time to aim, you just spray in an arc. The darts are finned, so there's no tumbling, and the gas pressure's enormous, so it has an effective range in still air of up to two hundred yards."

Harkins took another flat little gun out of the cabinet. "This is the one for serious killing—say an armed incursion by multiple intruders. It fires a stream of explosive microflechettes, two hundred to a clip. You can cut a man in half with it. Literally. Same range as the needle gun."

Jarls shuddered. Born and raised in a vacuum-sealed bubble city, he had a Jovian's true horror of firearms and explosives. There were no such things on Jupiter. Constables carried truncheons or disabling sprays. Planet-born people like Earthlings, with air to spare, were reckless indeed.

"Something bothering you?" Harkins said.

"No. Go on."

Harkins stared at him for an insultingly long moment. Then he showed Jarls a larger weapon with a folding butt that was meant to be tucked into the hollow of the shoulder. "Now we come to the heavier stuff. This baby fires little smart rockets about the size of your middle finger. That's what we call it—the finger. Once you lock onto a target, even for a microsecond, the finger's brain takes over. It communicates with the missile. The target can dodge, flee, or levitate. Doesn't matter. The missile will follow it. Around corners if need be. Same goes for your aim. You can be a lousy shot, or you could be knocked flat on your ass while aiming. The finger will pick out the likeliest hostile shape in the vicinity, whether it's an armored car or an armed man. Yeah, it can take out medium armor. For heavier armor, we go to a regular missile launcher that you carry in a back-scabbard, like a claymore." He showed an irregular row of teeth in a canine grin. "Incidentally, you scored well on the claymore. The laird liked that, with his Scottish roots."

"The laird is . . . following my progress?" Jarls said.

"Mister Karsen mentions you in his weekly reports. The laird likes to be kept informed."

"I see."

"But don't get too pleased with yourself. Proficiency with antique weapons is one thing. But you'll be tested on all these as well. Earth's a tough place."

"Are you . . . are you . . ."

Harkins gave him an angry grimace. "Yeah, I was born on Jupiter. My parents brought me here when I was fourteen. They wanted a better life. They didn't last long. Both of them died working on the transpacific tunnel. Even Jovians get the bends. I kicked around a while. Did strongarm for the *yakuza*. Ended up here. I work like hell, hours every day, to keep my Jovian muscles."

"So do I," Jarls said.

By fall, Jarls was well settled into his duties. He helped check the grounds on a rotating shift basis, filled in on gate duty, did his share of nightly perimeter patrol, and kept an unobtrusive eye on the children of the extended Hirakawa clan when they came visiting. The Hirakawas themselves were rarely in Scotland. They had town houses in London, Tokyo, Los Angeles, and Rome, an apartment in the Bern-Liechtenstein megalopolis, and country houses scattered through the world.

Despite all the ado about advanced weapons training, Jarls rarely found himself armed. He wore one of the big pistols for ceremonial occasions, and was issued the appropriate weapon for the occasional security scare. Most of them turned out to be false alarms. The Hirakawas' guests were thoroughly vetted before they arrived: visiting dignitaries were run through the computer, local tradesmen dealing with the estate implanted with identity transponders that could not be removed. The worst security flap that happened on Jarls's watch was a mentally disturbed man, a distant relative of the Hirakawas, who somehow got as far as one of the outbuildings before being discovered. He was easily disarmed, without any need to harm him, and packed off to a doctor's care in Osaka.

In early September, the estate was again abuzz with preparations for one of the Hirakawas' visits. "There's to be a grand weekend for about a hundred guests," Mary confided to Jarls. "There's to be foxhunting and a grouse shoot and a kabuki entertainment. All the most brilliant people will be there—the prime minister, and Bishop Burke, and Little Ricky the soccer star, and Lon Janeway the Omninet commentator, and some bigwig from Venus, and all sorts of theater people, and the *cream*, just the *cream* of London society. And they'll be there to meet, you can't guess! Go on, guess!"

"I give up," Jarls said.

"*Rudolph*!"

"Rudolph?"

"Rudolph of Triesenberg, the Megachairman's nephew. He has a shooting estate near Glenfinnan, but he pretty well cleaned out his own grouse moor in August and he still hadn't shot his fill, so Lord Hirakawa offered to have a grouse drive for him here at Strathspey."

"I see. So he's a nephew of Franz Joseph XXIV, is he?"

"Yes, but he hardly ever shows his face in Liechtenstein. He's not interested in politics. Or in the business affairs of the Pandirectorate. He's a sportsman. Still, he's fourth in line."

"Very exciting."

"Yes, it *is*! I think you're making fun of me." She made a face. "But you don't know everything, luv." She lowered her voice conspiratorially. "Lord Hirakawa's trying to arrange a merger between Solar Oxygen and EarthCorp, and he wants the Megachairman to issue him a new charter. Something to do with expanding EarthCorp's rights to Jovian hydrogen. So he thought it might help if he did the Megachairman's nephew a favor."

Jarls came to sudden attention at the mention of Jovian hydrogen. He thought of the EarthCorp orbital siphon that had almost killed him, and the peril to Jupiter's airborne cities. Whatever corporate skullduggery was hatching, it couldn't be good for Jupiter.

He forced a bantering tone. "If he curried favor, you mean."

"Oh, you!"

"How do you come to know so much about corporate secrets?"

"You'd be surprised at what a maid overhears from the guests. They think we're furniture." She leaned against him. "Will you come to my room tonight?"

"I'll try."

"The coast's clear. Missus Macintyre's in London today, opening the town house. Anyway, she knows about us."

"All right."

She gave his hand a parting squeeze. "And I used to think you were cold."

Jarls watched her walk back along the path toward the big house. Czoznek came and stood beside him. "Nice," he said. "Just don't get caught."

Jarls turned away. Czoznek laughed.


He was on perimeter duty with Czoznek and Stern, lopping branches that might impede a clear field of fire and planting remote sensors in inconspicuous places, when Karsen came by. He was moving so quietly that they did not know he was there until he was beside them.

"You're reassigned to house duty for the weekend, Anders," he said to Jarls. "Area A—foot of the main staircase from the Great Hall, first landing, and all access corridors."

"That's the approach to the owners' suite," Czoznek said. "Congratulations, Anders, you've come up in the world."

Stern was looking just as piqued. Jarls was used to taking orders without backtalk, but he said, "Are you sure I'm the man for the job, Mister Karsen? Maybe it should go to one of the more experienced men."

"Lady Hirakawa asked especially for you," Karsen said. "She's a bit nervous, with a lot of unfamiliar faces in the house, and on a hunting weekend when some of the more autocratic gentry can't be parted from their weapons. Irrational though it may be, she's taken into her head that she can trust her safety to you after your performance with his lordship's triceratops."

"But . . ."

"That'll do, Anders. Report to Mister Harkins. He's in charge of the household detail."

"Don't worry about it, Anders," Czoznek said. "You're only going to be a glorified hall boy."

"That's enough from you, too, Czoznek," Karsen said. "Get back to work."

"Yes sir."

Karsen turned around. "Are you still here, Anders? Get going."

"Yes sir," Jarls said.

He started down the path toward the house, with Karsen at his heels. When they were out of earshot of Czoznek and Stern, Karsen took Jarls by the arm.

"You're treading on delicate ground, Anders," Karsen said. "Keep your nose clean."

"Yes sir," Jarls said, puzzled. "Is that all, sir?"

Karsen looked at him as if he had something more to say. The moment passed. He released Jarls's arm. "Just stay out of trouble," he said.

"Not everyone will be going along on the grouse drive," Harkins told Jarls. "Just the chosen few. The rest will be fobbed off with the foxhunt. The prime minister couldn't be excluded, of course. But he was no problem. He was glad to have us lock his shotgun away until the morning of the shoot. Lord Chulmford presented a bit of a difficulty, however. Highly aware of his prerogatives, his lordship is. Has a twenty-second-century American repeating shotgun. Family heirloom. Valuable antique. Refuses to be parted from it. Doesn't sleep with it loaded, thank God. Not that much of a fool. I had a respectful talk with him. Put it to him as a gentleman. Asked him to keep it locked away. Strange servants in the house, disreputable journalists wandering about, and all that. He promised to cooperate. The gentleman from Venus was another story. Lord Chairman of Solar Oxygen. Arrogant young puppy. Told me to remember my place. He'd keep his weapon with him, thank you very much."

"Lord Chairman Paes?" Jarls said. "Here on Earth?"

"Yes—the young one, not the father. The old gentleman passed away several months ago. Is something wrong?"

"N . . . no. I was surprised to hear that Vanius Paes had been made Lord Chairman, that's all. I . . . I had a run-in with him on Venus."

"That so? I'm surprised he'd even notice a Jovian workie. Well, let's hope he doesn't remember you. Where was I? Oh, yes. We've checked all the maids and valets the weekend guests brought with them. Remote sensing. The laird's scruples about not violating the laws of hospitality doesn't extend to servants, of course. They all seem to be clean. And none of the other gentlemen brought their own weapons—they'll be issued shotguns by us for the shoot. That includes Prince Rudolph, believe it or not. Fine gentleman. Unpretentious. So as far as I know, there'll be only two weapons in the house. But keep your eyes open. You never can tell."

"I will."

Jarls took up his post at the foot of the grand carved staircase rising from the Great Hall, blocking the way to Lord and Lady Hirakawa's private quarters. Across the way, another uniformed Jovian—an iron-faced man named Wilberforce—stood sentry at the foot of one of the two staircases leading to the guest wings.

Jarls felt like an imposter in the black and silver uniform with the broad shiny gunbelt and the trademark big pistol. He tried to keep his face as stiff and expressionless as Wilberforce's, but it was hard not to gawk at the glittering company that filed between them on the way to the dining room.

The sprinkling of showcase celebrities that the Hirakawas had invited as conversation pieces included some familiar faces that Jarls had seen on the holovid in the guards' lounge. He recognized

Little Ricky, the soccer champion, and Reiko, the glamorous *onna-gata* star, resplendent in a revealing kaleidogown. Both of them were on their best behavior in the titled company that had included them as equals.

Janeway was another matter. The famed Omninet commentator was tastelessly dressed in a swallow-tailed coat and ruffled shirt that he evidently imagined was formal attire at Strathspey, and he spoke in a loud, intrusive voice. He had attached himself to an uncomfortable-looking Lord Chulmford, and as they passed Jarls he was booming insistently, "Come now, your grace, are you trying to tell me that it's mere coincidence that brought the Lord Chairman of Solar Oxygen and the Lord Chairman of EarthCorp together with the nephew of the Megachairman the week before the Jovian hydrogen charter is up for renewal?"

They passed on. Jarls could see Janeway trying to take Chulmford's arm, and Chulmford shrugging it off.

He strained for a sight of Rudolph, who was passing through on the other side of the hall, closer to Wilberforce's post. The man who was a distant fourth in the line of succession to the throne of Greater Liechtenstein was a bluff, ruddy-faced individual with the unmistakable Schellenberg jaw and nose. He was somewhere in his forties, with a blond mustache and the crinkly cornered eyes of an outdoorsman.

Rudolph looked like an amiable lightweight who would have been uncomfortable with the sober trappings of power, which was a good thing for him, since he was unlikely ever to attain it, no matter how many boards he sat on or how much family wealth came his way. On his arm was a stunning woman in jewels and diamond tiara, the wife he had been so famously unfaithful to. She glowed and looked fondly at him as they made their way through the hall.

Vanius Paes was late. He swept through the hall after the last of the guests had gone through with a gaudily dressed Venusian entourage of three men and two women, who entered the dining room with him as invited guests. At least one of them looked like a private bodyguard—an unforgivable affront to any host and hostess—and Jarls would have been willing to bet that the personal shotgun that Harkins had warned him about was not the only firearm in the Paes suite.

Paes's eyes had turned briefly in Jarls's direction as he passed, but there had been no sign of recognition on the narrow, spoiled face. To Paes, Jarls suspected, one uniformed Jovian guard looked much like another. It was unlikely that Paes would have bothered to trace him here, no matter how insane his grudge. When he learned that Jarls had been sold to a seedy labor contractor like Makay, that would have been the end of it for him. He would have assumed that a certified troublemaker like Jarls had been sold off to the Mercurian mines.

Jarls breathed relief. Even if Paes were to somehow learn that he was alive and on Earth, there was little he could do about it. One didn't mess with another's servants. It wasn't done in social circles.

From inside came the faint strains of a dinner orchestra warming up. It would be followed, after dessert, by the kabuki entertainment that Mary had told him about. It would go on for hours, while the guests wilted.

Across the hall, Wilberforce caught Jarls's eyes and grimaced. Both of them shifted their feet simultaneously and had a surreptitious stretch. It was going to be a long night.

Jarls had managed to have four hours sleep before reporting for duty with the shooting party. He trudged bleary-eyed up the path from the guards' barracks, past the elephant barn, where the grooms were still leading out the saddled and caparisoned pachyderms for the foxhunt. He could see Drummond and Bert, as they detained one of the beasts for some foot problem or other, as the groom stood impatiently by.

Drummond was kneeling on one knee, with the elephant's drumlike foot crooked over his other leg, while Bert prodded with a hoof pick. The groom was making expostulatory gestures at being detained, which Drummond ignored.

Jarls recognized the elephant—Dolly, one of his favorites. She was an expert at pretending to be lame to get out of work. Jarls missed the great animals, and wondered again why Karsen had assigned him to the grouse shoot instead of the foxhunt. It would have made sense to have a man who was used to handling the beasts working the hunt in case some problem came up.

Drummond shook his head and eased Dolly's foot to the ground. He raised himself to his full bantam height and gave her a scolding. Dolly twitched her trunk and looked the other way; the groom grew more overwrought.

At last Drummond released the elephant and groom. They started across the grounds toward the back lawn. Dolly limped along for a few more steps, then gave it up. Jarls smiled.

When he got to the house, he found a scene of pandemonium on the back lawn. Elephants and grooms were milling around as the hunt master and whipper-in tried to assemble them in some sort of order. The laird's guests, dressed in foxhunting finery from another century, were waiting their turn to mount the gray beasts, with the help of the grooms and little wheeled aluminum airplane ramps. Some of the more adventurous riders had opted for traditional saddles, looking ridiculously small on the enormous gray humps, and more ridiculous still when you took in the second riders—the Scottish mahouts who sat perched forward, behind the elephants' heads, and who would do the actual handling of the beasts. Other riders had more sensibly opted to be strapped into safety seats with high backs and neck rests, and twin pommels to grab onto.

There were even elephants bearing canopied howdahs, for the timid and infirm—and in one case for a randy couple who were already pawing one another, though the curtains of the howdah were still undrawn. The mahout, Jarls was sure, had been tipped to give them a bumpy ride.

Janeway, the commentator, was looking bloated and disgruntled atop one of the elephants equipped with a safety seat. He was wearing a pink riding coat that was too tight on him, a white silk ascot at his throat, and a silly little hat. He knew he was one of the laird's second-string guests, assigned to the hunt instead of to the smaller, more exclusive party invited to the grouse shoot with Lord Hirakawa and Rudolph.

The favored few included Lord Chulmford and Vanius Paes. Harkins had shaken his head over that. "Let's hope they're both poor shots," he'd confided to Jarls the night before. "The laird doesn't want to give Rudolph too much competition—just enough to make it look good. I've ... ah ... adjusted the sights on the shotguns we're supplying to the other members of the shooting party. Just enough to throw them off a bit. But Chulmford and Paes will have their own weapons." He'd looked sly and pleased with himself then. "Of course, I've supplied the shells for the gamekeeper's men to reload with. They'll make a satisfactory bang, but about two-thirds of the pellets will fall short. That ought to keep the odds at about the right proportion."

Jarls smiled at the memory. He'd been on Earth long enough to know that one had to lose to royalty, but lose gracefully.

He took a shortcut through the kitchens to the front lawn. The place was a steaming pandemonium. The footmen were clearing the remains of the enormous hunt breakfast that had been served in the dining room at the same time the kitchen staff was assembling hampers and pocket foods for the foxhunters and the shooters. Even the parlor maids had been pressed into service. Jarles squeezed past a long table where a row of aproned slaveys was putting up Scotch eggs and Cornish pastries in linen napkins, assembly line fashion. Mary was one of the drafted maids. As Jarls passed through, she flashed a smile at him and pressed a warm, napkin-wrapped parcel into his hand. He put it in his tunic pocket with a nod of thanks and continued on through to the outside.

Out front, a convoy of estate cars was waiting at the marble curb to take the shooting party to the butts. Rudolph was standing at the lead vehicle, chatting easily with Lord and Lady Hirakawa. Both the Hirakawas were dressed in baggy tweeds and matching tweed caps. Rudolph was dressed in an outfit that must have been native to the Swiss Alps—short leather pants that left his hairy legs exposed to the morning chill, and a little felt hat with a feather in it. His stunning wife was nowhere in evidence; Jarls didn't think she was the type to trudge dutifully over the moors with her husband.

Jarls looked for Vanius Paes and found him getting into the second vehicle, dressed in impractical Venusian finery. But then, Venusians had no experience of the outdoors. The door closed and the vehicle's curtains were drawn.

Karsen walked over to where Jarls was standing. "You're to follow the Hirakawas," he said. "The driver has instructions. You'll stand well back from the butts, and remain as inconspicuous as possible. The laird is not keen on having the illusion of a country weekend spoiled by the sight of a uniformed man, but he recognizes the necessity."

"I can't do much good at a distance," Jarls said. "Couldn't you use another man to keep an eye on the beaters? If there's any threat to Rudolph or the Hirakawas, that's the direction it's most likely to come from. You've already got sharpshooters stationed to the rear of the butts."

"Are you arguing with me, Anders?"

"N . . . no sir."

"Lady Hirakawa would like to have you nearby," Karsen said curtly.

He looked at Jarls and shook his head. Then he walked away to give instructions to a trio of guards who wore slim firing tubes slung across their backs. The lightweight launchers fired smart microrockets guided by individual ricegrain-size brains programmed to hit a human target precisely between the eyes, even if they had to get ahead of a fleeing suspect and make a U-turn.

Jarls glanced ruefully at the weapon that Harkins had issued to him that morning. It was one of the oversize pistols that were meant for show—good for blowing a hole through someone at close range, but not very useful in the present situation. He would have to fill out a report if he so much as unbuttoned his holster.

He got into the estate car that Karsen had pointed out to him. The back seats were crammed with Jovians—five of them, taking up more space than Earthlings would have done. Czoznek said to him: "You're covering the Hirakawas?"

"How did you know?"

"Word gets around. Me, I'm covering the Venusian." He patted the long flat scabbard at his belt. "Self-propelled tranquilizer darts. Long-range, and they've got a needlenose that'll penetrate heavy clothing. If you ask me, the only danger to the Venusian is himself. He's packing this expensive blunderbuss that he imported from Earth. But I doubt that he knows anything about how to use it. Where would you fire a shotgun in an orbital habitat? And what kind of game do they have there anyway? I tell you, Paes makes me nervous. Harkins wouldn't let me have anything lethal. Big diplomatic incident if anybody ever fired live ammunition past the Lord Chairman of Solar Oxygen."

Stern stirred heavily in his seat. The springs of the passenger bench creaked. "Nothing to fire at anyway," he said. "Who are you going to shoot? One of the beaters?"

"You never can tell," Czoznek said comfortably. He eyed Jarls's gun with a smirk. "I see Harkins issued you one of the horse pistols."

"I've got backup," Jarls said stiffly.

"Don't we all," Czoznek said. "Look handsome, Jarls, my boy."

The wagon dropped Czoznek off at the first butt. Jarls could see Vanius Paes, waving off the vehicle that had brought him there. He'd brought one Venusian flunky with him, a man in a crimson cape and pantaloons, looking preposterously out of place on the Scottish moors. The loader and the gamekeeper's assistant that Lord Hirakawa had provided, attired in shabby tweeds and sweaters, followed the Venusians to the butt, a shallow affair walled with rough logs and lined with peat. Czoznek disappeared behind a bush, about a dozen yards to the rear.

The wagon next let Jarls off at the Hirakawas' shooting stand, about fifty yards down the line. Jarls scanned the surrounding heath automatically, as he had been taught to do, but there was nowhere an intruder could have hidden.

Rudolph was showing off his antique shotgun, an early American model with an extended magazine that allowed it to shoot off fifty shells in succession with only a light touch of the trigger. Lady Hirakawa turned and looked at Jarls, and for some reason that made him blush. The only cover he could find was a low clump of heather, and he settled down behind it as best he could.

In the distance, he could hear the sounds of the beaters, people from the nearby villages who had been conscripted for the grouse drive. They were no security threat. On the contrary, they themselves were in danger from poor sportsmen who shot too low without waiting until the birds were in flight.

Jarls could just make out their position, about a quarter mile away, as their line advanced. Each carried a flag, a white rag tied at the end of a stick, to show the shooters where they were. They were hooting and howling and beating the brush with branches and sticks.

They drew closer and closer, flushing the hidden birds and sending them scurrying before them. Jarls could see them clearly now, thin people in ragged clothes. About half of them, from their size, were young boys and girls. Scattered through the adult ranks was a fair share of tottering oldsters.

All of a sudden, as if at a signal, the first flurry of birds exploded into the air like a great dark cloud. Jarls heard an immediate shotgun blast from the stand to his right, where Vanius Paes was stationed, but the birds continued to rise without casualties.

In the Hirakawas' butt, three gun barrels rose and shots rang out in unison. Birds rained from the sky by the score. To the right, the Venusian had his gun on full automatic, firing in a frenzy, but without visible result. Jarls could make out a little dancing figure, knocked about by the recoil. At last, a few of the shells that Harkins had left undoctored must have reached their target, because a few birds dropped from the sky in the direction he was pointing.

Rudolph was firing alone—the Hirakawas were showing a mannerly deference to their guest now that first blood had been drawn. To Jarls's newly educated eye, it looked as if Rudolph knew what he was doing. He was aiming at the densest part of the cloud and leading its direction of flight. He was keeping up a clockwork rapid fire, passing his gun to the loader when it was empty and accepting the alternate gun without a break in rhythm. He didn't seem to have a prejudice about using a borrowed gun for every other fifty-shot group. The birds pelted down with a dismal regularity; a businesslike slaughter that Jarls estimated at something like a thousand grouse so far.

To the right, Paes's firing was more erratic. There were long pauses between one emptied clip and another. Paes was being stubborn about using nothing but his designer weapon. His firing pattern showed a growing temper—emptying full clips without taking a moment to aim first. Even at a distance, Jarls could hear him yelling at his loader.

To the left, where Lord Chulmford and the others were spaced along a five-hundred-yard front, the shooting seemed more sportsmanlike. The shotgun blasts were mostly single shots and short bursts. The downpour of dead birds was reduced to a mere sprinkle here. Harkins's doctored shells and doctored guns were helping to keep the butchery to an accepted minimum. Rudolph would leave the field as undisputed marksman of the day.

At last the initial flight passed over. A straggling handful of injured birds fluttered down to the ground, to be collected by men with dogs. Out front, police whistles were shrilling maniacally as the gamekeepers regrouped the beaters. The beaters were closer now; Jarls could see them as individuals. One little girl had come upon a dead grouse and tried to stuff it under a baggy sweater. A gamekeeper caught her in the act. He took the bird from her and gave her a backhanded smack across the face that sent her sprawling. She scrambled to her feet and got back in line with her white flag and stick.

The beaters moved forward again, crowding the panicked birds before them for the next flight. When it came, it was almost as dense as the first flight had been. Lord Hirakawa's grouse heath could not have supported so many; he must have stocked the area in advance to give Rudolph a good shoot.

Again the guns went off. Birds dropped from the sky. Even Paes bagged a few. But he was growing more and more frustrated, continuing to spray the empty air in a fit of pique long after the flight had passed by.

By the fourth flight, the birds had thinned out considerably. There couldn't have been many of them left hiding in the thin strip of underbrush that now remained. Even Rudolph had dialed his selector to single shot, and was trying out old-fashioned marksmanship.

Now the beaters were only twenty or thirty yards away from the shooters. The line of pasty faces came into focus—missing teeth, stringy hair, gray stubble on the old men. Jarls spotted the little girl he had seen earlier trying to conceal the dead bird under her sweater. She was painfully thin, with legs like sticks. But the expression on her face was one of lively interest. She caught sight of Vanius Paes in his gaudy Venusian clothes. The crimson cloak, the puff sleeves, the multicolor sparkles must have been an astonishing vision to these starveling villagers.

The little girl nudged her companion, a small spidery boy with close-cropped hair, and pointed her stick at Vanius.

Jarls could somehow sense what was about to happen, but it was like a slow-motion dream that he was powerless to stop. Paes raised his shotgun and took almost leisurely aim. Twenty feet behind him, Czoznek rose from the underbrush to see what was going on, and his square body visibly relaxed when he saw that there was no threat to Paes, then jerked taut again when he saw what Paes was doing. He could have shot Paes with his tranquilizer gun then, but he didn't.

The little boy was quick. He dove for the ground and pressed himself into the soft earth like a small burrowing animal.

The little girl was not so quick. Or perhaps she wasn't worried. She was likely a veteran of other grouse drives. The gentlemen were always careful.

The shotgun went off like a clap of thunder and continued to thump in a rapid tattoo. The little girl's head disappeared. The rest of her toppled backward into the scrub.

Jarls was halfway there when she fell. He didn't remember running. He slowed to a walk. The moor was strangely silent for a moment, then a wailing of women started. The beaters started to converge on the spot where the girl had fallen.

Czoznek was trying gently to take the shotgun from Paes. The Venusian pushed him away. "Get away from me, you fool!" he snapped.

Czoznek backed away. He turned around and saw Jarls approaching. He spread his hands apart defensively. "There was nothing I could have done," he said.

Jarls turned his attention to the heath. He could not see the body, but a circle of beaters was standing around the spot, with more arriving. Some of the men had their caps off and held to their chests. Women were howling and tearing at their clothes. An old man in rags was trying to hold back a screaming woman. The children hung back, solemn and wide-eyed.

The little boy rose from the heather. He was bleeding from the scalp and looking scared. No one paid him any attention. He wiped his nose with his sleeve and went to join the other children. He tried to show off his scalp wound, but they edged away from him.

Lord Hirakawa was approaching the butt at a casual walk, surrounded by retainers. Jarls was suddenly aware that he had deserted his post behind the Hirakawa butt. But the laird didn't spare even a glance for him. He was dispassionately giving orders to those around him as he walked. One of the young gillies touched his cap and darted off in the direction of the gamekeeper who had been directing the drive.

Paes greeted the laird peevishly. "Damn fool little drab! She might have been pointing a gun at me for all anyone knew! See here, Hirakawa, don't your gamekeepers know how to train these people properly? And the bodyguard you assigned me! Just stood there without doing anything to protect me!"

Lord Hirakawa made soothing noises. Paes went on complaining.

The young gillie came back and whispered something in Lord Hirakawa's ear. Hirakawa took out his wallet and handed over a fat sheaf of banknotes. The gillie touched his cap and ran off again.

"That was a mistake, Hirakawa," Vanius Paes sniffed. "Coddle these people once and they'll expect to be indulged forever. I wouldn't put it past them to put another of their brats in harm's way just for the money."

Lord Hirakawa smiled vaguely. Jarls looked again at the circle of beaters on the heath. Lord Hirakawa's men were on the scene by now and taking charge. They had a tarpaulin spread on the ground and were sliding the small corpse onto it. Jarls caught a sickening glimpse of the shredded stump of neck, the riddled torso. Then the tarpaulin was mercifully folded over the body, and four gamekeepers' assistants lifted it by the corners like a stretcher. Other estate workers were holding the small crowd at bay. The head gamekeeper, Symington, was peeling off banknotes from the thick wad that Lord Hirakawa had sent him, and distributing them judiciously after brief interrogations. The recipients stuffed the money with furtive haste into trouser pockets or down frayed bodices. The woman who had screamed tried to attack Symington when he attempted to hand her a sheaf of notes, but she was held in check by the old man who had restrained her earlier. He accepted the money for her and deftly pocketed it and tipped his hat with one free hand while briefly pinning her wrists with the other.

The villagers were already dispersing, following the estate men with the tarpaulin, when Jarls heard Vanius Paes's petulant voice say clearly, "Can't we continue now?"

Lord Hirakawa replied in an absent-minded tone: "Hmm, I think we've had sufficient sport for the morning, don't you? Why don't we have a spot of refreshment? Lunch will be waiting for us at the house about now. Oh, here comes Lady Hirakawa. She'll have been in communication with the staff."

Lady Hirakawa came toward them, talking to the palm of her hand. She was still exquisitely beautiful, even in baggy tweeds and with her hair tucked up into the peaked cap. She did not look in Jarls's direction.

She closed her hand over the tiny object it held and smiled blindingly at her husband and Vanius Paes. "Monsieur has outdone himself," she said. "Foies de volaile sautes in Madeira sauce, champignons sous cloche, bisque de homard, ramuniku with hakka jelly. I don't know how he managed it."

The estate wagons arrived to pick them up, more quickly than Jarls would have thought possible. The Hirakawas led Paes, still grumbling, to their own vehicle, to ride with them and Rudolph.

The wagons drove off. Presumably Jarls and the other Jovians would be left to walk back on their own.

Jarls became aware that Czoznek was standing beside him. "You're in for it, Anders," Czoznek said. "You were there to keep an eye on her ladyship. You shouldn't have deserted your post."

Jarls was back on duty by eight. Harkins had juggled the schedule to allow him a few hours sleep, in view of the long night ahead, but Jarls still felt muzzy. The long Terran days took their toll when you'd grown up adapted to Jupiter's rapid rotation.

He found himself standing at the foot of the same grand staircase, facing his partner for the evening, Wilberforce, on the opposite side of the hall. The guests were in the dining room, telling stories about the day's foxhunting and grouse shooting, and pretending intermittently to pay attention to the kabuki performers. Jarls had overheard some of the conversation as they filed past him. Nobody had mentioned the shooting of the little girl, but there had been many comments about the remarkable day's bag racked up by Rudolph.

Jarls was mildly surprised to be here. Evidently Lady Hirakawa hadn't gotten around to complaining about him yet. When she did, he would be demoted. He could only hope that it would be to the lower ranks of the security force again, and not back to the stables.

Wilberforce looked around to make sure they were alone in the hall, then leaned forward and said, "Czoznek's on the carpet. Mister Karsen called him in for a talk this afternoon."

"He could have shot Paes with a tranquilizer dart," Jarls said. "He had time."

"Are you crazy?" Wilberforce said. "You don't interfere with a bigwig like that! Not in the slightest way. Czoznek held back so as to stay out of trouble."

"Then what's he in hot water for?"

"The Venusian complained that he didn't blow the girl away. That he had to do the job himself because Czoznek hesitated. Better to lose a beater than risk the life of a lord chairman."

"What's going to happen to Czoznek?"

"Mister Karsen will keep him out of sight for a while. Put him on some kind of menial duty. Tell Lord Hirakawa he's being punished. When the Venusian leaves Earth, he might start letting Czoznek out of the box, one small thing at a time—give him a chance to climb the ladder again."

"No flogging?"

"Not for a lapse like Czoznek's. A Jovian trained for security work isn't that easy to come by. Not everybody's suited for it. Mister Karsen takes care of his own. You'd have to do something really stupid. Something that would make the laird or her ladyship mad enough to order a flogging."

"And if that happened?"

Wilberforce's stoic face twitched. "Mister Karsen would deliver you trussed and ready for the bullwhip."

A servant came through with a tray, and Wilberforce stopped talking. Jarls devoted himself to the strenuous task of standing at rest and imitating a Jovian statue.

By midnight, most of the guests were in their rooms, getting a good night's rest for the morning activities at Strathspey. There was to be a boat ride, golf, tennis, or croquet for the early risers, followed by one of Lady Hirakawa's famous garden parties.

By three-thirty, even the most die-hard drinkers, card players, and talkative bores had called it a night. Jarls yawned, stretched, popped his muscles, and prepared to wait out the remaining hours until his dawn relief.

The shotgun blast came at four-fifteen. It was from somewhere in the guest wing, up one of the two flights of marble stairs across the hall from Jarls.

Wilberforce whirled instantly and bounded up the stairs, one hand unlatching his holster, the other reaching into his breast pocket for the little mayday transmitter. Jarls uncoiled to sprint after him.

He was twelve feet across the hall in one Jovian stride when a scream came from the top of the grand staircase behind him.

"*Tasukete*! What is it? Come here!" It was Lady Hirakawa's voice.

At the top of the stairs opposite, Wilberforce turned his head without breaking stride. "Go!" he shouted to Jarls. "I'll take care of it! Your job's with the Hirakawas!"

Jarls skidded to a stop. His momentum took him another twelve feet. He tumbled and reversed direction. In Earth's light gravity, his leaps took him to the top of the grand staircase in seconds. Lady Hirakawa was standing there in a gauzy robe, her face drained, holding onto the balustrade for support. She didn't seem to be hurt in any way, but she seemed rattled and confused.

A door down the hall opened and Lord Hirakawa appeared in the opening. He wore a long dressing gown and his face was puffy with sleep.

"*Do shimashita ka*?" he demanded. "What has happened?"

Jarls took in the state of affairs at once. Lady Hirakawa was paying her husband a nighttime visit when the shotgun blast had come from the guest wing. Neither of them had awakened to the dangers of the situation.

From the depths of the house, on the other side of the great hall, Jarls could hear the sounds of running feet, shouts, the flutter of explosive microfletchettes. There was activity outside, too. Floodlights had gone on, spilling light through the oriel windows in the hallway, and there was the sound of a heavy vehicle coughing into life.

"Your lordship, you can't stand there!" Jarls croaked. "You must get into your room at once!" He turned urgently to Lady Hirakawa. "Your ladyship! You can't stay here! Get out of this hallway!"

Neither of them moved. Jarls remembered how they had refused to flinch at the charge of the triceratops. People like these couldn't believe that anything could happen to them. Or perhaps they were simply slow to react.

"Please, my lady!" Jarls pleaded.

She remained clutching the balustrade. She seemed paralyzed.

Jarls did not stop to think of what the penalties might be for touching the gentry. He was suddenly aware that Lady Hirakawa was naked beneath the thin robe, and he tried to avert his eyes as he grabbed her and pried her hands from the balustrade. She gasped as he propelled her toward the bedroom door, almost lifting her feet off the floor. When he reached Lord Hirakawa, he grasped his shoulder with one meaty hand and manhandled the two of them inside.

He slammed the door shut, took in the room at a glance. There was a big, heavy oak wardrobe, about nine feet tall, against one wall. He picked it up, carried it across the room, and set it upright against the door. There was a casement window overlooking the lawn. He saw gray and silver uniforms running down the slope, and little twinkling flashes of microflechette fire. He picked up Lord Hirakawa's bed, an ornately carved Biedermeier monstrosity that was about six feet wide and eight feet long, and covered the window with it.

"You'll be all right," Jarls said. "Stay on this side of the room and keep low. Under the side table would be best. I'm going to squeeze past the wardrobe and leave it propped against the door. Lock the door behind me and don't open it for anyone until Mister Karsen gives the all-clear."

"No, you stay here with us," Lord Hirakawa said.

"But my lord, I should . . ."

"Be silent!" Lord Hirakawa hissed. "You will do what I say!"

"Yes, my lord," Jarls said.

Hirakawa felt his bruised arm and shoulder, where Jarls had grabbed him, and winced. "You are very strong," he said.

"He's a Jovian, Tommy darling," Lady Hirakawa said in her throaty voice. "I feel safer already."

"It's all right, my pet," Hirakawa said. "You don't need to be afraid anymore."

Lady Hirakawa didn't look at all afraid to Jarls. She looked thoroughly calm and competent, despite the fact that her robe had fallen open and she wore nothing under it. She didn't seem to care about Jarls's presence, and neither did his lordship. Jarls felt a brief flare of resentment; servants didn't matter to the rich and powerful—they paid them no more heed than a cat or a dog.

The sound of small arms fire continued outside. It seemed to be moving away from the house in the direction of one of Strathspey's meadows.

"So?" Lord Hirakawa said. "What is happening?"

"It's an incursion," Jarls replied. "By anywhere up to a dozen men, by the sound of it. I don't understand it. They couldn't have hoped to shoot their way into the house." He remembered the shotgun blast from the guest wing, and the sounds of strife that had followed. "But they had someone on the inside. Perhaps it was supposed to be an extraction."

Lady Hirakawa clutched her husband's sleeve. "Rudolph!" she exclaimed. "Oh, Tommy!"

"Well find out, fellow!" Lord Hirakawa snapped.

Jarls set his little transmitter searching the wavelengths. Everybody was very busy. But he got a few distracted replies that gave him a sketchy picture.

"Lord Rudolph's all right," he told them. "The guest wing's secured. And so is this wing. You're in no danger here. But it won't be safe to leave this room for a while longer."

He strained to hear the outside sounds. There was a faint throbbing in the sky. Then the sky exploded. There was a great silent flash that spilled around the edges of the bed that was blocking the casement window and lit up Lord Hirakawa's bedroom.

Jarls acted in the split second before the concussion came. He leaped at Lord and Lady Hirakawa, his thick arms spread wide, and bore them to the floor. His palms slapped the carpet on either side of them so that his weight would not crush them. Then there was a tremendous *whump*, the crash of glass, and the thump of the Biedermeier bed hitting the floor. Shards of glass rained on Jarls's back, but the mattress had taken most of the brunt as the bed was falling. Jarls waited a few more seconds, then helped the Hirakawas to their feet.

"My God!" Lord Hirakawa said.

"It was a helicopter," Jarls said. "Mister Karsen blew it out of the sky as it was trying to land. It must have come to take out the extraction team and the assassin. It would only have to hover at a given rendezvous for a few seconds. The defenses of a household like this are geared to repel people trying to get *in*, not people fighting their way out. Its transponder would have been programmed to fool the perimeter defense's artificial intelligences for a half-minute or so with a valid identity and a cover story about getting lost or running into mechanical trouble and making an emergency landing on a convenient meadow. But Mister Karsen didn't wait for it to land. He gambled that he wasn't shooting down an innocent aircraft."

"Mister Karsen cannot be accused of using an insufficiency of firepower," Lord Hirakawa observed dryly as he brushed crumbs of glass from his robe.

Jarls did not know how to reply. He stood mutely, feeling warm blood trickle down his back from the glass cuts. He hoped that Lord Hirakawa would not be upset about stains on his carpet. Or bruises on his wife's arms.

"Well, Jarls?" Lord Hirakawa said. "It is Jarls, isn't it?"

"He couldn't take chances," Jarls said. "There might have been anything aboard the helicopter."

Lady Hirakawa had an amused smile on her face. "So many conclusions from a few sounds outside," she said.

Jarls felt himself blushing. "I could be wrong, my lady," he said.

A look passed between the two Hirakawas. Lord Hirakawa sighed. "Very well, my dear," he said.

Fifteen minutes later, there was a pounding at the door. Karsen's voice came from the hallway. "Are you all right, your lordship? It's all over. You can unlock the door now."

Jarls stared down at what was left of Wilberforce. The upper half of the body was gone, leaving a red hash spattered on the walls and ceiling. The lower half was identifiable by the uniform. The right hand still clutched the butt of the oversize pistol, halfway out of its holster. The other body was in better shape, though. The shotgun blast had caught it in the face and chest. It lay in a puddle of coagulating blood.

"Who's the other one?" Jarls asked.

"Lord Chulmford, worse luck," Stern replied. "He tried to be a hero. The shooter was his own valet. From what we can reconstruct, he stole the lord's shotgun in the middle of the night and tried to sneak out with it. The lord must've woke up, followed the valet into the hall. You know what Chulmford was like. He probably ordered the valet to give him the gun, made a grab for it. The valet shot him, both barrels at point blank range. Then Wilberforce arrived and the shooter turned to face him. But the shotgun clicked on an empty chamber. No magazine. Chulmford had removed it, trying to be a responsible sportsman as Mister Harkins asked him to. The valet didn't know that. He'd counted on Lord Chulmford getting a loaded gun into the house for him for his assassination attempt."

"What happened to Wilberforce, then?"

"Lord Paes's personal bodyguard shot him. Heard the hullabaloo in the hallway, and instead of leaving it to us, inserted himself into the action. Probably Paes ordered him to. Anybody who'd smuggle an armed servant into a house without telling his host would be capable of that kind of behavior. The bodyguard opened fire without trying to understand the situation. Killed Wilberforce and let the assassin get away." He gestured at the mangled remnants of the Jovian body. "Just sprayed away. Explosive microflechettes, as you can see."

"So the assassin escaped?"

"Are you kidding? He got ten yards from the house. We caught him alive. Mister Karsen's questioning him now. An investigative team from Liechtenstein is on its way, but they won't be here for a couple of hours."

Jarls was startled. "From Liechtenstein?"

"Yeah. What do you think? Rudolph's fourth in line of succession. What happened here may be part of a major coup attempt."

Jarls nodded agreement. The helicopter and the armed invaders showed there was money and organization behind the incident. "How many infiltrators were there?"

"Nine. All dead now."

"How'd they get on the grounds?"

"They carried identity transponders the estate implanted in some of the village tradesmen who do business here." Stern shuddered. "I don't like to think about how they extracted them. They didn't have time for any fancy surgery. But they were able to fool the perimeter defense AI's long enough to get by them. They expected to be out of here in a few minutes—before there could be any human follow-up."

"To extract the valet?"

"Or shut him up. Mister Karsen found a suicide pill on him that he'd been given in case things went wrong—which they did. But he couldn't work up enough nerve to use it. They might have promised him extraction when they recruited him. Just to give him confidence. He was the only available tool. But they couldn't trust him."

"Who are 'they?'"

Stern shrugged. "Don't know. Mister Karsen is in touch with the Executive Guard data base in Liechtenstein. But they might not tell him everything."

Karsen briefed the security detail at morning muster. There had been no chance for sleep in the few hours that remained of the night, and the room was filled with bleary-eyed Jovians in uncharacteristically rumpled uniforms. Several of Jarls's cohorts sported bandages or patches of adhesive tape, and one man had his leg in a walking cast. Jarls wondered how that had happened; it was almost unheard of for a Jovian to break a bone in Earth's weak gravity.

The investigative unit from Liechtenstein had dropped out of the sky shortly after dawn in two screaming hypersonic craft that ignored Lord Hirakawa's private spacedrome across the valley and lowered themselves on their tails to the elephant pasture. Jarls had expected Executive Guard uniforms, but the Jovians who had spilled out and taken control of the estate wore civilian clothes. They were impressive men. They fanned out over the grounds without waiting to check in with Karsen, taking pictures and collecting expended ordnance and weapons. The fragments of the helicopter had been tagged and crated by intelligent machines that remembered their relative disposition and could later lay them out in the same configuration in some cavernous warehouse in Liechtenstein. A forensic team located the corpses and put them in cryogenic body bags. Karsen had taken the ranking officers into his office and turned over the would-be assassin to them. In the meantime, a team of interrogators had interviewed everybody who had seen or heard anything, including Jarls, for later analysis. The questioning had been surprisingly brief. The interrogators had shown no deference to rank or title. Even Vanius Paes had been questioned, despite his protests and threats, in front of a camera plugged into a blinking device that evaluated everything from pupil size and facial expressions to the moisture content of the air surrounding him. The two craft were gone only a few hours later, taking with them the bodies, the evidence, and the shackled prisoner, and leaving nothing behind but two scorched depressions in the meadow.

"We'll know more later," Karsen told them. "Or maybe not. The Executive Guard has bigger responsibilities than guarding a country house. For now, I can tell you that the target was almost certainly Lord Rudolph, and the attempt was part of a worldwide conspiracy. It was a busy night. Attempts were made on the lives of at least seven other members of the royal family, including some who were even lower in the line of succession than Rudolph. Three of the seven attempts succeeded, including the attack on the heir apparent, Prince Albert. So the heir presumptive, Count Steg, is now next in line to the throne and the megachairmanship. No attempt was made on the life of Franz Joseph himself, so that raises some questions."

Karsen clasped both hands behind his back, parade style. He looked tired and uncomfortable.

"Of course the dissident group may not have made an attempt on Franz Joseph simply because of the hopelessness of it. No assassin has *ever* gotten past the Executive Guard—not in four hundred years. And that includes nukes and one attempt, two hundred years ago, to drop an asteroid on the Bern-Liechtenstein megalopolis. But people keep trying. So maybe the conspirators figured that for now they'd concentrate on disrupting the line of succession, and hope to get a better shot at the Megachairman some time in the future."

Karsen's hands came into view again, and he started ticking off points on his fingers.

"That's one possibility. A second possibility, of course, is that the attack on Count Steg was bogus, and that the whole thing was a sham exercise meant to move the Count up one rung and assure the succession for him. But I'd discount that hypothesis. It's no secret..." Karsen chose his words delicately. "...that the Megachairman's popularity has been dwindling in recent years. There were four attempts on his life last year alone, and riots and demonstrations in all the major world metrocenters. Including the nasty one in Milan, just across the border in the Lombardian Dependency. The Executive Guards lost a lot of good men putting that one down, and worse, they lost a lot of popular good will." Karsen shook his head. "But Count Steg is even more unpopular than Franz Joseph, and there's even less public confidence in his ability to manage the affairs of the solar system."

Karsen ran his eyes over the Jovian ranks as if he were taking their measure. "And that brings us to a third possibility," he said.

Jarls was puzzled. Where was Karsen going with this? The room fell noticeably silent as weary men held themselves still in order to hear better.

"What if the attacks last night were intended to *keep* Franz Joseph in the megachairmanship by positioning the Count as an unacceptable alternative? To discourage assassination attempts by *other* terrorist organizations? Discourage reformist groups who might otherwise agitate for a more congenial administration. Discourage rivals within the Pandirectorate itself—especially those embarrassing members of the inner circle who've been hinting for the last year that the Megachairman ought to resign. They all have one thing in common. They have no place to go now."

The hairs rose on the back of Jarls's neck. Karsen was perilously close to implying that Franz Joseph himself, or those aligned with him, had had a hand in the night's events. Treasonous utterances carried the death penalty, even for a security chief. If there were any place in the world that could be kept swept clean of listening devices, it was Karsen's office, but even so, he was depending heavily on Jovian solidarity.

Karsen himself seemed to have concluded that he had said enough. "All that's conjecture," he said, "and it's not for public consumption. The Executive Guard has asked us to cooperate in downplaying this. I'll expect all of you to keep your mouths shut. Our Venusian guest, Lord Paes, is convinced that *he* was last night's target, and that's the story we're putting out."

Karsen detained Jarls after dismissing the rest of the security force. Jarls stood at attention, waiting to be reprimanded for his failure to back up Wilberforce.

But Karsen did not mention Wilberforce's death. Instead, he said dryly, "His lordship asked me to commend you for your performance last night."

"But I didn't do anything," Jarls said.

"You made the Hirakawas feel safer," Karsen said. "That's what the job's about."

"I could have been helping with the mop-up," Jarls said.

"All's well that ends well," Karsen said wearily. "We all might have been reprimanded for letting the valet slip by us in the first place. We might have been made an example of for letting nine infiltrators get onto the estate grounds, even though it took us less than an hour to dispose of them. But we weren't. Lord Hirakawa got a phone call early this morning from the Megachairman, thanking him for preserving the life of his nephew. Some of the other potential claimants to the throne were not so lucky, as you know. So instead of being humiliated for being careless, Lord Hirakawa came through this with a feather in his cap."

Jarls digested Karsen's words. "I see, sir."

"Of course, Lord Paes filed a complaint against us. Wants the whole security force flayed for endangering his life. But Lord Rudolph is happy with us. So the complaint won't go anywhere. And you've got your . . . commendation."

"Is that all, sir?"

Karsen gave Jarls a displeased stare. "No. You're being reassigned. Lady Hirakawa wants you as her personal bodyguard."

# 15

T HE MAID, Toshiko, found Jarls in the utility room, cleaning and oiling the ceremonial pistol, the *pistoru mhor*, that Lady Hirakawa liked to have him carry. She embarrassed him as usual by bobbing and bowing in the peculiar English fashion, and said in a twittering voice, "Her ladyship wishes to see you at once, Jaru-san."

"Right away," Jarls said. He snapped the slide back in place, stuffed the gun into its oversize holster, and stood up.

Toshiko giggled behind her hand and backed out of the room, still bowing. Jarls followed.

"What does she want this time?" Jarls asked as they threaded their way through the back corridors to the Hirakawa suite.

"I don't know, Jaru-san," she said, and that was all he could get out of her. Toshiko was an untutored local girl from Honshu, where the Hirakawas maintained one of their country estates, and her English was rudimentary. But she had become Lady Hirakawa's personal maid by dint of unwavering loyalty.

"Jaru-san," she said when they arrived at the entrance to Lady Hirakawa's apartment, "you must take off your boots."

Puzzled, he complied. It was no use arguing with Toshiko when her face was wearing the slight frown that indicated that she was under her mistress's orders. She rewarded him with a minimal smile.

Jarls was used to being received in the second drawing room,

248

which Lady Hirakawa had taken over as her study. He was surprised when Toshiko led him through the drawing room to an unobtrusive door at the rear, and ushered him into a small, almost bare room that was decorated only with floor mats and a few hanging scrolls. There was nothing to sit on—only a couple of flat cushions facing each other across a low table. The focal point of the room was a shallow alcove that contained a solitary vase holding a single flower. Jarls surprised himself by remembering the name of the terrestrial bloom. A chrysanthemum.

Lady Hirakawa was kneeling on one of the cushions. She had changed from the riding clothes that Jarls had seen her in earlier that morning and was wearing one of the elaborate robes that he had learned was called a kimono.

She looked up at Jarls and said, "Ah, so, Jarls. Come here, please." She indicated the cushion opposite.

Jarls was at a loss over what to do. He was obviously expected to kneel, not sit. Lady Hirakawa looked entirely natural and comfortable in that posture, but for a thick-bodied Jovian with massively bulging leg muscles, it was another matter. Jarls forced himself to a kneeling position, with a cracking of knee joints and a popping of tendons.

"Very good," she said with an amused smile. "We'll make a civilized person of you yet. Do you know why you're here?"

"No, my lady."

"You're going to learn about the tea ceremony. Tommy's away in London, and there are no suitable guests at Strathspey at the moment. You're not quite a servant and it's so bloody boring to go through the damn routine alone." She cocked her head. "Besides, you should know something of our customs if you're going to guard me properly."

Jarls already was familiar with the English custom of stopping everything for tea at inappropriate moments. He was used to sitting down with the others in the servants' hall, with a thick mug of black tea in his hand and a plate of ham sandwiches or buttered scones in front of him. He'd often thought it was a bit ritualistic. But he'd never heard it called a ceremony before.

"Yes, my lady," he said.

Lady Hirakawa clapped her hands, and Toshiko suddenly appeared with a laquered tray piled with tiny porcelain plates. She placed the tray on the low table, bowed once, and left.

"While we wait," Lady Hirakawa explained. "This is not a meal. This is only what we call a stone for the bosom."

She smiled at his hesitation. "Go ahead, dragon tamer," she said. "You must keep up your strength."

Jarls reddened as he reached for one of the miniature dishes. Lady Hirakawa liked to refer to him as her "dragon tamer" or "gladiator," sometimes, embarrassingly, in front of her guests. It was a reference to his stopping the charge of the triceratops on the day the mammoth had been killed. He could not tell if she was making fun of him.

He swallowed the diminutive morsel in one gulp. It was hardly large enough to chew. It seemed to be a shred of raw fish on a tiny ball of vinegared rice. There was a little paper-thin cucumber sandwich, and a thimbleful of a clear, sour broth, and some kind of sweet paste to be eaten with a little stick. He was finished almost as soon as he had started, and it had all added up to less than a mouthful of morning rice in the servants' hall.

He looked up to find Lady Hirakawa regarding him out of large, serene eyes. He realized with a sense of chagrin that she had sampled nothing from the tray herself.

She clapped her hands again, and Toshiko was there, unhurriedly arranging a number of objects one by one. There was a compact charcoal burner, already glowing, with a steaming kettle and a wooden ladle resting in a stand and a square lacquered box and a bamboo whisk. Toshiko placed a bowl of water and a tiny handleless cup in front of each of them, and then, at a nod from Lady Hirakawa, bowed and disappeared.

Lady Hirakawa fixed him with her disconcerting stare and said, "Now is the time to rise up and leave, if you detect anything disharmonious. It is considered a courtesy. Do you wish to do so?"

Numbly, Jarls shook his head.

"Everything must contribute to the repose of the moment. The proportions of the room—derived, by the way, from the Fibonacci sequence. The rightness of the flower in the niche. The cups—they are more than eight hundred years old, and come to us from the tea master, Rikyu. And I, myself. Do you find me disharmonious, dragon tamer?"

Jarls forced himself to look at her directly. "N-no, my lady," he said. Her kimono, he noticed, was decorated in a chrysanthemum pattern, the same flower as the one in the niche.

She raised the lid of the box, and used the wooden scoop to put powdered green tea in Jarls's cup. She added hot water, and with the bamboo whisk, stirred the tea three times, finishing each ritualistic motion by tapping the side of the cup with the whisk.

"Now you must take a sip," she said.

The cup almost disappeared in Jarls's thick hand. It was thin as a seashell. He handled it gingerly, afraid of crushing it. If it was really eight hundred years old, it must be a Hirakawa family heirloom, or have come from a museum—an object of incalculable value.

It was hard not to swig it down, the cup was so impossibly small, but Jarls managed to take a measured sip without disgracing himself. The green tea, plain and bitter, was nothing like the strong black tea that he was used to getting in the servants' hall.

Still holding the cup, he looked questioningly at Lady Hirakawa.

"Wipe the rim with the cloth and pass the cup to me, giving it a half turn," she said.

Jarls wiped the cup, rotated it as she had asked, and held it out to her.

"It would be courteous of you to admire the cup first," she said impatiently.

His ears red, he examined the frail object and noticed for the first time that it, too, was decorated with a chrysanthemum pattern. The colors were faded, and the porcelain was covered with a network of ancient cracks. Jarls groped for something to say.

"It's very beautiful," he said at last.

"It ought to be," she said. "It's an authentic Ninsei."

She took the cup from him, sipped delicately, wiped the rim as he had done, and passed the cup back. One more exchange and the cup was empty. She rinsed the cup in a bowl of water, and they began the routine again, this time with her cup.

Jarls waited for her to signal Toshiko again, for the next step, but she made no move, and Toshiko was nowhere in sight.

"My lady . . ." he began.

She put a warning finger to her lips and said, "You must not disturb the serenity of the moment."

She pushed the cup and implements aside and leaned across the table toward him, her lips slightly parted. The pupils of her eyes were enormous.

Jarls could no more have stopped himself than he could have chosen not to inhale after holding his breath past his limit. He leaned forward and met her lips halfway. Her kiss was greedy, brutal, at odds with her delicate appearance.

She broke away, leaving Jarls gasping. The blood pounded in his thick neck. Lady Hirakawa rested calmly on her heels, studying him—coldly, he thought. Jarls cursed himself for his idiocy and waited for her to press the implanted carpal switch that would summon Karsen's household patrol.

She rose with supple ease and took Jarls by the hand. A gentle tug brought him readily to his feet—the way, he thought crazily, he himself had managed obstinate tons of elephant without having to exert strength.

"You must have your way with me, eh, dragon tamer?" she said with indulgent mockery. "Come, we will see how strong you are."

He didn't see Mary for four days. She stopped him in the corridor, where she had been dusting the forty-seven marble busts of the former Earls of Strathspey. Jarls was on his way to the guardroom to report to Karsen. He gave a guilty start when he saw her. He told himself that he hadn't exactly been trying to avoid her, but he was forced to admit shamefacedly to himself that if he had known she was going to be working in the ancestors' gallery that morning, he would have taken another route to escape bumping into her.

"Well, Jarlie my boy," she said, shaking the feather duster at him, "I thought you'd vanished from the face of the earth."

"I . . . I've been busy," he said lamely.

"I'll bet you have, love. Her ladyship's been working you hard, has she?"

"You know how the gentry are," he said, his cheeks burning.

"Do I, now? I know you didn't come to me on Thursday, when Missus Macintyre was away and the coast was clear. And you haven't been coming to the servants' hall to say hello mornings."

"I . . . One of the underbutlers was hanging around the stairway on Thursday," he said. "Wilkins, the one with the big mouth. I tried to see you Friday, but you weren't there. Agnes will tell you."

"You know very well that I work Friday nights, Jarlie," she said sorrowfully. "They keep me till two in the morning. Agnes couldn't think why you'd taken it into your head to come around then."

"I thought . . . I thought . . ."

"You thought you'd dodge me without it looking that way, that's what you thought. Isn't it?"

"I'm sorry," he said miserably.

"That's nice, love," she said tartly. "What about tonight? I happen to know that Mister Arthur will be visiting Missus Macintyre for their monthly, and she always sleeps like a sow afterward, so there'll be no problem."

"I . . . that is . . ."

Jarls couldn't hide his dismay. He had grown fond of Mary, and he thought she was fond of him. Both of them had accepted their arrangement as a convenience—the best that could be expected for the time being in this place and under these circumstances. Jarls had allowed his memory of Kath, on faraway Jupiter, to grow dim, and Mary had done the same for someone in her past: a boy in Shropshire whom she'd been close to before her parents sold her into service and whom she hadn't seen for years.

But Lady Hirakawa had become a fire in his veins. She had

summoned him twice more since the day of the tea ceremony, sending Toshiko to fetch him in the middle of the night and sending him back to his quarters before the house woke up in the morning. He had never imagined a woman like her. At first he was afraid of injuring her, of bruising her with a careless grip or snapping fragile bones, but she would not allow him to be gentle with her. He learned quickly that she required him to manhandle her—to immobilize her in his iron grasp or hold her suspended in midair to create the illusion of helplessness. She contrived positions in which she would not be crushed by his weight. She was tireless in her demands, and Jarls lived for the crumbs of approval she doled out: "You are like a steel machine; how could one such as myself resist your strength?" she would say, pretending resignation. Or, sardonically: "Enough, Jovian satyr, you will wear me out!" She treated him distantly during the day, and would not allow him any familiarities, but at night she was voracious. Jarls felt himself consumed by her. He waited feverishly for those nocturnal summonses, in a panic that they might cease.

"Well, love?" Mary said, waiting.

"I ..." He sweated, thinking of Toshiko coming to fetch him, and not finding him there.

While he floundered, Mary stared at him with something like contempt. "I thought so," she said, and turned away from him to resume her dusting.

Jarls contemplated her starched back, and realized there was nothing he could say. He walked away, at first feeling sheepish, and then beginning to feel the first stirrings of alarm.

Mary could not possibly suspect, he told himself. How could she? Toshiko was the only one who knew about him and Lady Hirakawa, and she would die rather than betray her mistress. No, Mary was miffed at his neglect, that was all. Perhaps she suspected an affair with a rival in the servants' wing. And even if she had somehow guessed the truth, she would not dare to voice her suspicions and risk a flogging.

Karsen was another matter. Jarls sweated some more as he

swung round the bend in the corridor and took the staircase leading to the basement guardroom.

Jarls had expected to see Harkins, the weapons master, with Karsen. Harkins was, on the current assignment roster, supposed to be in charge of the household security detail, and this was his turf. But Karsen was alone in the room.

Karsen looked up as Jarls entered. He was sitting at Harkins's desk, scrolling through the weekly reports. He turned off the disposable screen and laid it face down on the desk.

"How is it going, Anders?" Karsen said without preamble. "Everything all right?"

"Yes sir," Jarls said. "No problems."

"Lady Hirakawa is happy with you, then?"

"Yes sir," Jarls said. "I think so."

"You've missed three of the last four morning musters. I thought I'd touch base with you as long as I was here to see Harkins."

"I . . . uh . . . had to be on early call. But I checked in with Mister Harkins. He said it was all right."

"I see." Karsen toyed with the screen, rolling it up, then letting it spring back into shape. "Your daily reports seem to be somewhat lacking in detail lately. Perfunctory, I'd call them."

"I'm sorry, sir. There hasn't been that much to report."

Karsen smoothed the screen flat and pushed it aside. "That's good then, isn't it, Anders? A security system is doing its job when there isn't anything to report."

"Yes sir, I suppose so."

"You've been assigned as Lady Hirakawa's personal bodyguard. But you mustn't forget that you're not the only one responsible for her safety."

"Yes sir."

"You're a part of the household security detail, and you've got to work hand in hand with them."

"I understand, sir."

"That means you've got to be fit and alert at all times."

Jarls wondered how much Karsen could tell by looking at him. The lack of sleep had left him bleary-eyed and leaden. He straightened up and tried to look sharp.

"Mister Harkins is concerned about your state of fitness," Karsen said. "He says you've been skimping on your conditioning sessions. You know what can happen to a Jovian in earth gravity. Without relentless exercise, that dense muscle mass can start to turn flabby. You carry around weight that isn't doing its job, leaving you worse off than an earthling. Bones begin to decalcify. The cardiovascular system loses its tone." He frowned. "Mister Harkins also says that you've missed your last two kendo sessions, and have not been keeping up the unarmed combat skills he was at such pains to teach you. Without daily practice, these skills deteriorate."

"I'll get on it, sir."

"See that you do. Mister Harkins is drawing up a remedial schedule for you. I'll clear it with Lady Hirakawa."

"Yes sir."

"You can go now." As Jarls turned to leave, Karsen said, "One more thing, Anders."

"Yes sir?"

"Get some sleep."

# 16

**J**ARLS PADDED barefoot to the window, wearing the light robe that Lady Hirakawa had loaned him—a *yukata*, she called it— and, drink in hand, looked out at a brilliant night sky, blazing with northern stars. Earth seemed almost unpopulated from here. He could see only a dim sprinkling of lights across the laird's valley to mark the nearer villages, and a few isolated gleams from some of the cottages where outside staff were awake for one reason or another. He knew that the great city of Aberdeen, with its population of ten million, lay somewhere to the east, and that Balmoral Castle, one of the royal family's residences, was only a few miles away across the low hills to the north, but their lights were not visible from here. This had been Hirakawa country since the laird's remote ancestor had bought the earldom in the twenty-second century from a strapped descendant of the original Earl of Strathspey.

He took a sip of the lukewarm stuff in the cup, and tried not to annoy Lady Hirakawa by making a face and risk being called a barbarian again. It was some kind of rice wine, and instead of sensibly chilling it, she served it heated. It was dispensed from a decanter that Toshiko had left for them on a small alcohol burner, and it had cooled to unpalatability while he had dawdled with it.

He finished it off gamely and turned to Lady Hirakawa. She was propped up in bed, wearing a man's silk pajama top, sipping delicately from one of the tiny cups. The bed was enormous—its gilt posts rising almost to the ceiling and hung with silk damask. A velvet settee with a facing chair and tea table rested at its foot. The bedroom, if it had not been so huge, would have seemed cluttered; it was a far cry from the adjoining bare and simple tea chamber. There was an elaborate marble fireplace, a lot of heavy carved furniture, and every flat surface was filled with antique gewgaws. One entire wall was given over to glass-fronted cabinets displaying Lady Hirakawa's doll collection—hundreds of them, in every conceivable style, and wearing every conceivable type of costume.

"It's beautiful out there," he said. "Nothing to see but the stars and the shape of the hills. You could almost believe we're alone on the planet."

"Perhaps it might be a good idea to get away from the window," she said.

"Sorry," he said, moving aside.

"More sake?"

"No thanks."

She raised an ironic eyebrow and put her own drink down on the bedside table. "Come back to bed, barbarian," she said, patting the comforter beside her.

Jarls made his way across the gaudy oriental carpet to Lady Hirakawa's side. He set his empty cup on the table next to hers and sat down on the bed. It creaked under his weight. "My lady . . ." he began.

"Oh, so formal," she teased him. She slipped a hand into his robe and ran it along his ribs and around to the ridged muscles of his back.

"So hard," she said. "Like a carving of solid mahogany."

"My lady . . ." he said again.

"He is talkative tonight," she said. "What's the matter, gladiator? Don't you like your privileges?"

"I was thinking that . . ."

"You are not here to think!" she said sharply. Then, softening, "All right, tell me what is worrying you."

"If Lord Hirakawa . . ."

"Ah, you are afraid that Lord Hirakawa will be angry with you, and that you will be flayed alive. Don't worry, strong man. Lord Hirakawa does not know, and does not want to know. He depends on me to be discreet. And I must trust you to be a sensible gladiator. Of course if Tommy were forced against his will to take notice, that would be another story. He could not allow himself to be humiliated in front of his friends or the servants. And especially he could not allow the slightest whisper of improbity to reach the ears of the royals here and in Japan, or the court in Liechtenstein. Honor is everything. *Meisi subite*, Tommy always says. But reputation is more than everything."

Once again, she had made him feel like an oaf. "I was only thinking of you, my lady," he protested.

"So gallant!" she said, stifling a yawn. "You need not fear for my place in Lord Hirakawa's affections. He is in no position to pretend outrage. Tommy has his own diversions. He's had a taste for Jovian women since he was a schoolboy. The family had a Jovian maid who bathed him. She bathed him a little too vigorously one day. The bruises couldn't be ignored. I'm afraid the rest of the story isn't too pleasant. The poor thing had to be reprimanded and . . . sent away. Tommy's parents were very old school—quite savage in their way. Tommy wept. But he always tries to keep a Jovian housemaid or two around now."

It was more than Jarls wanted to know. He could feel his face burning. It occurred to him that he was in possession of dangerous knowledge.

Lady Hirakawa laughed. "My poor bumpkin, I've embarrassed you, haven't I? Never mind, we earthlings are a wicked lot. Not at all like you virtuous giants."

Jarls was growing angry. "There's no need to go on," he said, his voice turning gruff.

But she would not be deflected. "Oh, don't be such a bloody innocent!" she said. "You must know all about Magda."

"Magda?" he repeated stupidly.

"The Jovian scullery maid. Don't tell me that you're not thick with her."

"N-no. That is, I know her to say good morning to, and so

forth, but Missus Macintyre doesn't encourage familiarity among the staff."

"Really, darling? I'd have thought that when two Jovians get within colliding distance of each other, they'd take advantage of it, like elephants in heat."

"Well we don't!" he said angrily.

"Do you know something, darling, I believe you. But surely the staff must gossip among themselves. About Tommy. And about me."

"They'll gossip about one another," he conceded. "But not about the master or mistress. Mister Arthur and Missus Macintyre wouldn't allow it."

"That's good to hear, darling. But you're allowed to hear gossip from me. You're absolved from a flogging."

It's only a joke, Jarls told himself, suppressing his repugnance at the callousness of the remark. But a chill ran down his spine as he thought of Mary and her outspokenness. "Spare me the gossip," he said, trying to imitate Lady Hirakawa's bantering tone.

She laughed and sailed blithely on. "Missus Macintyre's not pleased with Magda. She's clumsy and musclebound and breaks things. She's stronger than any of the men, and that doesn't sit well. She doesn't look good in a uniform—she's always bursting it at the seams. 'She's not suited, my lady!' That's what Missus Macintyre is always wailing to me. But I can't let her get rid of the creature. Tommy would be furious."

A scowl came and went across Lady Hirakawa's flawless face. "Tommy's courting disaster," she said. "The girl doesn't know her own strength. One day he'll get reckless and push it too far. And then there'll be a sorry mess to clean up."

Jarls was revolted. The desire he had been feeling for Lady Hirakawa turned itself off, and involuntarily he shrank away from her.

She eyed him with frank amusement. "Have I upset the dragon tamer? What a pity. We won't talk about such things anymore, darling." She opened the silk pajama top and pressed herself against his unyielding torso. Unwillingly, Jarls felt his desire return. "That's better," she said. "Now pick me up and carry me over to the refectory table in front of the doll cabinet. The bed's too soft. This time I'll have a try at being compressed between two hard surfaces."

Lord Hirakawa returned from his travels a week later, tired and cranky from his month-long inspection trip of EarthCorp properties in the Pacific and east Asia. He stayed another week, creating turmoil for the estate staff, then took Lady Hirakawa with him to London for a seasonal round of parties and theatergoing. Karsen took advantage of their absence to detach Jarls temporarily from his household assignment and put him to work helping to beef up grounds security for an expected influx of Hirakawa relatives and hangers-on.

"The same freeloaders show up every year about this time, and profess to be surprised that his lordship and her ladyship are away," Karsen said sourly to Jarls. "But they can't be turned away. They've got to be given the red carpet treatment anyway. It's part of the famous Strathspey reputation for hospitality, and Lord Hirakawa has to entertain them in absentia whether he likes them very much or not. They're a demanding lot—run the staff ragged. But they've got to be humored and cosseted. His lordship will have the hide of any servant his uninvited guests complain about."

Czoznek arrived just then with a floppyscreen. He passed it across the desk to Karsen. "Here's what Mister Arthur has for us so far," he said. He looked over at Jarls. "Off soft duty, are you, Anders?" he said. "One of the troops again?"

"Can it, Czoznek," Karsen said. He ran a finger down the list, frowning to himself. "Hmmm . . . the Chumford-Minamotos are here, as usual. Poor relations—I think they're fifth cousins of the Hirakawas. They're not even in the peerage. They bought a manorial title at auction some time in the twenty-first century. Got a rundown castle with it, but no privileges. They've been on their uppers ever since. Keep an eye on the children, Anders. They're light-fingered. Made off with a gold tea service last time."

"Yes sir," Jarls said.

Karsen continued down the list. "Here's bad news," he said, stopping halfway down. "Lady Hirakawa. The Dowager Duchess of Webrey. Flies into rages. Whipped a chambermaid with her cane last time over an imaginary wrinkle in the sheets. Laid the girl's cheek open, blood everywhere. Never apologized to her hosts. Nobody invites her anywhere these days, but she invites herself. Anders, tell Missus Macintyre to warn the chambermaids. Maybe we can head off another incident."

"I will, sir," Jarls said.

Karsen scrolled to the next page. "Hello, what's this? It's Sir Cyril Fujisaki, the laird's black sheep nephew. Now, *he* has no business here. He's been banished from Strathspey. Lord Hirakawa himself told him in no uncertain terms that he's not welcome here."

"Can't you evict him, sir?" Jarls asked. "If that's the case, that is?"

Karsen shook his head. " 'Fraid not. Not authorized. Only the laird can kick him out. Too big a scandal if a servant did it. We'll have to watch him, that's all."

"Could you at least call Lord Hirakawa in London?"

Karsen grimaced. "It would be worth my head. His lordship would not want to be bothered. We're supposed to handle these little things for him. Of course, we're on the chopping block if things go wrong."

Czoznek pursed his lips and said, "Fujisaki's trouble. Remember that business at the Duke of Cornwall's? Breach of the rules of hospitality. The man's ungovernable."

"What happened?" Jarls asked.

"He injured a Jovian maid. The Duke's younger daughter's personal maid, as it happens. The man's a Junophile. And with a taste for hurting them, unfortunately. The Duke didn't want to make a fuss, but the story got around. Fujisaki wasn't fazed in the least, though. He's an arrogant bastard. Knows we've got a Jovian scullery maid here at Strathspey . . . what's her name?"

"Magda."

Czoznek nodded. "Bothered her the last time he was here, he did. She was able to fend him off, fortunately. The laird got wind of it somehow. I guess that's why he read Fujisaki the riot act. Now the sod's after her again. Why else would he show his face here when he knows the laird's away?"

"That's enough, Czoznek," Karsen said mildly. "We'll keep an eye on Sir Cyril and try to head off any trouble as discreetly as possible."

"Couldn't we just arrange to move Magda out of Strathspey entirely while Fujisaki's here?" Jarls suggested. "Keep her out of sight in one of the outlying gardeners' bothies, or still better, spirit her off to the laird's fishing cottage in the islands? She could be assigned to the skeleton staff there."

"It's worth a try," Karsen said, rubbing his chin. "We'd have to get Missus Macintyre to cooperate. And that'd be touchy, interfering with her prerogatives."

"The fishing cottage would be better," Czoznek said. "Fujusaki would sniff her out if she were anywhere on the grounds. But Missus Macintyre would never agree to it. She runs a tight ship. I can hear her now. 'What, give the girl a seaside holiday with nothing to do? The lazy slut!' I've heard her. She has it in for the girl. She's looking for an excuse to get rid of her."

Jarls, remembering what Lady Hirakawa had told him, silently had to agree with Czoznek. But he said, "Missus Macintyre can't possibly want an incident with one of her kitchen slaveys."

"All right," Karsen said. "Anders, you go see Missus Macintyre. Put it to her as a security matter. Say the recommendation came from me."

"Yes sir," Jarls said.

The kitchen was still cleaning up after the enormous breakfast that had been served to the invading horde of freeloaders. A battery of kitchen maids was busy polishing the covered silver serving dishes and scraping the congealed remains off the engraved plates and into garbage cans. The guests' leavings—half-eaten lamb chops, grilled kidneys, smoked salmon, boiled eggs with rice, oatmeal, caviar-smeared toast, sticky puddles of honey—were enough to have fed the starveling inhabitants of the nearby village twice over.

Jarls saw Magda, lifting a heavy oak sideboard off the floor while another scullery maid mopped under it. Her corn-colored hair was knotted up in two thick braids, and there was a thin sheen of perspiration on her snub nose and florid cheeks. She was built like a barrel, with flat, dinner-plate breasts pushing at a uniform that was dangerously tight on her. Her arms bulged with Jovian muscle, turning her sleeves into sausages. She gave Jarls a side-long look as he passed, but did not attempt to greet him.

He found Missus Macintyre in the pantry, doing her accounts. She turned a pinched face in his direction and gave him a sour stare. "What are you doing in my kitchen?" she said. "Ye ha' no business here."

He was at a loss how to proceed. "It's about Lord Fujisaki," he said. "Mister Karsen says . . ."

"I know why ye're here," she snapped. "I will not have you saying things against the guests of Strathspey. I've a good mind to report you."

"But your scullery maid, Magda . . ."

"She's a wicked girl. She led Lord Fujisaki on the last time he was here. And I caught her talking to him in the passageway this morning before breakfast. She'll be punished!"

Jarls raised his eyebrows. "Lord Fujisaki was sniffing around here this morning?"

"That's enough! Lord Fujisaki came down for an early cup of tea before breakfast. The footman who was supposed to bring it to his room was tardy, and I'll speak to Mister Arthur about *that*! Now if ye're done interfering with the running of the kitchen, then I'll thank you to leave!"

Jarls saw that it was hopeless and turned to go. On his way out through the kitchen, he saw that Magda had a scratch down one cheek. He wondered what Fujisaki looked like.

Karsen was making his rounds, so Jarls didn't get to see him till almost noon. He found the security chief in the boat house, checking out the small fleet of pleasure craft that Lord Hirakawa kept for his guests.

"Give me a hand with this catboat, will you, Anders?" Karsen said. "It's one of the laird's antiques, made of solid wood. The homing beacon should be somewhere aft of the mast step."

Jarls helped Karsen turn the boat over. It only weighed a couple of thousand pounds.

"Homing beacon?" Jarls said.

"Safety precaution," Karsen said. "All of these craft have them. Some of the laird's guests think they're better sailors than they are. They'll run out of power or run out of wind, or not have the faintest idea of how to come about. The alarm blinks on the monitor screen here when they're about twenty miles downstream, and we send someone to assist. Can't have them being swept out into the North Sea."

"The North Sea? I thought the river ran to London."

Karsen laughed. "I can see you're not well versed in Earth geography. It's not at all like Jupiter, where there're no fixed landmarks, is it? London's some distance south of here, on the Thames. The Dee runs eastward into the North Sea. Not the kind of place where you'd care to be adrift in a small craft."

It was not like Karsen to be casually garrulous. Jarls had the feeling that the security chief was trying to tell him something, then dismissed the notion as foolish.

"Ah, here it is," Karsen said, holding up a small object that had been disguised to look like an eye bolt, and looked sturdy enough to serve the purpose. "Dead as a doornail." He screwed in a replacement, and turned to Jarls with a face that had gone stony again. "What is it, Anders?"

"I'm afraid Missus Macintyre wasn't in a mood to cooperate, sir. We'll just have to try to keep an eye on Fujisaki, as you said before."

"It doesn't matter anymore," Karsen said. "Lord Fujisaki was seen about half an hour ago at the Strathspey mag-lev terminal, boarding a capsule back to London." His voice took on a tone of grim satisfaction. "He was observed to be walking with a decided limp, and there was a swelling under one eye. Apparently he decided to leave rather abruptly, without bothering to notify the household staff."

Jarls digested that. "Will Magda be punished?"

"I doubt it. Lord Fujisaki will not be anxious to complain to his lordship."

The swarm of self-invited guests was long gone when Lord and Lady Hirakawa returned from their London holiday, like flies buzzing away from a picnic table before they could be swatted. Jarls was on hand when the Hirakawas arrived, waiting on the lawn with the rest of the security staff and the household servants who were lined up in twin rows to welcome their employers back.

A convoy of three hover limos arrived from the lord's private spaceport on the other side of the valley and settled to the grass with a subsiding wheeze of air cushions. Lady Hirakawa climbed out of the lead limo, looking flushed and in high spirits. Her arms were full of wrapped parcels, which she passed to the footman who had opened the door. Toshiko followed with more packages.

Lord Hirakawa emerged next, looking disgruntled. He had been riding up front with the driver instead of in the passenger compartment with his wife and her maid. He took his place dutifully beside Lady Hirakawa and gave her his arm. The remaining two limos disgorged a bevy of servants, presumably from the London town house, who were loaded down with more packages and shopping bags.

Lord Hirakawa dispensed with all pomp, waving aside a hovering Mister Arthur and a distressed parlor maid who was trying to present a bouquet of flowers to Lady Hirakawa. He seemed distracted, impatient, as he hurried Lady Hirakawa past the assembled ranks as if they were so much shrubbery.

Jarls stiffened as Lady Hirakawa walked past him without even a glance in his direction. He told himself that he was an idiot, that it would be unrealistic of him to expect her to show even the slightest awareness of his presence. But three weeks without her had left him in torment.

Lord Hirakawa was not as scrupulous as his wife. Or perhaps he couldn't help himself. As he strode past the little assemblage of curtsying kitchen maids, Jarls saw his eyes stray momentarily toward the rear rank, where Magda had been put.

Jarls suffered through the next week. It was bad enough to be deprived of the nighttime summonses from Lady Hirakawa—something he could not hope for anyway with the lord in residence—but Karsen for some reason had not reassigned him to his former spot on the household security detail, and he was denied even the sight of her during the day.

It was agony to be shut off from her this way. Jarls took stock of himself. He needed her like a drug—that much he could admit. He knew that his obsession was insane, but he could not help himself. He refused to think about the hopelessness of the situation or about its dangers. He dwelt only on the probability that sooner or later Lord Hirakawa would depart Strathspey for a day or a week or a month, without taking Lady Hirakawa with him, and there would once again be a middle-of-the-night invitation, delivered by Toshiko.

He got the first part of his wish—Lord Hirakawa's departure—in a way he had not imagined. He was busy with a routine early morning patrol near the rear facade of the house when he heard a familiar whipcrack in the sky. He looked upward to see the lord's transatmospheric ramjet swooping in to land at the spacedrome across the valley.

"Hello," said his patrolmate, a second-generation Jovian named Harrison. "Somebody got up early to call it in."

One of the estate wagons pulled up at the steps with an overalled maintenance man at the wheel, and a moment later Lord Hirakawa came out the front door, with Mister Arthur and the liveried house doctor at his heels. Lord Hirakawa was dressed in a light robe, worn over pajamas, and his right arm was in a sling. Jarls could see a patch of sticking plaster on his forehead.

Mister Arthur was wringing his hands, and the stout doctor was jabbering at Lord Hirakawa and trying to catch up. The doctor closed the gap and, still trying to get Lord Hirakawa's attention, grabbed him by the sleeve. That was a mistake. Lord Hirakawa stopped in his tracks, half twisted around, and delivered a hefty slap to the face with his good left arm. The doctor backed away in a servile crouch.

Mister Arthur helped Lord Hirakawa into the wagon and the vehicle took off in the direction of the spacedrome.

"What was that about?" Harrison asked.

Jarls said, "Stay here," and went round to the kitchen entrance at a lope. He slowed down to a saunter when he saw the little knot of servants gathered outside the door. Mary was among them.

"What happened?" he asked.

She gave him a look laced with venom. "What are you doing here?" she said. "Come round to sniff at your little Jovian trull, have you?"

His hand closed around her upper arm. "What happened?"

"Ow!" she said, and he let her go. She rubbed her arm and said, "I don't know. Big commotion before dawn. Mister Arthur woke up the doctor and sent him to Lord Hirakawa's suite. The lord rang down for some hot whiskey, and the maid that brought it to him . . . we're not supposed to talk . . ."

"Tell me!" he said, grabbing her arm again.

"Let go, you ape." she said, and he released her. "You know how they are. They'll forget we're in the room and talk in front of us as if we were furniture. Lord Hirakawa was in a temper, a real tantrum, it was. Giving the doctor a terrible dressing down. 'Think I'd let a quack like you put a cast on my arm?' he says. 'I'm going to London to see Sir James.' Then he says to Mister Arthur, 'You'll see to the girl. I don't want to see her stupid face again.' "

"What girl?" Jarls said, knowing the answer.

"Your precious Magda. Think I don't know? Don't mind taking the master's leavings, do you?"

She stopped, putting a hand to her mouth, turning her head to see if anyone had overheard. She didn't mind blackening Jarls, but criticism of the master, implied or otherwise, still wasn't permitted.

Jarls didn't bother denying the accusation. "What's happening to her?" he asked.

"They've got her locked in the pantry for now. They'll deal with her later, Mister Arthur says."

Jarls pushed his way through the door. Missus Macintyre was nowhere in sight, and nobody tried to stop him. The uniform he wore still gave him a modicum of authority.

A large Terran footman was guarding the pantry door. "You can't go in there," he said. "I've got my orders."

Jarls pushed him aside effortlessly. The pantry door was locked. Jarls pressed lightly on the door panel and the lock snapped. The door swung open with a bang, and Jarls stepped through.

Magda was at the far end of the pantry, huddled in a carved Jacobean chair. She looked up fearfully as Jarls approached her. Her face was swollen and wet with tears. She was in her under-wear, incongruously pink and frilly on her heavily muscled body.

"I didn't mean to injure him," she sobbed. "It was an accident. He wanted me to . . . to . . ."

Her accent was native Jovian, from one of the South Equatorial cities, Jarls thought. "How long have you been on Earth?" Jarls asked.

"Almost . . . almost two and a half years. They promised me a job at EarthCorp, a good job. But there was no job. Lord Hira-kawa's estate manager bought my bond from the labor contractor, a man named Stebbins."

"I know Stebbins," Jarls said harshly.

"Lord Hirakawa was so kind to me at first," Magda wept. "Mis-sus Macintyre hated me." She raised a tear-stained face to Jarls. "What's going to happen to me now?"

"I'll see what I can do," Jarls told her.

There was a noise behind him, and he turned around to see the Terran footman advancing cautiously into the room. He'd brought reinforcements—another footman and two hefty odd-men. But they were all earthies, and not anxious to tangle with a Jovian.

"You've got to leave, see?" the footman said in a strained voice.

Jarls shouldered his way past them. They moved aside hastily to give him room. An eavesdropping cluster of frightened servants outside the pantry door parted to let him through.

Behind him, the footman got back his courage and shouted after him, "Just you wait till Mister Arthur gets back!"

Jarls followed the passageways leading to the residence without meeting anyone. There was only one security guard on duty in the great hall, and as luck would have it, it was Jarls's sometime partner, Stern.

"Hullo, Anders, what's up?" Stern queried.

"Lady Hirakawa sent for me," Jarls replied.

Stern checked his thumbnail screen. "You're not on my list."

"It's a very confused morning," Jarls said.

"You can say that again. Lord Hirakawa stormed down the stairs with the butler and doctor in tow, at least two hours before his morning tea is usually brought to him, and stomped past me without a word. No orders, no anything. And then a couple of footmen run up the stairs past me, waving their passes. They never came down again—they must've gone down by the servants' stairs. What's going on?"

"Lord Hirakawa's flying to London."

"In his pajamas?"

"That's all I can say right now," Jarls said in a confidential tone. He started up the marble stairs, and Stern made no effort to stop him. He would have assumed, as Jarls had counted on, that Jarls had been reassigned to his household post, or was soon to be reassigned, now that Lady Hirakawa was back in residence, and that confirmation would come through Karsen later.

He let himself through the double doors to Lady Hirakawa's drawing room and felt an unexpected rush of expectation. It seemed an eternity since he had last been here, and the tall chamber seemed strangely unfamiliar. He paused momentarily at the entrance to the tea room, remembering that he was supposed to take off his boots here, and then, annoyed at himself, pushed his way through.

Toshiko was inside, kneeling at some task. She looked up in alarm at Jarls.

"Jaru-san!" she exclaimed. "You cannot be here!"

"Where is she, Toshiko?" Jarls said. "Is she in there?"

He headed for the bedroom. He heard Toshiko squeaking after him, "Jaru-san, Jaru-san! *Tomari nasai!* You must not to go inside!"

Lady Hirakawa was propped up in bed, sipping tea from a footed lap tray. "What is the meaning of this?" she snapped.

"My lady," he faltered, hearing his voice as if it were coming from a distance, "you have not spoken to me since you've been back at Strathspey. I didn't know what to think."

"And what's that to me?" she said. "It's not up to you to think! You were becoming a bore, darling. And now I think you'd better leave."

"But if I mean anything at all to you, can't you . . ."

"And now you are becoming insolent. Do I have to summon the guard?"

He pushed doggedly on. "I'll go, my lady. I only want to ask about the Jovian maid."

"How touching. You've come to intercede for the Jovian slut."

"What's going to happen to her?"

"She's going to be sold to Lord Hirakawa's nephew, Sir Cyril Fujusaki. He's had his eye on her for some time. I'll find Tommy another Jovian slut—one who's less clumsy."

"You can't do that!"

He took a step forward. Startled, she upset the tray. Tea, croissants, and a pot of honey spilled over the bedclothes. At the doorway behind him, Toshiko screamed. Lady Hirakawa narrowed her eyes and pushed her carpal alarm switch.

Jarls left in a hurry. But he wasn't fast enough. Before he could get halfway across the drawing room, the double doors burst open and Stern came rushing through, drawing his ceremonial pistol. Jarls bowled him over, tore the pistol from his grasp, and bent the barrel into a horseshoe shape so it couldn't be fired.

Stern flung his arms around Jarls's legs and tried to bring him down. But he was only a second-generation Jovian, and no match for Jarls. Jarls pried Stern's arms free, hearing a bone snap in the process, and gave Stern a jolt in the head that floored him altogether.

"Sorry, Stern," Jarls apologized, and fled from the room.

Again he was too late. Two more of Karsen's uniformed Jovians were already bounding up the staircase, guns drawn. Jarls slammed into them, sending them tumbling down the stairs, and ran past them. One of them had cracked his head at the bottom with a sickening thump, and was lying motionless, but the other one, though dazed, was trying to bring his gun to bear. As Jarls reached the front door, there was the *blam* of a great pistol, the *pistoru mhor*, and a bullet whistled past his head. It was poor marksmanship for one of Karsen's trainees, and Jarls thanked his lucky stars that the man had been rattled enough to try to bring him down with the ceremonial weapon instead of spraying him with the lethal little needle gun.

Then he was through the door and running at breakneck speed down the marble terrace and toward the maze of overelaborate shrubbery and painted statuary that bordered the vast expanse of lawn. An alarm was whooping somewhere, alerting the rest of the security force, and Jarls knew he didn't have much time.

His morning's partner, Harrison, came round the corner of the building and took in the situation at a glance.

"Stop, Anders, stop where you are!" Harrison shouted.

He was about a hundred yards distant. Jarls had another hundred yards to go to reach cover. He kept running.

There was no other warning. Jarls looked over his shoulder to see Harrison aiming at him, and remembered that Harrison, who tended toward overkill, had drawn a heavier hand weapon from the armory that morning in addition to the mandatory little *pistoru beg*.

Still running, Jarls waited until he saw a blink at the weapon's muzzle, then hit the ground rolling. The cloud of explosive microflechettes passed overhead and made a small fireworks display against the wall of shrubbery ahead.

Jarls's own weapon was drawn and in his hand without his thinking about it. The dial was already set to the nonlethal trank tank instead of the instant neurotoxin reservoir, the way Jarls habitually locked it in violation of procedure. He sprayed Harrison in a circular motion and hoped for the best. The range was extreme for the tiny finned darts, but the wind was with him and Harrison was facing directly toward him, presenting an optimum expanse of bare face and hands.

Harrison went down instantaneously, pitching forward on the grass, the flat little gun spilling from his hand. Jarls hoped he hadn't killed him. He had emptied the entire magazine of one hundred and twelve microdarts; it only took one hit to knock a man down, but there was a safety margin of at least ten or twenty doses before vital functions were in danger of being fatally depressed—and even more of a margin for a heavyweight Jovian.

Jarls wasted no time. He propelled himself to an all-fours crouch and sprinted for the garden border. There was a maze of paths in there, and the Hirakawa sense of esthetics had ensured that there was no continuous line of sight anywhere, despite the security department's strenuous objections.

The siren was still whooping and Jarls could hear the distant screaming of Toshiko at some open window. His former teammates in Karsen's security force would be fanning out across the grounds now, and there would be someone manning the monitors for the vid eyes and other remote sensing devices.

But Jarls knew the location of every camera, every electronic ear and seismic detector, every chemical sensor, by heart. He had planted many of them himself. He zigzagged through the gardens, trampling the laird's precious flower beds and knocking over ornamental bushes, while avoiding the scattered surveillance devices. A butyric acid sniffer disguised as a garden urn was in his path, more sensitive than any bloodhound. He veered and splashed through a shallow lilly pool, temporarily damping any scent from his boots, and cut across to a shaded avenue of painted statuary where he knew there were no spy eyes for several hundred yards.

The statues stared down at him with their painted eyes as he ran past them. They were singularly vulgar. Lord Hirakawa's landscape architect, an overbearing postneoclassicist he had imported from Calabria, had persuaded him that the ancients had originally painted their marble masterpieces, and that it would be fashionable of him to revive the custom. The result had been the colorization of the classic sculpture that had been standing in the garden all these centuries. Lips and nipples were painted a purplish red, Roman togas and Greek chlamyses were colored in garish hues of chrome yellow and puce, and the garden Priapus sported a livid purple erection.

He was making too much noise as he crashed through hedges and crunched on gravel walks. Something made him stop and listen. There were other sounds between him and the lawn's border—snapped twigs, the rustle of clothing brushing past foliage, muffled footsteps, the clink of metal. They would be spread out by now, closing in on him, spy eyes or not.

An amplified voice blared at him from beyond the screen of vegetation. "I know you're in there, you son of a bitch! Come on out before you get it right between the eyes!"

It was Czoznek. Jarls knew what he was talking about. It was the semi-intelligent mini-missile they called the finger. It would pick out the most likely moving target, whether a fleeing man or light armored vehicle, and stick with it no matter what kind of dodging or evasive maneuver was attempted. For a vehicle it would pick out any likely orifice—an exhaust pipe, an air vent, a gun slit—and do its exploding inside. For a man, its primitive visual recognition system would pick a spot right between the eyes. If the man were running away, it would zip past him, make a U-turn, and zero in for a sure kill.

Czoznek was not one to hesitate. Jarls heard the unmistakable whoosh of a finger leaving its hand-held launcher and popping its fins. It would be no good to try to stand stock-still and pretend to be an inanimate object. The finger could detect even a hair of movement that differentiated a target from its surroundings.

A spear of blue flame spurted past his head and for a fraction of a second the tiny missile hung six feet in front of his face like a metallic dragonfly.

Instantly, Jarls uprooted the marble statue next to him and held it at arm's length in front of him. It weighed about half a ton, and he wouldn't have been able to hold it motionless if he had tried.

The involuntary tremor in his arms created enough motion to interest the missile's flyspeck brain, and the painted eyes were realistic enough for its rudimentary visual circuits. It took half a tick to adjust its guidance fins, and then there was a stab of motion too fast to follow.

The statue's head exploded and showered Jarls with a hail of marble chips. But a cubic foot of stone had shielded him from the force of the explosion, and he suffered only a few minor cuts on his face and hands.

"Got him!" Czoznek shouted from somewhere behind the curtain of greenery.

At once there was the sound of heavy boots trampling down shrubbery and heading in the direction of the explosion.

"Over this way!" Czoznek shouted, and there were answering hails from down the line.

It was poor procedure, Jarls thought critically. Czoznek should have waited for backup to catch up to him. But Czoznek, though he had a high opinion of himself, had always been impetuous.

Jarls set the headless statue down in an overgrown bed of ferns at the edge of the path and flung himself prone behind a thick hedge. Czoznek appeared moments later, holding the missile launcher tucked under one arm and keeping a murderous little dumbgun sweeping back and forth with his free hand.

He stopped at the fallen statue, took in the situation at a glance, and spun in a full circle with the gun pointed in front of him. Jarls popped up from behind the hedge while Czoznek was still a quarter turn away from facing him, grabbed the statue by the ankles, and swung it two-handed like a great stone bat.

Czoznek tried to duck, but he was a shade too late. The statue swatted him at head and neck level with all its considerable mass. He had dropped the missile launcher and flung up an arm at the last instant to protect himself, but the tremendous impact lifted him off his feet and dropped him a couple of yards away, with the statue on top of him. Even at the last moment, he'd had the presence of mind to hang on to his hand weapon, and must have been trying reflexively to bring it to bear on Jarls, because a stream of microdarts made an arc of small explosions that chewed up the shrubbery but stopped short of its human target.

Czoznek wasn't moving. The upflung arm kept Jarls from seeing the damage to his head, and Jarls was glad of that. He briefly considered robbing Czoznek's body of its weapon and any spare magazines, but he didn't have the stomach for it.

He didn't have the time for it either. He could hear the other searchers beating closer to his position. They'd heard the finger explode, and they'd heard the stream of explosive darts go off, and they must have assumed that Czoznek had finished him off. So they wouldn't be hurrying. But he didn't have any time to spare.

Czoznek hadn't yelled to them again, and someone called, "Czoz, what's happening?" When he didn't answer, the man called again.

When he still didn't answer, they started to worry. Jarls heard a brief urgent babble of voices, and then the sounds of running feet.

Jarls took off at high speed, not caring anymore about the noise he was making. He was less than a hundred yards from the estate's security perimeter.

He made a beeline for the nearest blind spot he could remember from his training, making no effort to avoid the hidden camera eyes that would show him heading in that direction. Then, out of camera range, he changed direction abruptly and burst through the thick hedge marking the boundary.

He came out at a sheep meadow. There wasn't a shred of cover on the whole twenty or thirty acres. But if his little deception had managed to fool his pursuers, they would be wasting precious minutes on a patch of woodland that faced the exit that he had pretended to be heading for.

Karsen had a helicopter in the air now. Jarls could hear the flapping of the blades no more than a mile away and getting louder. It was flying low, but as the geometry improved, it would be able to spot him from the air.

He didn't stop running. He was fully exposed no matter what he did. With luck, he might make it to the far side of the meadow where there was a neglected apple orchard, a tangle of stunted trees and overgrown weeds that had been left untouched by the landscape gardeners.

He was in among the sheep now. They scattered, bleating. They were bigger and fluffier than the Scottish breeds of centuries past, bioengineered for size and ornamental value, but cloning hadn't improved their brain power.

He snatched one off the ground as he passed, and lifted it over his head. It struggled for a moment, then went limp, as the docility reflex that had been bred into it for shearing purposes took over.

The other sheep forgot their momentary panic and drew into a cohesive flock again. Jarls moved with them, crouched low to the ground, with his wooly burden lying passively across his back.

The helicopter burst into view, skimming over the hedge tops at a height of about forty feet. The sheep didn't scatter this time. The helicopter was not a predator in among the flock. Instead, they drew together into a tighter group. Jarls worked his way to the center of the flock, nudging sheep aside. They baahed at him, but obliged.

The helicopter circled the flock once, herding the sheep into an even tighter group in the process. Then it rose into the air again, overflying the bunched sheep as it veered to inspect the patch of woods that Jarls had previously feinted at.

The downdraft from the blades stirred Jarls's hair and riffled the wool of the sheep lying across his back, and then it was gone. The helicopter hadn't noticed him, either from above or from its low angle to the side, hemmed in as he was by the clumped animals. And, he was sure, infrared detectors and chemical sniffers wouldn't have been able to separate him from the living barrier that sheltered him.

Jarls breathed again. He began to move obliquely toward the edge of the meadow, and found that the flock of sheep tended to move with him, as long as he wasn't too abrupt. Either the sheep he had on his back was the bellwether, or the animals were suggestible to any purposeful movement by a member of the flock.

It took another fifteen minutes of vectored zigzagging before he reached the other edge of the meadow. Before he got there, a small armored vehicle pushed its way through the ornamental hedges on the garden side, came out a hundred yards or so for a perfunctory inspection, then turned on its treads and went back where it had come from.

Jarls lowered himself to his belly and slid out from under his sheltering sheep. He crawled flat to the ground through a fringe of tall weeds into the concealing underbrush that had taken over the apple orchard. The sheep that had camouflaged him came out of its trance, rose to its feet, and shook itself off. Soon it was grazing. The rest of the flock, deprived of its momentary purpose, began desultorily to disperse through the meadow again.

Jarls stayed in the abandoned orchard until nightfall, wedged under the trunk of a fallen tree. Insects plagued him, and once a curious squirrel came to have a look at him before scurrying off. The helicopter overflew the meadow twice more during the day, but nothing came of it. From time to time he could hear muffled loudspeaker commands coming from the direction of the manor house, and that was a great incentive to remain still.

After dark, he eased himself cautiously from his hiding place. He stretched found a few withered apples for his supper.

He knew from security protocol what would happen next. The starveling villagers would be roused at dawn to form a line of beaters to comb through the woods. Hannes Karsen would be relentless. There would be orders to shoot Jarls on sight, or still worse, to tranquilize him and bring him back for punishment. In that case there would be a summary trial before a tame court. The charges would be murder and attempted rape. Czoznek's body, and, possibly, Stern's, would be evidence enough of the former, and Lady Hirakawa's word of the latter. The penalty would be death if he was lucky, or life in the Mercurian mines if he wasn't.

He formed a threadbare plan, the only one he could think of. If he could get past the sleeping villagers while it was still dark, find another hiding place somewhere beyond the village and stay hidden through the following day, he could attempt to double back toward the river the next night. He knew the way Karsen's mind worked. Karsen would consider the territory between the village and the estate grounds to be well swept. He would then assume that Jarls had escaped overland—north toward Moray Firth or west toward Loch Ness—and issue a general alert to the constabulary. It wouldn't occur to him that Jarls would be so foolish as to choose to return to the estate grounds.

A light drizzle had started. The stars were obscured and a thin mist was rising from the ground. Good. That would improve his odds.

He worked his way in wary stages in the general direction of the village, moving from cover to cover. There were thick old trees, grown up in the centuries since this land had been denuded by earlier generations, the remains of ancient stone walls and rotting fences that had accumulated in the last century or two, the over-grown foundations of vanished cottages. Jarls took advantage of them all.

The village was only a couple of miles away, but it took him hours to reach its outskirts. Jarls was thoroughly soaked by now, but he ignored the discomfort.

He parted the foliage to have a look. There was enough light to see a dim outline of roofs and stone chimneys, and there were still a few people awake, judging by the pale yellow glow marking some of the windows. The laird's village was a miserable collection of hovels, with swaybacked rooflines and broken walls. But, Jarls reminded himself, people lived here. And they all lived by the sufferance of Lord Hirakawa.

He waited another hour, watching the lights go out one by one. When all the windows were dark, he moved out from cover, easing himself on hands and knees through the weed field surrounding the collection of cottages. He kept to the weeds, moving laterally to circle the village and come out behind it at a distance of a few hundred yards. Nobody would be heading in that direction in the early morning when the laird's gamekeepers rousted the beaters out of their beds.

Another quarter hour of inching himself along brought him to the rear of the village. Worse luck! It was a patchwork of individual garden plots, with no cover to speak of.

Jarls was exhausted. Even his Jovian body was depleted after a nonstop terrestrial day and half a terrestrial night. It was used to ten-hour Jupiter days, doubled back to back to provide a break in the middle.

He looked longingly at the row of tumbledown garden sheds at the far end of the vegetable patches and made up his mind. A couple of hours of sleep, out of the rain, and he'd be fit to find himself a hiding place for the next day in the scrub beyond. He'd be out of there long before the villagers woke up.

He looked over his shoulder at the village houses and saw no lights or movement. Moving at a half crouch, he swiftly crossed the garden plot to the likeliest of the sheds. A weathered door hung from one hinge. He eased it open and stepped inside, then pulled the door shut behind him.

It was dark inside. He felt around and his hands encountered rough-handled tools leaning against the walls, dented buckets hanging from nails, burlap sacks with unknown contents. There was a pile of rags in the corner. Gratefully, Jarls curled up on the floor, using the rags for a pillow.

He had just closed his eyes when someone yanked the door open. A lantern shone light in his face.

"Thought you could hide in here, did you?" a voice said. "Bloody stupid! Get up!"

# 17

J ARLS BLINKED and sat up. His discoverer was a gaunt woman with straggly hair. One hand held a lantern. In the other was a wicked looking sickle with a rusty blade.

He tensed. He didn't want to hurt her. And he wasn't sure anyway that he could move fast enough to grab her wrist before she could take a swipe at him. And then all she had to do was scream once to bring the men of the village running. He gave it up for the moment.

"There's a reward out for you," she said.

"I'm sure."

"You must have been raised indoors, ye puir witless loon, to leave wet footprints in the mud right up to the door and never think they'd be noticed. 'Twas lucky for me there was a weepon to hand by the door, but ye never noticed that either, I ken."

She brandished the curved blade at him, alarmingly close to his face.

"I didn't," he admitted.

He squinted at her. The shadows cast by the lantern gave her a flickering goblin's face. She looked somehow familiar, but he couldn't place her.

"Stay back," she warned, gesturing with the sickle.

He held himself still. "Are you going to turn me in?" he said.

She spat, "I have no love for the laird and all his rascal gillies and the birkie lot he brings to Strathspey." She was staring with loathing at Jarls's gray uniform.

And then he had it. She was the woman who the gamekeeper, Symington, had tried to pay off with a roll of banknotes during the grouse drive, after Vanius Paes had killed the little girl with his shotgun. She had refused the money and attempted to attack Symington, but an old man had held her back and taken the money in her stead.

He waited, not saying anything.

"My little Meg was buried without a head," she said.

"I'm sorry."

"You were one of them that day, one of the bulky men," she said tearfully.

So that was what the villagers called the Jovian security force. "Yes," he said.

"And now they're after you."

"Yes."

She sniffed. "I don't know what you did, and I don't care," she said. "It was against them, that's all I care about. I've seen wha' happens when they catch somebody. The puir devils. A flogging's the least of it."

He waited.

She sighed. "Come along wi' me, then. Old Henry will be out here in the morning. He'll do anything for a groat. I'll trample your footprints away on me way back."

She put down the sickle and blew out the lantern. Jarls followed her out the door. The drizzle was abating.

"Step softly now," she whispered at him. "Don't make so bloody much noise."

She led him into the underbrush beyond the gardens. A hundred yards farther on, he almost fell into a steep declivity that was disguised by a growth of brambles and weeds and close to invisible in the darkness.

"Take care now," she said, taking his arm and guiding him down the slope. There were tumbled blocks of stone that once might have been a foundation or a wall.

"This was an old cow byre, long time past," she said. "But there have not been cows here in living memory. The children play here sometimes, but they will not play tomorrow, what wi' the rain. Those of them who are too young or too feckless to be allowed on the drive. Oh yes, there's to be a drive for you in the morning, as if you were any game."

She dragged him by the arm through the brambles to a corner of the old foundation. It was four or five feet below the level of the surrounding land.

"You can crawl under those timbers," she said. "They're long rotted away to punk, but they'll hold their shape. I'll pile some thatch on top."

Jarls did as she said. He heard her rummaging around for straw and weeds.

"That'll do," she said. "It's two hours till dawn. Ye're not to move while it's still light. After that, ye're on your own. They won't be looking for you too hard by then, here near Strathspey. They'll have figured you've gone south. If ye're caught . . ."

"I won't say anything."

"That may not be up to you," she said dryly.

"I don't know how to thank you. If I ever . . ."

"Ye're not to know my name!" she cried in alarm. Then, more calmly, "Remember, ye're to lie still till next dark." He heard a faint rustle of weeds as she scrambled up the slope, and then she was gone.

He managed to doze fitfully in his burrow of straw and rotten wood, despite the clammy mist that seeped through. At dawn he was awakened by the sound of activity around the cottages as the laird's gamekeepers roused the inhabitants and got them organized into a ragged line of beaters. A light drizzle still persisted, and there were delays as the gillies rounded up those who had attempted to sneak away. At last the line began moving in the direction of the grouse moor and the bordering woods. The sounds grew fainter. Jarls risked a look, poking his face up to a gap between the riddled timbers. Through a fringe of dead weeds, he saw the little makeshift white flags moving off into the distance

At about noon, there was a rustling in the weeds, and the woman who had hidden him came scrambling down the slope with a burlap-wrapped bundle.

"They hae nae returned yet, but stay hid. Old Henry did nae go with them, and he is sniffing around. He knows I went out last night, and he asked if I had a man now, and I let him think what he thinks. I brought you a wee morsel to eat. It's only some drammach and cold collops, but I did not dare to cook anything."

She thrust the burlap-wrapped parcel at him, and then produced a heavy, coarse shirt. "This belonged to my man before little Meg died and he left. He was almost as big as you and perhaps it will fit. You'd best get rid of that jupe ye're wearing. The whole world will be looking for it." She fingered the fabric of his tunic and said regretfully, " 'Tis fine cloth."

"Do you want it?"

She recoiled. "Na, na! Get rid of it as soon as you can, and don't leave it here!"

He nodded. "I'm sorry I have nothing to give you."

"Wheesht, mon! Be off at nightfall. And good luck to ye."

When she had gone, he untied the burlap bundle and found a lumpy mixture of uncooked oatmeal and water and some fragments of an unidentifiable gray meat. He wolfed it down hungrily. It was hardly enough to fill a Jovian stomach, but he had not eaten for more than a day.

The villagers straggled back in the late afternoon. Jarls could make out the indistinct sound of voices for an hour or two as they went about their outdoor chores, but the chill rain drove them back inside their hovels long before sunset. Karsen's search helicopter, which he had been hearing intermittently through the day, made a final desultory circle around the village, then flew back to its distant pad and was heard no more.

When all the windows had finally gone dark, he emerged from his hiding place and stretched with a loud cracking of bones. He tried on the old patchwork shirt he had been given. It was a bit tight across the chest, but it would do. He turned his gray tunic inside out and wadded it up to be disposed of at the first opportunity. There was nothing he could do about his boots and uniform trousers for the moment, but they were muddied and disreputable looking, and perhaps would get by at a distance.

The rain had stopped by now, but there still was an oppressive mist in the air. Jarls made a wide circle around the village, then struck a straight course for the manor grounds along the river bank, keeping well to the concealing bracken.

He could make out the outlines of the boat house now—a low hexagonal shape with a cupola. Jarls moved inland another thirty feet to avoid the spy eye that he knew scanned the area near the riverbank. The next camera was three hundred feet farther inshore; Jarls knew because he had planted it there himself.

He breached the security perimeter halfway between the two cameras, with a margin of safety at least a dozen feet wide on either side. It was a gamble, but Karsen's guard would be down now that his security sweep had failed. The last thing he would be expecting was that his quarry would be so reckless as to double back after getting safely away.

No one was about. He vaulted over the verandah railing and in a few swift strides was at a side door. He broke the lock just by leaning on the door with his Jovian strength and let himself inside.

The laird's sizable fleet of sailing craft was in for seasonal over-haul. Jarls's eyes roved over a bewildering array of boats in all shapes and sizes, most of them on trestles or shrouded by tarps. He needed a boat that was large enough to be seaworthy, but not so large as to attract undue attention floating down the river Dee. He had no idea what constituted seaworthiness in a terrestrial ocean, so he looked for something that promised to be stout and simple to handle.

He settled on the antique catboat that he had examined with Karsen earlier. The mast was unstepped and lashed to the hull at present, but Jarls remembered that the sail arrangement was extremely basic, with no jib to worry about. There was a small cuddy forward for shelter. The boat was comfortably broad in the beam, promising stability, and about thirty feet long.

But more important, he knew where the homing beacon was.

He unscrewed the false eye bolt that contained the device and left it under the tarpaulin of a nearby sailing canoe. When the man on duty checked his board for the beacons, it would tell him that the catboat was still in the boat shed.

Next he raided the steward's pantry for supplies. The refrigerator and cupboards had been neglected since the last regatta, but he was able to find some stale bread and biscuits, cheese, tinned pate, and a jar of caviar. He filled as many containers as he could find with tap water, and stowed it all in the cuddy.

The boat was solid, the way people had made things in past centuries, with a heavy oak frame and planks that were correspondingly thick. It had taken two Jovians to lift it before, but Jarls dragged it off its cradle and let it fall to the floor with a thump that shook the boat house. He dragged it to the wide sliding door, broke another lock, and pulled it out to the boat ramp. There was no way to avoid noise, and he was out in the open now. He could only cross his fingers and hope for the best.

He slid the door shut behind him. It was unlikely that anyone would check the ramp door in the morning, unused as it was at present, and the other door that he had forced might not attract attention either, accidentally broken locks not being that uncommon when there were a lot of Jovians around.

He pushed the boat ahead of him down the ramp, picking up speed and vaulting aboard just before it hit the water. The push had sent the craft to the center of the river, and now it spun round, straightened itself out, and was picked up by the current. He rested a while as the boat drifted downstream, and when the rooftops of Strathspey were safely out of sight behind him, he set about stepping the mast. The mast was an antique, too; it was solid hardwood and taller than the boat was long. No two earthmen could have handled it without a block and tackle. Jarls wrapped both arms around it, levered it upright while the catboat heeled alarmingly, and with a grunt, dropped it into place.

The sail, fortunately, was not a heavy canvas antique, as it should have been. Out of consideration for Lord Hirakawa's usual lubberly guests, it was a lightweight modern synthetic, easily hoisted and handled. Jarls got it aloft after a brief struggle with the unfamiliar ropes, and watched as it was filled by a stiff breeze from the west. The catboat required minimum handling. Between the breeze and the current, Jarls found himself moving downstream at a pretty good clip.

Night traffic on the river was light. Jarls learned the rules of the road after being shouted at by passing helmsmen, and also learned, to his bemused delight, that sailboats had certain ancient privileges over powered craft.

The sun came up blindingly ahead of him. River traffic picked up in the early morning light. Jarls had his first good look at the river Dee. It was gray and impenetrable, dotted with busy vessels of every sort. There were enough small pleasure craft intermingled with the passenger and commercial traffic to make Jarls confident that the catboat would not be especially conspicuous.

He turned his gaze shoreward. He was on the outskirts of Aberdeen now. Buildings crammed either bank, getting taller and taller, jammed together in an unbroken fence of gray stone and bright structural plastics. There was no waterfront to speak of. A twisting skein of elevated roadways and concrete mag-lev conduits made a border between the river and the jumble of skyscrapers.

He stared at the soaring marvel, frankly agog. It was his first look at an Earth city. More people were crowded into this one place than lived on all of Jupiter. Jarls felt like a rustic indeed.

But Earthians evidently felt that there were never enough of them. Jarls was amazed to see flotillas of ramshackle boats anchored close offshore like floating hamlets, with whole families living aboard. A naked child sitting on the fantail of one of the makeshift craft waved enthusiastically at Jarls as he drifted past, until its mother, a skin-and-bones woman in ragged clothes, came out from the thatch-roofed shelter and dragged it inside. Jarls could not say he blamed her. Gentlemen in expensive pleasure boats who approached the floating slum were not to be trusted.

He could smell the sea now. Jarls had grown up with the stale fragrance of recycled air in his nostrils, but the sharp salt tang

awakened some atavistic instinct in him, and he immediately recognized the smell of the ocean for what it was.

He ate a little bread and cheese, and took a swig of water, keeping one hand on the tiller to steer with. The river was widening.
Soon he would be out on the open sea.

Now he had a new problem. So far the wind had been more or
less behind him, and the catboat's forgiving rig had done all the
work. But now he was going to have to somehow sail southward
along England's coast until he reached a jumping-off point for the
Continent. He knew there was a way for a sailboat to sail at an
angle to the wind. He'd heard some of the nautically inclined
manor house guests talk about it. It was called "tacking." But he
didn't have the slightest idea of how to do it.

He patted the letter in his pocket, the letter that Ian Karg had
given him so long ago on Jupiter. It was still there in its sealed
envelope. It had never left his person in all the time he'd spent in
the hellhole of Venus and in the purgatory of the Hirakawa estate.
It was addressed to Karg's old companion in Greater Liechtenstein,
an Executive Guardsman named . . . Jarls struggled to remember
without having to draw the envelope from its hiding place . . .
Leith Carnevan.

It was insane to try to reach Liechtenstein, when he knew nothing of Earth. But it would be more insane still to remain in Britain,
where he was a hunted fugitive. All of Earth cooperated in returning indentured workies. But Liechtenstein was crowded, and he
could lose himself there as well as anyplace else while he figured
out what to do next.

He had no idea whether he was still in the mouth of the river or
out to sea. At one point, a gigantic tanker, probably loaded with
fresh water from the Arctic, almost ran him down. But he escaped
with no more than a bad joggling from its wake and a thorough
drenching. He watched it slide by at a distance of less than twenty
yards, a monstrous metal cliff with no portholes and no sign of
human presence.

He sailed another couple of miles out to sea, or so he judged,
and, well out of sight of land, he attempted to learn how to come

about. He still had the sun in the sky to give him direction, and he steered the craft closer and closer to a southerly course until the sail began to flutter and at last held no wind. But at what he guessed to be another forty-five degrees or so, the sail, miracle of miracles, began to fill again on the opposite side. He swung the boat back to its old heading, and the same thing happened in reverse.

Jarls's elation faded almost immediately. He realized he knew nothing about navigation under Earth's night sky. He could find the Big Dipper and the Pole Star, after some hours of night duty at Strathspey, but other than that, he was at a loss.

Still, he told himself, it couldn't be that complicated. He could sail by daylight, keeping the coastline just within sight, and maintain his southerly heading.

It was a seductive thought. He'd had no sleep the night before. He yawned through the rest of the day, kept awake only by nervous energy. With his new-found skill at tacking, he found the coast again and followed it southward. The sun rose predictably until its high point at noon, then began to decline again.

The ocean was immense. He had thought it would be a little thing compared to the enormous scale of Jupiter, but the reality of this vast expanse of water was unsettling. Earth was a water planet, with three quarters of its surface covered by the precious stuff, some of it miles deep.

The gray water stretched as far as the eye could see, an awesome and frightening sight. It was flat, too, despite the choppy waves, totally unlike the familiar towering cloudscapes of his home planet. Jarls became all too aware that he could not swim. With his Jovian body mass, he was too dense to float. If he were unlucky enough to fall overboard, he would sink like a stone.

He shivered, and took refuge in the dim and misty vision of the Scottish shoreline, only a couple of miles away. It was no comfort at all. It was still too far, across that alien expanse of dark water. After some thought, he fashioned a harness and tether for himself out of a length of spare rope and fastened it to the mast.

He dozed, despite himself. He forced his gummy eyes open at least a dozen times through what was left of the afternoon, but when darkness fell over the sea, he sank into a sodden and irresistible sleep.

He was awakened after an eternity by raindrops hard as bullets falling on his face and head. The stars were gone. A brisk wind was rising.

The wind became a violent squall, then something worse. Jarls was not an experienced sailor. By the time he thought to take down the sail, it was too late. The wind was already tearing it to shreds.

The boat heeled over violently. The mast gave with a loud crack and toppled into the water, dragging the boat over still further. A mountain of water, dozens of feet high, appeared out of the night and crashed into the crippled vessel.

The next thing Jarls knew, he was in the water, gasping and choking. He had the presence of mind to draw a huge breath, and then he was under.

It was more frightening than falling through the helium depths of Jupiter. There, he had been inside a closed suit, still able to breathe, though he knew a swift end awaited him when the mounting pressure crushed the suit. Here, he was fighting his own lungs, unable to breathe. He had no idea if he was still tethered to the stump of mast, or whether the loop of rope had slipped off when the boat overturned.

And then there was a small tug on the harness, and he knew he had stopped sinking. He climbed the rope as he would have done on Jupiter in the syrupy atmosphere below the clouds. Just as he thought he could hold his breath no longer, he emerged into air and filled his burning lungs. He saw why the line had held; when the boat had rolled over, it had wrapped itself around the hull. If the boat had rolled in the opposite direction, the loop would have slipped off. He had been lucky.

When he had recovered, he pulled himself atop the overturned hull and lay there, gasping. He pulled on his lifeline to test it, and then, as a further precaution, he made another bight around the broken stub of the rudder post.

Now all he had to do was to stay where he was and hope that the upside-down hulk didn't sink.

The waves and the driving rain buffeted him for another hour, and then the gale started to move off. Another hour and he could distinguish what he took to be the horizon; the sea and the sky were both black, but the sea was blacker.

By morning the rain had stopped, and the clouds began to dissipate. A bleak sunrise revealed a heaving, inimical sea. Jarls found himself disoriented; the sun had come up from an unexpected direction. The floating wreck must have turned round many times during the night. No land was in sight. Jarls had no idea where he was. Currents might have carried him any distance into the North Sea.

Jarls could not even begin to guess how fast an ocean current on Earth moved; on Jupiter, atmospheric currents could carry you hundreds of miles in the length of time he had been drifting.

And now he had something new to worry about. The overturned hulk that he was clinging to was definitely lower in the water than it had been an hour before. Waves lapped at his feet and legs. He inched himself up toward what had been the keel, but there was nowhere else to go.

An hour later, the foundering wreck was lower still. The waves lapped hungrily at Jarls from all sides. He pried off his boots and let them sink. He knew it wouldn't make a particle of difference when he was finally in the water, but it was all he could think of to do.

When he estimated that he had a half hour left at best, he thought he could see a dot on the horizon. He kept an eye on it, and it grew.

Jarls dared to hope. The dot turned into a ship, a rather clumsy looking vessel topped by spiral towers of computer-controlled auxilliary sails. The sails were tightly closed now, like buds, and the ship was entirely under power. It came on fast, despite its lumbering appearance, heading in Jarls's direction.

Would it come close enough to see him? Jarls tried to think of some way to make himself more visible. The waterlogged mast and its sodden rags of sail were still attached to the wreck by the lines, but the secured ends of the lines were under water, with no way to reach them.

Jarls was still attached to the rudder post by his makeshift safety harness. Muttering a prayer under his breath, he undid the bight that secured it to the remains of the rudder post, made a bowline knot that gave him more slack, and played out the line until he had slid into the water up to his chin. He swallowed a mouthful of seawater and had a coughing fit. When he recovered, he fished underwater for any part of the rigging he could reach. His fist closed on a length of rope and he pulled himself one-handed up his safety line, dragging the broken mast with him. The rope held, and soon he had the broken mast lying the length of the hull with the broken end braced against the rudder post. He wrapped an arm around the mast and held on for dear life.

He blinked the water out of his eyes and looked for the ship again. It was only a quarter-mile away and about to pass his position, with no sign that it had seen him. It was not slowing down or changing course.

Jarls got to his feet and balanced himself precariously on the slippery hull. He waved and shouted to no effect. Despairing, he bent down and levered the heavy mast to a vertical position and held it there as long as he could. It was like balancing a tree trunk. Then a wave threw him off balance and the mast slipped. He watched helplessly as it slid back into the water. Worse still, it had knocked the rudder post loose, and he was no longer attached to the post by his safety line.

But the mast had done its work. Across the gray waters, the ship was slowing down. Jarls could see a churning of white water as bow thrusters came into play. The ship was riding low in the water, as though it had a heavy cargo.

They were lowering a boat now. Jarls watched as it swung from the davits and splashed down. There were tiny yellow figures in it. A motor sputtered into life, and then the boat was headed toward him.

By the time it reached him, he was up to his ankles in water. There was a gentle bump, and a hoarse voice shouting, "*Rask, rask!*" There were three of them, unshaven men in yellow slickers and hats.

Jarls leaned across and grasped the gunwale. He heaved, with a strength that pulled the rescue boat at least a couple of feet up the slope of the submerged hull and tilted it perilously toward him, and landed jarringly in the bottom of the boat. One of the sailors yelled in alarm, "*Forsiktig, vaer sa god!*"

The boat stopped rocking. The man at the tiller turned the craft around and headed back toward the ship. The sailor who had yelled at Jarls turned to him and said, "*Snakker de Norsk?*"

"I'm sorry, I don't understand," Jarls said.

The man shrugged, and they rode in silence the rest of the way.

When they reached the ship, Jarls saw that it was old, rusty, and unkempt. He climbed a ladder, with a sailor prodding impatiently at his back, and let himself be shoved along the deck toward a cabin at the stern. He looked around, trying to take in as much as he could. The entire deck seemed to be cluttered with junk—huge twisted girders, thick slabs of bent metal plate, long bundles of steel pipe that did not seem to be safely secured at all.

As Jarls plodded barefoot toward the stern cabin, the ship suddenly came to life with a shuddering of some hidden power plant. Jarls felt a slight lifting of the deck. But if there were hydrofoils or fans to make the ship levitate, they weren't powerful enough to boost the hull above the surface of the water. The ship continued its lumbering progress, wallowing in the North Sea's swells. Jarls was surprised; he didn't know what he had been expecting of Earth's vaunted technology, but this battered vessel, whatever its commercial errand in this desolate body of water, wasn't traveling any faster than a floater in Jupiter's hydrogen atmosphere.

"*Denne vei,*" said the sailor at his back, and got Jarls moving again. He thrust him into a cluttered cabin, where an older man with a neatly trimmed gray beard and wearing a blue, gold-trimmed jacket, which Jarls took to be some sort of uniform, sat at a small steel desk. The sailor saluted and left.

"*God dag,*" the man said, looking up at him.

Jarls shook his head.

"No Norwegian?" the man said. "So. Do you speak English?"

"Yes."

"I'm Captain Bjornson. This is the freighter *Solveig S.,* out of Trondheim. What were you doing out here in a small boat?"

Jarls said nothing.

The captain sighed. "You were in the middle of the North Sea, a hundred miles off the coast of Scotland. Are you a Scot?"

"No," Jarls said.

"I thought not." The captain's eyes strayed to the patched shirt that the woman at Strathspey had given to Jarls, then down to the soaked and torn trousers. The trousers still looked like what they were—part of a uniform—and they didn't go with the shirt. "You are very strong to have waved a mast at us. Are you a Jovian?"

Jarls did not know how to answer. He hesitated.

The captain sighed again. "It's none of my business. I don't want to know anymore. Then I'd have to report you by international law. The Scots don't like us very well. Neither do the English. They like to make trouble for us. They don't like our presence in these waters."

"What are you going to do?"

"We're always short-handed. You'll have to work your passage. We can use a set of Jovian muscles this trip."

"Where are you headed?"

"To Rotterdam with a cargo of scrap." He gave an enigmatic smile. "Rotterdam was the biggest oil receiving port in the world three hundred years ago. Now that there's no more oil, they're still living off the Magnus field and Ekofisk. One of the ironies, isn't it?"

Jarls didn't know what he was talking about. "Where's Rotterdam?" he asked.

The captain looked startled. "Why . . . it's Europe's major port on the North Sea. Still dry land after three hundred years, thanks to the international Zeeland project, because it was too important to be allowed to be flooded along with most of the rest of the Lowlands when the sea level rose." He shook his head in disbelief at Jarls's ignorance. "It was the engineering marvel of the twenty-second century, a legend to this day."

"Is it near Liechtenstein?"

The captain looked at him curiously. "No, my young friend. That's quite a bit farther to the southeast. You'll have to cross the Alps, and get past a few borders." He rose to his feet. "Come. We'll find some clothes for you in the slop chest and get you something to eat, and then you can start work."

Jarls stepped from the launch to the concrete jetty abutting the towering seawall and said goodbye in his few words of halting Norwegian to the sailors who had delivered him. "*God dag*, Herr Jarls," Lars, the coxswain, said, and they pushed off.

He headed for the long flight of outside steps leading to the top of the seawall. Captain Bjornson had told the sailors to bring Jarls here, to one of the less-used moorings, instead of to the customs shed where the *Solveig S.* was doing business with the port officials. There would be no fuss about papers as long as he stayed out of trouble. Rotterdam was used to foreign sailors filling the streets, and almost everybody spoke English.

Jarls looked like a sailor in his outfit from the ship's slop chest—a heavy jacket to conceal his bulk of torso, coarse-woven workman's pants, clumpy shoes, a knit cap. The uniform trousers had gone overboard; Captain Bjornson hadn't even wanted them in the slop chest where they might lead to questions.

He had money in his pocket, too—not much, but the first real money he had seen on Earth. The captain was a man of his word and had paid Jarls the going rate for an apprentice seaman.

The work had been brutal—beginning with tying up the dangerous bundles of metal pipe and seeing that they were properly secured. Cranes and heavy machinery were of limited value in that kind of work. Jarls came to understand why the captain had taken the opportunity to add a Jovian to his crew.

He also understood now why the captain had not been anxious to have any unnecessary contact with Scottish authorities. The scrap metal that he was transporting came from dismantling the old North Sea oil rigs from the twentieth and twenty-first centuries. There was a treasure trove of metal in that ocean, and the pirate outfits that sold the scrap to skippers like Captain Bjornson had not been overly scrupulous about distinguishing Norwegian drilling platforms from platforms that were still, theoretically, Scotland's property.

The captain must have had some residual scruples, though. He had been at pains to explain, without being asked, that the old rigs were of no use to anyone anymore. The geologists had lately been speculating that, miles below the exhausted oil fields of the past, there might exist a new bonanza of "nonbiological hydrocarbons" that had formed out of the carbon in the Earth's crust before life began. The North Sea might come to life again. But it would take new techniques, new kinds of ultradeep rigs, to reach mankind's second chance.

Jarls reached the top of the stone steps and looked down at the encircled city of Rotterdam from the wall that kept the sea at bay. It was huge—a crowded panorama that stretched for miles, with forests of residential housing, a patchwork of garden land, and the gray wastes of industrial areas. Rising from the center was a mile-high tower of glittering plastic that he had seen from far out at sea, and that Lars had told him was the Euromast.

The top of the seawall contained a roadway that was thick with speeding traffic, but there were footpaths leading down to the teeming city below. He stopped a pedestrian, an old man walking a dog, and asked if there was a way to the mainland.

"There's a ferry," the man said, "and a high speed tubeway. How far do you want to go?"

"As far as it will take me," Jarls said.

# 18

**T**HE MAN sitting across the narrow table released Jarls's arm. "There," he said. "All done."

Jarls looked at the little shaved patch on his forearm. The bar code looked like any other identity tattoo, with crisp black lines underscored by a strip of shifting holographic numbers embedded in the flesh. He rolled down his sleeve and buttoned the cuff.

"It's a valid number, too," the forger said. "At least it will pass muster at the central *gastarbeiter* register when it's scanned. Come back tomorrow and I'll have the rest of your papers, including a green card. That will be valid too—at least until the end of the year. Come back then and I'll give you another."

Jarls mumbled an assent.

"I don't know how you got by all these weeks on that phony dye transfer tattoo you walked in with," the little man said. "They must have seen you coming. Don't tell me. The steerer that got it for you was a big fellow with a blond mustache calling himself Emil, who met you at the Rhine crossing. The number that was on it doesn't even exist."

"I've only been stopped by the *polizie* twice. They looked at my arm, but they didn't bother to scan it."

"Good thing that Liechtenstein needs its guest workers so badly. But you wouldn't have gotten away with it for long. Well, you'll be legal tomorrow, or the next best thing to it, after I give you your *grune Versicherungskarte.*"

Jarls got to his feet.

"Wait!" the forger said, holding up his hand. He went to the window and peered round the edge of the shade. "Another armored vehicle going by. Executive Guards, I think. There, they're gone. Something big's going on. Nothing to do with you or me, but if I were you, I'd get home quickly and stay indoors tonight."

Downstairs, Jarls looked both ways for policemen before he stepped out of the doorway. It was late in the evening, but the streets of Liechtenstein's ordinarily sedate capital were crowded, and there was a kind of restlessness in the air that even an outsider like Jarls could notice. There was a knot of people milling about at the corner, and Jarls could hear voices raised in anger.

The forger was right; it had nothing to do with him. Jarls put his head down and started walking toward the slum district where he had a room.

The mountain air was bracing, even in the heart of this over-crowded metropolis, and the sky was clear and starry. Jarls paused for a moment to admire the magnificent mountainscape visible through the gaps between the buildings. From his line of sight down the length of the street, he could make out the long bare patches on the city's outskirts, where old rock slides from the Alpine slopes had been left sensibly unchallenged by the urban architects of the last few centuries.

He stepped a little farther out into the street to bring into view the fourteenth century castle where the Megachairman, Prince Franz Joseph XXIII, lived with his family. The von Liechtensteins had formed an unbroken royal line since their ancestor, an Austrian prince, had bought the country some seven hundred years earlier. It was a good thing that the castle stood some three hundred feet up the slopes of the Alps, because by royal decree—ostensibly for security reasons—no building in the densely packed capital could be built higher.

Tiny Liechtenstein had become the tail that wagged the Swiss dog—and the rest of the planet—some time in the twenty-second century, when its banks and its forgiving tax laws had allowed it to overtake Switzerland as a repository for the world's money. Today, the great megalopolis that stretched from Franz Joseph's capital of Vaduz to Zurich hosted the headquarters of most of the Earth's major corporations, and held a lion's share of the solar system's wealth.

Jarls was jarred out of his thoughts by a whooping siren. An armored vehicle was barrelling down the street, its lights flashing. Jarls stepped back just in time to avoid being run down, and tripped over the curb. As he caught his balance, a well-dressed man beside him, who had also had to dodge the armored vehicle, spat on the sidewalk and said, "That's the Executive Guard for you, racing all over the place, endangering the lives of law-abiding Liechtensteiners! They've just been getting out of hand this last week with their security sweeps! I don't know what's been going on. It was a mistake for the Megachairman's ancestors to entrust their safety to a band of barbarians from another planet, and I don't mind saying so! Prince Franz Joseph is right to have started a shake-up of the Guards' ranks. Heads will roll, mark my words! He should have done it long ago!"

Then he noticed Jarls's shabby clothes and Jovian build, and clamped his mouth shut. He turned on his heel and walked hastily away.

Jarls continued down the street toward the pedestrian walkway that bordered the Rhine, turning southward toward the poor district where the guest workers, from every nation on Earth and half the planets, lived their constrained lives. Switzerland lay across the river, but there were no guards or customs posts at the bridges, and the border between the two countries was largely theoretical.

An hour's walking brought him to a turnoff through a mountain tunnel, and then to a tract of cheap housing that had once been a scenic Alpine valley, but now kept the guest workers and other undesirables out of sight.

Another armored vehicle rumbled by—this time a police department tank with twin riot gun turrets on top—and Jarls pressed himself against a wall to give it more room to pass. Around him, others were doing the same. The streets were narrow here in this squalid neighborhood, and even if they had not been, the multinational inhabitants had learned to give the police a wide berth.

Jarls wondered what the tank was doing here. The urban *polizie* normally stayed out of the *gastarbeiter* slum except when they were called upon to quell some public disturbance. He wondered what kind of unrest they could be expecting tonight, and whether it had anything to do with the heightened activity of the Executive Guard the last day or so. He had passed Guard vehicles twice more this evening before leaving the downtown district. The Guard usually kept a low profile. Perhaps there was some sort of security threat that would be announced in a few days, when it had blown over.

He passed a hole-in-the-wall eatery and bought his supper: a half-dozen sausage rolls and a carton of beer. When he got to his *zimmerhaus*, the usual assortment of neigborhood toughs was lounging on the steps. They made way silently for him, not because they were afraid to tangle with a Jovian as he had come to understand, but because he lived there and was one of them.

"*Guten Abend, Herr Schwarzhorn*," said the scurviest of them, a shaven-headed hoodlum named Karl, who sported a facial tattoo of a snake emerging from the eye socket of a skull. Naming Jarls after a mountain was his little joke.

"*Guten Abend, Herr Karl*," Jarls said politely, and mounted the worn steps with his bag of sausages.

There was no lift. It had given out at least a century earlier, and no one had ever bothered to repair it. Jarls climbed the seven flights to his floor, trying to ignore the residual essence of a hundred years worth of boiled cabbage, stale beer, and mildew that seeped from under the doors that he passed. A man in an undershirt standing in an open doorway across the hall stepped hastily inside and closed the door when he caught sight of Jarls on the landing.

He unlocked the door to his room and let himself in. He had a bed, a chair, a scarred chest of drawers and a row of coathooks. He hung up his jacket and sat down at the table with his sack of sausages and beer.

He turned on the little holovid while he ate. The evening news was still on. Jarls learned about a hyperjet crash in Bolivia, food riots in Manitoba, a temporary shutdown of the Mars orbital elevator due to a minor accident caused by an especially close passage of Phobos, a dip in Solar Oxygen's profits attributed to an unavoidable slowdown in the Mercurian mines that supplied magnesium to Venus, and, closer to home, persistent labor shortages in northern Europe and southeast Asia.

Jarls grimaced sourly to himself. He knew all about labor shortages. They had gotten him from Rotterdam to Liechtenstein without being arrested as an escaped workie. There was no shortage of people on Earth. The problem was how to bind people to all the menial jobs that still needed to be done, even in a technological era. An industrial peasantry was indispensible, and human civilization, by one means or another, had followed its historic bent and seen to it that one evolved. That was why there were people like Vanius Paes and Lord Hirakawa at the top, and indentured workies at the bottom. Or people who were just as enthralled by economic necessity, without the legal rigamarole of a labor contract. And that was why when a Jovie without proper papers showed up at street corner labor exchange, he was able to get himself hired for a day or a week, no questions asked.

Jarls scowled as he remembered some of the jobs that had gotten him across Europe. In the Dutch delta, he had heaved three-hundred-pound concrete blocks, a job that usually took four men. In Greater Germany, he had hauled quarter-ton building panels up the side of a skyscraper under construction, a job that was usually done by a crane. In the Austro-Hungarian Federation, a jolly man in expensive tweeds had asked him if was willing to take a job that required muscle, nerve, and an absence of curiosity. Jarls had ended up escorting the man through the streets of Graz, carrying a reinforced suitcase that, from the weight of it, must have contained either gold or lead, and that no ordinary man could have carried and made to look effortless. When the suitcase had been delivered, the man had asked him if he wanted further work and if he was averse to rough stuff. Jarls had declined, and the man had paid him off without comment.

There had been other jobs—too many of them. Everywhere Jarls went, there had been people willing to give work to an undocumented alien—the hard jobs, the unpleasant jobs, the jobs you could save money on by giving them to someone who could do the work of four starveling Earthies, the shady jobs you paid off in cash. Some of Jarls's clandestine employers had even asked him to stay on. He had resisted the temptation. It was dangerous to stay in one place too long.

He studied the bar code imprinted on his arm. That would buy him time, until he figured out what to do.

The documents forger had explained to him what a valid code meant. Whenever the central computer caught up with him, the virus that the Liechtenstein underworld had planted in it would shift the number and all its pseudodata to another memory location that would be good for another few months or more.

But he had better find a new place to live as soon as possible, and shed the remnants of the shaky identity he had started to pile up here.

"... and the Pandirectorate information office has now issued an official statement calling the reports of new demonstrations in Milan and Genoa 'highly exaggerated,' and an attempt by Lombardian Dependency separatists to spread rumors undermining the public order ..."

The holovid snapped Jarls out of his thoughts. He gave his attention to the set's illusory window. An announcer was superimposed on a scene of a peaceful city street. But someone had forgotten to match the shadows. The announcer's shadow was shorter than the shadows of objects around him, and the angle was wrong. He was standing in a scene that had been recorded earlier in the season.

There were closeups of smiling Milanese, and then a new announcer came on, against a studio background. "... the Banking

Ministry has announced that corporate and individual assessments will rise by approximately fourteen percent in the next quarter. However, there are assurances from a source close to the minister that the increase is expected to be temporary, and should not affect long-term corporate planning . . ."

A quick montage of smiling board members around various conference tables, intercut with the imposing facades of a number of corporate headquarters, flashed by.

". . . and in a related development, a spokesman for the finance minister has denied that the Megachairman, in his role of Liechtenstein's head of state, is contemplating a devaluation of the Liechtenfranc. The Minister of Security, Count Steg, has issued a grave warning that such rumors constitute the crime of economic sabotage, and will be dealt with severely . . ."

A close-up appeared of an unsmiling Count Steg, the heir presumptive to Franz Joseph's throne and next in line to the megachairmanship.

". . . arrests have continued in the ongoing investigation of the death of the heir apparent, Prince Albert, and attacks on other members of the royal family. Sources close to the security minister have hinted at the involvement of prominent persons in Greater Liechtenstein and abroad."

Jarls pursed his lips as the holo window showed a trio of expensively tailored men in handcuffs and leg chains being herded into a security van. They didn't look like the kind of people who usually got themselves arrested.

The announcer's voice became still more somber. "The investigation is said to reach into the ranks of the Executive Guards themselves. A high-ranking officer in the Guards' palace detail has agreed to present himself for questioning at a time to be determined later . . ."

That one was really a shocker. Jarls forgot the remains of his supper. Wherever he had gone on his trek through Europe, and in the Liechtenstein capital itself, he had found that the Executive Guards were held in generally high esteem. They had always been a symbol of rectitude, and above suspicion.

Then he remembered the man on the street corner who had criticized the Executive Guards to him. Such criticisms would have been unheard of only a few short weeks ago. Was the news bulletin he had just heard part of a campaign to discredit the Guards? The Guards had for generations been charged with the protection of the Megachairman. Count Steg was supposed to be Franz Joseph's handpicked candidate for successor, despite his unpopularity with both the plebs and the influential upper crust. He ought to be courting the support of the Guards. This was a dangerous game he was playing.

Jarls shrugged and resumed eating. The antics of the mighty had nothing to do with him.

He switched to the Reward channel by snapping his fingers at the holovid set. The "Wanted" loop was nearing the end of its sequence and about to start scrolling again.

There was the usual exhortation by a public figure—this time the Prince Consort of Denmark—for citizens to do their duty and turn in wanted miscreants. Then came a breathless recitation by an insufficiently clothed holodrama actress of the prizes to be won, culminating in a shot of the previous day's big winner receiving a credit enhancement chip and the thanks of a grateful police chief in Bratislava for turning in an escaped serial killer who had eluded capture these last six months.

He waited patiently for his own reward notice to turn up. It was only about fifteen minutes into a nine-hour loop and getting pushed further and further back with each passing day. He noted with interest that the colorful swindler who specialized in impersonating corporate Lord Chairmen was missing from the wanted list—presumably having been apprehended—and a new superstar felon had been added, this time a gang leader who had blown up a bank in Zurich in the vain hope of destroying credit records and profiting from the confusion.

He himself, Jarls knew, was small potatoes. He was just one of the thousands of petty criminals listed on the loop, and the reward was correspondingly small. His wanted notice appeared for only a few seconds, once every nine hours. But he could never be sure that some bleary-eyed devotee of the channel wouldn't spot it.

There it was, following the familiar notice about the Carpathian strangler. Jarls had seen it too many times now, but he leaned forward in his seat anyway.

It showed his old identification photo, wearing the livery of the Strathspey security force, and with his hair closely cropped. He was a bit thinner now, though still of Jovian bulk, and there were new lines in his face. But a Jovian always drew a second look from passersby.

The charges were the same. Violation of labor contract. Murder. Mayhem. Attempted rape. Theft of a boat. Unlawful flight. The subject was extremely dangerous. It should be noted that he was a Jovian, abnormally strong and fast, and should be approached with caution.

Jarls smiled bitterly. Lady Hirakawa must have screamed bloody murder. It would be convenient for her if he was killed while being taken into custody.

He switched off the holovid and finished his beer. A violent knock rattled the door. Before Jarls could move, the door shattered and the room was full of Jovians.

He started to get up, but a hand as powerful as his own pushed him back in his seat. He looked up into the stony face of Hannes Karlsen.

"You had a pretty good run, Anders," Karsen said. "I'm impressed. But you couldn't hope to hide forever."

# 19

**J**ARLS RECOGNIZED most of the Jovians crowding the room. It was a shock to see Czoznek among them.

"I thought I killed you," Jarls said.

"You tried, you bastard," Czoznek growled. There was a dent in his skull, and his forehead was crisscrossed with angry scars.

Jarls looked at the ring of Jovian muscle and all the drawn weapons and gave up any hope of resistance. "What now?" he said.

"Get up. You're coming with us," Karsen said.

Jarls pushed his chair back and got to his feet under their watchful eyes. He reached for his jacket.

"You won't need that where you're going," Karsen said. They hustled Jarls downstairs and into a waiting limo with bulletproof screens over the side windows. Jarls was shoved brusquely into a rear seat, with a hefty guard hemming him in on either side, and two more facing him from jump seats. The guards directly opposite were new faces, and must have been recruited after Jarls's departure, but the man on his left was his old partner, Stern.

"Thanks for breaking my arm, Anders," Stern said.

"I'm sorry, Stern," Jarls said.

The limo whirred into life as the flywheel-powered generators engaged the electric motors, and the limo pulled out into a street that was empty of its usual traffic. A second limo, filled with Strathspey Jovians, followed.

Karsen was looking around at him from the passenger seat. "You're not a very popular fellow, Anders," he said.

"Is Harrison dead?" Jarls asked.

"No—not that it's any thanks to you. We were able to get to him in time and neutralize all the tranks you pumped into him."

"What about the man I pushed down the stairs?"

"You lucked out there, too—and so did he. Skull fracture. It looked bad for a while, but he pulled through."

Jarls remembered the Wanted loop he had just watched. "One of the charges against me is murder. Who was I supposed to have killed, then?"

"The Jovian kitchen maid, Magda."

"*What*!" Jarls started out of his seat, and was pushed back by the guards on either side.

"She was found strangled. A clumsy attempt had been made to make it look like suicide by hanging, but that wouldn't pass muster, and you made things wonderfully convenient for everybody by leaving a trail of mayhem behind you."

"I didn't . . . I didn't . . ."

"I know that, Anders. The laird had it done. He couldn't bear to sell her to Fujisaki. But it doesn't matter worth a damn. You've still got all the other charges against you. Dereliction of indenture, mayhem, unlawful flight, theft—including the boat, your own body as the laird's property through indenture, and Lady Hirakawa's jewelry for good measure. And then, of course, there's the attempted rape."

Jarls's sense of hopelessness deepened. "I didn't attempt to rape Lady Hirakawa either."

Karsen raised his eyebrows. "Oh, you're not charged with an attempt on Lady Hirakawa. The victim of record is her servant, Toshiko. It would be beneath Her Ladyship's dignity to be seen as the object of an attempted rape by a servant."

"How did you find me?" Jarls said bitterly.

"It wasn't hard. You've been popping up on our screen for months. Probable sightings from Rotterdam to Graz. You were smart to turn down that character in Graz, by the way. The police picked him up on his next bullion transaction."

"I don't understand. If you've been tracking me all this time, why wasn't I turned in?"

"It's not in our interest to do the work of the police for them."

"Who's 'we?'"

Karsen mulled over his next words, then answered obliquely. "Earth is a precarious place for Jovians, Anders. You've already found that out. The Executive Guards keep a register of every Jovian on the planet. We try to keep things from getting out of hand. We help one another if it's possible, and otherwise we try to steer our kind away from behavior that might reflect badly on us."

"And when one of us screws up?"

"We throw him to the wolves."

"You've come to take me back to Strathspey, then?"

Karlsen drew a deep breath. "That's what we told Lord Hirakawa. But we're reserving you for another purpose."

Jarls was confused. "What are you talking about?"

Karlsen chose his next words with painstaking care. "The Executive Guards are the finest mercenary force the world has ever known, but their numbers are relatively small. In the next forty-eight hours, they're going to need every man they can get. You did us a favor, Anders. You gave me an excuse to come to Liechtenstein with an arrest squad—nine of my best men." He bared his teeth in a sardonic grin. "You're very dangerous, you see. And Liechtenstein is filling up with hundreds of other Jovian security cops like me, here on any plausible excuse they can trump up. The police will have started to notice by tomorrow, but by then it won't matter."

"I still don't understand. What's all this about."

Czoznek, wedged in at Jarls's right, said, "I don't like this, Hannes. How do we know we can trust him?"

"Shut up, Czoz," Karsen said. He turned his attention back to Jarls. "We're going to remove Franz Joseph as Megachairman and install his nephew Rudolph in his place."

It took Jarls's breath away. "But that's insane. You can't depose the Megachairman."

"If we move quickly, it'll all be over before the opposition has a chance to react."

A bar of light crossed Karsen's face as the limo passed a street lamp, and Jarls saw that the security chief was staring at him intently.

"But . . . but it's the duty of the Executive Guard to protect the Megachairman. It always has been." Jarls could only think of old Ian Karg back on Jupiter, sitting in his walking chair, surrounded by his medals and memorabilia, and he blurted out, "It's their sworn trust!"

Karsen went on in a wintry voice, "There's no alternative. The Executive Guard isn't political. Yes, they're the power behind the throne, but they've always been content to leave the governing to anyone who can keep society humming. They'll forgive anything but incompetence." He sighed. "But Franz Joseph was a mistake. A megalomaniac and petty tyrant, and stupid to boot. Since he succeeded to the Megachair, things have been going to hell. Corporate balances are dropping, assessments are rising, and there's unrest in the streets. And now he's allowing that snake of his, Count Steg, to arrest members of the aristocracy on flimsy charges."

Karsen fell silent for a minute as the limo passed a clanking police department tank. The limo began to slow down. There was some sort of checkpoint ahead at a crossroads.

"You want I should run it, Hannes?" the driver said.

"God, no," Karsen said. "Put your guns away and look brotherly."

Czoznek jabbed Jarls hard in the ribs and said, "You keep your mouth shut."

The checkpoint was still a hundred yards away. The limo continued slowing. Karsen turned back to Jarls and went on unhurriedly.

"Where was I? Oh yes, Count Steg's little tinpot reign of terror. The Guards might even have overlooked that, but the last straw was the threat to the Guard itself. That couldn't be tolerated. No, the time to move is before the arrests start. Franz Joseph no longer has a majority of the board behind him. And the aristocracy is starting to worry about Steg. They'll wait to see if we're successful.

And once Rudolph is safely installed in the megachairmanship, they'll all breathe a sigh of relief."

"Does Rudolph know about the Guards' plans for him?" Jarls asked.

"Not yet."

"What if he says no?"

The flashing yellow lights in the road illuminated Karsen's face. He gave Jarls a wolfish smile. "He won't say no."

Jarls tried to remember what Rudolph was like. He recalled a sunburned face with a blond mustache, a sportsman's squint, and an amiable if distant smile.

"Count Steg was behind the assassination attempt on Rudolph at Strathspey, wasn't he?"

"Yes."

"Rudolph didn't seem all that much of a threat to Steg's ambitions. He didn't strike me as being someone who's particularly interested in running the world."

"He'll toe the mark when he understands that he has to. He's no intellectual giant, but he's levelheaded enough, and he's popular with the plebs. And he'll be acceptable to the aristocracy. He's not first in the line of succession, but he's got Schellenberg blood and he's the Count of Triesenberg. That gives him legitimacy, even if he spends most of his time at his shooting estate in Scotland and his hunting preserve in Alaska."

Karsen stopped talking as they reached the checkpoint. A policeman with a negligently held riot gun dangling at his side leaned into the window, saw all the uniforms, and gave only a perfunctory glance to the identification that Karsen held out. His eyes roved over Jarls in his workie clothes.

"What about him?"

"He's with us," Karsen said.

The policeman nodded and waved them on. A striped barrier swung open and armor-clad cops with handheld rocket launchers stepped aside to let the limo through.

"Amateurs," the driver said.

Karsen resumed his colloquy with Jarls. "So you see, Anders, the time is as ripe as it will ever be. It would be a mistake to delay. Steg is consolidating his power every day, and if the day were to come when he felt confident enough to move against Franz Joseph directly, society would be thrown into turmoil. We've had a *pax pecunia* for over three centuries, and we can't afford to let things break apart now."

"Pax pecunia?"

Karsen allowed a trace of amusement to creep into his voice. "Call it *pax corporatus.*"

Jarls was having trouble absorbing it all. "I was raised to believe that the Executive Guard was above politics."

"Throw power away, and power will throw you away. What the Executive Guard is doing is nothing new. It's been a human custom since the first clique of neolithic hunters threw their allegiance to a new chief when the old chief got too far out of touch to lead the tribe effectively. The Roman emperors were supposed to be protected by a Praetorian Guard. The Praetorians deposed and installed emperors for three hundred years, and ended up by selling the throne for money until Septimius replaced them with Germans and Britons, who were thought to be incorruptible because they were barbarians. Just like us Jovians, eh, Anders?"

Jarls remembered that Ian Karg had said much the same thing to him. "I've heard that Earthians think we're trustworthy, yes."

Karsen nodded in approval. "History's full of similar examples. There were the Janissaries, the elite guards of the Ottoman rulers. They were outsiders, too—Christian Slavs imported from the Balkans and forcibly converted to Islam. They, too, were thought to be more reliable than the sultans' own subjects, and they became the real power behind the Turkish throne for more than four hundred years. And then there were the Mamelukes . . ."

"Hannes . . ." Czoznek tried to interrupt.

Karsen waved him aside. "The Mamelukes were slaves. That's what the word means. The Egyptians brought them in from the Russian steppes. Some of the toughest people in the world. They were in great demand as royal bodyguards. But they became the ruling class themselves—a slave dynasty that lasted for more than five hundred years."

"Hannes . . ."

"And now we've got Jovians. The Executive Guards evolved from the Swiss Guards that protected the Pope in times past. Tough people, too—the best mercenaries in the world in their day. Their motto was, '*Point d'argent, point de Suisses*'—no money, no Swiss." He touched the slash of color at his sleeve. "Did you know that their uniform was supposed to have been designed by Michaelangelo? The Guard retained the colors, at least, and while the private security forces may imitate the uniform, we honor the colors themselves by not trying to copy them. The Executive Guards have levered Megachairmen into power before now—even though the general populace wasn't aware of what went on behind the scenes. When their purpose was accomplished, they always faded into the background."

"The Guards have done this before?"

"Yes. The last . . . ah, intervention . . . was only forty years ago."

Jarls's mind raced. That was within his parents' lifetime. When he had been growing up, his father and Uncle Hector had argued often about politics. But he had never heard them discuss anything like that.

He said thickly, "There's nothing like that in the history books."

"That's what makes it a successful coup, doesn't it?" Karsen responded.

Czoznek had reached the limits of his patience. "Enough talk, Hannes," he exploded. "Is he with us or not?"

Karsen nodded. "A fair question, Anders. Are you with us?"

A cold fist closed over Jarls's heart. He was not deceived by Karsen's dispassionate tone. Perhaps Karsen liked him well enough, but Jarls was there because Karsen thought he could use him. Jarls knew with utter certainty that if he gave the wrong answer, Karsen would regretfully have him shot and thrown from the speeding car.

He pondered his reply nevertheless. He had no particular loyalty to the Pandirectorate. Earth and Venus had been his exploiters. It was a rotten society anyway. It could stand a blast of fresh air.

"Yes," he said.

The tension went out of the men around him. There was an audible exhale from the man on his right.

Stern slapped him on the arm. "Good man," he said.

"Where are we going?" Jarls asked.

Karsen spoke without turning his head. "The Guard have a retreat up in the mountains. It's an old fortress that the Swiss once occupied. There isn't much traffic on the road leading there. They're using it as the staging area."

Jarls leaned forward to peer through the windshield. The mountains were dark except for a sprinkling of lights from some of the more remote villas. The limo turned onto a twisting mountain road and, with a small whine of complaint from its electric motors, began to climb.

The fortress's main hall was a gloomy cavern of a place, with a cold stone floor and ancient shadows high overhead amidst the oak rafters. At the moment, though, it was a buzzing wasps' nest of activity.

"Wait here," said the Guard lieutenant who had brought them in from the gate, and hurried distractedly off, leaving Karsen and his men standing in a cluster against one wall.

"What the hell!" Czoznek said angrily.

"They're busy," Karsen said. "They'll get to us when they can."

Jarls looked around. There were other groups of Jovians bunched along the walls, waiting to be assigned. Most wore some variation of the Executive Guard uniform, too—black or gray tunics with the copycat slashed sleeves showing a striped under-layer, though the actual colors of the slash did not presume to imitate the Guards' rainbow hues.

He turned his attention to the far end of the hall, where a committee of Guard officers sat at a long table on a raised hearth, in front of a fireplace that was big enough to roast a triceratops in.

There were eight of them—a row of clean-shaven faces that showed no details at this distance.

They were interviewing the volunteer groups one by one and passing out assignments, a process that was being continually interrupted by messengers arriving with dispatches, and by subordinates coming round the table to lay reports in front of them and whisper in their ears.

At a smaller table laden with esoteric equipment and an assortment of viewscreens, a little band of technical support people quietly went about their work. Once, Jarls saw them give what could only have been a lie detector test to one of the private security chiefs who was reporting with his men. The chief passed muster, and the officers' committee passed him and his team along to an adjutant who took them aside to give them a briefing and send them on their way.

There was another group of Guard personnel sitting unobtrusively to one side, on a double row of benches. Jarls could not make out their faces in detail either, but their posture was alert. They were watching the proceedings intently, and they were all helmeted and armed.

He found out what they were there for a few minutes later. Another contingent of Jovian volunteers was taking its turn before the tribunal. Things seemed to be going swiftly and efficiently as before. The group's leader had presented identification and had a brief interview with the examining officers, and his men were getting the usual one-minute grilling from the technical support people. Then there was a hitch with one of the men. A Guard technician looked up from his screen and made a sign to the officers at the table. The man being grilled did something stupid. Perhaps he thought he had a chance of getting out of the room. He whirled around and began running for the door, but two of the helmeted men on the benches had already started moving. They caught up with him before he had gone more than a few feet, grabbed his arms on either side, and before he could resist, shot him with a tranquilizer dart. He slumped at once, and they began dragging him away. In the meantime, another of the helmeted men had risen from the bench to confer briefly with the technician who had flushed the man out. The two disposal men paused to look over their shoulders at him, and he made a gesture of drawing a finger across his throat. The other two nodded and continued their removal of the unconscious man.

"Traitor," Karsen said in response to the questioning stares that Czoznek and the others were directing at him. He turned away and fell bleakly silent.

It was another half hour before it was Karsen's turn. The Guard lieutenant who had abandoned him returned, and said, "This way, Strathspey people."

Jarls followed the others to the table in front of the fireplace. He was conscious of the shabby workie clothing that made him stand out from the others, but he was not the only Jovian in the room without a uniform.

"Hello, Hannes," said one of the officers sitting at the table. "It's been a long time."

"I'm glad I was able to come, Hendrik," Karsen replied. "I brought some good men with me."

That was the end of amenities. Karsen presented his credentials, just as if he had not been recognized by one of the inquisitors, and had a retinal check, administered with a little electronic eye cup brought over by one of the technicians.

"You left Scotland with Lord Hirakawa's permission?" asked another of the seated examiners.

"Yes. When we return, I'll tell him that the fugitive we came to collect slipped through our fingers. He won't be happy, but that will be the end of it."

"Is this the man?" said a hawk-faced officer sitting farther down the table, swiveling cold eyes toward Jarls.

"Yes."

"Am I to understand that you're not taking him back with you?"

"Yes."

"Why not?'

"He doesn't deserve that. And he was one of my best men."

The officer frowned. "It would be better for all concerned if you took him back. We've got a limited reservoir of indulgence from the lords and masters of Earth, and so do you. And Lord knows, we're going to use a lot of it up in the next few days. We can't afford to be sentimental."

A chill went down Jarls's spine as he looked at the row of grim faces at the table. They were hard men, relentless men. They had to be. And they were all tense and tired. God knew how long they'd been without sleep.

Another officer spoke. This one was sandy haired with a deeply lined face. "Maybe he shouldn't go back, Mikhail. He knows too much already."

"What are you suggesting, *Obergruppenfuhrer* Lewis?" the hawk-faced officer said caustically. "That he be shot while being apprehended? Or that he be trusted to join us?"

Karsen broke in, his tone carefully neutral. "We have dangerous work ahead of us. We can use every man."

There were several frowns at Karsen's presumptuousness. The gray-haired officer whose collar insignia showed him to be senior said, "Leave it for the moment. Let's get on with the rest of Captain Karsen's candidates."

The exchange had not been lost on the disposal squad sitting on the side benches. The ones in the front row were eyeing Jarls speculatively.

The other Jovians from Strathspey were called one by one and asked a few terse questions. There was no pattern to the questions that Jarls could see, and some of the answers must already have been available from the records that were being called up by the technical people manning the data screens. Jarls learned to his surprise that his old partner Stern had a degree in Dolphin communication from the University of Southhaven in Jupiter's South Equatorial Belt, only a few thousand miles from Port Elysium at passage, and that one of Karsen's new men was a convicted killer who had been reprieved by some miracle from the Mercurian mines.

"All right," the tribunal's senior officer said when they were finished with the others, "you can step forward ..." He glanced at the flimsy desk screen lying in front of him. "... Anders, is it?"

"Yes sir."

"You got to Rotterdam by means unknown—not in that boat you stole from Lord Hirakawa—I take it?"

"No sir. I was picked up by a Norwegian freighter."

"No record of that. The captain didn't report you?"

"No sir. He was engaged in an illegal business."

The hawk-faced officer jumped in. "Illegal?" he said, leaning forward.

"Yes. He was transporting stolen salvage."

"And he enlisted you in this illegal activity?"

"I worked for him as a deckhand, yes."

The senior officer took charge again. "And then you somehow made your way across the length and breadth of Europe without being apprehended by police. A raw Jovian with no knowledge of Earth, sticking out like a sore thumb?"

"Yes sir."

"How did you survive?"

"I did odd jobs. Anything I could get."

The officer ran his thumb down the page, making it scroll. "I see that one of your so-called odd jobs was in the city of Graz, assisting in a criminal bullion transaction. What other criminal activities were you involved in?"

"I worked off the books, sir," Jarls said steadily enough. "That's a crime everywhere."

"And in all that time the police never picked you up? Forced you to work for them as an informant?"

That startled Jarls. "No."

"Show your arm."

Jarls reluctantly rolled back his sleeve. One of the technical support people was at his side before he knew it, running a portable scanner over the counterfeit bar code. There was a beeping at the technical table, and Jarls could see a flickering of transmitted data on the luminous pages before the members of the committee.

The technician who had scanned him raised his head and said

to the officers at the table, "That's the new one. The code remains static, but the central algorhythm keeps shifting to find safe hiding places. They haven't cottoned to it yet at the Labor Ministry."

The examining officer gave Jarls a sharp look. "I see that you were able to find the criminal element here, as well," he said.

"Sir . . ." Jarls began.

"But not quickly enough. You worked for weeks with the most rudimentary documentation here in the most sensitive area of the Bern-Liechtenstein megalopolis, and you were picked up neither by the police or Count Steg's security force. Steg's been trying to get himself Jovian informants of any stripe he can, in the hope of trapping the Executive Guard. What did they promise you? That they'd let you alone if you kept your eyes and ears open for them?"

"Sir, I . . ."

Two members of the disposal squad, burly even by Jovian standards, had risen from their bench and were edging toward Jarls.

Karsen spoke up quickly. "He's no squeaker. I'll vouch for him personally."

"We can't take any chances, Captain Karsen," the gray-haired officer said tiredly.

"I appeal to you, General Carnavan . . ."

Something rang in Jarls's brain. "Carnavan? *Leith* Carnavan?"

A hand like a hydraulic press gripped his arm. "Come along quietly," the guardsman said. A second member of the disposal squad fell in beside him, and they started to lead him away.

"Wait!"

The gray-haired general held up a restraining hand, and the grip on Jarls's arm relaxed.

"How did you know my name?" the general said to Jarls.

"I . . . I have a letter for you." Jarls attempted to reach for the letter he had carried on his person ever since leaving Jupiter, but the guardsmen pinned his arms and immobilized him.

"Hold it, friend," one of them said.

"Let him be," Carnavan said, and they released his arms, keeping a wary eye on him.

Jarls dug out the crumpled envelope. It was grimy and stained from his travels, but the tough waterproof skin was undamaged and the holographic seal was intact. He handed it over to Carnavan under the disposal squad's watchful gaze.

"It's from Ian Karg," the general told his colleagues, and broke the seal. He read rapidly, then passed the letter around. There was a murmur of voices around the table, as the others absorbed the contents.

"How do we know it's authentic?" the hawk-faced officer demanded.

"It's authentic," Carnavan said. "The seal can't be duplicated— there's a clock in it, and a forger couldn't reproduce the precise transformations as time elapses. They're specific to communications with me—one old comrade-in-arms to another. He doesn't use the seal lightly. I've had exactly four communications from him in the last twenty years."

"All well and good, General," the hawk-faced officer persisted, "but why should we take Karg's word for holy writ in a matter as insignificant as this?"

Thunder gathered on Carnavan's brow. "The Guard owes Ian Karg a blood debt. He's called in his markers. The price is a modest one for services rendered—'Show all consideration to the bearer of this letter, Jarls Anders.' Some of you would not be sitting here at this table tonight if it weren't for the sacrifice he made."

There was a lot of sober head-nodding at that. The objecting officer's face darkened, but he kept his silence after the rebuke. Carnavan turned to Jarls and asked, "How do you know Ian Karg?"

"He . . . he's a friend of my father's." That was stretching it a bit, but Jarls supposed that his father was as close to Ian Karg as anyone was.

"He speaks highly of you. Ian's trust doesn't come easily."

Jarls was bewildered. Perhaps Karg respected Clete Anders for his reputation—everybody did—but Jarls would hardly have supposed that Port Elysium's undisputed Great Man would have been aware of his existence: a boy growing up.

"General—what did Ian Karg do?" he ventured.

"He performed a very great act of heroism. He—"

Voices of protest at the table interrupted him. "Leith, you can't give him that information. It's restricted."

"It's old history," Carnavan said. "And it's not going to leave this room anyway." He turned to Jarls. "Is it, Anders?"

"N . . . no sir," Jarls said.

"Ian Karg kept a very dirty nuclear device from going off. He killed three . . ." He looked at his colleagues. ". . . let's call them terrorists . . . single-handedly, and then, instead of getting the hell out of there, as anyone else might have done, he stayed with it until, against all odds, he was able to neutralize the device. He kept the castle from being blown up, and with it the current Megachairman, corporate headquarters, Executive Guard headquarters and most of the Guard population, and half of Old Liechtenstein with a good chunk of the eastern Swiss megalopolis for good measure. And in the process, he took a radiation dose that ended his career."

"I didn't know," Jarls said.

"The public was never told of Karg's heroism. The matter was too sensitive. It wouldn't do for the world at large to know how close we came to disaster, or to encourage others to think they could get past the Executive Guard."

"But they didn't!" Jarls burst out.

"No, they didn't, did they?" Carnavan said. "Well, are you ready to become a part of this operation?"

"Yes sir!"

The general looked with distaste at Jarls's workie clothing. He turned to an aide. "See what you can do to get him properly attired."

"Yes sir," the aide said. He moved toward Jarls. "Come with me," he said. When Jarls hesitated, he elaborated, "That's all right. If your friends can't wait for you, we'll assign you to a Guard detachment."

"Just one moment, Lieutenant," General Carnavan called out as they started to leave. His voice softened as he said to Jarls, "How was Ian when you left him?"

Jarls called up the memory of an austere, gray-faced man sitting erect in his walking chair, surrounded by his medals and memorabilia, sipping the costly Burgundy from Earth that was his one indulgence, and ignoring the pain that had left the deep lines in his face.

"Well enough, sir," he said.

# 20

THE STAGING area was a villa in what had once been the Italian Riviera, but which for some three centuries had been a sovereign stretch of the Swiss seacoast.

Jarls sat with sixty other Jovians in the briefing room, converted from the villa's former grand *sala*, listening to Captain Stock, the unit's commanding officer, outline the mission.

"Our job is to pry a Lord Director named Berndt out of the Swiss naval base where he's holed up." Captain Stock said. He was a huge slablike man who still wore his Jovian strength with care in Earth's feeble gravity, keeping all his gestures tightly limited. "Lieutenant Rudenkov, you look like you've swallowed a lemon. Do you care to share your thoughts with us?"

Rudenkov spoke reluctantly. "Begging your pardon, Captain, but are we going to fight the whole Swiss navy?"

"We're not going to fight them at all if we can help it, Lieutenant. We're going to use speed, surprise, and overwhelming force, and hope that nobody gets hurt. We're going to have to live with the Swiss navy and Herr Berndt when all this is over."

Jarls stole a surreptitious glance at the overwhelming force he was supposed to be a part of. All of sixty Jovians. No body armor, no heavy weapons. He fingered the weapon that the sergeant had given him. One lightweight tranquilizer gun, set for single fire. It was sealed in a transparent bag, which he had been instructed not to open. Why, the sergeant had not told him. There was just enough play in the bag for him to grasp the gun by the butt and get a forefinger through the trigger guard. The first dart was supposed to be fired through the plastic for some reason.

For the rest of it, he was wearing a borrowed uniform with the silver collar insignia removed. They were willing to use him for his muscle, but you had to earn the right to wear the Executive Guards insignia.

"There'll be perimeter guards with powered suits," Rudenkov said dubiously.

"Then we'll be even, won't we, Lieutenant?" the Captain said sweetly. "Any other questions?"

Rudenkov shook his head. It occurred to Jarls that tranquilizer darts would be no good against men in powered suits, but he kept his mouth shut.

The Captain waited for a moment, and when no one else was foolhardy enough to speak up, he went on:

"Herr Brandt ran at the first sign of trouble, and the Swiss navy gave him asylum. They won't give him up—at least not until they're sure what side their bread's buttered on. And that's not going to be until a new Megachairman's installed and things quiet down. That made him our assignment. There are sixteen other directors in hiding, and other teams have been assigned to dig them out. We've got to have a minimum of at least seven of them to get a majority vote on the board. Herr Brandt was judged to be one of those who'll go along once he sees which way the wind is blowing. So that makes this operation important."

A brave hand went up, a young guardsman with no discernible mark of rank.

"Yes?"

"Excuse me, sir. What about Prince Franz Joseph?"

Captain Stock's furrowed brow gained another crease. "The Megachairman disappeared last night. We assume he's in hiding, too. He could be anywhere on the planet. The Intelligence section hasn't had any luck in tracing him so far, but they're still trying. That complicates the problem. Count Steg may be holding him in reserve, hoping to nullify the coup. We can only hope that he'll turn up before there's time for the opposition forces to rally around him. But that's not our concern. Our part in this is only to bring Herr Brandt back alive. We'll have to leave the rest of it to the political people."

Jarls shifted in his chair. It creaked under his weight. At the front of the room, Captain Stock was turning toward a ghostly image that was beginning to take shape in the air. After a moment, Jarls realized that Stock's adjutant, a Lieutenant Alves, was unreeling an almost invisible holo window from a cylindrical housing up among the carved cherubs decorating the *sala*'s ceiling. The tall windows looking out on the Gulf of Genoa began to darken, and the lines of an architectural plan, partially filled in by an actual aerial view, began to take shape.

"This is the front gate of the base," Stock said, pointing at the perimeter of the diagram with a glowing arrow that lengthened and shortened depending on the depth of its point within the holo. "There's a guardhouse here, and a pillbox for backup on the opposite side of the approach. We can be sure that it'll be manned by reinforcements in power suits. We don't want to get bogged down here, so we'll get inside by subterfuge."

Stock's arrow traced the roadway leading through the gate. "When everybody's in position, Lieutenant Alves and I will arrive unannounced in a staff car, with flags flying. We'll have a driver in front and two men posing as our aides in the second seats. That will make five of us—probably the maximum number that we can get in by pure bluff. We'll all be in dress uniform and ostentatiously unarmed."

Jarls caught his breath at the Captain's audaciousness. His respect for the Executive Guard went up a notch. Whatever the rest of the extraction plan, the Captain and the other four were putting themselves on the line, and without even a sidearm among them.

"There'll be a second car following behind us, and that one *will* have eight armed men in it," the Captain went on. "The Swiss won't like that at all, and their attention will be focussed on the second car. They're going to be very stubborn about letting it through the gate, and that will set the stage for my next move. I'm going to demand to see the base commander, Admiral Frisch. The admiral and I know each other very well, and we've had many a set-to on security matters, though we've maintained a cordial relationship in between. I'm going to be very up front about my purpose—to bring Herr Brandt back with me to the capital. He'll deny that he's harboring Herr Brandt, of course, and I'll make a terrible fuss—invoke our authority as the palace guard, and demand that I be received in the residence. That's where Herr Brandt will be—in the residence or in the underground warren beneath it.

"Frisch will finally give in, and allow me and my party through the gate, but he'll be adamant about keeping the armed squad outside the gate. I'll make a fuss about that, too, just to muddy matters, and insist that I need them to carry out a search. The admiral, being a typical Swiss polititian, will be reluctant to make the first overtly hostile move, so he'll seek to defuse the situation by inviting Lieutenant Alves and me inside for tea and cakes, while my driver and the two enlisted men cool their heels in the driveway."

He smiled, showing a row of white, even teeth. "Of course he'll have a couple of men in powered suits outside the drawing room doors, and that will lull the admiral still further. But a couple of men in powered suits are nothing Lieutenant Alves and I can't handle, eh, Lieutenant?"

Alves looked up briefly from his holo remote to flash a crocodile grin.

The Captain's self-confidence was impressive, but Jarls wondered how even a Jovian, with Jupiter-bred muscles, could stand up to a man in a powered suit. If a Jovian was three or four times as strong as an Earthian, an Earthian in a mechanically augmented suit of armor was at least four or five times as strong as a Jovian.

A second later, he had his answer.

"For those of you who've never gone up against a man in a powered suit and've let that part of your rookie training slip out of your memory, remember the story of Antaeus. Antaeus was the mythological character who was invincibly strong, because he got his strength from contact with Mother Earth. But Hercules outwitted him. He lifted him off the ground and held him in the air, where his strength didn't do him any good. Is it coming back? Your basic training instructor called it the Antaeus maneuver. Just be quick. Lift him overhead, front side up so the powered mitts can't reach you—a suit's clumsy and the arms can't reach backward—and smash him against any convenient hard surface. The elbow and knee joints are vulnerable. Dent them and you've immobilized your opponent. Remember that a man in a powered suit may be stronger than you, but he's also slower than you. You're fighting in your skin, in gravity that's a joke. Forget it and you're dead meat."

Jarls began to wonder what he was doing in an Executive Guard uniform—even one without insignia. The training he'd received at Strathspey, under the tutelage of Karsen and his combat instructor Harkins had been superb, but this barehanded operation of Captain Stock's was on another plane. He stole a glance at the seated men around him and wondered how he'd measure up.

"Now," Captain Stock was saying, "at the proper moment Lieutenant Alves and I will overpower the residence guards and take Admiral Frisch and any staff prisoner. In the meantime, our carful of armed men outside the main gate will have made a new ruckus and demanded again to be let through. They'll overpower the sentries who come out to deal with them and break through the gate. There'll be a fine brouhaha, and that will concentrate the attention of any reinforcements who show up. At the same time, the two supposed aides I've left outside the residence will quite naturally pound on the admiral's door to inform me and Lieutenant Alves of the riot. They'll bull their way inside and dispose of any additional personnel they see, and help the Lieutenant and I cope. The driver will remain outside, visibly pacing and checking his watch."

Lieutenant Rudenko was becoming more and more agitated. "Captain . . ." he began.

"Yes, Lieutenant," the Captain said. "You want to know what part you and the rest of the men are going to play in this operation."

The holographic arrow moved across the aerial map and came to rest at a point on the seaward side of the residence. Some kind of naval installation was there, but Jarls couldn't make it out clearly.

"I was just getting to that," the Captain said.

An hour later, Jarls was standing at attention on the villa's sandy beach with approximately fifty of the Jovian guardsmen, while a beady-eyed sergeant named Moy looked them all over with a fierce scowl.

"All right, you men, strip down to your skivvies and *unterhose*," the sergeant ordered. "Any free spirits here, you're out of luck. Fold your uniforms and leave them on the beach. They'll be here when you get back. If you get back."

Setting an example, the sergeant shucked off tunic, trousers and boots and laid them on the sand. The other men did the same, and Jarls followed suit, regretfully relinquishing the Executive Guard trappings he had been temporarily granted.

Sergeant Moy surveyed the resulting assembly of some ten tons of granitelike Jovian muscle critically. He himself resembled a primitive, thick-bodied stone statue that had been incongruously clothed in neatly pressed khaki underwear. Jarls noted the many scars that covered Moy's body, including a terrifying deep furrow all the way down one meaty arm.

"Any of you ever work under water before?" Moy asked.

Several hands shot up. "I worked on the transpacific tunnel, sarge," one of them said. There was an echo of similar voices.

"Awright. Good. Anybody here have experience working outside on Jupiter? Or in the Venusian atmosphere?"

More hands went up—a majority of those present. Jarls, feeling self-conscious, raised his hand with the other veterans.

"Good. This will be a piece of cake, then. We're going to stay in shallow water. The pressures won't be anywhere near what you're already used to. The main thing is to know how to move against resistance without wearing yourselves out."

Another hand went up—one of the men who had not responded previously. "I didn't work on the tunnel or anything, sarge, but I've done underwater walking on a Mediterranean archaeology project. When I was a graduate student. That count?"

The sergeant eyed him up and down. "You second generation?"

The archaeology student flushed. "Yes, but I passed all the Guard's tests for muscle fiber structure and low lactate buildup, and I've kept up with the weights and the penguin suit since I was a little kid."

The sergeant gave a little nod. "You'll do." His attention switched to Jarls. "You, the new man. You a native-born Jovian?"

"Yes."

"You raised your mitt. What's your experience?"

Jarls strove to recall the outside expedition that had killed Uncle Hector. "Soft suit on Jupiter. Down to about one hundred kilometers. About twenty atmospheres. A powered hard suit on Venus. But you had to work against it all the time."

He remembered, with a sudden stab of grief, how Herk had kept his suit moving by sheer muscle after the power had given out, and wondered if he could have managed a feat like that.

Moy nodded. "So I've heard. We get a lot of men who've worked downstairs on Jupiter, but we don't see many who've come by way of Venus. It doesn't work that way." He looked at Jarls with new respect.

Jarls thought that Moy was going to say something more, but the sergeant moved to a large packing crate lying on the sand, smashed it open with a blow of his fist, and bellowed at the waiting group:

"Awright, come up one at a time. Hang on to your plastic bag with the trank gun, because that's the only other thing you're taking with you."

When it was Jarls's turn, he got a pair of plastic goggles that were little more than eye cups, and some kind of respirator that resembled a surgical mask. The tank that came with it might have been charitably described as a sausage-shaped plastic balloon; it gave when he squeezed it. But it must have been made of some crystalline hypercarbon, like Mars's orbital elevators or Port Elysium's skin, because the contents would have to have been under tremendous pressure.

"No metal, not even my wristwatch," the sergeant said. "That's made of plastic too, with a plastic battery. The Swiss can detect a twenty-Liechtenfranc coin at a distance of half a mile. And that's *without* using a metal detector!"

Jarls and the men around him forced smiles at the tired joke, but the sergeant pushed on without pause:

"As far as the Swiss navy's concerned, we're nothing but biomass, and there's plenty of that in the Mediterranean. We'll have dolphin cover for our bubbles. It's all been arranged."

A hand went up. It was the underwater archaeologist. "But sarge, the Swiss navy has dolphins working for it."

"We've got dolphins on our payroll too. And we used our dolphins to bribe their dolphins. Both sides thought it was a great joke. Dolphins have their own sense of humor."

There were no more questions. Sergeant Moy glanced at his plastic wristwatch. "What the hell is keeping Lieutenant Rudenkov?" He raised his massive head and fixed the assembled ranks with an angry glare. "And remember one more thing. Lieutenant Rudenko is the officer in charge of this little excursion, so don't any of you get out of line. But you keep an eye on me, and follow my lead, and you'll be all right." He glanced at his watch again and frowned.

Rudenkov showed up about ten minutes later, wearing a regulation frog suit with lead weights around his waist and a pair of steel tanks strapped to his back.

"All right, sergeant, are we ready?" he said.

"Sorry, sir, but you'll have to get rid of the wet suit." Sergeant Moy said, his voice properly regretful. "It's too risky."

"That's ridiculous, sergeant," Rudenkov said. "The bottom's littered with scrap metal. One pair of tanks isn't going to make any difference."

"The bottom metal doesn't move," the sergeant said, as if placating a small child.

Rudenko's face tightened. "You're forgetting that I'm the one in command, sergeant," he said.

"Yes sir," Moy said without inflection. He stared unblinkingly at Rudenko.

The face-off lasted about fifteen seconds. Then Rudenko gave a petulant sigh and peeled off the wet suit and equipment. The sergeant silently handed him mask and goggles, and helped him secure the plastic balloon under his arm.

"Just squeeze it like a bagpipe, sir," he said. "You'll get the hang of it."

He got the men formed into a double line and said, "Stay close. It's easy to get lost out there. Anybody loses contact, don't try to catch up. Just walk for shallow water and stay under until your air gives out. Then you can go ashore and wait until someone picks you up. If I think anybody's done that on purpose, there'll be disciplinary action."

Then, with a last glance at the rear facade of the villa and its enclosing walls, he marched into the sea. The double line followed closely, with the men spaced almost within touching distance of one another.

Jarls was near the tag end of one of the lines, so he was able to watch as they disappeared one by one into the water. It was an eerie sight, all of those blocky overmuscled men wading steadily into the sunny blue sea, knee deep, waist deep, neck deep, until finally their heads went under and were gone.

Then it was his turn. The warmish water lapped at his legs and crept up his body inch by inch. He took an instinctive panicky breath as the water covered his face, but the simple breathing apparatus worked fine.

It was a little like walking on the surface of Venus. In fact, it was easier to walk under a terrestrial sea than to push your way through the soupy Venusian atmosphere, the powered suit notwithstanding. But the visibility was even worse. Jarls could see only as far as four or five men ahead of him before the column blurred into invisibility. He kept his eyes fixed on the pale back immediately ahead of him, afraid to lose contact.

After a while he picked up a rock he had stumbled over and kept it tucked in the crook of his free arm. The extra weight made walking easier. He noticed that two or three of the men within his field of vision had done the same thing.

A flock of shadows appeared overhead. It was the dolphin escort. They darted back and forth in what looked like a random pattern, but always returned to mask the marching column.

One of the dolphins swam down to have a look at Jarls. It hung beside him for a few paces, a long gray shape with a bulbous head, and opened its beak in a sawtooth grin. It was wearing some kind of harness with a tool kit attached. It gave him a playful nudge that almost bowled him over, then rose to rejoin its fellows on the surface.

The sandy bottom was cluttered with debris from other eras: bottles and jars, corroded anchors, pieces of broken statuary. The column was marching parallel to the shore, a few hundred feet out. The sergeant took a detour into deeper water to avoid a drowned villa that had gone under some time in the twenty-first or twenty-second century, when the ice caps had shrunk and sea levels had risen. A wrecked automobile was still parked in front of it. And now there was earlier debris—the bones of an ancient wooden ship from Greek or Roman times. The timbers had largely rotted away, but the shape of the hull could still be traced by the remains of the ship's cargo—a litter of clay wine jars, some of them still intact. Jarls felt sorry for the underwater archaeologist, having to walk by the wreck without stopping.

Jarls's sense of time had become distorted in the murky under-water environment, but he thought they had been marching for two or three hours when he bumped into the man ahead, and the remaining men in the rear bunched up behind him. It was not until he had stopped that he realized how fatigued he was. He wondered how much air he had left, and whether he and the other men would be up to the job that still lay ahead of them.

He waited. After a while the man in front of him handed him a waterproof slate that the sergeant had passed down the line. He read:

200 YARDS FROM SHORE

DOLPHIN SONAR SAYS MINIMAL ACTIVITY INSIDE PEN

GO IN FAST AND SPREAD OUT

That was all that was necessary. The Captain's briefing had covered all the details. Jarls passed the slate to the man behind him.

The column started to move, taking a sharp right angle toward shore. There was a slight upward slope, noticeable now. Jarls moved as fast as he could, straining hard against water resistance. The dolphins sported overhead, their turbulence masking any bubbles from the increased effort of the Jovians below.

The sergeant called a brief halt about halfway up the slope to allow for decompression, even though the gradual slope and the nitrogen-free breathing mix made any danger unlikely. Then the column resumed pushing shoreward, with maximum effort. The going became fractionally easier as the depth of the water decreased.

A great yawning cavern grew before Jarls's eyes—the sea entrance to the Swiss navy's submarine pen on the Gulf of Genoa. The brilliance of Captain Stock's strategy came home to Jarls; they were going to be able to get inside the Swiss naval base without ever having to leave the cover of the water.

He slogged on. The details of the submarine pen became clearer. The sandy floor leading into the cavern became a cleated steel ramp that presumably could be raised for drydock operations. The dolphins were gone, their job done. Jarls passed a length of massive chain that disappeared somewhere overhead, and then found himself enclosed by looming walls that rose on either side. The water grew ominously darker now that the bright Mediterranean daylight from above was cut off by the roof of the artificial cave, but the artificial illumination filtering through the depths still provided enough light to see by.

Another hundred yards and a steel cliff rose ahead of him. Jarls was glad to see that it was liberally provided with access ladders, dangling chains, and honeycomb recesses that could be used as handholds. Climbing it would be no problem for a bunch of

Jovians used to hauling themselves aloft in a gravity field two and a half times more powerful than Earth's.

He joined the men clustered around Sergeant Moy. Moy was making urgent hand signals; they had to move fast now, before someone spotted them from above.

Moy went first. He ripped off his breathing mask, clamped the plastic bag containing the needle gun between his teeth, and clambered up one of the chains. The men swarmed up the chains and ladders after him. Jarls, eschewing the sergeant's bravado, kept his breathing mask prudently on, and climbed one-handed, with an occasional assist from the hand encumbered by the bagged gun. The water's buoyancy nullified even his inconsiderable Earth weight as he drew himself from rung to rung; it was almost like pulling yourself along in free fall.

When his hand found the top rung, he yanked off the breathing mask and burst through to the surface. Seal-slick heads were emerging from the water all around him.

He had time only for a quick impression of his surroundings. Five or six of the small scout subs the Swiss navy used in the Mediterranean were moored at a row of finger piers that projected from a long concrete dock running the length of the cavern. A number of construction cranes and other pieces of heavy-duty equipment ran on tracks along the main dock. A yellowish illumination came from lamps high overhead.

There were no people around except for a half-dozen sailors in work fatigues busy with hoses and tools alongside one of the submarines. They didn't see the Jovians at first. Then one of them gave a strangled shout and pointed, and they all stared goggle-eyed at the heads popping out of the pool.

One man tried to make a run for it, and was brought down by a tranquilizer dart from somebody's plastic gun. The others milled around indecisively. The Jovians nearest to the sailors heaved themselves out of the water and surrounded them. In seconds, the Swiss were trussed up and immobilized.

Sergeant Moy was giving orders. "Get them out of sight. You,

Willy and Cheng, have a look down those corridors and see if they're clear. Garrigan, hand me the map."

Jarls helped drag the trussed sailors to a corrugated metal storage shed and lock them up. The men were too terrified to resist. When Jarls picked one of them up to hand him through to the Jovian inside, the man went rigid with fright. "Don't worry, nobody's going to hurt you," Jarls tried to reassure him, but the man didn't seem to understand.

When Jarls returned to Sergeant Moy, he found him surrounded by a mob of fidgeting Jovians at one of the corridor debouchments. "All right, men, get ready to move out," Moy barked. "Lieutenant Rudenko, I guess it's time to let the captain know we're on our way."

Jarls spotted Rudenko at the edge of the pier, lowering the end of what looked like a long plastic cord into the water by a length of thread. The Earthborn guardsman who had said he was an underwater archaeologist was doing the same thing a couple of hundred yards away. There were bulges at spaced intervals along the cord: plastic bags filled with some viscous substance. Rudenko fastened the thread to a cleat. The whole arrangement was in a straight line against the concrete, only a few feet under water.

"No metal, as you can see, Sergeant Moy," he said with heavy sarcasm. "Not even a detonator cap. All chemical. The captain thought of everything."

"What is that thing?" Jarls whispered to the man ahead of him.

The lieutenant couldn't have heard him, but he responded to all the puzzled looks he was getting.

"Radio signal wouldn't work with all this mass around us," he explained. "So we're going to use a modulated seismic shock. Very primitive. No precise timing. But the approximate intervals between the bangs will be good enough to provide a recognizable signal to the sensitive equipment in the vehicle waiting at the gate, and *they'll* beep the captain and Lieutenant Alves inside the residence. Here goes. You'll hardly feel a thing."

Rudenko reached down into the water and must have squeezed

the plastic bag at the end of the tubing. He withdrew his hand in a hurry. A few seconds later, the water gave a violent burp. Jarls could detect no shock or vibration through his bare feet. But then there was a succession of burps that traveled down the length of the pier, each one making a little fountain that splashed over the edge of the concrete. It was over in less than a minute.

Rudenko looked pleased with himself. "There we are. If all went well, the captain and the men outside have now started their diversion. We'll only be troubled by whatever personnel happen to be wandering about the tunnels. There'll be no reinforcements from elsewhere."

"Go!" Sergeant Moy shouted hoarsely.

The Jovian horde poured into the corridors. Jarls joined them, clutching the little trank pistol. It would have to be enough.

They ran into trouble at the first bend. A Swiss seaman in sentry gear, complete with helmet and transparent faceplate, came running toward them. He raised an automatic rifle without preamble and began firing.

Two Jovians went down. A hail of darts spent themselves harmlessly against protective clothing and the faceplate. A third Jovian reached the sentry, plucked the rifle from his grip, and broke his neck. Jarls, coming up fast, got a jolt when he saw that the man who had taken the sentry out so ruthlessly was Rudenko.

"How is he?" Rudenko said, turning toward the first of the fallen Jovians.

"Dead," said the man kneeling at his side.

Rudenko bent to examine the other downed Jovian. "How bad is it, guardsman?"

"I'll make it, sir," the man said through gritted teeth. "But I can't walk."

A spurt of automatic fire had stitched him across one leg, above the knee. He'd had the presence of mind to take off his skivvie shirt and wind it tightly around the wounds.

"We can't take you with us."

"I know, sir."

"You'll have to wait here until the Swiss come by. That might be a couple of hours. Surrender to them. They'll take care of you. We'll come by the hospital and reclaim you when all this is over."

"Yes sir."

Rudenko turned away. "Three casualties so far," he said to no one in particular. "Two of ours and one of theirs. The captain isn't going to like that."

But Jarls noticed that all the same, Rudenko had taken the automatic rifle from the man he had killed and discarded the little tranquilizer pistol.

The Jovians pushed on. There was another encounter farther down the maze, at an intersection that opened out into a guard station. The three men on duty must have had a couple of minutes' warning from sensors or security cameras, because they came piling out of their booth with their weapons at the ready.

When they saw that the corridor was thronged with half-naked Jovians, all of them armed with some kind of projectile gun, the Swiss threw down their weapons and surrendered. Rudenko looked disappointed.

The prisoners were unprotesting when Sergeant Moy had them tied up. Moy took a long look at all the communications equipment in the security booth, saw how lightweight and easily movable the chairs they were tied to were, and judiciously shot each of them in the neck with a tranquilizer dart.

It was easy going after that. The Jovians spread out through the maze of tunnels, breaking down doors and searching the bunkers. Some of the doors opened into dormitories, supply rooms, and weapons stores reflecting the centuries-old Swiss obsession with their historical defenses against a nuclear war that had never taken place. Some of the bunkers were luxury apartments, meant for top brass and government bigwigs.

But they flushed out only a handful of people—a janitor sneaking a nap in one of the bunkrooms, a hungover petty officer sleeping it off, an indignant storekeeper taking inventory in a supply room, a couple of sheet metal workers replacing a ventilation duct, an unfortunate sailor surprised finding his girlfriend in the bedroom of one of the VIP apartments. The Jovians herded them all into an empty hospital ward, with someone staying behind to keep an eye on them.

Jarls was checking out one of the side galleries when he heard a shout from the main corridor.

"We've got him! It's Berndt!"

He stuck his head outside and saw two Jovians escorting a balding man in a rumpled business suit out of a door that was hanging from one hinge. Herr Berndt was protesting furiously:

"Take your hands off me, Jovian swine!" he sputtered. "Do you know who I am?"

"That we do, Herr Director," Sergeant Moy said. "Don't worry, you won't be harmed. You'll be treated with all respect. Your presence is required at a board meeting in Vaduz."

"Board meeting? What board meeting? By whose authority?"

Moy ignored the question. "Take him outside, boys. Form a flying wedge around him. Our transport ought to be waiting at the gate by now. Captain Stern will have the admiral for a shield. When the admiral sees Brandt, he'll bow to the inevitable and switch sides like a good civil servant. Nobody's going to shoot."

A dozen Jovians boxed Herr Berndt in and hustled him off at high speed. The loud protests grew fainter and fainter as the forced cortege disappeared down the corridor.

Sergeant Moy put two fingers in his mouth and gave a piercing whistle. "Move out, move out!" he shouted.

"Just a minute, Sarge," a voice responded farther back. "I've almost got this door down!"

"That means everybody!" the sergeant yelled.

Lieutenant Rudenko's voice cut in. "Let him have a look. Who knows. The admiral may have another director stashed away in here."

"We're slicing it too thin, Lieutenant," Moy objected. "Our assignment was to look for Berndt, period."

"Are you arguing with me, Sergeant?" Rudenko said dangerously.

"No sir." Moy raised his voice. "Be quick about it, Garrigan! Catch up with us as soon as you can!"

Simultaneously there was a huge crash as a ton of steel door fell in. "Nothing, Sarge," Garrigan's voice called a moment later. "Just another store room!" There was no answer from the departing troop and next there were the sounds of bare feet slapping on the concrete floor as Garrigan ran after them.

It had all taken less than a minute. Jarls had been on the verge of abandoning the side gallery and following the others, but Rudenko's interference could be construed as permission of a sort. He took another look at the door he had been examining. It was as featureless as all the others, but there was a discreet seal on it in the form of a shield and a crown. That decided him.

He braced his bare feet against the floor and heaved with all his Jovian strength. Nothing happened. The door was as firm as a rock. He tried again. He thought he felt something give, no more than a sixteenth of an inch. He thought he might have bent the inner steel frame that much, but this door was tougher than most of them had been. It was going to take two or three Jovians at least to smash it down.

He thought about it for a moment. The Swiss had frozen their defensive posture in a dangerous nuclear age, centuries earlier. The doors in these underground tunnels were meant to withstand a blast from outside. Three bars of pressure, if he remembered the captain's briefing correctly. But that was pressure from outside, not the other way around.

He took another look at the door. It wasn't as featureless as it seemed. A foot-long rectangle of surface along one edge was something that looked like an access panel. Of course! For casual entry under conditions short of Armageddon, there would be an ordinary locking mechanism.

The panel was held in place by four hex bolts. He didn't have a hex wrench with him, but he had his Jovian fingers. He grasped one of the bolts between thumb and forefinger and exerted pressure. After a moment, the bolt gave a loud squeal of protest and started to turn. The turning became progressively easier, and the bolt came free in his hand. He had the other three bolts off in less than a minute, and the panel fell off with a clatter.

His assumption had been correct; there was a perfectly ordinary steel doorknob inside. He tried turning it, but it was immovable, locked from inside. He used more force, and the knob broke off in his hand.

But the rectangular recess left along the door's edge offered purchase for his fingertips. Jarls hooked the fingers of both hands inside the recess, planted his feet flat against the doorframe and heaved with all his might. He could feel the outer steel doorframe start to give. He heaved again, and this time was able to rip the door out of the frame. He let go and rolled to the side as the foot-thick slab toppled into the corridor.

He stepped over the fallen door and went through the opening. It was a luxury apartment, vip quarters with paneled walls and overstuffed furniture. He had just enough time for that to register, when he saw the headless thing that was waiting for him there.

It was a man in a powered suit, a heavy-duty model that was one continuous ovoid from top to groin, looking for all the world like a black-enameled egg with stumpy legs and stovepipe arms ending in three-fingered claws.

It moved at once toward Jarls, its arms extended. Jarls tried to remember what Captain Stock had said about fighting a powered suit bare-handed.

A claw made a swipe at him, but he was able to dodge it. The three fingers clicked together with a force that could easily have crushed granite, and would have squeezed Jovian muscle to paste. Jarls circled the armored man warily, looking for an opening. He feinted toward the cloudy dome where the man's head would be, hoping for a reflex. A claw snatched at his fist, fast but not fast enough. Captain Stock had been right; powered suits were a shade slower and clumsier than unassisted human reflexes. But Jarls knew that if those claws once got hold of him, he was finished.

The armored man made another swipe at him. He was trying to back Jarls into a corner. Jarls studied the smooth ovoid, but there was nothing that offered a safe grip. Then it dawned on him that the suit was unable to bend at the waist.

He tried to get around behind his adversary, but he was out of maneuvering room. He was boxed into the corner, barely out of reach, and the armored figure was advancing on him, arms outstretched. Jarls retreated until he felt his back against the wall.

His opponent lunged, and Jarls dropped to the floor. The claws ripped through hardwood paneling and punctured the concrete behind it. The egg was off balance for a fraction of a second. Before it could recover its center of gravity, Jarls thrust with his feet against the baseboard and shot like a catapulted boulder into the pierlike ankles.

The suit's enormous strength was no good to the man inside. His footing gone from under him, he crashed to the floor, face down. Before he could use the piston arms to push himself upright, Jarls had rolled past him, twisted around and grasped him by the ankles. Jarls scrambled to his feet, dragging his flailing opponent with him. He backed off to a clear space in the center of the room, where the snapping claws could find nothing to grasp for leverage. Then, the armored ankles firmly in his grip, he began to spin round and round like a shot put thrower.

The suit must have weighed three quarters of a ton, but as Jarls built up speed, centrifugal force made it easier. The claws groped blindly but were unable to reach him, and at last stopped flexing as blood pooled in the the unfortunate operator's brain and made him woozy.

With a final spin, Jarls slammed the walking egg against the wall. It slid to the floor, an arm and leg crumpled at the elbow and knee mechanisms. There was no detectable movement. Jarls hoped the operator had not been injured too seriously.

He pushed his way into the room beyond. It was a bedroom with silk tapestries hanging from the walls and a baronial four-poster bed centered in an alcove.

Jarls thought he heard a sound—a soft indrawn breath. He approached the bed. The heel of a slippered foot was sticking out from under it, poking through the coverlets hanging down from the side.

He grabbed the foot by the ankle and dragged out a portly man in a dressing gown. The face was unmistakable—the walrus mustache, the bristly gray hair, the bulging eyes, the protuberant jaw. It was the Megachairman, Prince Franz Joseph the Twenty-fourth.

The Megachairman stared at him, his mouth working mutely. Jarls took him gently but firmly by the arm and said, "It's all right, sir. But you'll have to come with me."

# 21

**W**AKE UP, Anders, you've got company." A hand was on his shoulder, shaking him roughly.

Jarls rolled over and sat up, aching in every joint. "What time is it?"

"Oh five three oh."

"Report isn't till oh six."

That's what they had told Jarls when they had walked him through the barracks by flashlight and assigned him a bunk. He'd had less than three hours sleep. He'd been held incommunicado for most of the day after delivering Franz Joseph, and then the debriefing had lasted until the early hours of the morning.

"Come on. They're waiting for you in the day room."

Jarls stretched with an involuntary wince of pain and a loud cracking of bones. The long walk underwater and the strenuous wrapup of the operation had taken its toll. "Who are they?"

"Visitors. How do I know? Come on, get going or you'll miss chow."

He showered, shaved, and dressed in under ten minutes. Another loaner uniform, freshly pressed and neatly folded, had been left at the foot of his bunk. Like the first uniform, it was without any Guard insignia.

The visitors waiting for him in the dayroom turned out to be Karsen, Czoznek, and Stern. They were sitting on one of the couches, watching an early morning newscast on the dayroom's holovid set. They were still outfitted in their Strathspey security guard uniforms, a little worse for wear after what must have been a taxing day and night. Stern had a stained square of gauze taped to one cheek, and Czoznek's right hand was swathed in bandages.

"Hail the conquering hero," Czoznek said without getting up.

Karsen came round the low table to meet Jarls. "In case you hadn't heard," he said, "Prince Rudolph's already been crowned. They flew him in from his shooting estate in Scotland last night. It was a private ceremony in the wee hours, but it was done with all due pomp, for broadcast later on."

"What about the Megachairman?"

"You mean the ex-Megachairman. Prince Franz Joseph's retired to his country estate on Lake Geneva. He's earned a richly deserved rest, and is delighted to have more time to devote to his favorite hobby, collecting stamps and other artifacts of bygone Liechtenstein. He doesn't want to be bothered by the public, and there'll be a special security force to guard his privacy."

"And Count Steg?"

"Oh, Rudolph's going to keep him on as his security minister. That will give him every opportunity to get himself convicted of treason—but some time in the future, when it won't stir things up again. The man's addicted to intrigue and skullduggery, and sooner or later he won't be able to resist the temptation to do something stupid."

Czoznek had turned up the newscast to catch an incoming bulletin. The incurvate holo window now contained a life-size man in sober gray business wear. It was the commentator who usually did the routine, unexciting news about stock prices and inconsequential corporate rearrangements. Jarls and Karsen turned to watch.

"... and in an early morning meeting of the Lord Directors, a vote was taken by the board to install Prince Rudolph of Triesenberg as Megachairman for an indefinite term. Prince Rudolph will be affectionately remembered as the winner, twelve years ago, of the Classic Ski Race at St. Moritz and as a former president of the Alpine Club ..."

"Herr Berndt voted for Rudolph, of course, along with a majority of the other Lord Directors who were rounded up for the vote," Karsen said with a small impeccable smile. "I believe you had something to do with seeing Herr Berndt safely to Megacorp head- quarters, as well as your involvement in the . . . other matter."

"I . . . they . . . yes, the Guard assigned me to that team," Jarls said. He wondered what work Karsen and his crew had been given during the fateful night, but he didn't think he ought to ask straight out.

"Sorry you couldn't be with us," Karsen said. "We had an inter- esting little to do at one of the Alpine passes. But it all worked out rather well, didn't it?"

Stern burst in enthusiastically. "The buzz is all over the place! All the auxiliaries are talking about it. They say you took out a man in a powered suit."

"The Guard is doing its best to damp those rumors," Karsen said dryly. "They'll never reach the general public."

"Yeah, they're holding a couple of guys from a Majorcan secu- rity force incommunicado," Czoznek said with a sour expression. "They're scaring the hell out of them right now."

The holovid was showing peaceful scenes from world capitals, and early reactions from Mars, Venus, and the Moon. The human race seemed to be going about its business as usual. An announcer's voice-over was droning on about Liechtenstein's long and stable history as the solar system's financial center, and its benign, centuries-old union with the Swiss Confederation. Then he started reciting Rudolph's family tree, starting with the original princely purchasers of Liechtenstein in the eighteenth century. Czoznek leaned across and turned down the sound.

"Let's eat," Czoznek said.

Jarls started to explain that the Executive Guards mess was not open to outsiders, when Karsen interrupted and said, "We're your guests."

Jarls said, "But I'm not—I mean, they gave me a ticket for breakfast, but—"

"It's all fixed up. You're excused from morning Report, and then you're going with us to HQ in the Rotes Haus."

* * *

"General Carnavan's waiting for you, Mister Karsen," the staff officer said. He pointed his chin at Jarls. "This Anders?"

"Yes."

The staff officer looked Jarls over. "The general's very pleased with you, son. We had a report that Prince Franz Joseph was holed up in the Carpathians. We thought he was out of our reach."

Jarls was saved from having to reply by a cheer from the corner of the anteroom, where a dozen Executive Guard officers were glued to a small holovid.

"Rudolph's already issued his first decree!" one of them called across the room. "He calls it the Jovian Repatriation Proclamation. It's going to offer financial assistance to indentured Jovians on Venus and Mercury who want to buy out their labor contracts."

Another officer watching the holovid said, "And that's not all. His pres sec says he's drafting an economic aid plan for Jupiter. First step is to help get the Deep Tap project off the ground!"

"Rudolph's moving fast," the staff officer said with a nod of satisfaction. "He let it be known on the flight from Scotland that he feels he owes a debt of gratitude to the Jovians. He knows that Count Steg tried to have him assassinated."

"It sounds like an early signal," Karsen agreed. "He's letting us know that we can expect an enlightened Pandirectorate."

"He needs us while he consolidates," the officer said emphatically. "And after that, he'll need a more prosperous Jupiter as a counterbalance to Venusian power."

"There's that," Karsen admitted. "But the Venusians won't like having their atmospheric mining monopoly threatened."

"We'll see," the officer said. He turned to Jarls with a smile. "In any event, my boy, it looks like good news for the folks you left back home."

"Yes sir," Jarls said.

"We'd better get moving. We're keeping the general waiting."

General Carnavan's office was not the orderly sanctum that Jarls had expected. The general's desk was a rat's nest of papers and flexible screens with dangling plugs. Five or six aides were at work at small tables and consoles scattered haphazardly around the room. A holovision set that no one was watching sat on a shelf with the sound turned down.

"Sit down, sit down," Carnavan said impatiently when Karsen and his entourage squared up at attention in front of the desk. They pulled up chairs, and the general motioned them closer.

"Well, my young friend," he said to Jarls. "That was quite a day's work you did yesterday."

Jarls wasn't sure if an answer was required, and he remained silent.

Carnavan turned to Karsen and said, "And your contribution at the Betterjoch Pass was invaluable, Chief Karsen. We're grateful to you and your men."

"Thank you, General," Karsen said.

"I understand you lost a man there. I'm sorry."

Karsen shrugged. "That's the price, General."

Carnavan returned his attention to Jarls. "You've been thoroughly discussed, as you can imagine. We think you're Guard material. I've been authorized to offer you a lieutenant's commission."

It was a thunderbolt. Jarls gaped at him.

Karsen interjected himself. "There's a problem, General. Anders is a wanted fugitive, if you remember."

"The problem's been taken care of," Carnavan said. "The Executive Guard takes care of its own. The old charges against him have been forgotten by the computer network. His labor contract balance has been readjusted to zero wherever it appears. He never worked at Strathspey. You'll find, if you care to check, that any reference to him in your own records has been erased."

"The laird will want to know why we didn't bring him back."

"I'm sure you'll think of something to tell him. The laird will soon forget."

Jarls felt as if the breath had been knocked out of him. "I don't know how to thank you, sir."

"Don't thank me," the general said. "The Guard always needs new blood from home. We lost some good men yesterday. That aside, our higher ranks are perpetually thinning out as we get older and soft with Earth gravity. You're still a child of Jupiter. You have a chance to go far."

He rummaged in his desk drawer and handed Jarls a small embossed folder. Jarls opened it and found a set of lieutenant's bars and the crossed silver pikes that were the Guard's collar insignia.

"Congratulations, lieutenant," the general said.

The others had risen as if on signal and surrounded him. Stern slapped him on the back and pumped his hand. "Congratulations, Anders," he said.

"Yeah," Czoznek mumbled. "Congratulations."

Karsen shook hands with him. "Forget about Strathspey," he said. "You're on your way."

Rudolph continued to move on the Jovian question. In rapid succession he followed up the Jovian Repatriation Proclamation with a series of reforms under names like the Articles of Indenture Act, the Interplanetary Transportation Act, and the Solar Labor Compact, that ostensibly applied not only to migrant Jovians, but the native inhabitants of the other gas planets and their moons and orbiting habitats—though it was obvious that Jovians would by far outnumber the other beneficiaries. The reforms gave bound workies better legal protection, better pay, and ended some of the more invidious practices, like physical punishment and exorbitant deductions for food, shelter, and air. Now indentured workies would have a fighting chance to pay off their labor contracts at term and go home with some money.

The labor reforms were only the beginning. Rudolph had also levered a new agreement with Venuscorp and Solar Oxygen. The atmospheric mining satellites that had been skimming Jupiter's hydrogen for generations would eventually be replaced by a permanent hydrogen siphon from Metis, Jupiter's innermost moon. Metis was less than eighty thousand miles away, with a diameter respectable enough to allow for major industrial development. The Jovians would get a larger slice of the hydrogen royalties and they would be in a position to have a hand in the Metis installation's day-to-day operation. The Venusians had not liked the implications at all, but Rudolph had smoothed their ruffled feathers by offering generous subsidies to Solar Oxygen.

And finally, promising to make even the Metis operation obsolete some day, there would be economic development aid from the Pandirectorate for Jupiter's Deep Tap hydrogen mining project. The Venusians didn't like that, either, but there was nothing they could do about it.

Rudolph's initiatives provided daily conversational grist at mess. The young officers at Jarls's assigned table talked of nothing else. Executive Guardsmen weren't supposed to be interested in politics any more than cats are supposed to be interested in pet canaries, but you couldn't keep them from speculating.

"There's a new day dawning for Jupiter," said one of the junior lieutenants at Jarls's table, his eyes shining with enthusiasm. He was a beetle-browed individual named Grigg, a product of one of the Guards' vicennial recruiting forays in the cloud cities. He had left Jupiter not long after Jarls had signed up for Venus, and he was still intermittently homesick.

"We'll see," said another of Jarls's messmates. "Don't get your hopes up." He turned to Jarls. "Pass the potatoes, Anders, would you?"

"Huth, you have all the imagination of a doorknob!" Grigg protested. "When the Deep Tap pays out, we'll have unlimited electromagnetic energy from the core, and access to unlimited metallic hydrogen itself. We'll finally be able to throw off the shackles of Earth and Venus. Jupiter will emerge from its backwater and take its rightful place in the solar system."

"Better watch that kind of talk, Grigg," Huth said, helping himself to more potatoes. "Or the Guard might decide to help *you* throw off the shackles of Earth."

"You're hopeless," Grigg said. He appealed to Jarls. "How about it, Anders? You've been on Venus. You've seen it all firsthand. When Jupiter gets control of its own hydrogen, things are bound to change."

"It may take a while," Jarls said cautiously. "It's unknown territory. Metallic hydrogen's tricky stuff. We don't know what kind of engineering problems we might encounter. Or even if the Deep Tap is possible at all." At the stricken look on Grigg's face, he relented, and hastily added: "But yes, with the new royalty agreements for atmospheric mining, and with a permanent siphon from Metis in the cards, things are bound to improve."

Grigg wasn't satisfied with that. The beetle brows contracted in a frown. He opened his mouth to protest, but couldn't think of a rejoinder right away.

Jarls offered a crumb to placate him. "But for now, the important thing is that there's a new deal for the Jovians working on Venus and Mercury. And *that* takes place right away."

Huth took a break from the task of shoveling food into his mouth. "Hooray for social justice," he said. "But they should have had better sense than to get caught in that trap in the first place." He realized what he had said, and apologized. "Sorry, Anders, I forgot. But you got out by yourself anyway, didn't you?"

Jarls smoldered in spite of himself, but the table's attention was already turned back to Grigg's unstoppable harangue, and he didn't have to reply.

"The engineering problems are overrated," Grigg said dismissively. "We've already got hypercarbon siphons strong enough for atmospheric mining satellites and orbital elevators, and the Metis project will give us still more know-how. Once we have access to that tremendous dynamo under Jupiter's skin, we'll have all the free energy we need for a super rail gun powerful enough to overcome Jovian gravity and shoot cargoes of metallic hydrogen directly to Venus."

"There's one thing more powerful than Jovian gravity," said a guardsman farther down the table.

"Yeah, what's that?"

"The power of Venusian financiers."

"All right, be a clown," Grigg said hotly. "But there's something in the deal for Venusian financiers, too, and you can bet that Rudolph will point it out to them. With all that metallic hydrogen being shot at them, the Venus terraforming project can go forward a couple of centuries ahead of schedule, and there'll be plenty of time for the money gnomes to figure out how to make a profit out of *that*!"

Jarls got up quietly and left them arguing. Nobody noticed his departure.

Venus was currently at inferior conjunction, and for the next few weeks there would be the chance to have something resembling a give-and-take conversation between the two worlds. The next opportunity was more than a year and a half away. Jarls's reservation had been in since early morning, and when he got back to his quarters to check the exchange, he found a flashing light indicating that they had located Yamaguchi, and that he was standing by.

Jarls hurried to one of the booths off the dayroom. He wanted to talk to a life-size Yamaguchi, not a miniature on his personal screen. He sat down in a chair facing the holo window and told the holding pattern who he was.

"Please make yourself comfortable," the illusory operator said. "Waiting time for the return transmission will be approximately four and one half minutes." The holding pattern was in the form of a pleasant middle-aged woman with graying blonde hair, looking remarkably detailed.

Jarls waited obediently. Just as he was losing his patience, the simulated woman faded away, and Yamaguchi was sitting opposite him.

"You must be rolling in Liechtenfrancs to spring for for a face-to-face like this," Yamaguchi said. "And is that an Executive Guard uniform I see? You've come up in the world, *tomodachi*. Go ahead, it's your debit. I'll talk as fast as I can when it's my turn."

Yamaguchi looked exactly the same. He hadn't changed at all, except for a new ropy-appearing scar running down the side of his massive neck and disappearing below the collar of his overshirt. Whatever had caused it hadn't disabled him in any way, Jarls was glad to see.

"Yes, I'm flush," Jarls admitted. "I got a recruiting bonus when I was inducted into the Guards, and a guardsman's credit rating to go with it." He gave a succinct account of the events that had made him a guardsman, leaving out his own role in the apprehension of Franz Joseph. Yamaguchi sat, immobile as a granite slab, during the recitation. He hadn't heard any of it yet.

". . . and that's about it," Jarls finished. "Guardsmen are indentured as a legal form, but I'm a free man, able to resign any time after a year's service, with no encumbering debt. The new decrees eliminate the thirty-year enlistment provision, but that's just to clarify our status—it'll continue to be a lifetime career for most guardsmen."

He took a deep breath. "It's a different story for you and the others bound to Solar Oxygen. It's too bad Herk's not alive. He could take advantage of the Jovian Repatriation provisions to get out of bondage and see Jupiter again. How about it, Taki? What are your plans?"

He'd timed it pretty well. He could tell by the change of expression on Yamaguchi's broad face that the opening words were just starting to reach him. It was Jarls's turn to sit like a granite slab and wait for Yamaguchi to respond. A couple of minutes later, Yamaguchi's face suddenly twisted with emotion; the reference to Herk must have come through about then.

"Herk wouldn't have taken the easy way out," Yamaguchi said. "He would have stayed on just to be a thorn in their side. I feel the same way. The situation may have changed, but Herk's work will never be finished. The torch passed to me after Herk died and you got shipped out with the incorrigibles." He flashed a wide grin, exposing a broken tooth that he must have acquired at the same time as the new scar. "The Uranians are resigned to the fact that I run things in the barracks now. With the new state of affairs, I might even get to be a straw boss myself."

Jarls didn't have to prompt Yamaguchi with questions and wait four and a half minutes for radio waves to make a round trip to Venus. Yamaguchi had anticipated what he would want to know next, and continued talking.

"Doolan's already packing up to go home. He doesn't have

any negative credit balance to pay off, and the repatriation provision will pay his fare. That boy will go far. If he was able to hang on to his money on Venus, he'll end up owning the solar system some day. Your other workmates, Arris and Bjorn, have opted to serve out their contracts and stay on. They've both toughened up nicely, and with Rudolph's labor reforms, they actually think they have a chance to go home with some money. I didn't try to talk them out of it. A surprising number of your old barracks buddies decided to do the same. Smithers is dead, by the way. An accident. They couldn't pin it on anybody. Herk had a lot of friends. A couple of the other Uranians took the hint and went back to their godforsaken planet under the provisions of Rudolph's Solar Labor Compact. Oh, and your friend Cam's gone back to Jupiter—Southhaven, wasn't it? She jumped at the chance. So did the other girl you saved from young Paes and his hyenas, Margriet. It was probably a good idea. Paes knows how to hold a grudge."

Jarls forgot about the time lapse for a fraction of a second and started to open his mouth, but Yamaguchi was still ahead of him.

"I knew there was somebody you'd want to talk to, so I put your call on hold till I was able to get her here. I know it's your credit balance that's draining away, but I didn't think you'd mind my inviting her in."

He reached out an arm to pull someone else into the call's target area. A red-haired, freckled amazon with shoulders as broad as Yamaguchi's came into view. She had a baby tucked under one muscular arm, a bright-eyed toddler who was unconcernedly sucking a thumb.

"Hello, Jarls," Maryann said. "I'm glad to see you're all right. We all thought you'd been shipped to a mining gulag on Mercury. We were afraid you were dead."

Jarls unaccountably felt his eyes go wet. The last time he'd seen Maryann, she'd been drawn and hopeless, exhausted by grief. The woman he was looking at now was showing something of her old spirit.

She held the child out at arm's length. It was a chubby, healthy looking infant, but somewhat longer-limbed and not as barrel-bodied as a Jupiter-raised baby of the same age might have been.

"I named him Brok, after his father," Maryann went on. "He's very strong, but of course he could never live on Jupiter. But he has a lot of Jovian aunts and uncles, and I'm afraid they spoil him." Yamaguchi, sitting beside her, beamed sheepishly at that, and she darted an affectionate smile at him. "These damned high-and-mighty Venusians can go to hell," she said defiantly. "At least my baby will grow up with some sense of what it is to be a Jovian, even in this wretched place!"

She paused to collect herself, and Jarls broke in even though he knew she could not hear him yet.

"Listen, Maryann," he said urgently, "you've got to get out of that hellhole. For the baby's sake, if not your own. Cloudhab is no place to raise a child. You can't go back to Jupiter, that's true. Your son's body was formed in Venus gravity. But you could take him to Earth. There're plenty of Jovians here to give him a sense of extended family. And he could make some sort of life for himself on Earth. It's not like Venus. The Executive Guard takes in Earth-born Jovians if they qualify. And there're a lot of private jobs where we're not expected to be just low-cost muscle machines. He'd have a chance to grow up on a level playing field. I know the repatriation provisions were written to give priority to Jovians who want to return to the home planet, but the rules can be bent. You're one of the special cases. I'll sponsor you. I can do that now. I'll pull strings. And I'll find you a job on Earth if it's the last thing I do."

Maryann's image had started to talk again, but Jarls squeezed in a last passionate rush of words:

"There are too many bad memories on Venus. I remember what Brok said before we left Jupiter on that cattle boat. Earth was the place he wanted the two of you to go in the first place. Do it for him."

He stopped abruptly to catch up with what she was saying. She was well launched into a fiery denunciation of Venusians and all their works. Jarls could not help smiling at her account of the stubborn tactics she and Yamaguchi and the others had contrived to thwart Venusian authority. She was doing her best to be amusing, but Yamaguchi's scar and broken tooth were mute evidence that life on Cloudhab and the surface bases was not a game. And she was staying far away from the subject of Brok's murder and the subsequent accident that had taken the life of the Uranian straw boss, Smithers.

She suddenly fell silent. Jarls's appeal about applying for passage to Earth had reached her. He watched as she listened. Her face was a mask that he could not read.

Then, at the end, Maryann's generous mouth widened into a face-splitting grin. "I'm still a damn good welder," she said. "And still as strong as any five inner planet creampuffs put together. Can you get me a job on the transpacific tunnel?"

Jarls was about to reply that there was a critical shortage of construction workers on such surface projects as the Gibraltar bridge and the Indonesian orbital elevator terminal, and that there was no need for her to work in undersea pressure conditions, when Yamaguchi broke happily in:

"Nice going, *tomodachi*! I've been trying to talk her into migrating to Earth for weeks and getting nowhere."

Maryann's face was shining. That was good enough for Jarls. There was no point in a prolonged exchange of goodbyes. It would take too long at interplanetary prices. "*Ausgang*," he commanded the booth.

Maryann and Yamaguchi faded out of existence, smiling and waving. The gray-haired lady materialized and said, "Thank you for your patronage. A charge has been deducted from your credit balance." Then she too winked out.

Jarls checked his balance. The little holo window on his bracelet flashed a figure at him. The call had eaten up a good chunk of his enlistment bonus, but there was more than enough left for a vidgram to Jupiter, including a reply.

He gave the necessary commands, and a few moments later was talking a mile a minute at a holo window filled with the neutral swirling mist that the communications experts had decided would be conducive to loosening a paying customer's tongue.

He was able to talk for all of twenty minutes before his bankchip gave a warning beep. Regretfully, he signed off.

The simulacrum of the gray-haired lady formed out of the mist and said pleasantly: "Jupiter is currently on the opposite side of the sun. All signals will have to be relayed through Vesta. Estimated minimum reply time is two and one quarter hours."

There was no point in hanging around. Jarls went back to his quarters and waited there, with a beer and a book to keep him company. It was a good four hours before the reply came through. Marth Anders must have been out when the vidgram announced itself, and Jarls's father wouldn't have wanted to accept the transmission without her being present.

Jarls opted to pick up on his personal screen instead of returning to the public booth. It was long after hours by now, and it didn't matter much anyway because vidgrams were sent flat. He gave the command for recording mode, because he knew he'd be playing his mother's message over and over, then told the gray-haired lady, now palm-sized and two-dimensional, to go ahead.

His mother popped into existence on the screen, the colors bright and artificial. She looked tired and her chopped blonde hair was a bit grayer, but the handsome, strong-boned face was as Jarls remembered it. She must have hurried back from an outside maintenance detail, because she was still wearing a pressure suit, and a bubble helmet was on the couch beside her, growing foggy. She was alone in the familiar, cluttered sitting room. Jarls could see no sign of his father.

"Hello, Jarls," she said, still breathless from her outside exertions. "We had no idea you were on Earth. We had those calls from Venus, saying you were doing well, and that was all. I couldn't believe my eyes when I saw you wearing an Executive Guard's uniform. Your father will be so proud when he sees it."

She bit her lip. "He . . . he hasn't been well lately. I didn't want to disturb him just now. But I know he'll want to brag about you to

Ian Karg." She shook her cropped head wonderingly. "Ian's been kept busy denying that the Executive Guard had anything to do with the . . . changes in Liechtenstein and the new deal for Jupiter, but nobody believes him. He's a hero around here, and you'll be one, too, when it gets around that Port Elysium has *two* sons in the Executive Guard! Oh, Jarls, I wish you could be here now!"

She fought to regain her equanimity, then went on. "You'd hardly recognize the place. People are walking around in a daze about what's been happening. Thousands of new jobs are opening up, here and in the other bubble cities. It's because of all the investment money that's been pouring in from Earth. The Deep Tap's been revived, and the Metis hydrogen siphon project is taking shape faster than anyone could have imagined. Your old foreman, Gord Murdo, is one of the Deep Tap contractors, and I do believe he'll be the richest man in Port Elysium some day. The Jovian League's announced that it's ordering two more orbital scramjets to accommodate the increased interplanetary traffic, and there's talk of eventually doubling the size of the present fleet. Or even tripling it."

Jovian reticence kicked in as she realized how voluble she'd been, and she abruptly broke off. Then Jovian frugality took over, and, determined to justify the expense of the vidgram, she doggedly resumed talking.

"And at least a dozen families in Port Elysium have already received vidgrams from kin on Venus and Mercury, saying they're on the way home. Ian Karg's denials aside, if the Executive Guard *did* have anything to do with Prince Rudolph's accession, you can be proud of being a part of it, however small."

Jarls fathomed from his mother's words that though the rumors were flying even on far-off Jupiter, the Guard had successfully squelched the details of Franz Joseph's apprehension, including Jarls's role in it. That was all right with him. He didn't need that kind of notoriety. Or the powerful enemies it might attract from the ranks of diehard Franz Joseph supporters.

His mother talked on for another five minutes. Jarls could see her surreptitiously glancing at her wristwatch. She dutifully gave him news of his uncle Jase, whose feud with Hector had driven somewhat of a wedge beween Jase and Jarls's father, but that was all over now, and Hector's death and Clete Anders's illness had drawn the two brothers closer again. She promised to give Jarls's regards to his old friend Torbey, but Jarls noticed that she avoided all mention of Kath. That was all right with Jarls, too. It was more than likely that he would not see Kath for years or decades, if at all, and she had a right to get on with her life. But it was more troubling that his mother said nothing further about the state of his father's health. There was no way he could press her on that subject now. Perhaps he could try to draw her out on some future vidgram to Jupiter.

The meter had run out. His mother's eyes flicked to what must have been an icon on the screen, and then her eyes strayed to her watch again.

"Goodbye, Jarls," she said. "Make the most of your new life on Earth. It's all we could have dreamed of for you. Perhaps one day I'll see you. I hope so. Remember that we love you."

Two weeks later, he was summoned out of the afternoon calisthenics session and found General Carnavan's aide waiting for him. "Hop to, Guardsman," the aide said. "The general wants to see you, *abreisen*."

Jarls's skivvie shirt was soaked with sweat; he'd already done thirty minutes on the treadmill, tied down by an elastic harness tightened to simulate two and a half gravities. "I'll get cleaned up right away," he said.

"Never mind that," the aide said. "He doesn't want to be kept waiting."

Jarls followed the aide down the corridor. "What does he want to see me about?"

"He'll tell you that himself."

"Can't you give me a hint?"

"Mum's the word," the aide said. But he stopped for a moment and turned to look at Jarls. Envy was plain in his eyes, but he obviously was torn by the desire to show off his inside knowledge.

"I'll say this much, though. How would you like to take a trip to Jupiter?"

"I don't have to tell you this assignment is a plum," General Carnavan said.

"No sir," Jarls said.

"It carries a promotion with it," Carnavan said, eyeing him judiciously. "Otherwise you'd be too junior in rank for the job."

"I appreciate that, sir."

Carnavan stared past Jarls to the tall window looking out at the Alps. "How about *Oberleutnant*? We'll make you subaltern to Colonel Wenzel. He'll be the offical attaché assigned to the commercial delegation. He's very political. And very good at it. But he hasn't been back to Jupiter for thirty years. You'll be the one doing the hard work."

"I don't know what to say, sir."

"Don't say anything. Your name wasn't exactly picked out of a hat."

Jarls could guess what Carnavan meant. He was being rewarded for being the accidental instrument who delivered Franz Joseph to Guard custody and kept the coup from becoming messy. Or he was being hustled discreetly offplanet to get him out of sight during the delicate transition period. Or both.

"Prince Rudolph is very anxious for this mission to succeed. If it does, it will be the crowning achievement of Colonel Wenzel's career. And the beginning of yours. It's a signal opportunity for a young man. Make the most of it."

"I'll do my best, sir."

General Carnavan harrumphed. "You'll be one of three junior attachés assigned to Colonel Wenzel, so don't let the appointment go to your head."

"I understand, sir."

The general relaxed. "Good. There's one more thing. You're to have an interview with the prince."

Jarls was stunned. "Sir, I . . ."

"You'd better get out of those exercise clothes and spruce up. And wear a dress uniform. With all the necessary decorations."

"Sir, I don't have any decorations."

"You do now. See my man on the way out, and he'll give them to you. Don't worry, you earned them."

Carnavan dismissed him by returning to the pile of work on his desk. Jarls saluted and headed for the door in a daze. As he reached for the knob, the general's voice stopped him.

"When you get to Jupiter, *Oberleutnant*, be sure to give my regards to my old friend Ian Karg."

Jarls was ushered into one of the sprawling castle's many drawing rooms by an elderly butler who opened the door and disappeared before Jarls could thank him. It was all quite informal. Prince Rudolph received him in shirtsleeves. Evidently he'd just been playing tennis in the castle's indoor court, because an expensive racquet lay carelessly on the brocade seat of a delicate antique chair, and he was still wearing white sneakers.

"Ah, Anders, come in, come in," the prince said, taking him by the arm and guiding him over to a spindly settee.

Jarls was a little uncomfortable. He'd been drilled about not sitting down in the presence of royalty, and not offering to shake hands or in any way touching them. But he'd not been told what to do if royalty itself was determined to be unceremonious.

Rudolph hadn't changed noticeably from the bluff sportsman Jarls had seen at a distance at Lord Hirakawa's grouse shoot. He had the same reddish outdoor complexion and crinkly cornered eyes, and the same bushy blond mustache. But perhaps there was more of a subtle air of command about him now.

"Thank you, your ... your ..." Jarls began, and stopped. He was chagrined to realize he hadn't been told the proper form of address.

Rudolph laughed. "Never mind all that. A simple milord will do."

"Yes sir," Jarls said without thinking.

Rudolph laughed again. Then he sobered and subjected Jarls's face to a keen scrutiny. "Haven't I seen you somewhere before?"

"I . . . I don't think so, milord." It didn't seem possible that Prince Rudolph could have noticed or remembered an obscure private security guard he had seen once, long ago when he had been a guest of minor nobility at one of an endless whirl of country weekends. But the thought was unsettling, all the same. The Jarls who had been erased from the world's memory banks was still, theoretically, a wanted fugitive. This was dangerous ground.

"Hmmm," the prince said absently. "Perhaps I'm mistaken."

Jarls remained on guard. If the prince remembered any of his country weekends, it would surely be the one where he had been the target of an assassination attempt. Minor details would tend to linger. And Jarls could not be sure how thoroughly the Guard had wiped out his past at Strathspey.

The prince became brisk. "I suppose General Carnavan's told you what this is all about?"

"Yes sir . . . uh . . . milord."

"I've been informed that you comported yourself meritoriously during the recent crisis."

He eyed the row of decorations that General Carnavan's aide had so offhandedly pinned to Jarls's tunic an hour previously. One of them was the Star of Liechtenstein, a gold sunburst dangling from a blue and red ribbon embroidered with the princely crown.

The prince's blue eyes sparkled with mischief. "I've also been confidentially informed about certain, ah, details of your prowess that don't appear in the official report. But we'll say no more about that, eh? Ever."

"No, milord," Jarls replied, thoroughly flustered now.

"Very good," the prince said. His attention strayed to a trophy cabinet filled with statuettes and framed medals on velvet.

"The third statuette on the left top shelf is for winning the Classic Ski Race at St. Moritz," he said, apropos of nothing. "And that medal in the silver frame is for marksmanship in the Lucerne games four years ago." He sighed. "There was some talk of my representing Liechtenstein in the Intersolar Olympic Games the following year, but my uncle vetoed it. Said it would be unseemly for a member of the family to compete in what's degenerated into a commercial circus."

Jarls made a polite murmur.

"We never know what strange turns life may take, do we, young Anders?" the prince went on in a remote tone of voice. "I never aspired to much more than adding a few more trophies to that cabinet. Now I can hardly find time to go skiing on my own mountain more than once or twice a week—and that only when the security guards are kind enough to let me." He gave a hearty laugh. "To say nothing of the difficulty of sneaking women into this ancient monstrosity of a castle."

Jarls was still less able to cope with that one. He settled for silence and a wooden expression.

Prince Rudolph's good humor seemed to have been restored. "And my poor uncle, who once had the solar system on a string, is reduced to playing with his stamp collection and dreaming of past glory," he said with an edge of malice.

Jarls was wondering if he ought to try to edge toward the door, when Rudolph took pity on him. "Has General Carnavan discussed any of the specifics of your assignment with you?"

"Uh, not really, milord. He said that I'm to assist Colonel Wenzel."

Rudolph nodded. "Yes, Wenzel's going to need all the help he can get. As attaché, he's the *de facto* point man for our commercial interests. To get anything done, he's going to have to butter up a lot of people. His diplomatic talents are outstanding—that's why he was chosen for the job. He's a born politician. But not so much of a nuts-and-bolts man. Fortunately he knows that, and doesn't get stubborn. How much do you know about politics, Anders?"

"Not much, milord."

Rudolph nodded again. "That's good. You won't get in Wenzel's way. But as a practical matter, you've worked in Jupiter's lower atmosphere?"

"Well, down to about a hundred kilometers. That's only down to the water ice layer. The hydrogen is still gaseous. Nobody's gone much more than about twice that and lived to tell it—not even the Deep Tap roughnecks who've been inching downward over the years."

Rudolph waved off the disclaimer. "But you've had practical experience?"

"Yes, milord. 'Most everyone in Port Elysium's gone downstairs at one time or another."

"That's what I was getting to. Your Port Elysium's always been in the forefront of Deep Tap exploration."

"Well—yes. Along with the other bubble cities in the South Equatorial Federation."

"Wenzel will set up residence in Polar City. It's the major portal for off-planet traffic, and besides being an important financial center, it's the current headquarters for the Jovian League. He'll be well positioned to push the Metis siphon project along from there. We'll post the other two assistant attachés there to help him cope. Do you follow?"

"Yes, milord."

"Don't look so downcast. Wenzel and I have decided to base you in Port Elysium to concentrate on the Deep Tap project. Wenzel will try to get to Port Elysium to show the flag as often as he can, but the major responsibility will be yours. You have family and friends there, you know the place, and you'll be in a better position to get things done. You'll miss all the glittering state banquets at Polar City, and you're going to work like a dog, and if you accomplish anything, Wenzel will get the credit. That all right with you?"

Jarls was staggered at the prospect of going home to Port Elysium. The small knot of homesickness that he'd kept repressed all this time burst loose in a sudden flood of emotion and threatened for a few seconds to overwhelm him.

"Yes, milord," he managed to say.

"Very good. You'd better start packing. The ship's docked at Eurostation now. You'll be leaving for Jupiter within the week."

# PART 4

# JUPITER

# 22

THE SCRAMJET flight from South Polar City to Port Elysium was uneventful. As a member of Colonel Wenzel's diplomatic staff, Jarls had traveled in first class comfort in a standard passenger spaceplane with all the amenities—a far cry from the stripped-down hernia factory that had originally lifted him off the planet.

Still, he was looking forward to a shower, a change of clothes, and a quiet reunion at home before presenting his credentials to the city fathers and assuming his new duties. His mother had promised to meet him at the passenger terminal when he'd called her from orbit, and had said she'd try to get in touch with Torbey and Kath as well.

So he was a little dismayed when he stepped through the lock into the passenger lounge and found the mayor, Councilman Mak, and a delegation of city officials waiting to greet him.

The mayor stepped forward, a wide official smile on her face, and clasped Jarls's hand warmly. "Welcome back, Consul Anders," she said in a formal voice that didn't go with the liveliness of her expression. "On behalf of all of Port Elysium, I am pleased and honored to receive you."

The office of mayor was largely ceremonial in Port Elysium, and Mei Lin had been its unchallenged holder for as long as Jarls could remember. She was a pleasant, gray-haired lady whose face at public events had been a familiar part of Jarls's growing-up. But this was the first time he had actually met her in person.

"Uh, thank you," he said, stumbling over the reply while he looked round to try to locate his mother. "But I'm not a consul. I'm just an assistant attaché."

Councilman Mak shouldered past the mayor. "Jarls, my boy," he said, pumping Jarls's hand. "You've come back in style. I always knew you had it in you. This is a great day for Port Elysium, with one of its native sons installed as emissary from Earth and the Pandirectorate."

Mak's demeanor was a little odd. Despite his effusiveness, he wasn't looking directly at Jarls. After a moment, Jarls spotted the newsnet reporter with the camera unobtrusively over to one side.

"Well . . . there's a lot of interest on Earth in taking a new look at the Deep Tap project," Jarls said carefully. "I'm here to help in any way I can."

"There's a bright future ahead for Jupiter," Mak said, looking directly at the camera, "and we're going to see to it that Port Elysium has a major role in that future."

He continued with a few more sentences of political boilerplate while Mayor Lin smiled in complicity and the other city officials edged forward restively. Mak finished with him, gave him a clap on the shoulder, and turned him over to the pack of municipal functionaries. They shook Jarls's hand in turn and recited brief insipidities for the camera while Mak stood by with avuncular proprietorship. Jarls gathered from all the gush that there was to be a banquet in his honor the following night.

Jarls nodded with half his attention and continued to search for his mother. He spotted her standing patiently in the small crowd that had gathered nearby, with Torbey at her side. There was no sign of Kath.

He started to edge tentatively toward them. Mak spotted his mother and Torbey at the same time, and helped pry Jarls free of the city hall group with a jovial, "We've had him long enough, people. Let the man go."

He followed Jarls for a few steps and, when they were out of immediate earshot, put his hand on Jarls's arm and said quietly,

"I'm sorry about your father, Jarls. He was a good man. The best. It's too bad you didn't get a chance to see him."

Home was as Jarls remembered it, the small wooden house facing the Middleville green, its eaves embellished by an embroidery of lacy curlicues that Clete Anders had painstakingly carved when he had built it in his youth. At the end of the short sidestreet, Middleville's outside bulkhead was partially screened by the trees and shrubbery that had grown up over the generations. There was little hint that Jupiter's roiling atmosphere lay behind the luminescent wall, or that the seemingly rock-solid little world that was Port Elysium was actually a carbon-based bubble bobbing about in the upper currents.

Marth Anders thumbed the homemade latch and let them inside. Locks and keys were not fashionable in Port Elysium, and especially not in Middleville, though the Jovian sense of privacy saw to it that closed doors were respected.

"Sit down, Jarls," she said. "Torbey, make yourself at home. I'll put some tea on."

Jarls settled into the familiar couch with its sagging cushions. Torbey hovered indecisively, looking uncomfortable.

"I'd . . . I'd better run along," Torbey said. "I know the two of you want to be alone."

"Nonsense," Marth Anders said. "Sit down. I'll just be a minute."

She bustled off—a little too hastily, Jarls thought. He looked over at Torbey, who finally—reluctantly, it seemed to Jarls—took a seat.

Torbey seemed to be chewing something over in his head. After a brief struggle, he blurted, "Jarls—I'm sorry!"

"Sorry about what?" He supposed Torbey meant about his father.

"About Kath."

"I don't know what you're talking about."

The words tumbled out. "You were gone. We didn't know if you'd ever be back. We both missed you. We spent a lot of time together. Mostly we talked about you. I tried to comfort her. After a while, we began to discover that we had more in common than our memories of you. We fought against it—you've got to believe that! Kath is a very loyal person. But you weren't there, and she had her own life to live." His eyes pleaded with Jarls. "We didn't mean anything to happen, Jarls, believe me."

"Take it easy, Torbey."

"Kath feels awful about it. She didn't want to face you. I told her I'd tell you."

"Tell me what."

"We got married," Torbey finished miserably. "About a year ago."

"It's all right, Torbey," Jarls said.

Torbey avoided looking at him. "We'd both like to be friends with you. Maybe you could come over. When you get settled in."

"I said it's all right."

Torbey's face was flaming red, but he looked relieved. Jarls's mother came in with a tea tray. She looked relieved, too. She wasn't a devious person, but it was obvious that she hadn't wanted to be the one to break the bad news about Kath.

She set the tea tray down on a table. "I made some *multerterte* to go with it," she said. "I remember how much you used to like them when you were a child."

Jarls was touched. He bit into one of the cloudberry tarts, the astringent, tangy taste bringing back childhood memories. He had been entranced then by the thought that cloudberries had some-how come from the billowy clouds that he could see outside Port Elysium's viewports. It was only later that he had learned that cloudberries—*multer*—were an Earth fruit, and had originated in the Arctic forests of his ancestral homeland.

Torbey sipped at his tea and nibbled at a tart, and made his excuses as soon as he courteously could. When Jarls and his mother were alone, she turned to him and said:

"Don't feel bad about missing seeing your father, Jarls. He held on longer than anyone expected. He knew you were on your way back to Jupiter those last few weeks, and that made him happy."

"I know, but—"

"It wasn't to be, that's all," she said firmly, closing the subject.

They gossiped inconsequentially for a while, his mother bringing him up to date on the news of Port Elysium. After all the safe topics had been exhausted, and conversation began to flag, she adopted the carefully offhand tone of voice that always indicated serious premeditated intent, and said, "Ian Karg's been asking after you."

"Oh?"

"He's called almost every day since your ship passed the outer moons and began its final approach. He's anxious to see you."

"It's not like Ian Karg to be anxious about anything," he said flippantly.

She was not to be deterred. "Are you going to go see him?"

"Of course," Jarls said as nonchalantly as possible. "I was planning to call on him anyway. It's only the courtesy that one Guardsman owes to another."

"When?" she persisted.

"I'll go over there first thing in the morning," Jarls assured her.

Ian Karg looked a lot older than Jarls remembered him, and not very well. His face was even grayer, and his eyes were bloodshot. Jupiter was catching up with him, as it had caught up with Jarls's father. Jovian gravity was not kind to the muscles and vascular systems of people who were chair-bound.

But he held himself as straight as before in his multi-legged walking chair, and he had dressed carefully in his old uniform with its rows of decorations and sleeves that were slashed to show the rainbow colors underneath the austerely gray outer fabric—the same colors that Michelangelo had chosen for the original Swiss mercenaries so long ago.

Jarls also was wearing his dress uniform—a mark of respect for the old Guardsman—though he hadn't been able to summon the courage to pin on the decorations that General Carnavan's aide had so casually dispensed.

"Well, *Oberleutnant* Anders," Karg said, looking him up and down and letting his eyes come to rest on Jarls's new insignia of rank, "you've risen rather quickly in the world, it seems."

"It's only a brevet rank, sir," Jarls said.

"Nonsense," Karg said. "It's richly deserved. From what General Carnavan tells me, you proved your mettle in a rather spectacular fashion."

Jarls was thrown into confusion. How much could Karg possibly know?

"Don't worry," Karg said, taking note of his discomfort. "It's still a Guard secret. Leith Carnavan and I stay in touch." He chuckled dryly. "They still haven't broken our code in all these years. So much for modern cryptography."

He had a coughing fit. He waved off Jarls's attempts to help him, and brought the fit under control.

"Leith was my aide, you know," Karg said. "A promising young man. I was glad to give him a push. I knew he had it in him to go all the way."

Jarls hadn't known that. His estimation of Karg went up a notch. It must have been a bittersweet satisfaction for the old Guardsman all these years to watch his protege on Earth scale the heights—heights that were forever denied to Karg himself because of the sacrifice he had made for his companions. No wonder Carnavan had spoken of an eternal debt.

And now Karg was seeing his own history repeat itself with especially poignant overtones. A young Guardsman to whom the corps also owed a debt—a debt that could not be publicly acknowledged.

Jarls felt that he understood Ian Karg a little better. But there was no hint in Karg's stony face of what he might be feeling.

"And what are your plans, Jarls?" Karg said.

The question caught Jarls by surprise. "I hadn't thought about it."

"You can write your own ticket on Jupiter, you know. When your tour as assistant attaché is over, you could apply for early discharge and take it here at home. Headquarters might grumble, but they never refuse requests like those. It's policy, for one thing—saves interplanetary fares. And then the sky's the limit. Ex-Guardsmen are heroes on this planet." He gave a small, sour smile. "I ought to know. And now, with the new pro-Jovian government on Earth and the lucrative new ties between the two planets, you'll be an especially valuable property. High government posts, indecently overpaid private consultancies—you can name your own terms."

It was a dazzling picture that Karg had laid out, but Jarls was uncomfortable with it. He couldn't see himself as some kind of politician, like Councilman Mak or one of Mayor Lin's stuffy, self-important deputies, or even as a lower-level bureaucrat, like the one that Torbey was on his way to becoming.

"I don't know, sir," he temporized. "First I've got to finish the job I was sent here to do."

Karg nodded. "I understand, Jarls. You feel a certain loyalty to the Executive Guard. They took you in when you were only another Jovian workie, with no expectations of anything else in your life. They opened your eyes to the larger possibilities—playing a part, however much a supporting role, on the stage of human history. Jupiter is a bigger world by far than Earth. But for now, Earth has wider horizons."

It was an unexpected burst of eloquence from a man who had always been miserly with his words. Jarls waited for more—for some sort of advice, or even some indication of what Karg really thought—but Karg was finished with what he had to say.

"I never . . . I haven't thanked you for the letter of introduction you wrote for me to General Carnavan," Jarls offered tentatively. "It . . . it made all the difference."

Karg waved the remark off. "It was no more than I owed to your father," he said. "I got the Guards appointment. He stayed on Jupiter." His brow darkened. "And had his accident."

Karg seemed to brood for a moment. Then he became brisk and cheerful.

"Let's have a toast," he said. The chair's rows of little tubular legs carried him over to a sideboard, where he busied himself with a bottle and glasses. "Burgundy from Earth," he said. "The same brand served at the officers' mess in Liechtenstein. I expect you've drunk your share of it by now."

"Yes sir, I have," Jarls admitted.

Karg raised his glass. "Here's to your future, Jarls Anders. Whatever it may be."

He took a small sip. Jarls followed suit. The Earthwine tasted thin, no longer the exotic experience it had been when he had first sampled it in this same room.

"Not the best brand in the universe, is it?" Karg said with a grimace. "The Guards' quartermasters always were frugal. But highly appropriate to the present toast, I think. A bit of nostalgia, eh, my young friend?"

"Yes sir."

The moment of joviality passed. Karg became his usual distant self. "I won't be attending the banquet in your honor," he said.

"That's . . . I'm sorry to hear that, sir."

"I don't want to steal your thunder. You'd better get used to being lionized."

"That's all right sir, I understand."

"Do you?" Karg said bleakly. He swirled the Burgundy around in his glass and took a ruminative swallow. Jarls left him sitting in the drab, bare room, sipping his sour Earthwine and staring at the cheerless walls.

"City bonds," Councilman Mak said. "That's where the money is. Port Elysium's going to be the hottest city on Jupiter, with your presence here to encourage outside investment. No matter whether or not the Deep Tap project itself ever pays off."

"It's going to pay off," Jarls managed to reply through an awkward mouthful of fried quadrachick and mashed potatoes. He swallowed hard and got the mouthful down.

"Of course it is, Jarls," Mak said soothingly. "All I'm saying is that for now, the important thing is that Prince Rudolph has you stationed here as a visible sign of his involvement. That will grease up the economic gears and get them moving."

Jarls was seated at the head table, sandwiched between Councilman Mak and Mayor Lin. He looked out over the sea of tables that had been crowded into the town hall, trying to locate his mother. He found her sitting at a table of friends and relatives with Torbey and Kath. She had been invited to sit at the head table, but had declined, saying that the evening belonged to Jarls, and that besides, Kath was feeling awkward and uncomfortable about the whole thing, and needed support.

The mayor leaned across to him. "Councilman Mak is right, Jarls," she said. "South Polar City may have the Liechtenstein legation, but you're our secret weapon."

Mak weighed in again. "I'm introducing a bill for a new bond issue in the council this week—the third so far. The first two are already on their way to being fully subscribed."

Jarls nodded politely. It had little to do with him. His mind was swirling with all the things he was going to have to do—working with the technical people and acting as liaison between them and the contractors in the front line; resolving potential conflicts among the participants.

His eyes strayed to one of the adjacent tables reserved for the bigwigs. Gord Murdo, his old foreman, was sitting there, looking uncomfortable in the formal wear that he had stuffed himself into. Murdo had put on weight since Jarls had last seen him, but he still looked rough-hewn and capable.

Murdo was looking his way. Their eyes met, and Murdo raised a meaty hand to wave. Jarls waved back, and Murdo went back to a conversation he was having with a stodgy-looking older man in a puffed shirt.

Mak never missed anything. "Murdo's one of our more prominent contractors now," he said. "He still goes out and works alongside his crews, though." He laughed. "Mrs. Murdo's trying to break him of the habit—turn him into a respectable businessman sitting at a desk. But he's very reliable. Maybe that's the secret of his success. He's been awarded a juicy contract for construction of Waystation Two. The funding comes from the Deep Tap Commission, of course, and if Port Elysium remains in the forefront, more capital will be funneled back to us than we contribute. Murdo's already working fifty miles deeper than anyone's gone before."

"Basically, it's the Jovian League versus EarthCorp, isn't it, sir? We're in a race with the Metis Siphon project."

Mak frowned. "Jupiter wins either way . . . but yes. EarthCorp is doing its best to muscle in on the Deep Tap. But it'll be easier for us to keep it entirely under Jovian control than a project that's based somewhere above the clouds."

Jarls was treading on delicate ground. "Colonel Wenzel was born a Jovian, but he has his duty to perform. He'll be pushing ahead on the Metis project with every fiber of his being and every resource at his command."

"I'd expect no less of him," Mak said sententiously.

"And the Metis project looks like more of a sure thing, doesn't it? It doesn't face the same kind of technological unknowns that we . . . that you do on the Deep Tap."

Mayor Lin leaned into Jarls's line of vision and fixed him with her bright, reasonable eyes. "That's why we're counting on you, Jarls. There's no conflict about your doing your best for us, and we know you're a loyal son of Port Elysium. Everybody's cheering you on."

She favored Jarls with one of her blinding smiles.

"I'm sure he understands, Mei Lin," Mak said. "Let the man finish his dinner."

Grateful for the escape route that had been offered, Jarls returned his attention to the plate in front of him. In addition to the quadrachick drumstick and the lumpy mashed potatoes with rapidly cooling gravy, it contained a megapea, baby carrots, soyacorn succotash, and assorted unidentifiable sprigs of vegetation from the biotanks.

He cut himself a slice of the megapea and tried a mouthful. It was a little too woody in texture, and he washed it down with a gulp of wine. The wine wasn't bad for a local bioengineered product; at least it tasted smoother to Jarls than the wickedly expensive Earthwine that Ian Karg had offered him.

"The rubber chicken circuit, my boy," Mak said. "You're irrevocably on it now." He turned to the mayor and said, "Why can't we have a decent menu for a change, Mei Lin? Something more imaginative?"

Mak himself, Jarls noticed, had barely touched his food. He had pushed it around on his plate and confined himself to the wine. Mayor Lin had done the same. They both must have been veterans of a thousand of these meals. Jarls suddenly felt like a yokel, and the food lost its appeal.

"Oh Mak," she said with a laugh. "If you had your way, they'd be feeding you on caviar and chateaubriand imported from Earth. And then what would happen to your plebeian image?"

"Just once, some tuna from the dolphin lagoon," he grumbled. "With a good tataki sauce to go with it."

"You know the dolphins charge a fortune for their tuna," she chided him. "The city budget can't afford it."

Mak nodded glumly and pushed his plate away. He drained his wine glass and tapped its rim with a spoon until he had the room's attention. The buzz of conversation and the rattle of dishes died down, and Mak stood up with a suddenly convivial expression on his face.

"May I have everyone's attention, please . . ." he began.

Jarls sat stoically through the flowery speeches that followed, and rose to his feet on cue to say a few words himself. He hadn't thought to prepare any remarks, but he managed well enough by simply saying how happy he was to be back home in Port Elysium among his friends and neighbors, and telling a couple of harmless anecdotes about life in Liechtenstein. He was embarrassed by the inordinate applause that any mention of the Executive Guard brought, and became a little self-conscious about wearing the gray and silver dress uniform among people who'd seen him grow up. In Port Elysium, the uniform had always been the prerogative of Ian Karg, the symbol of Terran power that had set Karg apart. Jarls finished with a reference to Prince Rudolph and his determination to forge new links between Earth and Jupiter, and was amazed at the round of cheers that Rudolph's name elicited. When he sat down, Mak, in a whispered aside, said, "Good job, Jarls. We'll make a politician of you yet."

After dinner, there was a reception in one of the antichambers to the hall. Jarls's mother was one of the first to reach him, pushing Torbey and Kath ahead of her.

Torbey hung back. Kath looked trapped, but she managed a wary smile.

"Hello, Jarls," she said.

"Hello, Kath," he responded just as carefully.

"I . . . I'm glad to see you back. I'm sorry I wasn't able to come to the passenger terminal yesterday with your mother and Torbey to greet you. I couldn't get the time off."

"I understand, Kath."

She looked over the trim Executive Guard uniform. "My, don't you look impressive! Who'd have dreamed that you'd go so far in such a short time."

He laughed, but was unable to keep a tinge of bitterness out of his reply. "They shipped me to Venus as a workie," he said. "I didn't think I'd get to where I am now, either. You were wise not to come with me, Kath. Venus wasn't a very pleasant place. Neither was Earth, at first."

She flushed. "I'm sorry, Jarls. I . . . I just wasn't made for travel. I'm not very adventurous."

"Don't apologize. I should have understood your feelings."

She was saved from having to respond further by the intrusion of her awesomely imposing mother, Kristen av-Greta. She looked exactly like Kath, with the same shining blonde hair and chill blue Nordic eyes, but thirty years older. She herself was a clone of her own mother, Greta, making Kath a third-generation clone. It was a family that didn't have much use for men, until Kath had come along. Perhaps the genetic trait of needing to be always unassailably beyond criticism had taken a different form in Kath—a drive to be conventional and compliant.

But in Kristen av-Greta, the trait had resulted in perfect confidence and a steely disdain for those who failed to measure up. "Well, Jarls," she said, "you've certainly surprised us all."

He could see her icy eyes measuring him against Torbey, and perhaps regretting her previous dismissal of him.

He forced a laugh. "I surprised myself," he said.

"Kath, darling, we must make our Jarls welcome," she said. "I'm having a small party next week to celebrate First Landing Day. Some of the best people will be there. I'll need you to help with the preparations."

"Yes, mother," Kath said obediently.

"And of course you'll come," Kristen av-Greta said to Jarls, giving him a surgical smile.

"I'll try," he said.

"You must try your best," she said. "You're going to be in great demand. Every young woman in Port Elysium will be after you."

"Oh, mother!" Kath said, her face reddening.

It didn't seem to have dawned on Kristen av-Greta that it was too late for matchmaking. There was the awkward fact of Torbey's existence that would have had to have been undone. Jarls felt sorry for Torbey; he didn't envy him his terrifying mother-in-law.

Kath shot Jarls a surreptitious glance of apology, and Jarls returned a fleeting grimace of sympathy, both of which went totally unnoticed by Kristen av-Greta. The exchange made them allies and wiped away any remnants of tension between them. Kristen had done that for them, at least.

Poor Torbey shuffled forward to do his duty. "That was a swell speech you gave, Jarls. Really outstanding."

"Thanks, Torb."

"Say, my department's involved in drafting the city construction contracts, including the ones that involve subsidies to the private contractors working on Deep Tap projects. Let me know if I can be of any help."

"I'll do that."

Torbey seemed relieved to have made his contribution to the social amenities. He looked at Kristen av-Greta for her approval, but she ignored him.

"Speak of the devil," Torbey groped on, "here comes Gord Murdo."

Murdo was shouldering his way through the crowded room like a boulder rolling downhill, pushing everything in its path aside. There were no boulders on Jupiter, and Jarls, with his experience of Liechtenstein's alpine slopes, was probably the only person present who could have made the comparison.

Murdo reached him, with a broad, jagged grin on his face, and an empty glass still swallowed up in one thick fist. He nodded to the others and addressed Jarls gruffly.

"I always knew you'd get yourself out of the clutches of those labor crooks and come back, Jarley boy. I held a job open for you. Too bad you've already got one."

"I wouldn't mind working downstairs again," Jarls said. "Thanks anyway. I appreciate it."

"What you're doing now is more important than wrestling steel. Even Hec would have told you that, in spite of all his speeches about not trusting the Earthies."

He fell silent for a moment, out of respect for Hector's memory.

"Things have changed now," Jarls said softly.

"Yeah," Murdo said. "You know, I filed a complaint about that accident that knocked you overboard. Mak got the Jovian League to lodge a formal protest. Nothing ever happened. EarthCorp wouldn't even compensate us for damage to the pumping station. There were two more close encounters after you left. One of them was a hair-raiser. Came within twelve miles of Southhaven, and ripped up one of *their* pumping stations. No loss of life, fortunately, but if it had hit Southhaven itself, or any of the other cities at that latitude, including us, we could've seen a repeat of the disaster of '32."

"My God!" Jarls said.

Murdo nodded soberly. "But things changed in a hurry after Franz Joseph retired and Earth dealt itself a new Megachairman." He looked at Jarls shrewdly. "What did you have to do with that, Jarley?"

"Not much," Jarls said.

Murdo raised a skeptical eyebrow, but did not pursue the subject. After a pause, he said, "The mining satellite that caused the trouble was suddenly taken out of service and so were all the other satellites with skewed orbits that took them into inhabited zones. No explanation. Technical reasons, they said. There are no plans to put them back in service. They'll make do with whatever assets they have within their alloted five degrees of the equatorial band until they can get the Metis siphon up and running. They say that Metis is too big and stable to ever pose a risk, and that there'll be all kinds of safeguards as well. According to them, it'll be as predictable as an astronomical table and as safe as a sunrise."

"That's comforting."

"Maybe. But I don't trust them. Maybe some of Hec's skepticism rubbed off on me. That's why I'm betting everything on the Deep Tap. If we get there first, we'll make the Metis siphon obsolete before it gets started."

"If the Deep Tap is possible at all."

"There's no problem that can't be solved with enough sweat," Murdo said firmly. He frowned. "Right now, we're stuck. We keep losing pipe. But if we can only break through past the layers of atmospheric turbulence, we'll have a clear shot to the depths where molecular hydrogen begins to dissociate."

"Do it by remote," Jarls suggested.

"Won't work. Molecular hydrogen is an insulator—gas, liquid, or solid. We need hands-on roustabouts who can work at, say, twenty or thirty gigapascals of pressure."

"You know that's impossible. Even for men in suits."

"Yah, I know," Murdo said.

"Even in some kind of work pod with external waldos. You'd still have hollow spaces, and then—kerr-runch!"

"I know that, too."

"Then what are you going to do?"

"Keep trying. Maybe we'll get lucky."

"And then," Jarls mused, "even if you manage to thread the needle, there'll still be a need for endless maintenance from then on."

"I'll tell you what," Murdo said. "Why don't you come along and have a look? I'll take you along on my next descent."

Jarls suppressed a shudder at the thought of the depths at

which Murdo was now working. What had Mak said? Fifty miles deeper than anyone had ever gone before.

"Sure," he said. "Just tell me when."

"I'll fix it up," Murdo said. He apologized to the others for having monopolized Jarls for so long, then walked off.

People were crowding around Jarls, waiting to shake his hand. He was soon engulfed in a sea of prattle and getting groggy with the effort of coming up with some appropriate gracious response to each well-wisher when he became aware that Councilman Mak had appeared in the front wave of the congratulatory swarm. Mak was shepherding a broad, stubby man with coarse black hair and flat Siberian features, guiding him through the crowd with a hand in the small of his back.

"Friend of yours," Mak said. "Something he needs to talk to you about."

Jarls recognized the stubby man with a stab of guilt. "Doctor Chukchee!" he exclaimed.

"I gather you two have some unfinished business," Mak said. He removed his hand from between Chukchee's shoulder blades. "Nice to talk to you, Doctor. I'll do what I can on that research grant, but money's tight these days for pure science studies. Everything's going to the Deep Tap proposals."

Mak gave a nod and smile to two or three faces he recognized in the crowd, and departed.

"I'm sorry I broke our appointment, Doctor Chukchee." Jarls apologized. "I left you a message, but I was on the passenger manifest for an off-planet flight. I just found out that morning. There wasn't time enough to see you."

Actually, Jarls knew, he could have called Doctor Chukchee the previous day, when he had signed up for what he thought was to be a three-year hitch on Earth. But it wouldn't have made any difference, and he didn't see any need to go into a complicated explanation.

Doctor Chukchee waved his apology aside. "Never mind. It was a long time ago. The important thing is that you're here now. I've been keeping my data bank on *Laganum volatilis* active all this time. In fact, I've added fourteen new *Laganum* encounters while you were gone. None as intriguing as yours, unfortunately, but every scrap of data helps fill in the picture."

Jarls had to remember not to call the creatures by their common name of flapjacks. Doctor Chukchee had a prejudice against the term.

"My encounter with the ... um ... native that rescued me was pretty brief," he said. "Not like some of the other encounters I'm sure you have in your files, where the creatures stayed with a disabled floater or work pod for hours to nudge it back to safety."

"The difference is that none of the other encounters ever involved anything that could be defined as communication!" Chukchee said fervently. "There's your experience and any number of ancient tall stories coming out of the so-called shadow trade—if you can believe half of them."

"Well—I'll help if I can," Jarls said. "I don't know how much I can remember after all this time."

Doctor Chukchee smiled the gentle smile of a true fanatic. "I'll have a dolphin there to prompt you," he said.

"Hello, Jarls," the dolphin said. "It's very nice to meet you. I know your mother."

It was leaning over the side of its travel tub, its head out of water. Its words were perfectly intelligible, though its voice was somewhere in the piccolo range, like a human baby's, and intermixed with a few extraneous squeaks, clicks, and whistles.

"You do?" Jarls said.

"Yes," came the squeaking reply. "I work with her on the outside maintenance crew. I'm a structural integrity inspector."

The curved beak opened in a sly dolphin smile, and Jarls had to fight off the impression that the dolphin was laughing at him. The smile, he told himself, was simply a natural feature of *Tursiops* anatomy.

"I'm sonar certified, of course," the dolphin added in what came across as a raucous bleat.

"Of course," Jarls said.

"My human name is Nemo," the dolphin said. "That will do for air-talking. My dolphin name is . . ."

Nemo ducked under water and used the end of his snout to tap a couple of buttons on a keyboard. His long jaw opened, and a loudspeaker on the laboratory wall emitted a series of high-speed clicks and squeaks. At the same time, a holo screen next to the loudspeaker lit up with a burst of rolling three-dimensional graphs.

"You're not getting it all, of course," Doctor Chukchee said, standing beside him. "There's an ultrasonic component that's beyond human hearing. The computer modulates some of it downward, and compresses it into a narrow band at the top of our auditory range, just to give us a subjective impression. But most of it becomes part of the translation program."

"I see," Jarls said.

"And of course we don't get the sonar part of it at all, except for computer-generated pictures. But it all works surprisingly well. The dolphins make a conscious effort to use lower pitches and to edit, and the computer dictionary does its best to translate human speech into delphinese whenever ambiguities crop up."

"Don't worry about it, Jarls," Nemo piped, his head out of the water again. "It gets to be second nature after a while. We don't get everything you say, either. The computer translates the fuzzy parts for us."

"Shall we get to work?" Doctor Chukchee said.

For the next two hours, Jarls sat in a padded chair, surrounded by spidery equipment that monitored his pupil size, read the levels of stress in his voice, measured skin moisture, tasted his pheremones, and sampled the electrical activity of his brain. He did nothing but talk to Doctor Chukchee and the dolphin, while watching the feedback generated by the lab's artificial intelligence program and Nemo's sonar retelling of his descriptions.

"No, Jarls," Nemo said at one point. "There's something missing. The flapjack told you to back off from that hammered metal badge by knocking you away from it, is that correct?"

"Yes."

Doctor Chukchee was scowling at the unscientific use of the

word "flapjack," and Jarls realized that the dolphin was deliberately needling him.

"And then you tested it by trying again, and it knocked you down a second time?"

"Yes."

"And then you offered it your tool kit in payment for its saving your life, and it . . . hesitated . . . before accepting it to make sure you really meant it. Is that so?"

"That's the impression I got."

"Was it like this?"

Nemo dove to the bottom of his travel tub, and began chirping at his equipment. Jarls could tell that the chirping was only incidental to a battery of sounds he could not hear, because the version coming out of the loudspeaker was interwoven with a medley of transposed squeaks and clicks at the upper limits of his perception, and the screen in front of him was going wild.

Real time for a dolphin evidently operated at a higher speed than human senses were capable of. The images on the screen settled down into a sort of slow-motion replay. Jarls saw a ghostly gray delineation of a flying pancake with a tiny mote riding on it, a mote which grew into the recognizable shape of a man, as Nemo zoomed in on it. Dolphins could paint with pictures as well as words, and show things to their fellows instead of merely describing them.

"Well?"

"Yeah, you're right. I backed away from the tool kit, and the flap- the *Laganum* took that as permission to accept it."

Nemo submerged, twittered at length, and the ghostly holo image corrected itself.

"More like that?" the dolphin said.

"Yes."

Doctor Chukchee was dancing around. "At that point, your communication was in the form of human body language. And your rescuer was able to interpret it."

"Pretty basic body language, doctor," Jarls protested mildly. "Any species knows what it is to back off, whether it's crawling, creeping, swimming, flying, or sending out pseudopods."

"It doesn't matter," Chukchee insisted testily. "It constitutes a quantum breakthrough."

His fingers were dancing over a keyboard as he called up old data from his files.

"Let him be," the dolphin said tolerantly. "Jarls, aside from that great shrug, or twitch, or whatever you want to call it, that bowled you over, did you notice anything?"

Jarls thought it over. "Well, immediately before that, I think I saw those scalloped edges they use for flight control and for carrying things sort of curling up. Sort of an involuntary flexing."

"Grasping motions," Doctor Chukchee said smugly. "But you wouldn't expect a dolphin to know anything about that."

"Grasping motions with an interrogatory," Nemo countered. "And you wouldn't expect a human to know anything about *that*."

Jarls hastily interceded. "I wouldn't even begin to know how to see a question mark in what I observed," he said apologetically.

"You did well enough, Jarls," the dolphin said. "Bravo to you. The interrogatory might not have been in the motion itself. It might have been a sonar subscript. Or it might have been a gesture on another part of the creature hundreds of yards away from you, and out of sight. Or it might have been something twitching somewhere in the creature's interior, and visible only to another flapjack. Or to a dolphin."

"Enough for now," Doctor Chukchee said. "We have the beginnings of an answer. It needs more study. More observational data. But we know that *Laganum volatilis* is capable of interactive behavior. We know they have an ethical sense—the shadow trade told us that long ago. And now we know they have the desire to communicate."

Nemo propped himself against the rim of the travel tub with a flipper, looking for all the world as if he were leaning on an elbow. "Humans will never be able to talk directly to flapjacks," he said. "But we can. And you can talk to us."

# 23

IT WAS noisy inside the hard suit. An incessant rumble of thunder from the ammonium hydrosulphide clouds overhead reverberated in Jarls's helmet and rattled his senses. Murdo worked his riggers and roustabouts only four hours at a time at this depth. He limited them to one shift per ten-hour Jupiter day, letting them take the rest of each day-night cycle off to recover in the floater's quieter cabin. It was an expensive way for him to operate, but it cut down on accidents.

There was a loud crack from a nearby lightning bolt, and Jarls almost jumped out of his skin. He caught his breath, and turned back to Murdo, who was hanging beside him on the floater's outside scaffolding.

"What did you say?" he asked.

Murdo grimaced at him from behind the thick faceplate. "I said I wasn't expecting you to bring a friend along."

He glanced pointedly at the cylindrical pod dangling beneath the floater on an improvised tether. Jarls knew Murdo was miffed at the extra weight resulting from some sixty cubic feet of water and dolphin in the pod. It displaced the equivalent of about half a million cubic feet of the hydrogen they were floating in, and compromised his slim margin of buoyancy.

"I hope he won't get in the way," Jarls apologized. "I know it's a lot to ask, but Doctor Chukchee heard that the flapjacks swarm around the new construction sites, hoping for a handout of metal, and he thought that Nemo might get lucky."

"Yeah, we've been seeing more of them lately," Murdo admitted. "Two or three sightings a day, sometimes. But they don't hang around long."

"He's developing a new theory of flapjack communication," Jarls said.

"That old pipedream! Hec was big on it! He was sure that one day we'd be talking to the beasties, just as sociably as you please! As if we had anything in common with them. We're further removed from those animated flying carpets than we are from an oyster. When was the last time you tried to talk to an oyster?"

"Doctor Chukchee's doing important work. At least, Mak took him seriously enough to get him a research grant."

"God bless the scientists. What would we do without them? I just wish Mak had sent us someone doing research in how to keep a buckytube pipe from flexing at the thirty gigapascal level."

He peered out along the the mooring line toward the growing construction complex the floater was tied to. Jarls followed his gaze.

A gang of riggers in accordian armor was maneuvering another section of the Deep Tap into place. The section was at least a mile long, and its upper end was lost in the dark clouds above. Somewhere above that, totally invisible, was the enormous flotation rig from which the section was suspended.

It was brutal work. Jarls watched them wrestle the end of the fabricated span into place by sheer muscle power, aligning it with the cross section of the long stem that disappeared into the clouds below. Its horizontal inertia must have been immense at the distal end, but that made it all the more dangerous.

Murdo echoed his thoughts. "This is where we're vulnerable to pendulum effects triggered by turbulence," he said. "A thousand miles below, it won't matter anymore."

It must have been bad luck to mention it. Jarls thought he saw the enormous shaft quiver along its length, and then there was no doubt that an oscillation had started. Its arc was small, considering the length of the shaft—no more than about twenty feet—but it was enough to rip clean through a guardrail and swat one of the armored figures off the deck.

"Damn!" Murdo said.

A safety net slung under the platform caught the falling roustabout neatly. There was a lifeline attached to his suit as well, in case he had missed the net, but the question now was, was he still alive? The shaft's tremendous inertia, despite the brevity of its arc, was enough to have crushed his suit—or pulverized him within it.

Jarls held his breath, knowing Murdo was doing the same, until the motionless shape stirred and sat up. Then, moving like an arthritic, the roustabout pulled himself hand over hand up his own safety line, swearing colorfully over the general wavelength until Murdo told him to watch his language.

"Good man," Murdo told Jarls over the proximity circuit. "Going right back to work instead of claiming a paid break at time and a half, as he's entitled to do."

Jarls watched in admiration as the mob of riggers damped the oscillation with ropes and clamped a collar around the junction of the two lengths of hypercarbon shaft. Separate teams working around the circumference ratcheted the collar tightly into place with eight-foot-long wrenches. The tap was only as strong as its weakest link, and this was a job you couldn't trust to machinery.

There was a wait while the tightness of the fit was tested by eyeball and special equipment, and then Murdo gave the okay for the completed section to be lowered.

The Tap eased down still another mile into Jupiter's depths. Riggers in bulbous constant-volume suits were lowered on hyper-filament pulleys to attach flotation devices intended to take some of the strain. The neck of the new section of pipe was secured at deck level to await another length from above.

Murdo gave crisp orders to the unseen roughnecks in the clouds above. Then he switched off the general frequency and gave his attention to Jarls again.

"Only another four thousand miles to go," he sighed. "Maybe I'll be around to see it."

He looked up at the cloud layer, but nothing was visible yet.

"It'll take a while," he said. "They've got to fiddle the next casing into position. We won't see the guide rope for another half hour. Good pilot on the lifting vehicle scheduled for this lift. Fellow named Rebikov from New Kalingrad. A real artist. He'll drop that baby into place with close to zero deviation and zero vibration."

Jarls's eyes were still fixed on the growing tower below, looking like some improbable plant poking up through the clouds, with the entire sprawling industrial complex at its end for a Brobdingnagian blossom. He could see the yellow-suited men swarming over it like aphids on a stem. One of them came free, swinging out on his near-invisible pulley ropes and starting to rise, his part of the job done. A small cloud of vacuum bubbles was already drifting upward to mark the places where the heavy-duty lifters would be attached.

"Yeah, when we get it down to four thousand miles, its weight will keep it immovably rigid," Murdo went on. "And the greater buoyancy we'll get at the denser hydrogen levels, and the upward pressure we'll get when it's in operation will keep us from losing it. It'll be a stable structure. There for the ages. But till then, it's touch and go. For one thing, we're going to lose those balloons when we get deep enough. They'll pop like soap bubbles. Too bad we don't have roustabouts who could go down there and hang new ones."

"It's hard to believe that all the problems are in the upper regions, and not in the lower depths," Jarls said.

He smiled wryly at his own words. It was still a matter of mild astonishment to him that he had come to think of these stormy deeps, dangerously below Port Elysium's benign realm above the clouds, as part of the "upper" regions.

"There's no weather down there," Murdo responded. "It's like the situation they're facing in building the orbital elevator on Earth, only upside down. An ocean of molecular hydrogen getting heavier and heavier is a dampening medium, even when it starts to turn to slush. And even when it starts to turn into a brew of diatomic molecules mixed with the monatomic form, the situation doesn't change. The pipe's still under tension. It might as well be set in concrete."

"The tensile strength—" Jarls began.

"The new buckytube composites can easily take the stress. There's a four or five times safety factor. And don't forget, there's no moving parts down there to go wrong. The pressure differential just sucks it up the pipe. We get a gusher and filter out the metallic hydrogen up here. In some ways, it's easier than trying to get a space elevator anchored and operating, even on a lightweight planet like Earth. I don't envy the poor bastards."

Jarls nodded. Mention of the space elevator made him think of Maryann. He had promised to get her a construction job on Earth. The Executive Guard had pulled strings for him at the Indonesian elevator terminal site in Sumatra, but he still hadn't heard anything when he had left for Jupiter. Maryann must be on Earth by now, with her baby. It was about time for him to check, and see if anything had happened yet.

Murdo was shading his faceplate with a thick gauntlet and peering into the distance. "Your dolphin just got lucky," he said. "Here come the flapjacks."

It was a flight of six of the circular creatures, maintaining a V formation and coming up from the white cloud deck, no more than a mile or two away.

"That little accident a while ago must have alerted them," Murdo said. "That section of safety rail and probably a few small objects fell downstairs. They've come up here to see what's happening."

"They don't beg," Jarls said.

"No, they don't. I'll give them that. But anything that falls overboard is fair game."

"I guess this site is a bonanza for them. Do they ever go after Tap sections that you lose?"

"No, they're not interested in carbon. No way for them to work it. They're only after metal. They're mad for it. They'll go after anything made of it, no matter how small."

"But they won't steal it."

"No—but that's no indication of human-level intelligence. I've never seen a real dog, but they say a well-behaved dog won't steal either, not even an unattended steak."

"I wouldn't know. I didn't have much contact with dogs when I was on Earth."

That wasn't strictly true. There had been Lord Hirakawa's fox-hounds, and from what Jarls had seen, they had abided by the gamekeeper's rules of etiquette. But he wasn't about to admit that to Murdo. Murdo's stubborn prejudices were softening somewhat, but he still refused to admit that the flapjacks' use of primitive tools proved their intelligence. Tools, he pointed out, were used by chimpanzees, birds, elephants, and even ants. To the argument that the flapjacks shaped their tools instead of merely using convenient objects at hand, Murdo replied that chimpanzees did the same.

Instead, Jarls contented himself with saying, "Doctor Chukchee thinks that flapjacks have an ethical sense."

"Maybe. Whatever that proves. They've got a sense of curiosity, anyhow."

Down below, the flapjacks had gathered in a circle around the dangling dolphin pod. By leaning out, Jarls could see them clearly. They were maintaining a polite distance of about a quarter-mile from Nemo's little cocoon. Their size, as always, was impressive: some four or five acres of leathery surface, glistening wetly from the cloud moisture that had condensed on their hides. All six of them carried spears and nets. Only one of them, though, wore any ornament—a cross-belt with a badge of foil-thin hammered metal at the intersection.

"Look at that," Murdo laughed. "It looks like *they're* studying *him*!"

The circle had opened out into a wide semicircle, with the end of the pod, where Nemo's head was located, at the focus. Every once in a while, one of the flapjacks would break ranks to view the dolphin pod from another angle, then return to its position.

"If they're using sonar, they can see Nemo inside the pod," Jarls said. "And vice versa."

"Yeah, I hope the good doctor gets his money's worth," Murdo said. "Come on, I'll show you what the caisson derrick looks like. We can see it better from up top."

Dutifully, Jarls followed Murdo up the scaffolding to the floater's broad crest. The layout of the unfinished terminal was spread out before him in a checkerboard of storage tanks, cranes, piles of gargantuan pipes, jerrybuilt living quarters, and untidy mountains of supplies and components. The parked vehicles and ancillary floating facilities of a dozen of the participating bubble cities stretched for miles. This would be mankind's most ambitious engineering project till the next one came along.

Murdo spent the next hour explaining it all to him in excruciating detail. Jarls learned more than he wanted to know about pressure valves and their idiosyncrasies, monatomic filters, van der Waals force inhibitors, and ambient pressure additive injectors.

"That big ring-shaped foundation," Murdo explained proudly, waving a glove at one of the checkerboard squares, "is where the stabilizer plant is being built. Luckily for us, it takes a lot less pressure to metallize the fluid state than the solid state, so that's what we'll get without having to go all the way down. The metallic liquid and the metallic solid have about the same density. If we quench the fluid quickly, inject the additives, and give it a little timely squeeze, we can get a stable solid metallic form, a lot lighter than aluminum. And a lot more useful. Shipping the liquid form to Venus will be our bread and butter. But it's the solid stuff that'll make us rich."

He noticed that Jarls was getting restive, and said, "But I guess you've heard enough talk. I'll take you across to the platform now and see if I can get you a ride in the bathysphere. It'll take you down to the present terminus. It's as deep as man has gone so far on Jupiter. You can tell them that you've been there personally. It'll help when you're lobbying."

He started to climb down the scaffolding, and when he reached the bulge of the floater's equator, checked the view below.

"The flapjacks are still there, looking your dolphin friend over. Two of them, anyway. That's strange. Usually they lose interest after a few minutes."

Jarls caught up with Murdo and leaned out for a look. The two flapjacks who still remained had closed the distance to the pod, and were hovering only a few hundred yards away. One of them was the big flyer who was wearing the ornamental badge. The other, holding a thousand-foot spear at the vertical with a scalloped projection curled around the shaft just above the center of gravity, was flapping slowly in place beside it, hanging back slightly like some kind of attendant.

As always, the colossal monsters were exhibiting a surprising delicacy, taking care not to brush the pod or disturb it unduly with the breezes generated by their flapping.

"Something's going on," Jarls said.

The big one tilted its broad expanse briefly to face Jarls and Murdo as they emerged from behind the floater's bulge, then righted itself again. A few moments later, Jarls got a call from Nemo.

"Jarls, it recognizes you," the dolphin squeaked.

"Recognizes me?" he exclaimed in disbelief.

"It's your old friend. The one who rescued you when you fell overboard that time."

Murdo sputtered inarticulately, then got a few words out. "Are you having some dolphin fun with us? How could they possibly tell any of us apart?"

Nemo spoke slowly and deliberately, pitching his voice as low as possible to make it easier for someone who wasn't used to dolphins to understand him.

"Hello, Gord. Or would you rather I call you Mr. Murdo? Flapjacks are very observant and attentive to tiny details. All of us pack hunters are. We have to be. The flapjacks hunt mostly by sonar, as we do. They can see right through the suits to the meat underneath and the bones and organs inside the meat. They know human anatomy better than a first-year medical student. And they can identify human individuals, if it's important enough for them to care, by your gross physical characteristics—say a dolichocephalic skull and an enlarged liver. The hard-shell suits make it even easier for them. The sonar waves travel from the compressed atmosphere outside, right through the twenty atmospheres of pressure you maintain inside. They've scanned me inside this water-filled pod the same way."

"Wait a minute! Are you trying to tell me that . . . that oversize dishrag could *recognize* Jarls in particular out of all the other human fleas around it? And after all the time that's elapsed?"

"It was a very important encounter. Jarls gave it his tool box."

Jarls cut in. "How do you know it recognized me?"

"It showed me."

"Hold on!" Murdo roared. "This is preposterous."

"It *showed* you?" Jarls said.

"Yes." Nemo sounded as smug as his chirping dolphin voice would allow. "With a little prompting from me, of course."

Murdo was beside himself. "Let's get this straight," he said. "You're claiming you talked to a flapjack?"

"Not exactly."

"People have been trying to figure out how to communicate with the beasts for a couple of hundred years, and you claim you learned to talk to them in a couple of hours. Do you expect me to believe . . ."

Nemo cut him off in an uncharacteristic lapse of dolphin courtesy. "The important thing, Jarls, is that the flapjack wants to talk to *you.*"

"How?" Jarls managed to say. How is that possible?"

"I'll translate," the dolphin said.

Ten minutes later, Jarls was climbing down the hypercarbon cable that attached the dolphin pod to the belly of the floater. Murdo had objected, telling Jarls it was too dangerous. He had finally given in, but had made Jarls wait until an improvised safety line could be rigged up. "It's my neck if anything happens to you," he had complained.

It wasn't as bad as Murdo had made out. A sturdy communications umbilical was wound round the tether, with enough give so that Jarls could use its loops as handholds. He made the descent while Murdo scolded him from above.

". . . and it's a damnfool thing to do! Just because an overimaginative trained dolphin thinks it's heard something intelligible in a lot of sonar noise."

"It isn't like that, Gord," Nemo replied cheerfully. "There's no such thing as a vocabulary or grammar to learn. You name a thing by showing a picture of it. But it's not exactly a picture, either. It's an imitation of the echolocation you got when you beeped it yourself, so that the person you're sending it to gets approximately the echolocation he would have gotten if he'd been the one who beeped it. That's how we tell another dolphin that we've located a school of fish. Instead of a lot of stupid words, there's one quick burst that shows the size of the school, its distance, the speed and direction it's traveling, the species of fish, and everything else, as though *he* were the observer himself. And we can modify the sonar message to show what you human people call virtual images. Like how the other dolphins should position themselves to herd the fish into a bubble trap. And *that's* elementary. We can retell all the old dolphin epics, or make up new dolphin poetry. The flapjacks do the same thing. Oh, flapjacks and dolphins have different sonar conventions—it isn't as if the images were literal transcriptions. But we adjusted to one another. It only took a few seconds, like you tuning something in on a dial. I'm afraid it's beyond the ability of humans, even with computers."

Jarls paused in his downward climb. "I think I can understand," he said by way of mild reprimand. "We stupid humans have a long tradition of using sign language and pictures in the sand to communicate with other tribes."

"Good point, Jarls. We're only using a kind of pidgin sonar to communicate. Very limited, but we're making do. Flapjacks are very sophisticated. They can draw on a variety of senses we don't even have."

That got Jarls's attention. "Like what?" he pressed.

"They're able to read the changes in electrical potential caused by muscle movement in their prey—and one another, of course. Sharks back on Earth can do that. But of course sharks are too dumb to use it for conversation."

"What else?"

"Having evolved on Jupiter, they also have a strong magnetic sense, just as migrating birds do on Earth. My visitor seemed quite surprised that I didn't have it too. But he decided to treat me as a hearing-impaired person and shout all the louder in the sonar range."

Jarls resumed his descent. He still had another fifty feet to go, and he had the distinct impression that the living landscape looming below was getting impatient.

Nemo was still chattering away with typical dolphin talkativeness. "Doctor Chukchee will have to sort it out from my data, of course. But they must use their infrared vision to read body language the way we use our eyesight. And they must use their chemical senses, the way we dolphins use taste and you humans use smell." There was a sly pause. "I gather that pheremones play a part in human mating rituals and male dominance games." He hurried on before Jarls could comment. "And they may use very long radio waves. Or very deep subsonics, like your elephant friends. The point is that no matter how much we learn, we're never going to have anything resembling a flapjack dictionary."

"Then we'll just have to rely on dolphins, won't we?" Jarls said dryly. "At dolphin prices."

Nemo emitted a warbling imitation of human laughter. "Now you've got it, Jarls," he chirped.

Jarls climbed down the last few feet and straddled the capsule, keeping a grip on the cable with one hand. He gave the capsule a thump to signal his presence. "All right, I'm here," he said. "What now?"

"He's scanning you now. He just added a high-speed burst similar to what you humans call dolphin 'signature whistles.' It may mean something like, 'Thank you for coming.' With your permission, I'm going to copy it back to him and sign your name—that is, with the symbol we've assigned to you attached. I hope he'll take it to mean, 'You're welcome.' Flapjacks are very polite, and they expect us to be, too."

"You *hope*? I thought you said you could talk flapjackese."

"Pidgin flapjackese, Jarls. I explained all that. I swear that talking to you is sometimes like talking to a tuna. Even though I take care to slow way down and use only sounds in the range you humans can hear. The flapjack and I are doing the same thing. Don't worry, it will work fine."

Jarls didn't enjoy being scolded by a dolphin. He held off replying and looked across uneasily to where the great flattened beast hung in the sky, its scalloped edges undulating slowly. Again, he had a definite sense of being scrutinized, though the creature possessed nothing resembling eyes. Perhaps Nemo's surmise about deep subsonics was correct, and that was where his feeling of unease was coming from.

"Explain to me again how you and this levitating leviathan got so cozy with each other," he said.

"Oh, Jarls, you're getting to be a pain in the blowhole!" Nemo expostulated. "All right. The flapjacks—excuse me, *Laguna volatilis*—were attracted in the first place by the echolocation pulses I was sending out to probe the clouds. After I found them, I could sense that they were using their own sonar to probe the source. They came over to have a look. When we found that we could 'see' one another's sound images with a little adjustment, they decided I was an intelligent creature, even though I was deaf in the rest of their total communications spectrum. So they asked what I was doing there. They asked by beeping me a picture of myself in the work pod, and alternating it several times with an empty pod, and following it with a high-frequency snort that was unmistakably a question mark. I answered with a scenario showing a falling man landing on a flapjack's back, and the flapjack bearing it upward to safety. I added your little tableau about the toolbox, and the flapjack gave me a replay that made it clear that he was the other player. So I told him that one of the two human minnows up there on top of the floater happened to be you. He flew up higher for a better look and checked you out. Then he asked to talk to you. Jarls, he's being very patient. So far."

Jarls turned his attention to the living island opposite. It seemed to him that the flapjack was starting to fidget, if the random twitching he could observe across that huge expanse of rippling flesh could be interpreted as fidgeting.

"So let's get to work," he said.

Two hours later, he was exhausted. Flapjacks were as prolix and discursive as dolphins in their own way. The two of them together were calculated to leave the poor human in the middle with his head spinning. Some of the long digressions seemed puzzling and irrelevant to Jarls, but evidently were important to the flapjack and dolphin, so Jarls doggedly went along with them until they were satisfied.

"Jarls, he wants to know if the . . . bone . . . hard stuff . . . metal in the tool box came from the body of a living thing."

"Tell him no."

A pause. Some indecipherable dolphin burbling. Then, "That's good, because he neglected to perform the ritual purification, and he's been afraid all this time that he's committed a . . . sin . . . no . . . an offense against . . . the gods . . . no . . . the sun . . . That's it. In their experience, the only entity they can sense above the clouds is the sun, so they think that the sun is what dispenses the never-ending rain of organics from above . . ."

And:

"Jarls, he's noticed that your bladder has been filling up while we've been talking. I explained to him what a bladder is—they have no comparable organ—and he asked if you were uncomfortable."

"Tell him no, I'm game to go on talking for a while longer."

"Jarls, you ought to ask him about *his* comfort."

"Go ahead, do it."

A pause. Then: "He says he's okay. Not tired yet. Plenty of heated hydrogen in his interior spaces to keep him aloft."

And:

"Jarls, he still doesn't understand about metal. *All* the debris that falls from the clouds has an organic origin. Metal didn't start to appear till a couple of hundred years ago, when they first became aware of the bubble cities floating out of reach above them."

"Explain to him about mining."

"I don't think that's a good idea, Jarls. Too complicated. He has no comprehension of solid planets or asteroids. You'd have to get into astronomy. Save that for later. Think of something else."

"Tell him the sun has children. Since we dwell above the clouds, we are able to reach the children. And we get the metal from them."

"Not bad. Do you mind if I interpolate a little of the old dolphin creation legend about where dry land came from? It might make some kind of sense to a flapjack, even though they have no conception of dry land."

"You know best. Go to it."

And:

"He wants to congratulate you on the clever artifacts you've made of the bones of the unimaginable animals that dwell with you above the clouds. He means the sections of Deep Tap pipe. They can . . . taste? . . . smell? . . . the fact that they're carbon-based, like their spears and other implements, though the form of the carbon is strange to them. They're particularly impressed by the threaded ends—they never thought of joining things together that way. Some of their younger hunters are starting to experiment with carving screw ends in cartilage, to make spears with a longer reach. They're very bright."

"Good. Are you listening, Gord?"

Murdo's voice came over the open circuit. "All right, I'm eating crow. But I still don't see how all this alien ethology gobbledegook matters one way or the other."

"You still don't have it, Gordo," Nemo chided him. "Ethology is about *animal* behavior. Doctor Chukchee would call it ethnography."

"Stuff it, you overgrown fish," Murdo said rudely.

Nemo made a rude noise back, and resumed talking to Jarls.

"Your flapjack rescuer—his name translates to something like 'Big Beacon,' by the way—admires your piety in attempting to reach the Thick Sea with your staff of bones, but he regrets to inform you that your efforts are doomed to failure."

"Why?"

"Your staff must be guided and braced where it passes through the Place of Bending, and the bubbles that cling to it like sucker beasts must be replaced when they are crushed by the high-pressure cells that weather brings at that intermediate depth. Deeper down, there's no problem."

"Huh? Are you listening, Gord? That's essentially what you told me."

But Murdo had switched off. Jarls returned to his three-way conversation with the flapjack.

"Are you able, then to fly . . . to swim so deep as the Place of Bending?"

Nemo had his reply for him a minute or two later. "Easily, Jarls. It's their preferred environment. In fact, they descend still lower to fish with baited lines for creatures that live even lower than that, at depths that even a flapjack can't reach."

"How is that possible? We can't even get a bathysphere down that far without its being crushed."

"The same way that creatures of the abyss exist in the ocean trenches of Earth, at pressures of three or four tons per square inch. Same pressure inside as outside."

"Jupiter pressures are of another order entirely. How much can a living organism stand before the molecules it's made of start to dissociate?"

"Jarls, they've evolved for billions of years, same as we have. They've adapted to their environment, as strange as it is. They continually adjust the pressure of their internal hydrogen to suit their depth. It's not even conscious. It's what keeps them alive. It's no big deal. On Earth, cephalapods like nautiluses migrate nightly from the ocean bottom to the surface, which is why our dolphin cousins there occasionally enjoy a gourmet treat that's denied to you humans. Sure, Big Beacon here starts to get uncomfortable at the point where the squeeze and the heat threaten the molecular integrity of his kind of life form, but otherwise he can do what your bathysphere can't."

"Then I guess we're in business," Jarls said. "Ask him if he'd like to earn some metal."

Negotiations began in earnest. They took a long time. Flapjacks, Jarls found, drove a hard bargain. In the end, they had a detailed verbal contract that would have impressed even the nit-picking lawyers of Greater Liechtenstein.

Jarls called Murdo to seal the contract.

"Gord, I want you to drop a girder overboard."

Sputtering sounds came from his helmet speaker. "Do you know what those things cost?"

"It's important."

After an interval of obligatory grumbling, Murdo gave in. "Oh, all right, you're running this show. Mak said to give you full coop-eration. But I'm billing the city for it. And you're going to initial the bill."

"Thanks, Gord."

It took a few minutes for the order to be relayed to the con-struction platform hovering opposite, and then more minutes for the order to be confirmed to the incredulous foreman. And then Jarls saw the end of a girder appear past the edge of the platform and inch gradually out as the roughnecks slid it along.

The two flapjacks were watching too, with whatever they used for senses. They were tense, poised. Their body language was unmistakable, as alien as their bodies were to the human eye.

As the girder inched closer to its center of balance, the second flapjack—the one Jarls took to be Big Beacon's attendant—flapped over and positioned himself beneath it. It tumbled, and the flap-jack caught it neatly in his folds.

Big Beacon waved a salute, and Nemo's voice came over the radio in a burst of dolphin twittering.

"He says thank you, Jarls. The bargain is sealed. He speaks for his . . . people . . . tribe . . . clan . . . pack . . . whatever you want to call it."

The two creatures banked and sideslipped, and dived abruptly into the cloud banks below.

Jarls found that he was drenched with sweat, despite the suit's cooling unit and dehumidifier. He took a deep breath, willing his racing heartbeat to return to normal. The departure of the two behemoths had rocked the dangling pod and set it slowly swinging. He clung like a fly to the cable, waiting until the swing died down, then began the long upward climb.

Murdo helped him get his footing as he hoisted himself to the duckwalk atop the floater's curved back. "What was that all about?" Murdo demanded.

A skein of lightning flared in the overhead cloud layer, and Jarls had to wait until the thunder died down before answering. "I've got you your roustabouts," he said.

A message from Earth was waiting for him when he got home. It was a budget message—print only, with no voice and no picture, low priority transmission, and his mother had left a note pinned to the family screen so that he wouldn't miss it.

He got himself a beer and sat down in front of the screen. "Go ahead," he said, and the screen came alive with words.

It was from Maryann. Jarls would have liked at least a still photo of her, but she was being frugal. He couldn't blame her; Venus had taught her a harsh lesson, and she couldn't have been on Earth long enough to trust the new state of affairs.

He leaned forward and began to read.

*Dear Jarls,*

*Little Brok and I have been in Indonesia about a week now. The trip from Venus was not as difficult as I feared—certainly not as bad as the terrible journey that brought us there from Jupiter. The other passengers were mostly Jovians, going to new jobs on Earth, so I felt quite at home. In fact, several of the passengers were headed for Sumatra too, to work on the orbital elevator terminal.*

*I will never be able to thank you enough for what you did for little Brok and me. The red tape was cut like magic, and all of a sudden I had a visa, a work permit, and a contract specifying that I was to be employed by EarthCorp as a welder, at welder's pay, on the space elevator project. There was even an Executive Guard escort from the local bureau to meet me at the Jakarta spaceport and smooth the way to*

*Padang, which is the staging area for the construction site in the western mountains. He was a nice young man named Lieutenant Grigg, who said he knew you in Liechtenstein. I thanked him, and he said it was only a courtesy to any Jovian sponsored by a fellow Guardsman, and he was happy to be of help.*

*Sumatra is beautiful. I never imagined how wonderful it was to walk around under an open sky, breathing natural air that smells only of vegetation. Little Brok is in a constant tizzy of discovery over the wonders he sees every day—banks of flowers, birds, insects, mountains, an ocean stretching to forever, and most of all, a glorious golden sun in a blue sky instead of the malignant furnace hanging over Cloudhab One or the tiny bright dot he'd see if he were able to live on Jupiter. He's going to grow up happy here. He may be a child of three planets, but he'll be a citizen of Earth.*

*Enough mother's chatter. I'm looking forward to seeing the Singapore-Kuala Lumpur metacity—it's closer than Jakarta, and the usual destination for weekend furlough. You can see the three-mile-high towers from across the Malaccan Strait—it's a wonder they don't collapse of their own weight, even in Earth gravity. The locals on the other side of the strait boast that it's going to become the hub of the solar system once the orbital elevator's in place, never mind that the elevator terminal's technically on the Indonesian side of the line because that's where the equator is. Emotions run high here. Don't tell me that Malay-Indonesian rivalry's been stilled by two hundred years of federation.*

*Jarls, I wish I could look forward to seeing you in person some day, my dear. Little Brok and I owe you so much, and Brok would want to thank you, too, if he were here. Maybe it's not an impossibility. Your friend Lieutenant Grigg says that if the Deep Tap can ever be put in place, Jupiter could even have a space elevator of its own, though I can't understand how it could be done, with Jupiter's gravity and the killer zone of radiation that passengers would*

*have to pass through. Lieutenant Grigg tends to let his
enthusiasm run away with him. But who'd have thought a
few hundred years ago that people could live on Jupiter at
all? Anyway, it's a sweet daydream.*

*Have to stop now. Running out of word allowance. Wish
all success for you. I'm glad that one of the three of us could
make it back to Jupiter.*
*Your friend,*
*Maryann*

Jarls stared at the frozen page a long time. He found the phrase
that had stuck so vividly in his mind and read it again: "He may be
a child of three planets, but he'll be a citizen of Earth." It was a
fine, brave sentiment. He hoped that things would work out for
Maryann and her child.

Something else she had written nagged at him. Grigg's nonsense about a space elevator in Jupiter's gravity, even with hyper-
materials and the unlimited energy that inexhaustible metallic
hydrogen would provide. What did one impossible project have to
do with another?

He sipped his beer and thought about it. He allowed himself to
daydream for a few minutes.

Colonel Wenzel, back in Polar City, was busy trying to make the
Metis siphon a reality. People had turned it into a race with the
Deep Tap. Or a veiled contest between EarthCorp and the gnomes
of Venus. But if you could anchor one end of an eighty thousand
mile siphon on Metis at all, the other end didn't have to stop at
merely skimming Jupiter's hydrogen atmosphere a few dozen
klicks below the cloudtops. You could anchor it to a deep structure
like the Tap. What had Murdo said? "It might as well be set in concrete." And the flapjacks had confirmed it.

No, that wouldn't work. Metis was too far from synchronous
orbit. Its period was less than a third of one of Jupiter's ten hour
days. That was too much to ask even of the new, miraculous
hypercarbons, with their buckytubes laced with boron and alu-

minum atoms. If the strain didn't snap the elevator, the drag would inevitably slow Metis down and lower its orbit. You could have a moon fall on the people beneath.

He thought about it some more. Amalthia or Thebe? Still not high enough. Amalthia had a period of about half a day, and Thebe circled her hostile grandfather in about two thirds of a day. Jupiter would still be tugging at her leash too hard.

But between Thebe and Io was a godforsaken rock named Antiope, originally known as Jupiter XXIII. Antiope was only decimal points above synchronous orbit. The tug would not be extreme. The drag of the anchor would eventually bring it closer to what passed for equilibrium. But it didn't matter a whole lot anyway. Jupiter was not a solid planet like Earth or Mars. Jovians had lived for generations with bubble cities that floated past one another all the time, and with ad hoc spaceports that did the same. A wandering orbital elevator would be welcome to the club.

Of course, it still remained to be seen if a tether some two hundred thousand miles long could be constructed. But that wasn't Jarls's department. The Metis engineers had already certified a tether of up to eighty thousand miles as practical. It was up to them.

He got up and got himself another beer. His mother came in while he was opening it. She was still dressed in her outside maintenance suit, her helmet tucked under her arm.

"Oh, you're back," she said. "I didn't expect you for at least another day. How did Nemo work out?"

"Just fine," he said. "Just fine."

He sat down in front of the screen to answer Maryann. He had a lot to say.

# 24

**J**ARLS RODE the dolphin pod, waiting for the signal from Murdo and feeling like some kind of giant crab in his armored suit. There was enough flexibility in the suit's legs for him to straddle the pod's broad back, but it wasn't a very comfortable position.

He surveyed the scene around him. It was a fine clear day for Jupiter, at least at this level. The lightning was mostly far above, and veiled by the intervening layers of clouds. The sky here was blue and transparent, with an oceanic vista of water-ammonia fog below.

To his left was the colossal shaft of the Deep Tap's Station Two, climbing almost four thousand miles from its roots beneath the fog to pierce the multicolored clouds overhead. Floaters of all shapes and colors swarmed around it, looking like toy balloons at this distance. Improbable tethers dangled from the clouds above, bearing the house-size attachments that still had to be installed. The tremendous construction complex that had spawned it all was more than a hundred miles above this last roof of clouds. This was about as deep as a human being could safely go, even when packaged and sealed in a rigid buckytube suit.

Away to his right was the VIP floater with the observation gondola slung underneath. The faces at the portholes were pink dots from here, but each of the dots was some bigwig deemed important enough to be included in today's junket.

It was strictly a ceremonial occasion. The real breakthrough had been made weeks ago, but Murdo was putting on a show for them. At some point he would give them a thrill by lowering the floater an extra mile or so, so they could go back to their constituents or money people and say that they had descended deeper than man had ever gone before, to personally witness this landmark event in human history.

Jarls could hear Murdo giving them the treatment now, through the pickup he had thoughtfully left on for him.

"... and we have every expectation that the extra miles of pipe we're adding today will put us over the top. Or under the bottom, if you prefer. We already were beginning to find evidence of monatomic hydrogen mixed in with the diatomic slush, when we lost our upper stage impellers at what the flapjacks—pardon me, our native Jovian friends—call the Place of Bending . . ."

Jarls smiled to himself at Murdo's tactful circumlocution. Doctor Chuckchee, of course, would have been included among the dignitaries; it was his work with Nemo and the other dolphins that assured the success of the project, and the underwriters would be waving his name like a flag in front of the eager investors. Nobody wanted to offend his academic sensibilities by using the word flapjack in front of him.

Jarls watched with a professional eye as the additional mile of pipe streamed past his vision, the effect enhanced by the barberpole stripes Murdo had had painted on it. There were oohs and ahs from the dignitaries. Murdo had timed it nicely. It was good theater, though a few extra miles of reach would make little practical difference at this point.

Murdo went on to explain what the Place of Bending was. "We get a zone of counterrotating eddy currents at that depth, caused by the differential in temperature gradients. The energy of the eddies is fed into the sustained eastward and westward wind patterns at different velocities. As you can imagine, on Jupiter the wind shear is enormous. But fortunately, below that level, where the word 'atmosphere' becomes a joke, the influence of the gradients becomes adiabadic, and essentially negligible. Our large friends have reason to be quite familiar with the phenomenon, and gave it a name long ago."

Someone in Murdo's captive audience was asking a question, but he was too far away from the pickup for Jarls to make out the words. Murdo answered, "Yes, that's the reason we lost our upper stage impellers. It was a blow. We had to suspend processing operations temporarily, though of course there was no interruption in the job of lengthening the Tap itself."

Jarls made a face at all the malarkey. Murdo had purposely shut down the separation plant after processing a few ingots for demonstration purposes. There was enough unprocessed slurry in the holding tanks to keep the plant busy for weeks, but Murdo had seen no point in continuing until he could get a richer mixture.

"But we hope to get our gusher today," Murdo went on shamelessly. "Jarls, have you and Nemo been able to contact our indigenous labor force yet?"

More nonsense. Big Beacon and his clan were already waiting below with their instructions, probably puzzled by the human delay in getting on with the job.

But that had been Murdo's signal. Jarls supposed he couldn't blame him for trying to milk the moment for a little drama. He dutifully chinned the transmit button and said, "Not yet, but we're still trying. If they're anywhere within a thousand miles, they should respond."

He clicked off and switched to Nemo on the private channel. "Okay, you can go ahead," he said.

"I heard him," Nemo said. "I'm way ahead of you."

Jarls heard a few creaks and whistles, but knew they were incidental to the actual give and take of dolphin-flapjack conversation. Then the sounds stopped, and there was nothing to do except wait.

The wait was long enough for him to begin to get nervous himself, when to his relief a scattering of black specks burst through the sea of fog below and rose toward him, rapidly growing in size.

The flapjacks wasted no time. A small work party surrounded one of the dangling impellers and hovered there with slow, powerful whole-body strokes that almost folded them in half, while one of their number detached the housing from its tether.

They caught the barn-sized structure in one of their circular nets and bore it away. Jarls watched them as they swooped downward in diminishing spirals until they disappeared into the fog. Another work party was already deploying a net under the next impeller housing, as an agile colleague, his body drawn almost into a purse shape to bring all his edge scallops to bear on his task, unfastened the suspended unit.

"Amazing!" a disembodied voice said in Jarls's ear. It was some member of the Deep Tap Commission or one of the honored guests who must have wandered near Murdo's mike. Jarls could hear what sounded like party noises. Murdo would be breaking out the champagne about now.

The flapjacks were all gone within half an hour. When there was nothing more to see, the observation floater started slowly to rise. "See you back at base camp, Jarls," Murdo's voice came through the helmet receiver. "There's a reception in the big conference room. The Commission's laying out the refreshments. Nemo's invited, too."

Murdo was pretty sure of himself. By the time he got there with his cargo of dignitaries, there'd be something to celebrate. Down beneath the sea of fog, the flapjacks were already beginning to install the impellers. As big as the devices were, they only had to be clicked in place and secured against Jupiter's violent forces.

The flapjacks knew what to do. They'd been well instructed, and they'd installed the units before, some of them a lot farther down, when the Deep Tap's gargantuan foot valves were worming their way past the turbulent regions. Murdo would only have to throw the switch with a flourish, wait for the green light, and announce that the impellers were working.

Only a party pooper would want to spoil the celebration by pointing out that it would take a lot more than an hour for the hydrogen cocktail to work its way up four thousand miles of pipe and get its monatomic component separated out and stabilized.

"Are you ready?" Jarls asked Nemo. "I'm taking us up."

"I hope they'll save me a fish," Nemo said.

The festivities were well along by the time Jarls arrived. The guests had been well lubricated on the way up, and had continued at the buffet table. Jarls helped himself to a glass of cheap champagne and sized up the gathering.

He knew most of the guests. He'd been thrown together with them often enough during the last fourteen months—the commissioners and investors and the assorted politicians from Port Elysium and the other participating cities, and the onboard newspeople and the businessmen who were happily making fortunes by providing the Deep Tap with the stuff of which it was made.

Doctor Chukchee and a couple of human assistants were over to the side of the room, ineffectually trying to sanitize an interview an overaggressive reporter was coaxing out of Nemo. Nemo had been wheeled in through a side door in his travel tub, had been given a round of applause which went to his head, and was enjoying the party too much. Doctor Chukchee had made the mistake of mixing him a cocktail of vodka and clam juice, though everyone knew that dolphins got silly when they drank.

Torbey was present, one of the miscellaneous bureaucrats who had attached themselves to the excursion, and unfortunately for him, so was his domineering mother-in-law. Kristen av-Greta was on some committee or other connected with the Deep Tap.

But the luminary of the event was indisputably Colonel Wenzel. Wenzel had taken a scramjet flight from Polar City as soon as Jarls had alerted him to the impending fruition of Murdo's efforts, and he was busy taking credit for the accomplishment in Prince Rudolph's name.

Jarls listened to Wenzel now as he rapped on a glass for attention and beamed at the gathering, with Councilman Mak and Deep Tap Commissioner Fiske at his side.

"Congratulations to all of you for the part you've played in making this moment possible," Wenzel said. "Today's signal achievement may go down in history as marking the success of the most monumental engineering project the human race has attempted to date—at least until we mine the sun itself. Greater even than the Martian or Terran orbital elevators, or the transpacific tunnel. And, I might add, we've come in ahead of two of these, against all odds and all expectations. It's a tribute to the perseverence and hard work of Jovians, and makes me proud of my own Jovian heritage."

He beamed at them some more, his gaze traveling all around the room to include everybody there. "Ladies and gentlemen," he said, raising his volume another notch, "we've got ourselves our gusher!"

He got a round of delirious applause for that. Wenzel was good—that was why General Carnavan had persuaded Prince Rudolph to choose him. He had deftly flattered everybody and singled out nobody—not even Murdo. The glory went by default to Prince Rudolph.

"He should have mentioned you," Torbey grumbled, sidling over to stand next to Jarls. "And Nemo, too."

"Shut up, Torbey," Jarls said.

The applause died down. Having set the essential tone, Wenzel went on to recite a catalog of names that included Murdo, Jarls, and Doctor Chukchee along with everybody else, from participating mayors to junior underwriters. Mak and Commissioner Fiske moved closer to Wenzel and got a sentence or two of special mention when their turn came.

"How do you like that Mak?" said a voice behind Jarls. "He doesn't care if Wenzel gets the cake; he's going to be there to catch the crumbs. Hello, Torbey."

Jarls turned. It was Murdo, his fist wrapped around a whiskey tumbler that he had obtained from someplace other than the buffet table.

"Mak's all right," Jarls said, uneasy at the gibe. "And Wenzel's just doing his thing. He was sent to Jupiter to get the ball rolling, and he did."

"You got the ball rolling, Jarley," Murdo said. He was a little drunk but holding it well. "Wenzel is still tiptoing around trying to get the Metis project off the ground without stepping on the Venu-sians' toes too much."

"It's a delicate situation. He's got to tread softly to look after Jupiter's interests."

"Yeah, yeah," Murdo said. "Now that he's sopped up all the credit here, he'll be back to Polar City to take up the diplomatic wars again. We won't see him around here in a hurry. He doesn't want to get his hands greasy. Do you know he got together with Fiske and the big boys to choose a tame Deep Tap Administrator to keep the work going, now that we're safely on our way. They offered the job to me."

"What did you tell them?"

"I told them no thanks. I'm no paper pusher. I'm a contractor."

Torbey was goggle-eyed. "You turned it down? That's an important job!"

"Maybe. But not for me," Murdo said.

"Torbey's right," Jarls said. "It's going to be the best job in town."

"I'd go crazy," Murdo said. He took a swig of his drink and wiped his mouth on the back of his wrist. "I better go over there and see Chukchee and his fish. I've got to make arrangements for a dolphin crew to work around the clock."

He sauntered off in the direction of Nemo's travel tub. Torbey stared after him, shaking his head.

"I've never understood him," Torbey said. "He'd be in charge of all the other contractors."

"That's just what he doesn't want," Jarls said.

Torbey was looking at Jarls, a little enviously. "Well, you're going to be the toast of Port Elysium when word gets around, no matter what kind of speeches get made. What are you going to do now?"

"I don't know. The project can pretty much run on its own steam now. I'll work with Murdo till he can get his dolphin crew and train some human interpreters. There's not much for me to do. The fundraising can take care of itself, and so can the political stuff. I guess I'll be running errands for Colonel Wenzel on the Metis project. I have a few ideas I want to talk over with him."

Colonel Wenzel was bringing his speech to a conclusion. "And now I've been informed that the moment we've all been waiting for has arrived. Mr. Murdo, if you please."

But Murdo had written himself out of the act. He remained stubbornly glued to the floor in the vicinity of the dolphin tub, looking on with remote, polite interest. Instead, a white-smocked technician from, Jarls guessed, the separation plant, hurried over to Wenzel, carrying a gleaming silvery cube in each hand.

Wenzel didn't miss a beat. "Thank you," he said to the technician, and took the cubes. They looked as if they ought to have weighed twenty or thirty pounds apiece, but from the way Wenzel handled them, they must have been as light as foamed plastic.

"Here are the very first ingots of metallic hydrogen produced by the Deep Tap," he said, holding them aloft. "I am pleased to accept one of them for our generous patron and Megachairman of EarthCorp, Prince Rudolph of Liechtenstein."

There were cheers and whistles, and someone made an abortive attempt to sing a few bars of "Shining Stone," the Liechtenstein anthem. Wenzel waited for silence, and turned to the Deep Tap commissioner.

"And the other, I present to Commissioner Fiske for his faithful shepherding of this project to completion."

Fiske accepted the ingot with a stony bureaucratic face. A few more ragged cheers broke out.

"This is only the beginning of a bright new future for our planet," Wenzel said, displaying the ingot. "The metallic hydrogen was brought up, atom by atom, from the bowels of Jupiter, strained out from a brew of diatomic slush, pressed into a temporary solid form and stabilized by an additive consisting, so the metallurgists tell me, mostly of aluminum and boron. We've got here a metal that will float in water, is strong enough to replace aluminum as the lightweight metal of choice in manufacturing, makes an excellent room temperature superconductor, and that, because its density allows it to pack approximately eight times as much energy into a fusion reaction, is destined to replace frozen deuterium and tritium in fuel pellets. We were only able to produce these sample ingots today, of course, but when we're up and running, Jupiter will be able to fill the needs of the entire solar system."

The technician from the processing plant was frowning, but he didn't say anything.

Jarls whispered to Torbey, "Hogwash! Those ingots were processed three weeks ago. And it took a couple of million gallons of slush to get enough of the metallic stuff to make them. Some gusher! Murdo thinks he'll have to go down another two hundred miles before the mixture is rich enough to start real production. It'll take another year, at least."

"It doesn't matter, Jarls," Torbey said. "You never really understood politics. The word isn't just the father to the deed. It's a stand-in for it."

Jarls sighed. "You're right. I've seen enough this last year to know how it works. I just don't believe it yet."

"You'll learn. You'll *have* to learn, now that you're back on Jupiter with a promising government career ahead of you. Or a private sector career for that matter, if the Guard will let you go. You ought to settle down, raise a family—"

He stopped abruptly, as he realized how thoughtless his remark had been.

"It's all right, Torbey," Jarls said gently. "I'm happy for you and Kath and the new baby. I'm glad it worked out."

Torbey began babbling to cover up his blunder, making it worse. "You'll find someone, Jarls, I know you will. Why they've been swarming around you like flies. One of them's bound to turn out to be the right one. Is there anyone special?"

The only one Jarls could think of was Maryann. The image jumped into his mind, unbidden and unexpected. But that was ridiculous. He and Maryann had never been anything but friends. And there was the memory of Brok between them. And she was on Earth, and doomed by her Venusian baby to remain there.

"No," he said. "Not yet."

Torbey was hardly listening. He had begun extolling family life, and he couldn't stop, indiscretion or not.

". . . and there's nothing that compares with being a father, Jarls. Little Thor is really a remarkable baby. He never cries, and he doesn't talk yet, but I can tell he's taking in every word. And he's very strong—just try to pry him away from his crib when he doesn't want to go. Kath is really very happy about having a son instead of the daughter her mother wanted. I know it breaks the clone line that she comes from, but he's got half her family's genes, doesn't he? That's how life is supposed to go on. What's so great about cloning anyway? No surprises. What really matters is that Thor's a fine, healthy baby. Kath says so herself. After all, it isn't as if she can't have other babies later by cloning herself if she wants to."

He'd gotten himself into hot water again. Kristen av-Greta had been standing behind Torbey for the last part of his recitation, and she'd heard every word, despite Jarls's attempts to warn Torbey by poking him.

"One would hope so," she said icily. "Surprises are what one worries about. Hello Jarls. Congratulations. This is quite the triumph today, isn't it?"

Torbey had turned a bright red. "I didn't mean to imply . . . that is, there's nothing so great about a man contributing his genes either . . . I mean, it all depends on what the genes are that are being contributed, doesn't it?"

She ignored him. "And I'm sure there are more triumphs ahead for you, Jarls. Perhaps there's something to be said for the Y chromosome after all. The committee is having a little tea next Tuesday. We generally have a speaker. Would you care to give a brief talk? Oh, you needn't worry about preparing anything. It's all quite informal. Perhaps a look ahead at the new Deep Tap era."

The stricken look on Torbey's face told Jarls that he had expected to be asked to give the talk himself. Jarls put on his best expression of regret and said, "Oh, I'm sorry. I'd like to very much, but I'm afraid Mr. Murdo is going to need me all next week."

"What a pity," Kristen said. "I'd ask Colonel Wenzel, but he's leaving for Polar City tomorrow."

Torbey cleared his throat and made another mistake. "Uh, Kristen, if you like, I could . . . that is, my department's made a comprehensive study of the expected economic impact of the Deep Tap. There's a lot of technical data, too. We enlisted some of the scientific experts—Dr. Singh, the metallurgist we just saw, and . . ."

"Oh, I don't think so," Kristen said. "The committee's interested in hearing from the movers and shakers, not a dull functionary. Perhaps I could get Commissioner Fiske."

Torbey's ears turned an even brighter red, if that was possible. Jarls tried to think of a graceful excuse that would get him away from this eerie replica of Kath whose son-in-law he had so narrowly escaped becoming.

But he was rescued before the situation could become even more embarrassing. One of Wenzel's other assistant attachés came looking for him, and said, "Sorry to interrupt, Anders. The Colonel wants to see you."

"Excuse me," he said. He followed the assistant attaché across the floor to where Colonel Wenzel stood with Commissioner Fiske, Councilman Mak, and a couple of steely eyed political types who Jarls vaguely recognized as having something to do with the Jovian League.

"Ah, Anders," Colonel Wenzel said. "We need to have a chat with you. Splendid job you've done, by the way. I've written all about it in my report to Prince Rudolph."

"Did you get my memo about anchoring a space elevator on Antiope, sir?" Jarls asked.

"Oh, that. Yes, I did. Interesting idea. We'll have to look into it further. But that's not what we wanted to talk to you about."

"Sir?"

Wenzel looked at the two Jovian League men. One of them gave a small nod.

"We've demonstrated the feasibility of the Big Tap. We'll be mining great quantities of metallic hydrogen in the near future. It will change the destinies of Jupiter and the rest of the inhabited solar system immeasurably. It's going to be an enormous enterprise. We'll need someone to run it on a day-to-day basis. It's time to appoint a permanent Deep Tap Administrator.

"It's a big job, Jarls," Mak broke in. "And you deserve it."

One of the Jovian League representatives spoke up. He was an older, sharp-nosed man with thin lips and shaggy gray eyebrows. "The consensus around here seems to be, Lieutenant Anders, that you're the one who can handle it."

"What do you say, *Oberleutnant?*" Wenzel said, looking fatherly and expansive.

It had come too quickly. Jarls was not ready for it. He took refuge in temporizing. "What about Murdo?" he said, already knowing the answer.

"Mr. Murdo was one of the names under consideration." the League man said. "But we believe that you're the most suitable choice."

"Don't be modest, Jarls," Mak put in. "There's a lot at stake here."

Jarls had a vision of himself sitting behind a desk entrenched in paperwork and growing soft, while Jupiter howled around his cubicle and men like Murdo and Hector and his dead father struggled outside, doing the work. He'd seen too much of the universe for that. Then, uninvited, a countervision crept into his brain: the blue skies of Earth and the solid land beneath. His mind filled in the details; the generalized landscape became the rich green tropical vegetation of Indonesia, with a smiling Maryann in the foreground, holding her baby.

The vision was so exact that he had to blink several times to clear it out of his head. Wenzel and Mak were looking at him curiously.

"Do you need more time to think it over?" Wenzel said. "It's a civilian job, of course, and the Guard can't insist that you take it, but . . ."

"We were counting on you, Jarls," Mak said.

"I'm sorry," Jarls said. "I'm not a good fit for the job. But I can tell you who is."

Wenzel tried to cut him off, but one of the League men stopped him with a look.

"Sir, the Deep Tap Administrator has to be someone who knows his way around the system, who doesn't make waves, who knows how to work with all sides without ruffling feathers. Maybe I helped get things rolling, but now you need someone who can roll with the ball."

"Get to the point."

Jarls took a deep breath and used all the eloquence he could muster to eulogize Torbey. He helped himself along by remembering the stricken look on Torbey's face when Kristen av-Greta had belittled him, and by imagining the look on Kristen's face when she learned that Torbey had been appointed Deep Tap Administrator.

". . . and I've worked with him for the last fourteen months on some of the knotty problems that came up, and he always came through. Friend or not, I believe he's the most qualified person for the job."

One of the visitors from the Jovian League turned to Mak. "Do you know this Torbey person, Councilman?"

"He's a career bureaucrat in the contracts division. He's capable at what he does. He worked his way up in only a couple of years to head the division."

"But he's dull, is that what you're trying to say?"

Mak had trapped himself. Never criticize a constituent was his creed; it always gets around, and you may need his good will later.

"Well, I wouldn't say . . ."

The other Jovian League man, the one who had remained silent, spoke up. He was an imposing man with a standard political face, but a touch of humor played about his lips as he interceded.

"Maybe dull is what we need, Edard," he said. "And the contracts division sounds good. Lord knows, we'll be up to our necks in a sea of contracts."

Edard turned back to Mak. "Can you vouch for him?"

Mak, ever a realist, knew when to switch sides. "Yes. I've known Torbey for years. He's dependable. And he's sound."

Nothing showed in Colonel Wenzel's face. He said to Jarls, "All right, Guardsman, it's settled then. I hope you've made the right decision. Your work here is over, and Prince Rudolph has made it clear to me that you're to be given the assignment of your choice. He seems to have taken an interest in you. You're a very lucky young man."

Jarls had automatically brought himself rigidly to attention as the colonel spoke. "You can continue here on Jupiter as one of my assistant attachés, and I can assure you that you'll be given useful work to do," Wenzel continued, "or you can get yourself reassigned to Guard headquarters on Earth and choose some new berth there. Where do you want to go?"

"Earth," Jarls said.

# 25

**T**HERE WERE only his mother and Torbey to see him off. Jarls had arranged his departure to cause as little fuss as possible. Murdo might be a little hurt that he hadn't been informed of Jarl's embarkation date, but he'd get over it. And Mak wouldn't have come anyway; Jarls was old business.

The three of them were standing around in Port Elysium's departure lounge, waiting for the ferry that would take Jarls to the scramjet anchored some fifty miles away. The scramjet would connect with the passenger ship now orbiting Callisto more than a million miles away and beyond the worst of Jupiter's deadly cloak of radiation. If he missed the connection, he'd have to wait a month or more for the next flight to Earth; the passenger ship would not linger long at Callisto.

"Kath was really sorry she couldn't come," Torbey apologized. "She couldn't leave little Thor. But she sent her best wishes."

"Tell her not to worry," Jarls said. "Give her my best too."

His mother frowned at the wall clock and said, "I told your uncle Jase, and he said he'd try to be here. I guess he changed his mind."

"That's all right," Jarls said. "Jase hasn't exactly been close to us all these years, and it's a little late to start now. What's that you're holding?"

She looked at the package in her hands and said, "Oh, I almost forgot. It's from Ian Karg. He found out somehow that you were leaving today, and he sent this along with a nice note."

"He keeps tabs on all the Earth traffic," Torbey said. "He's been doing it for years. I used to send him the manifests when I was a dispatcher."

Jarls tore the wrappings off the package and found himself holding a bottle of the sour Earthwine that Karg imported for his own use. He handed it over to Torbey. "You better take this, Torb. I've already got a weight penalty with this one small bag."

"Oh, I couldn't," Torbey protested.

"Go on. There'll be plenty of Earthwine where I'm going."

Torbey reluctantly accepted the bottle. "Marth, you come back home with me afterwards. We'll drink a toast to Jarls. I know Kath will want to, too."

"What does the note say?" Marth Anders asked.

Jarls opened the envelope and read: *Once a Guardsman, always a Guardsman. Ave atque vale. I.K.*

What does *Ave atque vale* mean?" Jarls asked.

"It's Latin," Torbey said. "It means 'Hail and farewell.'"

"Not farewell," Marth Anders said, taking her son's hands. "You'll come back to Jupiter for visits, won't you?"

"I'm sure of it," Jarls laughed. "Jupiter's getting rich. Space travel's going to be a lot easier from now on."

"Jarls, listen," Torbey said earnestly. "Kath and I can never thank you enough for what you did for us. You sacrificed yourself for . . ."

"Forget it," Jarls said. "It wasn't a sacrifice. You'll make a fine Deep Tap Administrator. The floating rail gun to launch interplanetary freight traffic is your next project. And then, one day, the Jovian space elevator."

"Will you bring your children back?" Marth Anders whispered.

Jarls grew somber. "I don't think that's going to be possible," he said. "Assuming there *are* any children."

"Then I'll just have to come to Earth and visit *them*," she said firmly.

"We're getting ahead of ourselves," Jarls said, laughing again.

He'd had another exchange of messages with Maryann. He'd take a month's leave in Indonesia to see her, and then he'd see what strings he could pull to get her a job on Prince Rudolph's new project to construct a water tunnel through the Bergamasque and Rhaetian Alps to the Adriatic Sea to give Liechtenstein direct access to the Mediterranean. She'd brought up the subject herself. It would put her within an easy weekend jaunt to Liechtenstein, she'd said.

A chime sounded overhead, and people started lining up in front of the departure gate. "I'd better go," Jarls said, picking up his bag.

His mother hugged him, and Torbey shook his hand, and then he was in the line, moving forward toward the gate. A few of the passengers turned their heads to look at him, obviously recognizing him, but nobody was so impolite as to intrude on him. Jovians were not a demonstrative people.

He had a last look at Port Elysium from a couple of miles away, through one of the viewports on the ferry. It filled the porthole, a gigantic shimmering pearl set amidst the clouds, and then dwindled to a distant speck. In the days ahead, he knew, Jupiter itself would dwindle to a bright jewel in the sky.

And then, as the ferry rotated and fired its retros to mate with the looming scramjet, even the speck disappeared from view. Jarls retrieved his bag from the overhead rack and strapped himself in for the docking.

"Excuse me, sir," the steward said. "We've completed mating with Eurostation, and we'll be ready to disembark soon."

"I'll be along in a minute," Jarls said.

He wanted a few more minutes to enjoy the specacular view from the spaceship's observation deck. Earth was a marbled blue sphere overhead, and by twisting his neck, he could see the pitted face of the moonlet they'd towed in from the asteroid belt. The beginning of the space elevator, a few hundred miles of plaited moonshine projecting from its surface, pointed straight at the center of the Earth.

By using it as a pointer, Jarls thought he could make out the